A loving husband and father, a CA, and a financial leader in his sector. Sylvester Alex Bosch's view on life is drawn from diverse cultural backgrounds. He is a strong believer in philosophy, mystery, fantasy, history and religion. He believes nothing just happens; that we all came from somewhere; are here for a reason and season, and when our time here is up, we continue to exist in a new dimension that includes fighting mysterious battles we barely knew existed during our life time. Success in these unknown battles that lie beyond the grave is predicated on diligence, shrewdness, perseverance, humility and excellence.

To my father, a man full of wisdom; and to the most gorgeous and exceptionally smart women in my life and their strong belief in me. My wife, Alexina, and my parents, Patricia and Boston (senior) – this is for you.

SYLVESTER ALEX BOSCH

THE UNKNOWN BATTLES THAT LIE BEYOND THE GRAVE

AUSTIN MACAULEY PUBLISHERS™

LONDON • CAMBRIDGE • NEW YORK • SHARJAH

Copyright © Sylvester Alex Bosch 2023

The right of Sylvester Alex Bosch to be identified as author of this work has been asserted by the author in accordance with sections 77 and 78 of the Copyright, Designs and Patents Act 1988.

All rights reserved. No part of this publication may be reproduced, stored in a retrieval system or transmitted in any form or by any means, electronic, mechanical, photocopying, recording or otherwise, without the prior permission of the publishers.

Any person who commits any unauthorised act in relation to this publication may be liable to criminal prosecution and civil claims for damages.

This is a work of fiction. Names, characters, businesses, places, events, locales and incidents are either the products of the author's imagination or used in a fictitious manner. Any resemblance to actual persons, living or dead, or actual events is purely coincidental.

A CIP catalogue record for this title is available from the British Library.

ISBN 9781398487062 (Paperback)
ISBN 9781398488533 (Hardback)
ISBN 9781398487086 (ePub e-book)
ISBN 9781398487079 (Audiobook)

www.austinmacauley.com

First Published 2023
Austin Macauley Publishers Ltd®
1 Canada Square
Canary Wharf
London
E14 5AA

I would like to thank my wife, Alexina, and Paige Lawson, for their input.

Table of Contents

Chapter 1: Settling Among the Natives Under a Veil	11
Chapter 2: When Misfortune Comes Knocking	14
Chapter 3: Missing the Forest for the Trees: Sexy Stories	19
Chapter 4: Children and the Supernatural	21
Chapter 5: The Impact of Parental Issues on Children	27
Chapter 6: Guilt and Grief	33
Chapter 7: The Power of Confrontation	39
Chapter 8: The Silver Lining	46
Chapter 9: New Level, New Devils 1	54
Chapter 10: New Level, New Devils 2	58
Chapter 11: The Tiny Steps that Lead to Death	65
Chapter 12: A Place Where Nothing Is Hidden	69
Chapter 13: The Gliding Blood Sucker	74
Chapter 14: Trial by the Jury of Consuming Fire	79
Chapter 15: Self-Defence in the Unknown Court	88
Chapter 16: The Intervention	92
Chapter 17: Seeing Things Hidden from Mortals	98
Chapter 18: Combat Ghosts from the Dead	104
Chapter 19: Choosing the Acts (Assignments)	109
Chapter 20: Assembling Team Combat Ghost	113

Chapter 21:	The Stubborn King and His Kingdom	128
Chapter 22:	The Natural Disaster Weapons	136
Chapter 23:	The Wings Warehouse	145
Chapter 24:	The Warrior's Creed	152
Chapter 25:	Meeting the Combat Ghosts	156
Chapter 26:	Military Strategies	162
Chapter 27:	The War Speech and Military Training	174
Chapter 28:	Good Angels, Bad Angels	183
Chapter 29:	The Silence of God	193
Chapter 30:	Inside the Invisible Door	198
Chapter 31:	Incursion into the Revolutionary Kingdom	204
Chapter 32:	Heroic Episodes	207
Chapter 33:	Fighting in Retreat	211
Chapter 34:	The Point of No Return	217
Chapter 35:	The First Natural Disaster Weapon	225
Chapter 36:	First There's Calm, Then Disaster Strikes	231
Chapter 37:	From Best Friends to Worst Enemies	233
Chapter 38:	The Second Natural Disaster Weapon	238
Chapter 39:	The Third Natural Disaster Weapon	242
Chapter 40:	Asking for Help	246
References		257

Chapter 1
Settling Among the Natives Under a Veil

Trump Bloomfield was the oldest child in a family of two children. His father, Kennedy Bloomfield, migrated to Africa as a Christian missionary, just before the start of the First World War, in 1913.

It is a widely held belief amongst contemporary historians that most white settlers migrated to Africa under the auspices of spreading the gospel but had ulterior motives and ended up committing some of the most heinous crimes ever recorded in human history.

The dichotomy to these supposedly surreptitious dark motives mainly lies in the meaning of the word gospel, which comes from the Old English god meaning 'good' and spell meaning 'news, a story' and in Christianity, this 'good news' refers to the story of Jesus Christ's birth, death, and resurrection.

Did Kennedy fit this mould? Perhaps. Kennedy Bloomfield abandoned his original mission of spreading the gospel to the 'dark continent' within a few years of arriving in Africa. He tactically married a local girl named Muswana and settled amongst the natives.

According to some schools of thought, historians have traditionally looked at Christian missionaries in one of two ways. The first church historians to catalogue missionary history provided hagiographic descriptions of their trials, successes, and sometimes even martyrdom. Missionaries were thus visible saints, exemplars of ideal piety in a sea of persistent savagery.

However, missionaries were viewed quite differently by the middle of the twentieth century, an era marked by civil rights movements, anti-colonialism, and growing secularisation. Instead of godly martyrs, historians now described missionaries as arrogant and rapacious imperialists. Christianity became not a saving grace but a monolithic and aggressive force that missionaries imposed upon defiant natives. Indeed, missionaries were now understood as important agents in the ever-expanding nation-state or ideological shock troops for colonial invasion whose zealotry blinded them.

Within a year of their marriage, the Bloomfields welcomed their first child, Trump Bloomfield, born on the 30th of April 1915. He was a lovely mixed-race boy with a mixture of features inherited from both parents. Trump's sharp blue eyes and long fingers were a genetic stamp from his father; whereas his dark thick hair and his long, round, artfully curved semi-flat nose were a combination of his parents in varying proportions.

At the age of five, Trump was enrolled in a local school run by the Catholic missionaries, and he seemed to fit in quite well. Growing up, Trump was prone to several minor and serious tragedies. This could have been his modus operandi for testing and establishing his identity and simply to find answers to the numerous questions that lingered in his small head for which he did not attempt to share with his parents or his teachers.

In Trump's 'world', action almost always carried the day and spoke louder than words. One summer afternoon, Trump's mother, Muswana, picked him up from school and left him with their maid momentarily to go to the shops with his younger sister, Joanna, who was now aged three. After changing his school uniforms, Trump wore his favourite red vest, which had a big pink label at the front that read 'JUST DO IT IN THE DIRTY!' and his brand-new shorts, which were made of polyester and nylon materials.

As the saying goes, "An idle mind is the devil's workshop." Trump started to wonder what would happen to him if he sat on a brazier full of red-hot coal used as a backup for cooking the family meals whenever there was an electric power outage. After consulting the left and right faculties of his brain, he anecdotally concluded that his bums would endure hot coal fire. While their maid was busy ironing, Trump swiftly instigated the manoeuvres necessary to bring his crudely crafted experiment to life. He sat on the brazier full of red-hot coal fire and got a rude shock.

No sooner than Trump sat on the flaming red hot coal that was burning at temperatures above 1,100 degrees Celsius (2,012 degrees Fahrenheit) than he instinctively garnered all the strength in his small legs to help him jump off the brazier higher than he had ever jumped before, at least not up to that date, while screaming in excruciating pain and anguish. He ran to the nearest tap at full speed to soak his burning bums in cold water, but it was too late. His polyester shorts melted slowly on his backside, causing deep burns. By the time the maid rushed to Trump's rescue, damage had already been inflicted, and the fire left an indelible scar on his backside for future reference, one would hope.

Three months down the line following the 'red-hot-coal-gate' incident, Trump had completely obliterated the painful experiment from his memory. One afternoon while alone near the grass thatched fence surrounding the family's vegetable garden, Trump started wondering what would happen if he set fire to the grass thatched fence and then poured hot water on it. "Would hot water make the fire burn more in the equation: hot + hot = more action, or would it stop the fire altogether?"

"I do not think so," he concluded on the basis that only cold water would stop the hot fire and not otherwise.

Trump therefore proceeded and designed his experiment to confirm two possible outcomes. Step one, steal the match box and stealthily start the fire. Step two, pour hot water on the fire and checkout the outcome. Finally, if step two didn't stop the fire, quickly navigate to step three and pour cold water on before anyone could notice.

It was summertime, and the grass was dry. Immediately after Trump set fire to the grass thatched fence, there was a huge blaze, and the wind that was already blowing made things worse. Trump was so shocked that he could not even execute any of the other steps laid down in his blueprint, not even pouring hot water on the fire that was now burning wildly and out of control. He just stood there stone frozen as the neighbours frantically battled to stop the fire, taking turns to pour water on it. After battling the fire for a while, the helpful neighbours finally managed to quench it. There was calm at last, though the thick black smoke continued for several hours until Trump's mum returned from her shopping errand.

No one quite knew how that fire was started, and that's how Trump escaped punishment. Suffice to say, the unfortunate incident shocked and shook Trump to his core.

Chapter 2
When Misfortune Comes Knocking

During that same week of the fire incident, while Trump's father, Kennedy, had gone to meet his white friends at a local pub for a drink, his sister, Joanna, wandered away from home and accidentally fell into a septic tank. Joanna intended to jump over the asbestos covering to the septic tank, but she couldn't stretch the full length and landed on top of the asbestos lid, which failed to sustain her weight and gave way. The asbestos lid broke into pieces, and Joanna fell into the septic hole full of water and human waste. Her whole body was submerged in the watery human waste except for her head which she occasionally popped above the sewer water as she struggled to catch a breath.

Fortuitously, the moment Joanna fell into the septic tank, her aunt, and the best friend to her mum by the name of Manku, witnessed what had happened and frantically rushed to her rescue while screaming at the top of her voice, leading the neighbourhood train of mums, dads, uncles and aunties to mention but a few, all headed in the same direction. Upon reaching the septic tank, Manku put her head into the dark hole and called out Joanna's name several times, but there was no response. After calling out her name continuously, Joanna finally responded in a choking voice amidst fearful groans when her head popped above the watery sewage material.

Joanna sounded very scared as she fought for her dear life while splashing water in the dark and stinky abyss of human waste. She screamed uncontrollably as she shouted for help whenever her head popped above the stinky sewer water.

Manku was renowned for always thinking on her feet, so while the men that were present jostled about looking for a rope to pull out Joanna, she asked four clueless men who stood closest to her to lower her into the septic hole while holding her legs so that she could stretch her hands and reach for Joanna. The four men sheepishly complied without asking any questions as desperate situations indeed call for desperate measures. Two of the men securely held her right leg while the other two did the same to her left leg while Manku guided them to gently lower her a little further down, headfirst, and both arms fully stretched towards Joanna's location.

Because it was dark inside the septic hole and Joanna had disappeared under the sewer water once again, it took a few minutes before Manku's hands could locate her. Manku made several 'feel and hold' attempts until she finally felt something solid in her hands, and she knew she had located the young girl. She grabbed Joanna by her jersey and hollered to the four men who held her legs to pull her out. The four strong men managed to pull her out with Joanna's motionless body in her hands.

No one knew whether Joanna was dead or alive. Confused and curious at the same time, most of the women and children around were screaming in horror while others around shoved and pushed through the people that surrounded Joanna just to have a glimpse of her motionless body.

Some studies show there are reasons why human beings can't look away from tragedy. There is a science to why death and destruction command our attention. What happens to our brains when we see destruction? According to Dr John Mayer, a clinical psychologist at Doctor on Demand, the process is one that actually triggers our survival instincts. "A disaster enters into our awareness – this can be from a live source such as driving by a traffic accident or from watching a news report about a hurricane, a plane crash or any disaster," he explains. "This data from our perceptual system then stimulates the amygdala (the part of the brain responsible for emotions, survival tactics and memory). The amygdala then sends signals to the regions of the frontal cortex that are involved in analysing and interpreting data. Next, the brain evaluates whether this data (awareness of the disaster) is a threat to you, thus judgment gets involved. As a result, the 'fight or flight' response is evoked. This acts as a preventive mechanism to give us information on the dangers to avoid and to flee from," he says. Once we go through this process and deem what we're witnessing a non-threat, psychiatrist Dr David Henderson says that we continue to stare as a way to face our fears without risking immediate harm. Further, one study published by the American Psychological Association found that we react to and learn more from our negative experiences than we do positive ones. "Humans are prone to negative bias and negative potency," explains psychologist Dr Renee Carr. "Negative bias is the tendency to automatically give more attention to a negative event and negative information than positive information or events." Psychologically, negative events activate our brains more than positive ones. "Negative potency describes the higher amount of psychological arousal that is experienced when a person is exposed to a negative or traumatic event compared with a positive event," Dr Carr explains[1].

Muswana was convinced that her daughter, Joanna, was dead as she vigorously shook her motionless body, which lay on the ground covered in human waste. In the hustle and bustle of the moment, the neighbour to the Bloomfields, who was a nurse by profession named Gift, arrived at the scene and compassionately requested Muswana to move aside for him to administer CPR (i.e., Cardiopulmonary Resuscitation) on Joanna. He tapped Joanna on her shoulder and shouted her name in her right and left ears. "Joanna! Joanna!" he called frenetically. There was still no sign of life or response from the young girl who lay motionless on the ground. Gift then asked Manku (who was standing close to him) if anyone had called the emergency line 911. To Gift's astonishment, no one had yet called the emergency line, so he instructed Manku to immediately call 911.

The good Samaritan nurse, Gift, opened Joanna's airway while she lay on her back, tilted her head slightly to lift her, and listened for breathing sounds for about 10 seconds. He couldn't detect any, so he placed his right hand on top of his left hand in the middle of Joanna's chest and used his body weight to help administer compressions that were at least two inches deep at a rate of at least 100 compressions per minute. With Joanna's head still tilted back slightly and her chin lifted, he pinched her nose shut and placed his mouth over her mouth to make a complete seal, and he blew into Joanna's mouth to make her chest rise, but it did not rise with Gift's initial rescue breath. So, Gift re-tilted her head before delivering the second rescue breath.

Yet still, Joanna's chest did not rise with the second breath, so Gift realised she might be choking, but he decided to administer another set of 30 chest compressions before attempting the third rescue breath. Joanna's chest remained still and did not rise. Gift then intuitively dipped his two left fingers down Joanna's throat and felt an object which he gently but quickly pulled out. It was a sanitary towel that had blocked Joanna's airway, and he realised that's the reason why her chest was failing to rise when he breathed in her mouth.

While waiting for the medical respondent, Gift continued to perform CPR steps, and within a few seconds, Joanna coughed and vomited out some thick dark green water that was mixed with human waste very much to the relief of her grief-stricken mum, Muswana, and all the bystanders who, out of excitement, started to jump up and down in exhilaration and ululating jubilantly.

Muswana took the cotton material she wore around her waist and wrapped it around her daughter in order to keep her warm. Within a few minutes, the ambulance arrived. Joanna was connected to an oxygen tank and whisked away to the hospital with her mum. After the ambulance had left, Manku took the opportunity to thank Gift on behalf of her friend Muswana for administering CPR on Joanna, without which she could have died.

Although some people mistakenly think CPR is a new technique, it has been in use since the mid-1700s (1740), when the French Academy of Sciences recommended mouth-to-mouth resuscitation for drowning victims. Dr James Elm first demonstrated the technique and worked with Dr Peter Safar in proving the effectiveness of CPR and its many advantages compared to other emergency procedures. The first attempts to deal with sudden cardiac arrests or heart attacks started in the mid-1700s in Amsterdam, where wealthy and civil minded citizens organised a group named Society for Recovery of Drowned Persons. The organisation formed a set of rules to follow if a person may drown. It became such a success that similar organisations were founded across Europe and later migrated to America. The CPR movement has gained massive popularity since, saving approximately 92,000 lives each year.

The soused and inebriated Kennedy returned home from his drinking spree late at night, only to be greeted by the stunning and shocking news about his daughter, Joanna. He at once jumped onto his motorcycle and headed for the hospital. Sad days lay ahead for the Bloomfield family as Joanna's condition deteriorated in the hospital.

Kennedy finally arrived at the hospital to his hysterical and despondent wife. She was shouting and crying uncontrollably, laying the blame on him. She pointed the accusing finger pregnant with sorrow straight at him and screamed, "Had you been home to help me look after our children instead of being out drinking with your good-for-nothing-racist mates, our daughter would not be lying in the hospital fighting for her life."

Kennedy was deeply touched as streams of tears rolled down his frozen pale cheeks from his bewildered eyes like a waterfall. Drawing on his natural charm apologetically, the devastated Kennedy wrapped his hands around his wife Muswana and held her tight close to his body to comfort her. However, she was inconsolable as she continued wailing and levelling accusations at him on top of her voice, very much to the amusement of hospital staff and those around.

Dutifully, the senior hospital receptionist led Kennedy and Muswana away from the waiting area into a private room adjacent to the reception to help them recuperate and come to terms with the predicament surrounding their daughter.

After Kennedy had managed to calm down his wife, Muswana, a lanky grey-haired Asian doctor walked into their room to detail their daughter's prognosis. Dr Chanda apprised the couple to prepare for the worst as their daughter was in a very serious condition. The doctor explained to Kennedy and Muswana that Joanna had taken in too much sewer water, which exposed her to several potentially deadly bacteria.

In order to drive the point home, Dr Chanda mentioned some of the pathogens Joanna's body was contending with, which included the *Campylobacter jejuni* bacteria – a bug commonly found in animal faeces and one of the most common causes of gastroenteritis; Salmonella, which could cause gastroenteritis, typhoid fever and paratyphoid fever, all potential killers; *Escherichia coli* or *E. coli* a bacterium commonly found in the lower intestine, also found in sewage; Listeria bacteria which could cause a potentially deadly infection called listeriosis etc.

The detailed explanation by Dr Chanda was intended to prepare Joanna's parents for the worst possible outcome as Joanna lay dying in her hospital bed. The only tantalising signs of life from Joanna's body were the eerie groans she produced each time she breathed in and out, which seemed to be in chilly harmony and in tandem with the sound from the oxygen machine she was attached to.

Chapter 3
Missing the Forest For the Trees: Sexy Stories

In an idyllic and epitome world, Manku should have naturally been touted as a heroine for her fast thinking, which led to the rescue of Joanna out of the sewer pit. However, all her good works were overshadowed by the sordid and salacious gossip doing rounds, mainly among the male folk of the compound.

The red-hot saucy chatter among the concerned gossip peddler male folks, which was carefully kept under wraps and away from the hearing range of their 'pious' wives, was that on the day Manku rescued Joanna from the sewer hole, she wasn't wearing any knickers. You guessed it! Therefore, it was alleged and claimed by the dubious eyewitnesses that the four men (and those close by) who dipped Manku into the dark sewer hole actually got more than they 'bargained for' during their rescue mission.

It was alleged the quartet and a few others were made to feast their eyes on Manku's nakedness for as long as the rescue mission lasted. Some among the four rescuers who held Manku's legs while she stooped into the dark pit to salvage Joanna went on further to claim that for the sake of the X-rated entertainment, they ensured they pulled Manku out of the sewer hole extra slowly. If true, one would rightfully deem it a callous act given Joanna's survival depended on the length of that rescue mission. Each second that ticked by was extremely valuable and meant the difference between life and death for Joanna.

Others derisively and sardonically added that as ever, Manku was so task-focused that she was oblivious to the X-rated movie she was making other people's husbands watch free of charge. Yet still, others stocked the fire by adding that it was habitual of Manku not to wear knickers.

Unfortunately, much of this gossip was done within Trump's hearing range, who seemed to be flabbergasted about the whole thing and wondered why these gentlemen were so intrigued by what they saw in the process of rescuing his sister.

Following the gossip, the young Trump strongly suspected Manku was a magnet for controversy. One day while eavesdropping, he overheard Manku ask his mum to lend her a knicker. Though he wasn't old enough to construct a mountain out of the molehill of that information, nevertheless, he suspected there was something weird, uncanny and bizarre about that request. This was especially so because at one time, his mum chastised him for inadvertently coming home while wearing a jersey that belonged to another boy from his school. "You should never ever wear other people's clothes because clothes carry germs!" Trump's mum scolded him in a low but firm voice.

From that stern admonishment which remained entrenched in his mind on pain of punishment if he ever disobeyed, Trump inferred there was something yucky and distasteful about Manku's request to borrow his mother's underwear. Where was Manku planning to go while wearing his mother's underwear? he pondered and marvelled.

It was not long after the 'knicker-saga' when while eating his lunch in their kitchen one Friday afternoon, Trump overheard Manku confide in his mum that she caught her stepdaughter red-handed peeping through the opening of their master bedroom door while her father was dressing in readiness for work. Manku continued that she became curious and quietly moved closer behind her stepdaughter to see what had caught her attention from their master bedroom. Upon drawing closer, she said she was shocked and discombobulated to discover that her stepdaughter had actually been gazing at her own father's nakedness.

Manku claimed she did not know what to do or to make out of the unfortunate situation and whether or not to inform her husband or simply scold her stepdaughter. She also wondered why her stepdaughter would be drawn to watching the naked body of a man, let alone her biological father. There was a whisper followed by episodes of silence as the two women pondered the best course of action. After a few minutes, Muswana stood up and shut the door to their living room, where she was seated with the 'storyteller' Manku. Trump was somehow glad not to hear the conclusion to that unusual incident because Manku's stepdaughter, Muzo, was his friend.

Chapter 4
Children and the Supernatural

Trump's home life was so littered with unwarranted and, in some cases, avoidable dramatic events that to say he underwent a normal childhood growth process would be a misnomer. This is so because of what he saw and heard while growing up. One would rightly conclude that Trump had a troubled childhood. The fact that he had a black mother and a white father with different cultural backgrounds and perspectives did not help matters. While Trump's mother was religious and loved him and his sister to bits, she was bipolar and prone to punishing them for the smallest of infractions. Her physical punishment was very much dependent on her mood.

Trump's father, Kennedy, loved the bottle a little bit too much and spent a considerable amount of time away from home with his white friends in the black man's land where they shared 'white peoples' problems' and experiences while constantly validating their decision to migrate from Europe to Africa. During their alcohol imbibing convocations, they also took time to console each other that settling in Africa was the right thing to do given the stiff competition and ongoing upheaval in Europe.

Kennedy was also an emotionally distant man and usually kept Trump and his younger sister at arm's length. However, he was quick to show disapproval and resentment towards anything Trump did.

The marriage of Trump's parents was a tortuous and labyrinthine affair that fuelled their bad behaviour towards each other and their children. While some traumatic experiences were maybe obvious, like physical chastisement, other things like emotional abuse were surely not so much, and this was the side of life that Trump experienced growing up.

At the tender age of five, Trump was exposed to the supernatural world by his grandfather, Dilaso, who was the biological father to his mother, though he was unaware. Some scholars define the supernatural as events or things that cannot be explained by nature or science and are assumed to come from beyond or originate from otherworldly forces. Different people from different parts of the world bear testimony to real-life encounters with the supernatural world. These testimonies are often passed on out of their own free volution from the lowly ranked to the noble men and women of our diverse societies, thereby tossing out the possibility of collusion as to the realism of the paranormal, mystical or supernatural world.

According to a BBC article that was authored by David Robson, *'Psychology: The truth about the paranormal'*[2], soon after World War II, Winston Churchill was visiting the White House when he is said to have had an uncanny experience. Having had a long bath with a Scotch and cigar, he reportedly walked into the adjoining bedroom – only to be met by the ghost of Abraham Lincoln. Unflappable, even while completely naked, Churchill apparently announced, "Good evening, Mr President. You seem to have me at a disadvantage." The spirit smiled and vanished. His supposed contact with the supernatural puts Churchill in illustrious company. Arthur Conan Doyle spoke to ghosts through mediums, while Alan Turing believed in telepathy. Three men, all known for their razor-sharp thinking, could not stop themselves from believing in the impossible. Some paranormal experiences are easily explainable, based on faulty activity in the brain. Reports of poltergeists invisibly moving objects seem to be consistent with damage to certain regions of the right hemisphere responsible for visual processing; certain forms of epilepsy, meanwhile, can cause the spooky feeling that a presence is stalking you close by – perhaps underlying accounts of faceless 'shadow people' lurking in the surroundings.

Not only was it rumoured, but it was also a well-kept family secret, at least from the 'foreigner' Kennedy Bloomfield by his wife Muswana and the rest of her family, that Muswana's father, Dilaso, was a high-profile wizard who travelled between countries and continents in the wee of the night on his sorcery missions. Unbeknown to both Muswana and Kennedy, their own son Trump accompanied his grandfather on some of those sorcerous tours. The act of involving an innocent child in such diabolical operations, albeit unawares, one could argue, has the potential to entrench the realism of the supernatural underworld in their subconscious mind from a tender age.

History is pregnant with a plethora of facts about children and their involvement or close shave with witchcraft. According to an article by Francis Cronin, 'The witch trial that made legal history'[3]. In recent years, children as young as three have given evidence in court cases, but children under 14 were seen as unreliable witnesses in the past. A notorious seventeenth century witch trial changed that. Nine-year-old Jennet Device was an illegitimate beggar and would have been lost to history, but for her role in one of the most disturbing trials on record. Jennet's evidence in the 1612 Pendle witch trial in Lancashire led to the execution of 10 people, including all of her own family. In England at that time, paranoia was endemic. King James l was on the throne, living in fear of a Catholic rebellion after Guy Fawkes' gun powder plot. The king had a reputation as an avid witch-hunter and wrote a book called *Demonology*. At the time, Lancashire had a reputation for being full of troublemakers and subversives. Jennet lived with her mother Elizabeth, her grandmother Demdike, older sister Alizon and brother James in the shadow of the Pendle hill. Villagers dubbed Demdike a 'cunning woman'. In March 1612, Alizon cursed a pedlar who would not give her any pins. The pedlar collapsed, and his son reported it to an ambitious local magistrate, Roger Nowell. He interviewed Alizon, who confessed to bewitching the pedlar but also accused their neighbours, who the family was having a feud with, of bewitching and killing four people. The neighbours pointed the finger straight back at Demdike, accusing her of witchcraft. Nowell was extremely zealous. He arrested Alizon, Granny Demdike, as well as their neighbours Anne Whittle (also known as Chattox) and her daughter Anne Redferne. In his book *Demonology*, King James l wrote: "Children, women and liars can be witnesses over high treason against God." This influenced the justice system and led to Nowell using Jennet as his key witness. This wasn't the only case involving children in witchcraft.

By the start of the seventeenth century, many children were being punished and put in prison for taking part in witchcraft. This usually occurred because of their alleged participation in Sabbats. It was a common belief that witches' children inherited witchcraft from their parents. It was often the practice to charge a whole family of witchcraft, even if only one individual was suspected. Witches who confessed often claimed that they learned witchcraft from a parent. Pierre de Lancre and Francesco Maria Guazzo believed that it was enough proof of a witch's guilt if they had parents who were witches. They believed witch parents introduced the children to Satan, took the children to Sabbats, married children to demons, inspired the children to have sex with Satan (devil) or had sex with Satan with the child present. Many times, the child accused of witchcraft, due to being shunned, threatened community members, thereby enforcing their beliefs that the child was a witch[4].

Trump's unintentional involvement in his grandfather's sorcery antics and frolics was, therefore, not an isolated incident that was unique to him but simply a case of history replicating itself. As soon as his head hit his pillow at night, Trump would sense and feel as though he was flying at a very high speed; but because all this was so foggy and hazy, he always attributed the experience to a bad dream bordering on a nightmare. Trump never made any attempt to confide in his parents or anyone for that matter about his fiendish and malevolent encounters at night. As the saying goes, "What you tolerate, you allow." Because he told no one, the wizardry encounters became a constant feature of Trump's dreams or, rightly put, what he did after going to bed daily, till after he was six years when it suddenly stopped, and he started having normal nights again.

Trump's wizardry encounters usually started with an ominous sound of an unsettled wind which steadily increased in tempo and velocity until it attained its highest momentum, at which point Trump would take off flying at full speed. He couldn't figure out exactly what It was, but it felt as though he was riding on the back of something like a bird, and he would always hold tight to it around what felt like its neck in order not to fall off.

Flying at an astronomical speed, Trump's mysterious mode of transport would often leap up and down but always tended upwards until it had climbed to a certain height before becoming stable as they cruised through thick clouds and strong turbulences without causing an iota of damage to the invisible supernatural plane.

In the natural world, while most encounters with turbulences are fairly routine and aeroplanes are designed to cope with the forces and pressures placed upon them during these minor occurrences, it is the unpredictable nature combined with the low visibility that makes them a danger to pilots, aircraft and passengers, and this can cause double trouble if a pilot is not skilled enough or experiences extreme levels of turbulence because this can cause them to lose control of the aircraft. This is a particular concern around Cumulonimbus clouds (thunderstorm clouds) which can be concealing severe turbulence, strong vertical motions, severe icing, thunderstorms and hail. This is the exact reason pilots do not choose to fly through clouds if they are avoidable and plan their flight path to avoid certain weather patterns involving large and dangerous cloud formations and for larger passenger aircraft, this means flying up above the cloud base. Trump's mysterious plane seemed impervious to all these forces of nature, and he did not have to worry about Cumulonimbus clouds or landing his plane safely.

After a tour of duty, Trump's plane would without notice in the end head for the earth (home) and on approach, on its descent, he would start seeing houses appear, and they would eventually fly past his house onto a plain field that was covered with tall, thick green grass. One significant thing Trump noticed was that when descending, the grass would always bend over as they flew past, and the place behind them would immediately become dark so that nothing behind them was visible but only what lay in front of them.

The apex or peak moment of those recurrent sorcery and shamanism shenanigans was what happened each time or whenever Trump and his 'transport' flew over and past the graves of dead people, both ancient and modern graves. The horrifying and harrowing experience caused Trump to conclude that two sets of people lay in those graves. The first group was composed of the Satanists who were only interested in the 'here-and-now' and wanted nothing to do with life or what happened after death, whereas the second class of dead people, who Trump simply termed non-Satanists, had something to do with life after death.

His tender age and mind aside, Trump did not arrive at that conclusion anecdotally or without reasons. It was precisely because the graves that he saw were labelled on some wind-tossed, seemingly smoky transparent coverings or banners that distinguished the occupants of the graves. Each time they flew past the graves of the class Trump termed 'the Satanists', he noticed that his flying experience was distinctly very bumpy, and he would hear a loud voice, as though through a huge loudspeaker which echoed miles and miles away saying, "Doom, gloom, and death hangs over the earth, here's to the worship of life, Satanism is for the living. If we can, we will cheat death at every turn, to continue living well, we enjoy the here and now, and do not look for a fictive afterlife."

Conversely, Trump heard a completely different, quiet and calm voice akin to someone trying to whisper something yet doing so very clearly and loudly each time they flew past the graves of the group Trump termed 'non-Satanists'. The other astonishing thing that Trump noticed while flying past the graves of this latter group was that the ride was extremely smooth, and the words he heard were also completely different. They were words of hope beyond death and the grave saying, "Happy are the dead who die in the master, they rest from their labour, lo and behold their good deeds follow them."

To mark the end of each sorcery mission, it would suddenly become quiet, and when Trump opened his eyes, it was dawn, and he would be glad that it was over.

Each time it was bedtime, Trump would hesitate to go to bed, but his parents could not fathom his reasoning, or perhaps like most parents, they simply paid no attention. One would argue that how else would they know except if Trump let them in on his secret, but that's something he was determined not to risk sharing with anyone for fear of reprisal from the 'underworld'.

Chapter 5
The Impact of Parental Issues on Children

Considering Trump's tribulations at night, one would wonder why he simply never asked for help from an adult.

According to an article that was authored by Teresa Buchanan titled '7 Things You Need to Do So Your Kids Come to YOU When in Trouble'[5], One of the most confounding things to parents reading the Harry Potter series to their children would be '*why doesn't he ask an adult for help*'. Arguably this is easier said than done. The characters in the series would find themselves in dangerous, frightening or difficult situations that could be easily resolved with a word or act by an adult, but they never asked for help. And perhaps that's one of the reasons why that series is so popular, as it accurately portrays a universal childhood problem. Many young people say they cannot talk to their parents. They believe there is no adult in their life that will listen or understand. And this was also Trump's problem.

According to some schools of thought, when parents don't love each other as much as they should or if either or both of them are addicted to alcohol or some other form of substance, it's often a time difficult to realise their children may be in need of help as it was in Trump's case with his encounter with sorcery at a young age.

Trump's father, Kennedy, could not bring himself to face that he was addicted to alcohol. He fell into the category called 'functional alcoholics'. According to an article by Melissa Bienvenu, 'Are You a High-Functioning Alcoholic?[6]' from the WEBMD archives. The classic picture of an alcoholic is someone who always drinks too much and whose life is falling apart because of it. But that's not always the reality. Some people seem to be just fine even though they abuse alcohol. Experts call these people 'functional' or 'high-functioning' alcoholics. "You can still be one even though you have a great 'outside life', with a job that pays well, home, family, friendships and social bonds," says Sarah Allen Benton, a licensed mental health counsellor and author of *Understanding the High Functioning Alcoholic*. Benton says that a functional alcoholic might not act the way you would expect him to act. He might be responsible and productive. He could even be a high achiever or in a position of power. In fact, his success might lead people to overlook his drinking. He could also be in denial. He might think "I have a great job, pay my bills, and have lots of friends; therefore, I am not an alcoholic," Benton says. Or he might make excuses like, "I only drink expensive wine" or "I haven't lost everything or suffered setbacks because of drinking." But he isn't doing fine, says Robert Huebner, PhD, of the National Institute on Alcohol Abuse and Alcoholism. No one, he warns, "Can drink heavily and maintain major responsibilities over long periods of time. If someone drinks heavily, it is going to catch up with them."

Others maintain that not all alcohol use is a problem, ranging from non-problem drinking to addiction. Some people say they can't stop drinking, and this is called an 'addiction' to alcohol. When someone is addicted, they keep drinking alcohol even though bad things start to happen. In some cases, stress or other mental health problems may lead to drinking more alcohol.

In the case of Trump's father, Kennedy, the issue was convoluted and quite complicated. The genesis of his woes ranged from being a white settler in a land where few people looked like him or shared a similar background or upbringing to his unwillingness to fully subsume his cultural background into that of his wife's and other people who looked like her, and they were in the majority. These are the people who he chose to settle amongst, the black natives, out of his own accord.

It was this polarised situation that relegated Kennedy to an ambivalent personality. This meant he was usually uncertain, tentative, cautious or lacked the ability to make confident decisions on a number of family life issues. To cope with the inevitable, Kennedy employed a variety of coping mechanisms ranging from alcohol to spending vast amounts of time away from his family and other local natives who tried to befriend him. Instead, he 'voted' with his feet and chose to hang out with his fellow white folk at a pub owned by a Scotsman called Jolly Fisherman's.

While Jolly Fisherman's was not exclusively for white people, the culture inside and around the pub resonated very well with the implied philosophy of a 'white only' pub which intentionally made most natives feel unwelcome, leading them to avoid it altogether. It wasn't uncommon for Kennedy and his friends to use coded language to cleverly pour scorn on the natives' primitive culture and way of life in most cases and then ironically, at least in Kennedy's situation, later return to his native wife to play family.

The state of affairs was further compounded by Kennedy's early years and his upbringing, which he desperately tried to forget and never shared with anyone he had come to know in his new life in Africa, away from the land of his upbringing in Ireland; not even his wife Muswana knew anything about Kennedy's childhood.

Kennedy grew up in a troubled home, but his parents always found a way to circumvent divorce which was not by resolving issues but by exchanging 'fists of fury' and bottling up their problems whenever the situation presented itself. His Irish father and Colombian mother, Mr and Mrs Bloomfield, had multiple sexual partners and occasionally participated in swinging sex, which they kept a secret from each other.

One unfortunate night while at a swinging session, having lied to his wife that he had a work assignment that required him to travel out of town, Mr Bloomfield Senior, while adorned in a mask to disguise himself, spotted his wife also in a mask, in full action with four men, and she clearly made it known to him that she had also seen him (in action with two women). Bizarrely, each one of them continued unperturbed as though they were strangers till the end of that sexually explosive group event of consenting adults.

Unsurprisingly, though he tried to pretend, the situation was too overbearing for Bloomfield Senior to handle, and he failed to fully enjoy himself that night. He carried on nevertheless, and so did his wife. Research into the 'World of Swingers' shows that not all swingers think swinging means playing side by side with their spouse. It seems every swinger has their own definition of what swinging is and their own rules regarding playing. For some, swinging means planning an evening with their spouse and making a date with another couple. Their course of action usually involves getting to know another couple by having dinner at a restaurant or meeting for drinks before initiating any sexual contact with them. Others prefer the swing club approach, which is generally meeting another couple while at a swing club and heading either into the back room or meeting outside the club to have sex.

Research also shows that most swingers will agree that being in the lifestyle has brought their couple closer to the belief that they must have a tremendous amount of confidence in each other and their relationship to make this work. It is said that trust is extremely important because, without it, swinging won't work. For many couples in the lifestyle, a big part of the 'thrill' is watching their partner with someone else while they, too, are enjoying themselves.

What Bloomfield Senior's philosophy was when it came to swinging was anyone's guess. It was clear that Bloomfield Senior deemed swinging to be strictly out of bounds for his wife, as can be deduced from the fateful events that followed.

After scoring an 'own goal' that night, so much ignominy, indignity, humiliation, and rage, all mingled together in Bloomfield Senior. According to his state of mind that night, he had caught his wife red-handed violating their marriage vows. Bloomfield Senior completely removed himself from the picture as his way of doing things. He was absolutely convinced he had done nothing wrong in his own mind. Inversely, she had gravely wronged him as both her husband and head of their household.

Bloomfield Senior retired home earlier than his wife on the material day. His wife arrived home just before sunrise and knocked hesitantly on the window of their master bedroom. She avoided knocking on their front door out of fear, but also in order not to disturb their son Kennedy who was still asleep.

It was as though Bloomfield Senior had been waiting for his wife's arrival. He quietly opened the door but never uttered a single word to confront his wife about her presence at the 'swingers'. Within a few minutes of Mrs Bloomfield's arrival that fateful morning, Kennedy was awakened by some wild, loud bangs and when he rushed out of his room to wake his father up, he was shocked to find both his parents lying there in a pool of blood.

Kennedy later learnt from the police and other media channels that his Irish father Mr Bloomfield, who was incongruously and oddly well-loved and respected in his local community, aged 35, shot dead his Colombian wife, Luciana Bloomfield, who was aged 40 at the time, before gunning down their cat and dog and then turning the gun on himself. The question that often lingered in Kennedy's mind afterwards was why his father never shot him dead after killing every living thing in their house. A caretaker at a foster home where Kennedy was later temporarily accommodated managed to answer Kennedy's question unflinchingly. He looked straight in young Kennedy's big eyes and said in no uncertain terms that his lucky escape could only be attributed to the intervention of the supernatural forces who spared his life for a reason.

Though he grew up to be a normal person somehow, the grisly childhood events he experienced contributed towards shaping the man that Kennedy grew up to become; the man who migrated to Africa as a missionary and married a native African girl, Muswana, who later became Trump's mother.

As a consequence of his appalling childhood experience involving his parents, Kennedy suffered from a medical condition known as dissociative identity disorder (previously known as multiple personality disorder). Dissociative identity disorder is said to be severe thoughts, memories, feelings, actions, or sense of identity. Dissociative identity disorder is thought to stem from a combination of factors that may include trauma experienced by the person with the disorder, and that was the origin of the 'demons' that Kennedy had to deal with. One would not cast a shadow of a doubt that Kennedy's ordeal must have affected Trump's upbringing and his relationship with his father.

Another unsettling incident that left an enduring scar on Trump's mind was remembering his father, Kennedy, returning from one of his numerous drinking sprees just before 9 pm. He walked past his family seated in the living room without greeting them and went straight into their master bedroom. Trump's mum continued reading them the storybook without paying attention to what had just happened partially because, truth be told, that was not an isolated incident. Kennedy had behaved in the exact manner on countless other occasions except that night he did something very weird.

After spending some 10 minutes or so quiet in their master bedroom, Kennedy emerged and walked slowly into their family living room, where his wife Muswana was reading a storybook to their children. He was completely naked with his overgrown blonde pubic hair around his genitals on full display. He idiotically stood in the middle of their living room and called his wife's name in a sexually suggestive manner, "Muswana oooh Muswana, Muswana oooh Muswana…" while dancing erotically and simultaneously shaking his willy from one side to the other and then round and round in the shape of a circle.

Caught unaware, Muswana was so shocked she nearly passed out. That also meant her reaction to rectify the situation was slower than one would expect in the circumstances. By the time she sprung on Kennedy and aggressively hounded and dragged him back into their bedroom, the damage had already been done. Unfortunately, the bemused, mystified and perplexed young Trump never looked away during the entire incident. He saw everything! The whole family was spooked. This was also done in full view of Muswana's younger sister and Kennedy's sister-in-law, Jane, visiting that weekend. In an attempt to register her displeasure and save her sister from humiliation through her presence having seen the size of Kennedy's undergarment 'fathering-equipment', Jane cut her visit short and left very early the following morning before Trump and her sister could wake up.

All Trump remembered following that foolish 'naked-stunt' by his father was that the over the top vicious, rancorous and rambunctious actions that his angry mother Muswana employed to deal with his father's imprudent behaviour was more than enough to ensure there was no repeat of not only that particular stunt but also other analogous stunts that might have been work-in-progress in Kennedy's imperceptible 'psycho-assembly bay'.

Chapter 6
Guilt and Grief

"Words are like soft feathers, easy to drop but hard to pick," goes the old adage. In the case of real feathers, it's precisely because the wind would have blown them away. The guilt trip that Muswana put on Kennedy blaming him for Joanna's accident due to his absence from home on the day she fell in the sewer hole never left his ears. Her sharp and piercing words kept ringing in his ears day and night, 24hrs a day, seven days a week, and the guilt was eating him big time. Grief Counsellors often say that the grief journey is long, winding, uncharted and at times torturous. Two of the most common emotions experienced on the grief journey are times of anger and times of guilt. Guilt is insidious. It creeps under our skin and becomes a part of us before we realise it's happening.

Although Kennedy tried hard to wear a façade of being strong on the outside, especially when talking to his work mates and other people about their daughter's condition in the hospital, he was crushed on the inside and constantly blamed himself. He also experienced times of anger and times of guilt interchangeably.

Replaying Muswana's livid and irate words that were hurled at him at the hospital that night, he was convinced that had he been home instead of the pub on that tragic day, perhaps he could have prevented what happened to Joanna. And it ate him deep to his core. Further, he thought God was having a go at him not only for his countless past sins but also for being a dreadful Christian who migrated to Africa on the pretext of being a missionary and later revealed his true colours as an egocentric, ungrateful and churlish man. The 'monkey' on Kennedy's back did a fairly good job castigating him!

In accordance with her upbringing and family tradition, Muswana continued to attend church throughout the period when their daughter was hospitalised. Muswana could be overheard agonisingly pleading with God to heal their daughter in prayer during mass or church services. She also rallied her fellow Christians to stand with her in corporate prayer; the term used to describe praying together with other people – in small groups or in larger bodies of people.

Corporate prayer is understood to be an important part of the Christian church, and in Acts 2:42, it is recorded that the early church prayed together. The bible does not indicate that corporate prayers are more powerful than private prayers. Some bible scholars allege that perhaps the misconception that some Christians have about the increased power of corporate prayer is based on Matthew 18:19–20, "Again, I tell you that if two of you on earth agree about anything you ask for, it will be done for you by my father in heaven. For where two or three come together in my name, there am I with them." The bible scholars further point out that it is important to read these verses in the passage context. The context addresses church discipline of a sinning member. When Christians think that these verses give them a 'blank cheque' to ask God for anything, it is a deep misinterpretation of the passage. Just because two or three people are gathered together in Jesus' name, they don't acquire some magical power that assures God will answer their prayer according to their wishes. Yes, Jesus is present when people pray together, but He is equally present when a believer prays individually. The scholars conclude by saying corporate prayer isn't about getting enough people together to pray until God bends His will to our will. Instead, prayer (corporate and private) is about cooperating with God, abandoning our desires, and submitting to God's will. In fact, Matthew 6:8 says, "…for your father knows what you need before you ask him."

Setting religious semantics aside, Muswana saw to it that her fellow Christians were actively engaged in pleading her daughter's case with God.

While Joanna was critically ill in the hospital, Trump had a hard time concentrating at school or on anything because he really missed his little sister. In his mind, he thought she was going to die. He kept daydreaming about her funeral and all the good times and adventures he experienced with his sister.

One Sunday, before Joanna fell into the sewer hole, on their way to church, after walking for a distance of about three miles from their home, Trump recollected his mother whispering to him and his sister and their mum's young sister Jane to keep quiet as she lowered her stature behind a shrub. They were all scared, thinking perhaps she had spotted a dangerous wild animal, and they panicked even as they quickly complied with Muswana's directive.

Muswana then quickly but quietly unwrapped the cotton clothing she was wearing around her waist and spread it wide with both arms to their maximum full length as she crawled forward, after ordering Trump and his sister Joanna and their aunt, Jane, once again to remain still and silent. Trump watched attentively as his mum sprang in one leap with her cotton clothing fully stretched, and she landed onto some unsuspecting birds, about 20 of them in total. She managed to trap about half of them, which was good.

It turned out that it wasn't actually a wild animal that Muswana had spotted. She wanted to ambush a swam of birds, a traditional delicatessen her father Dilaso introduced her to when she was about Trump's age which her family often ate with meals as a relish. That evening trump and the family feasted on the newly introduced relish, 'junior chicken'. After acquiring the taste for wild birds, Muswana and her siblings often referred to them as 'junior chicken' because their meat tasted just as nice as the real chicken.

While Joanna was in the hospital, Muswana continued attending church services three days per week. She attended mass on Sundays and Bible study on Wednesdays and Fridays. Besides attending church three days per week, their senior Pastor by the name of James, accompanied by church elders, came to their house either on Tuesday or Thursday (depending on how busy the Pastor's schedule was) around 7 pm to conduct a special healing service for Joanna. They would start with songs of praise and worship, and this would be followed by speaking in tongues and calling upon the name of Jesus to heal the young girl who lay dying in the hospital.

According to the Christian Bible, the gift of speaking in tongues is a spiritual gift. It means speaking with words or in a language one doesn't know to edify both oneself and others and make special requests to God. Some preachers go further to clarify the gift of speaking in tongues as the art of speaking in an encrypted language that the devil can't understand so that there's no way for him to thwart the requests being made of God; in this case, the healing of Joanna. The Bible records that Jesus foretold of speaking in tongues: *"And these signs will follow those who believe…they will speak with new tongues."* Mark 16:17. The first time anybody spoke in tongues was on the day of Pentecost, when the Holy Spirit was poured out on the apostles, as related in Acts 2:1–12. The apostles spoke the gospel to the crowds in Jerusalem, and what they said could be understood by people speaking many different languages: *"…We hear them speaking in our own tongues the wonderful works of God."* Acts 2:11. It is believed that the passionate, sometimes rhythmic, language-like patter that pours forth from religious people who 'speak in tongues' reflects a state of mental possession, many of them say. Now Researchers have some neuroscience to back them up. Researchers at the University of Pennsylvania took brain images of five women while they spoke in tongues and found that their frontal lobes, the thinking wilful part of the brain through which people control what they do were relatively quiet, as were the language centres. The regions involved in maintaining self-consciousness were active. The women were not in blind trances. "The amazing thing was how the images supported people's interpretation of what was happening," said Dr Andrew B. Newberg, leader of the study team, which included Donna Morgan, Nancy Wintering and Mark Waldman[7]. "The way they describe it, and what they believe, is that God is talking through them," he said.

Further, contrary to a common perception, some studies suggest that people who speak in tongues rarely suffer from mental problems. A recent study of nearly 1,000 evangelical Christians in England found that those who engaged in the practice were more emotionally stable than those who did not. Researchers have identified at least two forms of the practice of speaking in tongues, one ecstatic and frenzied, the other subdued and nearly silent.

Each time Pastor James and the church elders visited the Bloomfield's home to conduct healing services for Joanna, Kennedy would excuse himself and leave the house to meet his friends at Jolly Fisherman's. After imbibing a few pints of his favourite beer, Castle lager, Kennedy would every so often start to complain indignantly to his white friends about the situation at his home. In his drunken rants, he loudly disapproved of the visits to their home by Pastor James and the church elders and described the healing services as a wanton 'trespass' that hindered the right of his family to enjoy peace in their home. His fellow white friends would spur him on as they took turns insulting the Pastor using the 'n' and 'f' words interchangeably as some form of soothing balm to Trump's psyche.

To the Christian Muswana, no doubt the unsanctimonious 'balm' that was clandestinely administered to her husband at the Jolly Fisherman's pub by his wayward friends each time he ran away from their home would have stood in stuck contrast to the 'balm' contained in the hymn that often preceded Joanna's healing services conducted by Pastor James and the church elders. It was a hymn written by Nana Mousouri and Roger Loube, 'Balm in Gilead':

There is a balm in Gilead
To make the wounded whole
There is a balm in Gilead
To heal the sin-sick soul
Sometimes I feel discouraged
And deep I feel the pain
In prayers the holy spirit
Revives my soul again
There is a balm in Gilead
To make the wounded whole
There is a balm in Gilead
To heal the sin-sick soul
If you can't pray like Peter
If you can't be like Paul
Go home and tell your neighbour
He died to save us all
There is a balm in Gilead
To make the wounded whole
There is a balm in Gilead
To heal the wounded soul

Further, to feed his bigotry and narcissistic ego by playing to the gallery, it was during those same wild rants at the Jolly Fisherman's pub that Kennedy often disrespectfully referred to Pastor James's church as 'the Kaffir sanctuary'.

Kaffir (Arabic: 'kaffer'/'kæfər') is an ethnic slur used to refer to black Africans in South Africa. In the form of *cafri*, it evolved during the pre-colonial period as an equivalent of 'negro'. The term was later used to refer to the Bantu peoples in Southern Africa. This designation came to be considered a pejorative by the mid-twentieth century, and it is regarded as extremely offensive[8].

As the drinking continued deep into the night on the days when the healing services were taking place at his home, Kennedy's angry, nasty and sarcastic tirades and outbursts would often zero in on how he loathed the loud singing and the speaking in claptrap, twaddle, baloney and gibberish languages (i.e., speaking in tongues), and how it was really driving him insane. He also alleged the healing services were not making their daughter's condition any better; if anything, he claimed she was getting worse by the day. He would then switch from drinking beer to spirits just before retiring home to make sure he was completely sloshed and befuddled. By the time he got home after midnight, the church people would have long been gone, and Muswana would be fast asleep.

Chapter 7
The Power of Confrontation

Muswana was so focused on securing divine healing for her daughter that she was completely oblivious to Kennedy's stupid and irresponsible behaviour. She intentionally resolved to ignore him. The more she ignored him, the more horrendous Kennedy's behaviour became.

One day, Muswana decided she'd had enough of Kennedy's silly and absurd behaviour because it wasn't like she had tasked him with anything during the healing services with Pastor James and the church elders other than simply being civil. On the day she chose to implement her plan, Muswana petulantly and querulously confronted Kennedy about his behaviour, and he nearly died of a heart attack when she revealed that according to a prophecy by Pastor James, God was punishing their family because of him.

According to the un-cut details of the oracle offloaded by Muswana, without foreknowledge, Pastor James prophesied that Kennedy was once a good Christian who migrated to Africa as a missionary, but he purposely wandered away from God after He had blessed him with his family in countless ways including surviving a dreadful car accident in which Kennedy was the sole survivor. According to Muswana, Pastor James further prophesied that instead of seeking the face of God with his family during a very difficult time, Kennedy opted to spend valuable family time with a bunch of white atheist friends of his at the Jolly Fisherman's pub. According to the prophecy allegedly delivered by the Pastor, Trump's behaviour was a direct consequence of why their daughter suffered that terrible accident and lay dying in the hospital and that the only way God was going to heal their daughter was if Kennedy repented and turned back to the Lord.

Up to that point, no one besides Muswana had directly blamed Kennedy for Joanna's accident, so the prophecy cut deep into Kennedy's consciousness and his very persona, and it didn't matter whether it was true or not. In the few days that followed, Kennedy somehow recovered from the crippling prophecy, but the guilt was crushing him. Kennedy started hearing voices in his head asking him to repent to heal his daughter. Kennedy had never acquainted himself with Pastor James, but he dreamt about the Pastor one night. In the dream, Pastor James repeated the exact words Muswana narrated to him regarding the prophecy on why God was punishing their family. He woke up drenched in a cold sweat and thought some supernatural force or power was trying to communicate with him. Could his wife be right regarding the prophecy she relayed to him from Pastor James? Kennedy pondered and shuddered because he now had corroborative evidence from his dream.

While some psychologists have argued that dreams provide insight into a person's psyche or everyday life, others find their content too inconsistent or bewildering to reliably deliver meaning. Virtually all experts acknowledge that dreams can involve content that ties back to waking experiences, although the content may be changed or misrepresented. However, the meaning of real-life details appearing in dreams is far from settled.

The whole dream thing really distressed Kennedy greatly. In the weeks that followed, Kennedy started to pray privately before sleeping, and after waking up, and whenever he was by his daughter's bedside. He secretly prayed for his daughter and family and, above all, for God to forgive him. The prayers weren't done consistently or logically, but he got an inch deeper each day. Then one day, Kennedy surprised his wife when he decided not to go to his favourite pub Jolly Fisherman's, on both Friday and Saturday. He woke up very early on Sunday and further surprised his wife when he told her he wanted to accompany her and Trump to church. Trump, in particular, was very excited. He always loved spending time with his father, although he seemed aloof and distant.

The impact of a father's personality on his children may be imagined, both for good and bad. It's called the daddy factor – the impact of fathers on their children's development. Research shows that secure attachments have positive benefits that last into adulthood. Children who are securely attached do better academically; they are also more sociable and well-liked throughout early childhood than children who do not have secure attachments. Research also shows that Fathers who are actively involved in their children's lives – helping care for them, playing with them, and teaching them – tend to experience less conflict with their wives. This not only benefits children, but also strengthens the marital relationship, and it also has long-term benefits for children. Further, new research shows that fathers may have an even greater impact on children's language development than mothers. When fathers use more words with their children during play, children have more advanced language skills a year later. This is especially important because language skills are correlated with academic success.

After Kennedy had begun spending more time with his family, his relationship with his wife also improved tremendously. He also cut down on his drinking though he still found time to meet his friends' fortnightly on Fridays but had started returning home at a sensible time. Kennedy's attendance at church also improved, and he slowly started making friends with men of good standing in their church and locality, most of whom were educated natives, men who seemed to know how to look after their wives and family well. This bunch of Kennedy's new friends also religiously followed biblical principles in running their family affairs. One thing Kennedy desperately tried to avoid, though, was attending the bible study with his newfound friends from church. Nor did he want these people to know that he migrated to Africa as a missionary in obedience to the great commission launched by Jesus when he commanded his disciples, "Go ye therefore, and teach all nations, baptising them in the name of the Father, and of the Son, and of the Holy Ghost." This was to remain a top secret, and he made his wife promise to him that she would never let the cat out.

Joanna had now been in the hospital for close to six months, and with time, her condition started to improve, albeit at a slow pace. In the 8th month following her accident, Joanna came out of her medically induced coma. It appears Pastor James's prophecy was slowly but steadily coming to pass, and the guilt that had overwhelmed Kennedy had dissipated, making way for increased hope and faith instead.

The Christian bible defines faith as the evidence of things hoped for, the substance of things not seen. 'Faith' (*al-iman*) in the Arabic language means to affirm something and to comply with it. Ibn Taymiyyah writes: "It is understood that faith is affirmation and not merely belief. Affirmation includes the words of the heart, which is belief, and the actions of the heart, which is compliance[9]."

In line with his newfound faith, Kennedy held on firmly to the unseen evidence that his daughter was completely healed, and it was only a matter of time before his strong belief could bear fruit. Kennedy believed that through the unction of the holy spirit, God was calling him back to the fold, and he was reaping the reward of that obedience through receiving the gift of healing for his daughter.

Three months after coming out of her coma, Joanna was well enough and on the cusp of being discharged.

A week before their daughter got discharged from the hospital, while attending church service with his family on Sunday, Kennedy was so touched by the sermon that was preached that when Pastor James made an altar call at the end of his sermon, Kennedy did not even consult Muswana but sheepishly stood up and went to the front to rededicate his life back to Jesus. The sermon was on why Jesus heals, and the reason was to bring glory to his father. The mainstay of Pastor James's sermon was a passage he read from the book of Matthew 15:30–31, "Great crowds came to him, bringing with them the lame, the blind, the crippled, the mute, and many others, and they put them at his feet, and he healed them, so that the crowd wondered, when they saw the mute speaking, the crippled healthy, the lame walking, and the blind seeing. And they glorified the God of Israel."

"The power to heal the sick," the Pastor rammed the point home, "is still available to those who believe in Jesus."

Throughout the sermon, Kennedy was quietly thanking Jesus for healing their daughter while silently repeating the words, "I believe…I believe…I believe all things are possible in the name of Jesus."

The Pastor also preached on a subject that deeply permeated to the core of Kennedy's inner being to melt whatever hitherto had hardened his heart. It was on the wages of sin from Romans 6:23. "For the wages of sin is death; but the gift of God is eternal life through Jesus Christ our Lord." By the time Pastor James was making the altar call, Kennedy had already made up his mind to surrender his life to Jesus, and the rest was simply a formality.

Kennedy's rededication of his life back to Jesus didn't come as a surprise to Muswana; she knew he was changing, but she didn't think he was convicted sufficiently enough to surrender his life publicly as he preferred to operate 'underground'. Kennedy saw himself as a missionary who had fallen too far away from the grace of God and now in hiding. Further, Kennedy was a proud white man who felt he occupied a special place among the black natives. Therefore, he had enough pride to stop him from making a fool of himself in front of the natives, most of whom were poor and uneducated and had never witnessed a white man crying.

Seeing the unashamed Kennedy in front of the church (which he once upon a time referred to as 'the Kaffir Sanctuary') packed to capacity with black natives and his cheeks drenched in a pool of tears was in itself a great miracle, mused Muswana, with a grateful heart as she joined into the chorus with great Jubilation as they all sang the hymn 'There's power in the blood' (originally authored by Jones E. Lewis in 1899) led by Pastor James. And they continued to sing:

"Would you be free from the burden of sin?
There's power in the blood
Power in the blood
Would you o'er evil a victory win?
There's wonderful power in the blood
There is power, power, wonder working power
In the blood of the Lamb
There is power, power, wonder working power
In the precious blood of the Lamb
Would you be free from your passion and pride?
There's power in the blood
Power in the blood
Come for a cleansing to Calvary's tide
There's wonderful power in the blood
There is power, power, wonder working power
In the blood of the Lamb
There is power, power, wonder working power
In the precious blood of the Lamb."

It was now more apparent than ever to his wife Muswana and their close relatives and family friends that Kennedy had turned a new chapter in his life and had embarked on a new spiritual journey. The moment Muswana had long yearned for finally arrived, Kennedy completely severed ties with his white folks, who were his long-standing friends and drinking buddies he often mingled with every Friday and Saturday at Jolly Fisherman's.

Kennedy started to spend a large portion of his time with his wife, Muswana, and their son, Trump, after work and over the weekend. It seemed as though Pastor James's unrelenting fervent prayers for the Bloomfields had played a major part in Kennedy's transformation. Pastor James's advice was based on the old crèche that 'bad company corrupts good morals' and that if Kennedy was serious about his new walk with Jesus, he needed to cut loose his old sinful friends. Pastor James also quoted a few prominent biblical principles to Kennedy, including the famous one found in the book of Amos 3:3 "How can two walk together unless they have agreed." Pastor James also threw in street advice by quoting sayings such as 'if you hang around the barber shop long enough you are bound to get a haircut', i.e., don't hang around bad friends or else you will join in the mischief.

Kennedy's favourite biblical passage and one that played a major role in his conversion was about the two paths (one narrow and the other broad) recorded in Matthew 7:13 of the Christian Bible: "Enter ye in at the strait gate: for wide is the gate, and broad is the way, that leadeth to destruction, and many there be which go in there at. Because strait is the gate, and narrow is the way, which leadeth unto life, and few there be that find it." In Kennedy's own words, during his confession to Pastor James, he wanted to be counted among the few that found the way to life, so he chose the narrow path.

There were tangible and very fruitful results following Kennedy's decision regarding his family life. He was in love with his wife again, and people would often see them walking together while holding hands, and they showed up at the hospital to visit their daughter together. Each time they visited the hospital, they would kneel by their daughter's bedside, hold hands and pray together. They had made up their minds to be selective in what they chose to believe from the doctor's reports which usually contained words contrary to what they believed for.

According to an article titled 'Time Together and Time Apart'[10], authored by Rob Pascale and Lou Primavera Ph.D., Partners who do things together become more closely connected and come to enjoy each other's company. That's because shared experiences give them something in common; that helps make them feel good about each other. However, in heterosexual relationships, husbands and wives may have different ideas about how much time should be dedicated to the couple and the individual. In many couples, the wife tends to want more couple time, usually because she regards it as important for bolstering a marriage and making sure there's solidarity as a couple. On the other hand, her husband may tend to prefer more time on his own. That's not to say men aren't that interested in spending time with their wives. Rather, it may stem from the fact that men tend to have more and better-quality leisure time than women. Men tend to excel at compartmentalising, so issues they're dealing with in one part of their lives don't interfere with the other parts. It's easier, then, for them to put their work and home responsibilities aside and enjoy whatever else they're doing. Perhaps more importantly, however, many husbands still expect their wives to take care of their home and family. Consequently, they don't feel as much pressure to sacrifice their personal time as their wives might.

Chapter 8
The Silver Lining

The day finally came when the doctor delivered the message Kennedy and Muswana had believed for. Their daughter, Joanna, had become well enough to be discharged from the hospital. Joanna would continue treatment from home and see the doctor once per month to assess her progress.

Within five months, Joanna was completely healed and started attending school in the sixth month. As a result of their daughter's miraculous healing, Kennedy and Muswana's faith grew to a whole new level of strength, and it was for a good reason too. They believed Jesus had performed a miracle for their daughter.

According to the philosopher David Hume, a miracle is "a transgression of a law of nature by a particular volition of the deity, or by the interposition of some invisible agent." In the Old Testament of the Christian Bible, it appears that God's miracles, such as the parting of the Red Sea, were meant to show God's care for his children and lead them back to him. They were supposed to be a visible sign of God's presence in the world. Similarly, in the New Testament, Jesus is incarnate, and his public ministry is full of miracles. He heals the sick, walks on water and casts out demons. The *Catechism of the Catholic Church* explains how Jesus' miracles served a similar purpose. Furthermore, miracles in the Old and New Testaments are supernatural occurrences that only God can accomplish. This is most clearly expressed in the 'showdown' between Moses and the magicians of Pharaoh, as well as Elijah and the priests of Baal. Both times it was proven that God was the one behind the miracles and that he alone possessed supreme power.

Sometimes miracles are dismissed by scholars and scientists as a literary device used by the biblical authors that express a naïve understanding of science. They see a natural explanation for all the reported 'miracles' in the Bible and believe God was not behind any of it. Obviously, Kennedy and Muswana's interpretation of the word miracle was from a biblical point of view. The healing of their daughter Joanna was against the backdrop of the doctors' gloomy and bleak prognosis.

After abandoning his original mission to Africa of spreading the gospel (missionary work), Kennedy joined an American copper mining company whose headquarters was in Washington and had branches in Africa and South America.

One day, about fifteen months after Joanna's discharge from the hospital, Kennedy had just returned home from work, and after a warm bath, he was ready to sit down and relax with his family over a game of monopoly. Within a few minutes into the monopoly game, he received a communique from his boss, Mr Fitzgerald, to go back to the office for an urgent meeting with him. Kennedy thought that was rather odd because he had never been asked to return to the office after he had knocked off. Muswana looked at her watch incredulously and noted that it was after 6 pm and concurred with her husband that that order from Kennedy's boss had some elements of idiosyncrasy. Resisting the urge to confess negative words, they each secretly harboured a premonition of imminent disaster. Was Kennedy about to lose his job? Had they become too relaxed about the things of God and erred in their walk with Jesus? The whole situation was confounding, and Kennedy felt sick to the stomach. He nevertheless quickly jumped into his office attire and wore a warm jacket, and within a few minutes, he was riding his motorcycle to the office.

Upon arriving at the office, Kennedy went straight to the toilet, closed the door behind him and knelt to pray to Jesus, asking him to dispel any impending bad news or, if that was not possible, to give him sufficient grace and strength to bear it. Kennedy decided to lean on the words of encouragement that were spoken to Saul as recorded in the Christian Bible (in 2 Corinthians 12:9) when his prayer request for sight was not granted right away; instead, he received the words of encouragement: "My grace is sufficient for you, for my power is made perfect in weakness."

After his secret prayer session, Kennedy stood up and walked straight to his boss's office. The corridor was quiet as all employees had already been knocked off except for a few admin staff and the secretary to his managing director by the name of Patricia. When he reached outside the door to Mr Fitzgerald's office, Kennedy decided not to knock right away as his heart was pounding fast and felt out of rhythm, so he waited for some fifteen seconds, and after he had calmed down, he knocked gently on the door.

Mr Fitz, as his staff usually called him, had a natural poker face. He never gave anything away in terms of facial expression, so it was almost impossible to read his mind. He had dry blue eyes that shone more like poisoned precious stones than living tissue; his eyes were piercingly sharp, and he rarely blinked when talking. Or as his secretary, Patricia, once put it at a staff Christmas party after downing a few shots of tequila and letting her hair down. "That son of a bitch Fitz sees everything…he has eyes like those of a pitiless judge that seems to go to the very bottom of all mistakes to elucidate the reasons and intentions behind."

With his eyes looking straight into Kennedy's eyeballs as though to test how firmly they were held in place by his eye muscles, Mr Fitz gawkily and awkwardly stretched his hand towards Kennedy so they could shake hands.

Handshake enthusiasts claim that a handshake can tell you everything you need to know about someone even before a word is spoken. Grip long, grip hard. That's what we're usually told from the moment we're old enough to greet someone with a handshake. It doesn't matter how much success we've had or what we're about to achieve. Those few seconds in which we physically connect will reveal more about our character than any letters after our name or the title on a business card.

Research conducted by psychologists at the University of Alabama in 2000 tested the handshakes of 112 volunteers and compared the impressions they made with the psychological reports the volunteers completed afterwards. The researchers found that a 'firm handshake' corresponded to personality traits that included extroversion and 'openness to new experiences', while those with a weak handshake were more likely to show higher levels of shyness and anxiety on their psychological reports. Women generally had weaker handshakes than men, but women who shook hands firmly were rated positively. Even among women, a strong handshake suggests a strong personality.

The firm handshake aside, there was no doubt in Kennedy's mind about the strength of Mr Fitz's personality as it was common knowledge amongst all staff. The man brooked no-nonsense, and he was on point and meant business any time of the day or night. Kennedy silently sighed a sigh of relief after Mr Fitz finally loosed his grip and released his hand, which seemed to be dancing to freedom.

Mr Fitz gestured to Kennedy to sit down on one of the leather chairs. Kennedy sat down quietly with pressure slowly easing on his mind. Mr Fitz then cleared his throat and slowly parted his lips which were conspicuously disproportionate and lopsided in size as the upper lip was approximately two and half times thicker than the lower lip. He said in a hoarse, croaky, husky and bossy voice, "*Before we get on, I have to start by apologising to your wife and children for asking you to come and see me at this late hour. Will you please relay my apology?*" Kennedy nodded emphatically without uttering a single word.

Mr Fitz then continued slowly but assuredly, "*I have an announcement that I'm delighted to make. I'm very happy to inform you that the board of directors has approved my decision to promote you to Head of Metallurgy. This well-deserved promotion comes following your management of three phenomenally successful smelter modification projects at three different sites, and the triumph of your implementation has helped increase our copper production and revenue. I am also aware that you did all this at a difficult time when your daughter was still in the hospital. I'll be sending a memo tomorrow morning to all staff about your promotion. Congratulations once again. You are now free to go and share the good news with your family, and don't forget to convey my apologies for stealing you away from them. Hopefully, this should serve as a good reason for them to forgive me. And by the way, I know the answer is yes, so I didn't ask you.*"

Kennedy was pleasantly surprised because that's not the news he was expecting, and without asking for permission, tears took turns pouring down his joyful face. After hugging Mr Fitz and recounting how grateful he was, Kennedy headed straight home with his hands shaking uncontrollably while muttering words of thanks and praise to Jesus.

Muswana was increasingly becoming anxious at home as she didn't know what to expect. Her mind conjured up the worst-case scenario on what would happen to their family if her husband got laid off from his job, more so because there were few international companies in the country that employed white people. The other part of Muswana emboldened her to remain hopeful. After all, there hadn't been anything to suggest to her that Kennedy was in some form of trouble, or his company was doing badly. But given the misfortune that had befallen their family in the recent past, Muswana wasn't ruling out anything. The more she tried to dismiss her anxious and fiendish thoughts, which she construed as stemming straight from the pit of hell or from evil spirits, the louder they rang in her mind. She was also aware that bad things could happen to God's children, for example, the misfortune that befell an upright man by the name of Job in the Christian Bible contrived by the devil and executed by evil spirits.

Emanuel Swedenborg's writings about Spirits and Men argues that "Man is not responsible for all his general states. A child is not responsible for his/her childishness, and no adult can be blamed for having passed into maturity or old age. Neither can any arguments or any deliberate effort bring a woman into the state of a man or a wife into the state of her girlhood. Whenever our bodies grow tired after a day of activity, our minds inevitably come into new states, less strenuous; until we sink into oblivion of all cares, and spirits of a celestial type environ us. Men commonly blame many of their disappointments on 'bad luck', or ascribe their windfalls to a lucky chance. It is easy to see that the real causes behind man's general states lie in the presence with him of spirits of different types, and thus in the different spiritual mediations which modify the influx of the Lord's life into men. We can also see that evil spirits could lead men into many kinds of accidents and misfortunes. Certain spirits, by their arts, have a special skill to produce a sphere from which unfortunate circumstances naturally flowed in a way which wholly resembled pure chance. Unforeseen misfortunes are nothing else than the perpetual endeavours of evil spirits[11]."

Muswana was not given to reasoning by appearances. She was a staunch believer in the fact that 'those who trust in the Lord continually receive good from Him; and that for whatever happens, whether it appears as prosperous or not, is still good for them and conducing to their eternal happiness'. In succinct, she could comfortably or uncomfortably, as the situation dictated, navigate between the two paradigms. It was these firmly entrenched beliefs in her spiritual psyche that helped her calm her nerves as she patiently waited for her husband to return home.

After what seemed like an eternity, there was a knock at the door, which sounded like Kennedy's style of knocking. They say everyone has their own style of knocking. Some people start with a gentle tap progressing to a louder, firmer knock, while others go straight in with a good strong bang. Kennedy's style started with two loud knocks followed by three gentle well-spaced knocks. Muswana, therefore, knew who was at the door right away and leapt for the door and energetically flung it open, instantly separating the door handle from the rest of the door; but she didn't let that incident bother her. Kennedy immediately hugged her as tightly as glue, and she noticed he was shaking. She couldn't quite make out what he was exactly saying because although he naturally spoke with a lisp and also stammered from time to time, especially when under pressure. One thing that stood out was that in betwixt what Kennedy was saying while speaking fast and laughing, he had mentioned the word promotion. Muswana wasn't expecting to hear the sweet 'P word' so her brain was still trying to process the meaning of the word as Kennedy kept her imprisoned in his warm embrace, loaded with some terrific news.

Talking about brain processing speed, studies suggest that the speed of information processing changes with age along an inverted U-shaped curve, such that our thinking speeds up from childhood to adolescence, maintains a period of relative stability leading up to middle age, and finally, in late middle age and onward, declines slowly but steadily. Muswana hadn't yet hit middle age, so her information processing capability might have tittered somewhere before the apex or zenith of the inverted U-shaped curve.

Finally, Muswana's brain relayed to her what Kennedy had just said, and it was nothing short of a eureka moment, or the Aha moment.

People from all walks of life have attested to the significance of 'eureka! or aha!' moments in their lives and how in some cases, that has not only affected their individual lives but thousands or millions of other people. One of the most famous eureka moments in history involves none other than Albert Einstein. While working in a patent office at the tender age of 28 in 1922, Einstein was daydreaming and was suddenly struck with an idea: "If a man falls freely, he would not feel his weight. I was taken aback. This simple thought experiment made a deep impression on me. This led me to the theory of gravity[12]." And what a 'aha!' Einstein's 'eureka' moment has turned out to be through the ages of human history.

Just like Muswana took long to process and finally realise the meaning of what had been uttered by her husband (aha! moment), Einstein's theory wasn't complete for eight more years, so the moment wasn't so much a eureka moment as the beginning of a long train of thought and experimentation. Einstein didn't come up with the whole thing in an instant, struck by mathematical equations in the patent office. He was, more believably, struck by a simple notion that was powerful because of how he considered it.

It had now sunk in for Muswana that it wasn't bad news, after all. It was, in fact, excellent news for the entire family, Kennedy had been awarded a well-deserved promotion to become the head of metallurgy, and that meant more money. The only twist was that the new job was in another part of the country, the second-largest commercial town after their country's capital city. Kennedy detailed the full implications of his promotion to Muswana. They were going to shift from the town where they had become so accustomed to, leaving their spiritual family and friends behind.

According to a poll carried out by Anxiety UK, two-thirds of people rate moving to a new house as more stressful than divorce. In 1967 a pair of psychiatrists made a list of life events and assigned each one a numerical value based on how traumatic it was. They then worked out how likely one was to develop a stress-related illness based on these experiences. According to the scale, moving to a new house increased one's chances of developing a stress-related illness to 30%. And if paired with something like a divorce or starting a family – both of which are common reasons to move to a new house – then that figure got pushed up to 50%[13].

No doubt this was great news for Kennedy and Muswana, but one that had unintended consequences, albeit potentially favourable, especially from a financial point of view. In the end, they both came to terms with the implications of Kennedy's promotion to the post of head of metallurgy and started making arrangements to relocate. Most children easily adapt to change, so naturally, the decision to relocate to a new town didn't bother Trump and Joanna that much so long as their parents were okay with the decision.

Time passed quickly, and the day came when the Bloomfields finally packed their belongings, bade farewell to their family and friends and moved to the new town.

The Bloomfields did everything possible to ensure a smooth settlement in their new town. It was a much bigger house than they previously had, just by a busy roadside. There was also a small stream of water lined with shrubs and trees that flowed parallel to their house. From time to time, Trump and his sister Joanna would vanish into the thick green shrubs and jump into the shallow waters of the stream, picking up tadpoles and dumping them into their bespoke version of baby ponds which happened to be empty strawberry jam bottles filled with water. The only problem was that the poor creatures would die within a few days of being domesticated because the crudely tailored baby ponds contained dirty water and lacked the necessary food.

The pair made several attempts but couldn't quite figure out how to prevent the premature deaths of their little aqua creatures; neither did they know what sort of food to feed them. In all fairness, they made every effort to keep their imprisoned creatures alive, ranging from dropping pieces of bread and meat into the water to pouring the creatures out of the jam bottles onto the lawn of their backyard for them to catch some fresh air and stay alive, alas, all that effort was in vain, and the impoverished creatures still died. Being fast learners, Trump and his sister Joanna got notification that their creatures had died each time they saw their lifeless bodies floating in the dirty water and that was their inadvertent first encounter with the meaning of death.

Chapter 9
New Level, New Devils 1

Within two weeks of their relocation, Trump was enrolled in the fifth year at a nearby school about one mile eight hundred yards from their home. Muswana escorted him to school the entire month following his enrolment and picked him up after school. The family only had one car, which Kennedy used to go to work, so Muswana ensured they always started off from home in good time.

One day while coming from school, Muswana noticed a pair of twin boys a couple of times (also enrolled at Trump's school) walking to school and back home unaccompanied. The twins always walked past their home, making Muswana conclude that they lived a few blocks down the road. She decided to befriend them and also introduced them to Trump. The twins were both in year six, one year higher than Trump. Upon asking the boys further, Muswana discovered the twins started walking to school by themselves when they were just in year four, and she was quite impressed because they seemed sharp and very streetwise. She asked if they could stop by the following day to pick up Trump so they could walk with him to school, and the twins accepted with great enthusiasm, "Yes, Mum, yes Mum, not a problem!"

The following day, the twins arrived 20 minutes earlier than agreed, looking sharp as ever and eager to pick up Trump. After a month of walking to and from school with the twins, Trump was confident enough to start walking by himself and didn't have to wait for the twins.

After school, Trump would spend a bit of time with his sister Joanna then sneak off to the back of their house to watch cars as they drove past their house. He was especially drawn to the red cars, and he would often count them and keep a tab of how many red cars had driven past each day. Trump discovered he had a lot of free time on his hands, and it wasn't long before his old naughty ideas started forming in his head. It is said that often people mistakenly think they have left their old habits way behind them, whereas they have always remained on a parallel path all along.

One day, provoked by his old demons, Trump wanted to find out how far a wire spring could fly into the road if stretched fully and then let loose. He waited patiently for a red car before executing his plan. As soon as he set off the spring, it flew straight through the open window of a passing red car and smashed deep into the driver's left cheek and threw him into a state of shock and panic. The poor driver pounded heavily onto his breaks, fearing he was under attack from some unknown source as the tyres of his fancy red car screeched and skidded on the tarmac bringing the car to an abrupt halt. The result was a pile-up as cars smashed into the backside of each other. A total of four cars were involved, and one passenger was seriously injured.

Unable to bring himself to check and assess the full extent of the chaos he had just caused, Trump emerged from the long grass he was hiding and bolted into the house. He went straight into the toilet and locked the door behind him as drivers yelled and screamed at each other outside.

After a while, Trump flushed the toilet and slowly walked out on the pretence he had been relieving himself in the toilet. Muswana, busy ironing in their dining room, was interrupted by a knock on their kitchen door. She hurried to answer the knock as Trump followed her, curious to see who was at the door. *Could it be the police?* he wondered. Trump was dead afraid of the police, so his heart was pounding heavily against his chest wall and cold sweat slowly rolled down his back into the intersection of his tight bums and beyond.

Muswana opened the door and in front of her stood a huge white man in a short-sleeved shirt with a red tie and his face red with anger. Trump peeped past his mum as he heard the angry man scream some unpalatable syllables while pointing his flab finger at him, saying what a stupid boy he was for causing the road accident pile up. Trump impetuously and vehemently refused he had done anything inappropriate because he had been in the toilet.

Luckily for him, his mum was also convinced she had seen her son come out of the toilet and protested that it was a question of mistaken identity. The outraged white fella standing at the door was absolutely convinced he had seen Trump carry out the unholy act and then ran away after realising what he had done. Muswana wasn't having it as she strongly believed in her version of the truth, which corroborated with Trump's alibi. The man insisted Trump was the culprit and threatened to report the matter to the police.

At that point, Muswana lost it! She upped the tone of her voice and accused the man of being a racist, wanting to blame his misfortune on the poor 'coloured' boy who just happened to be her son. The fact that the man had a strong Afrikaners (Boer or Dutch) accent didn't help matters at all; if anything, it just made Muswana more animated in lambasting and deriding him. The 'race card' that Muswana threw into the altercation seemed to have done its trick because as soon as the indignant man heard the word 'racist', he started to walk away while protesting.

Research shows that, ironically, ideas about racism are often kept current by attempts to avoid or criticise racism. Being accused of racism can feel like the worst thing in the world. For many, it feels like a huge attack, as though they are being accused of being a horrible person, which would be right if that were the truth, but in some cases, it just isn't the case, and the word is merely used as a weapon to disarm someone.

After a while following the mishap that Trump had orchestrated, the Police arrived at the scene of the accident. When Muswana peeped through their living room window, she saw the Police taking down statements from the three drivers whose cars had kissed the backside of each other and the man who had accused Trump seemed to be the main culprit as he was the centre of attention and was gesturing energetically as he spoke to the police in what appeared to be an attempt to exculpate himself.

Hiding in his bedroom and involuntarily trapped between his mattress and his linen bed sheets, Trump was so scared that he wetted his pants and beddings. He expected the police to knock at their door anytime and take him away. His mum was secretly worried, too, but was determined not to let that show partially because she wanted the whole thing to go away. That was only going to happen if Trump and herself stood united as to what they believed had transpired, which was that Trump had been falsely accused by that egotistic racist white fella.

Minutes turned into hours, and three hours had now elapsed since the accident happened, but there was still no sign of the police anywhere near their door. The next time Muswana peeped, this time through their dining room window, she saw the recovery vehicle driving away, towing the last car that had been badly damaged. The other cars were towed away soon after the Police took down statements from the drivers.

Like any good parent would, later that afternoon, Muswana confronted Trump to find out if he had anything to do with the accident per the accusation from the angry driver, but he stuck to his guns and flatly refused. That was the end of the drama, and Muswana never brought up the issue again.

Chapter 10
New Level, New Devils 2

The days and months that followed were trouble-free for Trump. He was slowly but steadily trying to understand the connection between cause and effect and was determined to avoid having difficult conversations, especially with his mother, by intransigently trying to stay out of trouble. The narrow escape from the consequences of the accident that he engineered remained fresh in Trump's mind and served as a reminder of what could go wrong. The creche that 'old habits die hard' has stood the test of time and has proven to be true through different chapters of the human race.

Some studies show that as human beings, we usually imagine that we've travelled so far from the things we left behind when, in reality, the wrong track is always running alongside the right one. If we get on it, we're quickly zooming along in the wrong direction. Before we know it, we can be doing things we swore we never would and wondering how we got so lost again. As the Alcoholics Anonymous saying goes, "You pick up where you left off."

The psychiatrists warn that to successfully kill bad habits, it's important to create good new habits to replace bad ones. True repentance is not merely eliminating the negative but replacing it with positive attitudes and actions. This advice was also at the heart of the parable of the empty house that was told by Jesus as recorded in the Christian Bible (Mathew 12:43–45), 'When the unclean spirit is gone out of a man, he walketh through dry places, seeking rest, and findeth none; but when a man speaketh against the Holy Ghost, then he saith, I will return into my house from whence I came out; and when he is come, he findeth him empty, swept and garnished; for the good spirit leaveth him unto himself. Then goeth the evil spirit, and taketh with himself seven other spirits more wicked than himself, and they enter in and dwell there; and the last end of that man is worse than the first. Even so shall it be also unto this wicked generation'.

Therefore, it goes without saying that because Trump had formed very few good habits to replace his old bad habits of stirring up trouble, he was back into mischief again within a short time. This time Trump was fascinated with 'drinking from the poisoned chalice' that was dangled at him by the twin brothers who used to walk him to school. In the first phase of their friendship, Trump's relationship with the twins never lasted. As soon as he had gained a flicker of confidence to walk to school by himself, he simply cut them loose largely because they were fond of siding with each other. The twins also made fun of Trump's big ears, which he construed to be bullying.

However, Trump later changed his mind about the twins and was eager to rekindle their friendship after they impressed him so much with their swimming skills during a combined PE session at school. Trump was keen to find out how and where the twins learnt how to swim, but the twins refused to disclose, saying it was a secret, something which Trump found rather bizarre. *How was that supposed to be a secret?* he wondered. One of the twins nearly let the cat out of the bag but quickly covered his mouth based on one stern look from his twin brother. Trump was now even more determined to know about this secret so that he could learn how to swim and impress a girl he fancied from his class.

According to psychologists, there are two aspects of secrets that seem pretty intuitively obvious: First, keeping secrets probably makes you feel worse than you would if you were not keeping a secret. Second, the most stressful part of keeping a secret is hiding it from the people you don't want to tell. They suggest that a potential problem with keeping secrets is that you have a goal to keep the information secret. Goals that have not yet been achieved are often easy to think about. That is how our motivational system gives us opportunities to achieve our goals when we see something related to the goal in the environment.

Needless to say, the twins were equally bothered by this secret of theirs because Trump kept pestering them. With time, the twins grew weary with holding on to their swimming secret following Trump's persistence, so they liaised with each other and came up with a plan. The plan was to 'tax' Trump's lunch box. If Trump would agree to give up the contents of his lunch box during their lunch break, then the twins would be willing to tell it all.

After assimilating the twins' uncouth and crude proposition, Trump reminisced, trying to remember how it felt like the last time he starved and withstood the pangs and paroxysms of hunger and how he survived. He found a handful of examples in his archives, so he welcomed the proposition. He devised a backup plan, though, to sneak into their kitchen after his parents had gone to bed to pack extra lunch for himself. He planned to first eat his extra meal before surrendering his lunch box to the twins and then pretend to be hungry.

The following day, the plan was executed perfectly. When the secret was finally out, Trump couldn't believe his ears; the twins learned to swim in a nearby river renowned for being infested with crocodiles. The twins justified their seemingly reckless behaviour by quickly pointing out that the crocodiles only habited certain parts of the river; the lower bank, which was quite far from the 'safe' section of the river where they learnt how to swim.

Afterwards, the older twin half-heartedly added a caveat without making eye contact with his younger twin brother as he mumbled, "Our uncle once told us that about 15 years ago, a crocodile strayed into the 'safe waters' and a boy was killed, but that was before any one of us was born; and since then there have been no such incidents." Trump was impressed by that seemingly honest caveat, and it increased his trust in the twins. He felt that their vulnerability in relaying that unfortunate incident was a sign of their genuine interest in ensuring the success and safety of their clandestine 'swimming project' and not only in his lunch.

According to Bryan Kramer, often, people think that opening up and being vulnerable comes after trust, but actually, once you switch this equation around, it can be vulnerability that leads to trust and more meaningful relationships. Expecting perfection will lead to a very disappointing set of circumstances and encouraging people to cover up their weaknesses will lead to damaging behaviours and a detrimental impact on esteem[14].

What the twins demanded next would have completely eroded whatever little trust Trump had built up in his internal 'twins-trust-account-with-Trump', but it didn't. After spilling their carefully caveated swimming secret and seeing that they now had Trump in their 'claws' the twins made another demand, a pair of Trump's school stockings for each of them in exchange for them drawing up a swimming timetable for Trump. Trump accepted right away though he had already fulfilled his side of the bargain by 'delivering' his lunch to the twins. This was not only because Trump was so eager to learn how to swim, but also because he had no personal boundaries, which was a sign of low self-worth although he had high self-esteem, and his upbringing was partially to blame.

According to an article authored by Ida Soghomonian on Boundaries and why they are important, she says, "Personal Boundaries are guidelines, rules or limits that a person creates to identify reasonable, safe and permissible ways for other people to behave towards them and how they will respond when someone passes those limits. They are built out of a mix of conclusions, beliefs, opinions, attitudes, past experiences and social learning. Personal boundaries help to define an individual by outlining likes and dislikes and setting the distances one allows others to approach. Healthy boundaries are necessary components for self-care. Without boundaries, we feel depleted, taken advantage of, taken for granted, or intruded upon. Boundaries help us take care of ourselves by giving us permission to say NO to things, to not take everything on. Boundaries draw a clear line around what is ok for us and what is not. When someone behaves in a way that doesn't feel ok to us – that crosses our line, we need to take care of ourselves by letting them know and making that line much clearer[15]."

In the days that followed, Trump delivered his second 'consignment' to the twins: a pair of stockings to each twin, starting with a pair for the older twin that same week and the final pair of stockings to the younger twin the following week on a Friday during break time. The trio then agreed to commence the swimming lessons in the third week. It wasn't only going to be them attending the swimming rendezvous, there was going to be a few other kids there, and they would all share one thing in common, taking swimming lessons 'undercover' hiding from their parents on the pretext of remaining in school to attend extra lessons or revision classes. The twins advised that those were the two main excuses that sold well with parents, and they were to be used in tandem in the initial week and juxtaposed the week after and so on and so forth.

Other requirements needed fulfilling in order for them to successfully conceal their swimming lessons arrangement from their parents. Trump was tasked to bring with him some Vaseline to be carefully wrapped in a piece of paper, and the paper put into a plastic covering so as not to mess up his books. Further, Trump was also asked to bring a box of matches to light fire using pieces of wood and dry shrubs from nearby trees in order to warm and dry themselves after finishing their swimming lessons. The fire was also intended to dry their underwear and clothes. The final requirement was for each of them to bring extra underwear. No towels were required as that would raise suspicion from their parents.

Trump managed to cleverly organise all the requirements in phases. He packed the match box immediately after he got home from school, the Vaseline when he went to bath and the extra underwear just before going to bed. All these items were hidden underneath Trump's school books in his bookcase. The whole plan was predicated on telling one lie after another without being caught, or else the whole swimming arrangement would suddenly grind to a halt.

According to research, all children lie, and the extent of those lies depends on the age group but can also crisscross between age groups. The good news is that if parents take a strong lead on a no-lying policy, most children will learn to walk the straight and narrow path. As the primary role models in their children's lives, parents play a vital part in showcasing honesty. They also have the most influence when instilling a deep-rooted commitment to telling the truth. As children mature and acquire a more sophisticated understanding of social etiquette, parents must help children differentiate between little white lies told to spare people's feelings and downright dishonesty.

Further, according to the American Academy of Child & Adolescent Psychiatry, children and adults lie for similar reasons: to get out of trouble, for personal gain, to impress or protect someone, or to be polite. At a young age, children will experiment with the truth, and they continue to do so through all the developmental stages, with varying degrees of sophistication and elaboration. For maximum influence at each developmental stage, parents ought to address the subject of lying in an age-appropriate way by learning how to respond appropriately to children of different ages when they're caught telling a lie[16]. However, one would argue that if the lies are well concealed, it's hard to see how parents can exert any positive influence or take corrective action until the offending child is caught red-handed.

On the day that the swimming lessons were earmarked to start, the trio headed straight to the river after knocking off from school. Upon arriving at the river, they found a few other boys there, but the twins had a special spot following a narrow path that led through the tall grass onto the sandy beach. Some sections of the riverbank were covered with reeds as tall as two metres above the water except for that special spot. The name that was given to that special secret swimming spot, the twins, explained, was 'Paka dyie' which literally meant 'dying place' or a place where people die. The name was only known to a few people and passed down in 'history' amongst the boys their age. No one knew the exact reason why that secret swimming spot was called 'Paka dyie'; however, rumour had it that in the past, several boys drowned in that same spot while learning how to swim after running into trouble either because they had accidentally dived into the deep end or had strayed into the deepest part of the river.

The water at 'Paka dyie' was so dark that the twins called it 'the-place-where-the-waters-run-black'. The twins recounted to Trump that underneath the 'Paka dyie', the water was so dark that if someone drowned, they would simply disappear into the water and most likely die before a rescue could arrive. The message was meant to warn Trump to pay careful attention to the swimming instructions and never attempt swimming to the deep end before he was ready. Upon viewing the scenery and absorbing the history associated with 'Paka dyie', Trump was scared and started having second thoughts as to whether he should go along with the swimming lessons. In his mind, Trump had expected to see clear sky-blue swimming water with no gloomy history behind the secret swimming spot.

The younger twin added context to the seemingly troublesome message that was abruptly delivered to Trump by stating the obvious, and he said, according to a reliable source, the reason why some boys died at 'Paka dyie' while learning how to swim was that they were so eager to explore the deep end before perfecting the art of swimming in the shallow waters. The older twin then emphasised that he had nothing to fear as long as Trump abided by their instructions. Following that reassurance, Trump eased up marginally and managed to put on an unwieldy phoney smiling face for a few seconds.

The older twin continued explaining to Trump that his swimming lessons would be done in stages starting from the shallow waters then proceeding to swim in the middle waters before venturing into the deep end. That way, further continued the older twin, Trump would learn how to swim without risking his life. Trump felt sufficiently reassured, and the fear vanished almost instantaneously.

According to Research, almost every swimmer, no matter how experienced, has some sort of mental block regarding open-water swimming. For many, it's anxiety was distracting enough to make them swim off course, miss drafting opportunities or over-exert themselves. But for an unfortunate few, it can be a real fear that disrupts their breathing to an extent that might ruin their swim and risks causing a panic attack. It's easy to oversimplify the problem as a general dislike or fear of open water, but chances are there's a specific aspect of it that triggers your anxiety. Some classic 'triggers' include murky water, deep clear water (causing a feeling of vertigo), plants or fish brushing against them, swimmers nearby etc.

Per the debrief and the swimming plan that the twins carefully drew up, Trump being a novice, started his swimming lessons from the shallow part of the river. The first lesson was learning how to keep afloat and preventing water from gushing into Trump's mouth to avoid choking. The second lesson was learning the art of using both the hands and the legs in order to remain afloat.

The trio continued this routine under cover, and Trump proved to be a fast learner. With time, Trump progressed from splashing water while static like a boat trying to take off in a high gear while still anchored to using both his hands and legs and moving about in the water while being very cautious not to stray to the deep end.

After each swim, the boys would gather some wood and dry branches from surrounding trees and grass and then start a fire to warm and dry themselves while shivering vigorously like reeds tossed about in the wind. The boys would remain by the fire long enough until their bodies and undies were dry. They would then take off for their respective homes to arrive at a sensible time so as not to rouse suspicion.

One day, Trump nearly got caught by his mother, Muswana. Upon arriving home, he found his mother in the kitchen washing dishes, and as his eyes caught hers, he immediately looked away, but Muswana noticed that his eyes were quite red, so she asked if he had been crying or had problems with his eyes to which Trump casually responded, "No I'm fine, Mum." Trump realised that the brevity of his response didn't augur well with his mother, so he quickly attributed the strange colour of his eyes to the extra reading he had put in after knocking off from school, and that was the end of the conversation.

In the days that followed, Trump made it his goal to avoid looking into his mother's eyes upon arriving home from his secret swimming lessons. He would start by peeping through their kitchen window to ensure Muswana wasn't in the kitchen before opening the door and walking straight to his bedroom shouting, "Hello, Mother, I'm home," shortly before closing the bedroom door behind him.

Chapter 11
The Tiny Steps that Lead to Death

In the fourth week of Trump's swimming lessons and in exchange for the contents of his lunch box, the twins proposed to teach Trump how to trap birds using a glue-like sticky paste called 'bulimbo' extracted from a rubber tree. The process of extracting 'bulimbo glue' started with cutting the trunk of the rubber tree in several places and then tapping the white milk-like liquid that oozed from the tree into small containers. When the containers were full of bulimbo, the boys would then start stirring the bulimbo glue with a stick until it became thick and very sticky. The boys would then apply the bulimbo glue around carefully selected straight sticks of about 30 centimetres in length and then climb some nearby trees (usually two adjacent trees), and using strings extracted from special fibre trees, they would fasten the sticks that contained the bulimbo glue to tree-top branches to protrude above the other branches.

The boys would then climb down the trees and wait in ambush for the unsuspecting birds to land onto the protruding sticks that had the sticky bulimbo glue around them. Upon landing on the bulimbo sticks, the feet of the birds would get stuck, and the boys would then quickly climb up the trees and catch the birds and snap or squeeze their necks to death. As expected, the birds died the moment their neck got snapped between the thumb and the index finger, following which they were dumped in a black bag. When the dedicated 'bloody' black bag had enough dead birds, the boys would go back to swimming, knowing they had secured their meal to replenish their strength after the swimming was over.

After the swim, the boys would roast the birds over the fire while drying themselves and their clothes. The division of labour was always the same from one week to the next, resulting in specialisation. The older twin would pluck the feathers from the birds, and the younger twin would stuff the birds and also sprinkle pepper and salt on the bird meat while Trump's role was to dry their underwear and clothes (i.e., school uniforms). At first, Trump thought the roasted birds tasted somewhat weird, but then he remembered acquiring the taste when his mother Muswana trapped some birds on their way to church when he was much younger. He, therefore, quickly notified and persuaded his 'taste buds' that he actually loved the taste of roasted birds. It was a different taste from chicken or duck meat, but he thought it was an unusual, scrumptious, and delicious delicatessen. This became the routine for the trio, and Trump succumbed to surrendering a few more 'lunch box meals' to the twins along the continuum of his swimming lessons.

Within three months, Trump graduated from swimming in the shallow waters to swimming in the middle waters, i.e., the section before the deep end. This continued until shortly before the rain season when the river was flooded. Due to the health and safety hazards posed by floods, the twins suspended the swimming lessons, and Trump was fully in agreement. By then, Trump had already started to swim close to the deep end without any difficulties. In that part of the world, the rain season lasted for about five months, and the trio suspended all swimming lessons for the entire period.

Near the tail end of the rain season, in the fifth month to be precise, one day at break time, the twins approached Trump 'wide-eyed' with some big, exciting breaking news. The news was that some boys had actually started swimming in the 'big waters', meaning in the flooded river. The twins added that although the water current was stronger than usual, that simply elevated the fun and thrill to a whole new level compared to the associated risks. In other words, contextualised the younger twin, the adrenalin-fuelled fun of swimming in 'big waters' far outweighed the health and safety risks associated with the floods so long as they took extra care. And the older twin added that, after all, swimming was all about mastering the art of keeping afloat regardless of the floods, water current generally or rip currents even. The twins were so convincing that Trump got swept off his feet and was left with no room to voice out any doubts. After psyching themselves, the boys were all agreeable that swimming in 'big waters' would be adventurous and exhilarating and something worth doing, so they decided to press ahead.

It was such a perilous decision because the boys' secret swimming spot called 'Paka dyie' was situated close to the river mouth commonly associated with rip currents. In most parts of the world (including that part), the majority of water incidents involve rip currents which are a major cause of accidental drowning on beaches. Rips are strong currents running out to sea, which can quickly drag people and debris away from the shallows of the shoreline and out to deeper water. Rip currents tend to flow at 1–2mph but can reach 4–5mph, faster than an Olympic swimmer. Rips are especially powerful in larger surf, but the power of any water should not be underestimated. They are also found around river mouths, estuaries and man-made structures like piers and groynes. Rip currents can be difficult to spot but are sometimes identified by a channel of churning, choppy water on the sea's surface.

After talking to their other friends and considering all the associated risks, the boys' minds were made. They covertly and furtively arranged to go to the river to test their swimming prowess the following day. Trump packed the relevant swimming requirements the night before. After knocking off from school, Trump linked up with the twins, and they started off for the river.

The heavy rains over the five months caused the river to break its banks and flood the surrounding areas. The water current was so strong that their favourite swimming spot, 'Paka dyie' and a large section of the beach were completely submerged under water, and the rip currents continuously flowed out to cover the whole beach with water and back to the river again. The trio led by the older twin opted to find another swimming spot along the riverbank after analysing the situation and the impediments it posed to the fun they were seeking. They managed to find an alternative location where a few other boys were trying to swim but seemed exasperated by the strong water current. Trump and the twins joined in, but they could only swim in very shallow waters, which wasn't the sort of adrenalin fuelled fun they were searching for, so they started to venture a bit further into the deep water. As would be expected, Trump was very cautious because he wasn't as experienced as the twins.

After a while, the dare-devil spirit in Trump, which remained dormant since the start of his swimming lessons, was somehow stirred up and became fully awake and alive. So, he gathered an ounce of courage and dipped himself into the fast-running water while holding onto the nearby reeds. As soon as his body was halfway into the water, the strong water current, much of which was running underneath, swept him away like a piece of paper in the wind. He frantically and feverishly tried to firm his grip and hold on to the reeds in order to resist being taken, but the reeds got ripped off by their roots, and the fast-moving water helplessly carried him away towards the choppy waters in the deep end section of the river.

Trump was in deep trouble, and he started to scream above his voice vociferously. Within a few seconds, his vision became blurred as a result of the troubled waters, and through the corner of his eye, he could see that his friends were in a great panic, running along the riverbank jumping up and down while waving their hands and shouting his name and calling for help, "Somebody please! Help! Please help! Trump is gone! Trump is gone! Somebody, please help Trump is gone!" In the mayhem and turmoil that ensued, Trump soon lost sight of the twins and the other boys who were calling for help, and all he could now hear was the sound of the raging waters as he tried to swim but in vain. Water was gushing violently in and out of Trump's mouth and ears, and when he felt his undies get ripped off his body by the strong water current, he realised he was about to die, and he saw life flash before his eyes.

In a moving study, Israeli scientists shed light on what happens moments before a person dies by interviewing people who nearly died. They learned from intimate conversations that flashbacks don't happen in chronological order like what's conventionally thought. The doctors behind the study from Hadassah University in Jerusalem suggest that these memories replay in a person's final breaths because the part of the brain that stores memories may be the last to go. The researchers call it LRE – life review experience – which is the vivid account of a person's life-long autobiographical memories.[17]

After Trump's version of his life review experience (LRE) was over, suddenly everything went quiet and black.

Chapter 12
A Place Where Nothing Is Hidden

Trump suddenly woke up as though from a slumber, but he was no longer in the rough and choppy waters anymore. He was in this incredibly beautiful place he had never been to before. He couldn't feel himself breathing, but at the same time, he wasn't gasping for breath. Another thing Trump realised was that his body was different. It was between transparent and translucent but not opaque. He also soon realised that he was not alone. There were other people there, all of whom had the same body type as his; not clothed, yet no private parts were visible, so he couldn't tell their sex. He also noticed there were no young or old people there. They were all of the same height and body mass and seemed the same age.

It seemed as though conversations in that magnificent place were not conducted in words but in this sweet and very soothing music. Trump tried to speak to one of the individuals walking past him, but instead of the words, he heard a very sweet sound of music proceed effortlessly out of his mouth. The response from the other fella was also in the form of music, and as their music blended, it produced a higher level of 'musical conversation' which harmoniously reverberated into all the four main vocal ranges of soprano, alto, tenor and bass, and it was simply magical and amazing. The only problem was that Trump could not interpret the response from the other individual although he enjoyed the music. The 'encrypted' response from the other individual was, "It's great to see you, welcome back home. Someone will be with you shortly."

Trump checked out the place around him in wonderment and admiration; it was subtly glistening and luminescent, white all over and enshrouded in an alluring layer of a seamless bright cloud. The rivers in the gardens flowed with silky water, and the streets were made of gold. It was a gorgeous place decorated with elegant trees, gardens, ponds, rivers, gems of all kinds and charming flowers and populated with good-looking individuals whom he couldn't tell whether they were men or women. The individuals there went about their business quietly, and the beauty about each one of them was so perfect that none of them seemed to be attracted to each other. Everyone looked youthful, and Trump thought they must have felt youthful on the inside, too, because that's exactly what he felt.

Three huge stars were shining from what seemed like the sky, yet Trump never felt the heat. The three prominent stars produced such a beautiful and gentle form of light and Trump could see it flowing into and out of everyone's translucent bodies.

As Trump stood there in awe and disbelief as to what was going on around him, he was suddenly surrounded by seven individuals adorned in bodies similar to his; the only difference being their bodies were much shinier than his. The seven individuals stood still and quiet around Trump for a while without saying anything to him, but they seemed to be talking to each other after looking at him from time to time as though reading his life. Trump couldn't hear a single word they spoke as it was different from the individual he spoke to on arrival to that place, it was music nevertheless, like music in Russian played to another nationality with zero knowledge of the Russian language, that he gathered, was the language of that place.

Finally, one of the seven individuals signalled to Trump as though asking him to look at his own body. Trump looked, and he realised that something about him had changed. His body had become a 'movie screen' review of his own life story on earth. Clips and clips of his life on earth kept flashing up in his body, including the time and year of each event; everything about his life was there for the seven individuals to see, and that seemed to be the core of their conversation.

From the life history clips playing from his own body, which had become some form of screen, Trump saw all the six stages in the human life cycle of himself, starting with him as a foetus growing inside his mother's womb. Shockingly, he also noticed something disturbing just short of macabre. It was that he wasn't conceived with his father's sperm, meaning Kennedy wasn't his biological father. To his astonishment, Trump discovered that his biological father was his dad's long-standing friend, a gregarious priest who went by the name of Father Greenleaf.

When Kennedy migrated to Africa as a missionary, he attended a local church and struck an instant connection with the parish priest, Father Greenleaf, and they became close friends, both of whom were white settlers in Africa.

Unbeknown to Trump's father, Kennedy, Father Greenleaf was a proper philanderer who not only had a long-standing relationship with his wife Muswana but also had affairs with other black African women from his Parish, and it didn't matter to him whether the women were married or single. When Muswana informed him that she was pregnant by him, Father Greenleaf and Muswana orchestrated a plan to implicate Kennedy.

To execute their cleverly crafted plan, Father Greenleaf 'innocently' introduced Kennedy to Muswana. In the days that followed, and in keeping with the spirit of the plan, both Muswana and Kennedy were separately invited for an evening meal at Father Greenleaf's parish apartment. On the night, one thing led to the other, and after the trio had downed an assortment of spirits, including countless bottles of red wine meant for the church's holy communion, Muswana and Kennedy woke up from the same bed in Father Greenleaf's house the following morning. It was evident to Kennedy that he and Muswana had unprotected sex the previous night, and that was the start of their relationship, which quickly culminated in their marriage officiated by none other than the 'wolf-in-the-skin-of-a-sheep', Father Greenleaf himself.

As the clips continued to play, Trump saw himself at birth after spending nine months and two weeks inside his mother's womb. He also saw Father Greenleaf, his biological father, come to visit his mother while she was still in the maternity wing of the hospital. He held him in his hands, said a prayer, and then gave him back to his mother, Muswana.

Trump also noticed that his father, Kennedy, for some reason, did not visit his mother in the hospital until two days after his birth. Bizarrely, Kennedy spent both the two days his wife Muswana was in hospital with another woman, and it was no other than the best friend to his wife, Manku! The same woman who rescued Trump's sister, Joanna, from the sewer hole. Trump was flabbergasted by the drama that surrounded his parents' relationship and his birth. It was as King David in the Christian Bible lamented, "Behold, I was shaped in iniquity; and in sin did my mother conceive me."

Trump then saw himself in his childhood, learning to walk and talk, including when he set fire to the family's grass-thatched fence and the heart-breaking moment when his sister Joanna fell into the sewer hole. Oddly enough, he saw himself on the same spot where his sister fell into the sewer hole…he was right there with her shortly before she fell in.

Then something else captured his attention. It was about the chilly revelation of the true diabolical forces behind the strange dreams he dreamt as a child about himself flying at full speed as though riding on something he couldn't see. In fact, it was not actually him riding on something but the other way round; It was his grandfather, Dilaso, the father to his mother Muswana, who rode on him in the wee of the night when everyone was asleep. Disturbingly, Trump learnt that Dilaso used him at night as some form of magical plane. His grandfather, Dilaso, derived the magical power to fly 'his plane' from the blood of the people that he killed every now and then using his wizardry tools.

From the flashing clips of his life history, Trump surprisingly noticed that before setting off on a sorcery flying mission, Dilaso would enter Trump's bedroom through the thick walls at night as soon as he jumped into his bed and fell asleep. He would then induce Trump into a deep sleep by casting a spell on him. The spell caused Trump to lose all consciousness and crossover into the supernatural world to which only those with special wizardry power had access.

After crossing with Trump into the mystical and paranormal world, Dilaso would then produce a horn-like instrument, which was actually a dead, dry penis of a human being and filled it with fresh human blood he had drawn from people he had killed the previous night. It had to be fresh human blood for it to work.

Pondering on the 'invisible' power contained in human blood, Trump recalled a lesson he was taught at Sunday school while he was still on earth on why God forbade the Israelites from eating blood as recorded in the Old Testament of the Christian Bible (Leviticus 17:11...), "For the life of the flesh is in the blood, and I have given it to you to make atonement for your souls upon the altar; for it is the blood that makes atonement for the soul. Therefore, I say to the Israelites, none of you may eat blood, nor may any foreigner living among you eat blood." Trump now realised the plausibility of that lesson on the power that was in the human blood upon seeing how his grandfather, Dilaso, was able to diabolically take advantage of that power.

Upon filling the embalmed foot long dead dry penis with the blood of his victims, Dilaso would then insert it in Trump's mouth and drain it down his throat akin to someone filling the fuel tank of an automobile. The dead, dry penis, only comparable to that of Rasputin, was detached from one of Dilaso's victims who was killed because he had an affair with his wife. The brief history is that Dilaso's wife was mesmerised by the victim's huge private member, and despite repeated warnings from Dilaso, the illicit relationship persisted. Dilaso had no option but to kill the adulterous man and severed his penis, which he added to his wizardry tools box.

Chapter 13
The Gliding Blood Sucker

As Trump continued to view clips of how his own grandfather abused and exploited him as a young boy during his witchery and necromancy adventures at night, he saw that after the tank of Dilaso's mysterious plane (i.e., Trump) was filled with fresh human blood, Dilaso would then jump on Trump and set off on his malevolent missions.

On one of those missions, they flew to Tonga Island and, while there, headed to one of the country's most notorious prisons called Tolitoli. Upon penetrating the prison walls, Dilaso cast the spell of an evil spirit he named 'Give-us' on one of the inmates on death row by the name of Cush. The evil spirit like creature called 'Give-us' immediately entered into Cush and, once inside of him, literally took over his senses and overall control of his actions and caused him to kill his cellmate (who was also on death row due to be executed the following morning at 10 am via lethal injection) for no reason. Cush started by slamming the head of his poor victim to the floor, then stomped on his throat repeatedly before strangling his lifeless body.

After Cush had completed his gruesome act, the evil spirit that had entered him on Dilaso's command, Give-us, laughed loudly and uncontrollably while four strong prison officers desperately tried to pull Cush away from his victim whom he had just killed. In the eyes of the prison officers and following the incident report they later filed. "Cush laughed wildly and disdainfully after killing his victim." But little did they realise it was actually the evil spirit inside Cush, Give-us, that was behind that outrageously eerie laughter.

As Cush's victim lay dead in a pool of blood, Dilaso disembarked from Trump to collect blood for fuel. He dipped the dry, dead penis, which was in the form of a horn, into the pool of blood and with a single sip, it sucked all the blood and replaced it with water. The water still seemed as though it was blood to the prison officers. Afterwards, Dilaso beckoned and ordered Give-us to jump back into his small wizardry container, which was skilfully knitted with grey human pubic hair and off they flew away.

Because the blood he collected from Tolitoli prison that night wasn't enough, Dilaso's next destination was Mauritius, an island located in the glittering Indian Ocean, off the southeast coast of Africa.

The island of Mauritius is part of the republic with the same name, alongside Cargados Carajos, Rodrigues and the Agaléga Islands. Surrounded by the world's third-largest coral reef, the island prides itself with a ravishing natural beauty capable of seducing even the most pretentious of travellers. In addition to miles of white sandy beaches, lush tropical forests, emerald waters with beautiful lagoons, and plenty of national reserves, Mauritius features lovely mountainous landscapes that give it a truly special charm no wonder it's a popular destination for honeymoons for newly married couples.

After hunting for a potential victim to 'devour' for blood, Dilaso finally spotted his target victim. It was a couple from Singapore during what was supposed to be a romantic honeymoon getaway. Upon entering their chalet while the young couple was fast asleep, Dilaso disembarked from Trump and invoked the evil spirit 'Give-us' to enter the young groom by the name of Aidan. Upon entering inside Aidan, Give-us possessed and took over the control of his spirit, and while sleep walking caused him to kill his beautiful bride by the name of Adela. It was a savage and brutal murder that was committed in cold blood. Under the influence of the evil spirit Give-us, Aidan shattered his wife's head with a flowerpot, leaving shards in her scalp, dislocated her arm, punctured her with a plastic fork, fractured her wrist, ribs, jaw, facial bones and skull, and, wielding a pocketknife, left five gaping stab wounds on the back of her neck. While Adela lay helpless and dying in a pool of blood, Dilaso collected her blood into the horn and off they went.

The blood was still not sufficient for Dilaso's near-future evil missions, so they had to collect some more and headed to Madagascar, the fourth largest island in the world after Greenland, New Guinea, and Borneo, and an incredible biodiversity hotspot.

Both nature enthusiasts and adventure travellers in Madagascar are greeted with outstanding national reserves. One of the most renowned is Andohahela, a very unusual paradise spread over 80,000 hectares. Featuring three different ecosystems, Andohahela is also home to the spectacular trees called baobabs.

Upon arriving in Madagascar, Dilaso headed for the city of Toamasina to the home of a local and well-respected Baptist preacher, Pastor Gaetan. Pastor Gaetan was in a troubled marriage with his combative Russian wife Kristina of 27 years.

To gain respite from his belligerent wife, Pastor Gaetan had several illicit affairs and often arranged overseas trips on the pretence of spreading the word of God in far-flung places. The Pastor had a son from a previous relationship, a Junior Pastor in the same Church, and both the pastor and his son were shamelessly having affairs with the same other women. Pastor Gaetan was so close to his son that the father-son relationship was non-existent. They knew each other's indiscretions and worked very hard to cover up for each other to their wives.

Pastor Gaetan's Church had a debt that was causing a lot of anxiety and desperately needed some hush money. Dilaso sensed in his spirit that he could capitalise on that polarised situation in order to acquire the coveted treasure for himself, blood.

After analysing the evil act, he was about to commit, Dilaso rationalised that after all, all the parties to the evil act he was about to commit would benefit as Pastor Gaetan and his church would also 'miraculously' find a solution to their perplexing financial difficulty. So Dilaso invoked the power of the evil spirit Give-us to enter into Pastor Gaetan and possessed his soul and took over control. Suddenly the Pastor had a light bulb moment and crafted a plan to resolve their church's financial problems.

To execute the vile plan, the evil spirit Give-us moved Pastor Gaetan to enlist his son, Gael, to kill his stepmother in what seemed like a murder-for-hire plot in order for them to collect 500,000 Malagasy Ariary (MGA) (equivalent to U$ 127,891) in life insurance policy. The plan had to be executed that same night while she was asleep. Pastor Gaetan's conceived alibi was that upon returning from a short trip to the store, he discovered his wife had been shot to death. Following their wicked plan, Pastor Gaetan's wife was killed with a single bullet to her head by his son and junior pastor, Gael, in her sleep, and Dilaso was able to collect the budgeted amount of blood for the night.

Following the evil deed, Dilaso packed up his apparatus and returned home on the back of his grandson, Trump. As he stood there spooked in that strange place in a strange cinematic luminous body, Trump could not bring himself to fully comprehend what he was seeing.

Trump observed that that evil night proved to be the bloodiest, in part because Dilaso had decided to collect blood far from home as almost all the nearby targets seemed to have this 'protective veil' far superior to his evil powers. The protective veil that deterred Dilaso from killing his victims inside as well as near his hometown on that particular bloody night was red in colour and watery in form. Trump wondered what that veil was, seeing it had successfully deterred Dilaso from killing the people under its covering or protection.

One of the seven translucent individuals seemed to have read Trump's thoughts, and he explained to him that the red veil was the covering of the blood of the son of Theo Lesa (a god) who died as a martyr in order to save his people. The Translucent individual went on further to explain to Trump that the blood of the son of Theo Lesa provided the only protection against any witchcraft fatal attacks that resulted in the premature and untimely death of the naïve, often foolish and unsuspecting human beings who left themselves exposed without the covering of the blood of the son of Theo Lesa.

The seventh Translucent individual continued speaking to Trump and added that although some deaths amongst human beings appeared to be natural, in reality, it was evil men like Dilaso who struck the fatal blow in the quest to suck their blood. "Mortals," one of the other seven Translucent individuals continued, "are born into a fallen world, resigned to participate in a degenerate existence with no hope of recovery. The pain of sin and death immediately attaches itself to all men the moment they are born and ushers into perpetual motion the ravages of death, each passing day drawing them closer to their eternal demise."

To illustrate the power that resided in the blood to Trump, the third Translucent individual of the seven conjured up a vision accompanied by a bright flash of light which momentously scared Trump as he wasn't expecting anything fairylike in nature. The motion images seemed to depict some eminent historical event as the people's appearance seemed very strange; all men had a long beard and were all dressed in long gear resembling gowns, and they seemed to be on a journey headed some place. The people also seemed to be panicked about something as though they were anticipating some catastrophic incident of the magnitude of a cyclone or tornado.

All these images that Trump was seeing were encapsulated in a huge transparent balloon-like bubble, and he saw that there was someone who looked like a leader and main character amongst them, and he was busy giving instructions to others who listened carefully to each and every word that fell from his lips. The third Translucent individual explained that it was Moses of old imparting knowledge to his people, the Israelites, on the protective power found in the blood. Then Trump saw and heard Moses' call to all the elders of Israel and said to them, "Pick out and take lambs for yourselves according to your families and kill the Passover lamb. And you shall take a bunch of hyssop, dip it in the blood that is in the basin and strike the lintel and the two doorposts with the blood that is in the basin. And none of you shall go out of the door of his house until morning. For the Lord will pass through to strike the Egyptians, and when He sees the blood on the lintel and on the two doorposts, the Lord will pass over the door and not allow the destroyer to come into your houses to strike you."

The third Translucent individual then explained that the images Trump had just seen were a mere demonstration of the hidden power found in the blood, and that it was because of that power that some enlightened individuals among the human race still celebrated feasts such as the Passover because it was due to the blood that the death angel passed over their ancestors but killed whoever did not have blood on their doorpost.

Trump was overwhelmed with fear and started trembling as he didn't know what to make out of all this. Then the fifth individual among the seven Translucent fellas with a high note of music pitched in what sounded like tenor turned off the 'movie' about Trump's history.

Chapter 14
Trial by the Jury of Consuming Fire

After seeing the shocking scenes of his life story on earth, Trump still had a lot of unanswered questions. For instance, he didn't know where he was and why he was shown the secret things that hitherto had been hidden from him.

The seventh Translucent individual spoke again and explained to Trump that he had actually died on earth by drowning in the river. He then switched-on Trump's historic movie again, and Trump was able to see his death. The seventh Translucent individual further explained that the beautiful place Trump now found himself was called Nebuparadiza.

Further, the seventh Translucent individual explained to Trump that Nebuparadiza was a place specially reserved for human beings who had lived sacred lives during their lifetime on earth. It was a place reserved for holy men and women. "However," the seventh Translucent individual continued, "once every 1000 years, there was Ubereora (Jubilee or commemoration) in Nebuparadiza, whereby one human being called 'The Chosen One or The Sheela', upon dying, was offered admission temporally into Nebuparadiza regardless of how evil they lived their life on earth and a decision was made whether to grant them another opportunity for them to alter their destiny before being condemned to Gehenakumbo." Gehenakumbo, he explained, was a place underneath the core of the earth in which evil souls were subjected to perpetual anguish and pain and suffering untold.

The seventh Translucent individual further explained that whether or not to grant permanent admission into Nebuparadiza depended on how The Chosen One (The Sheela) died and whether their good deeds during their lifetime on earth outweighed their evil deeds.

Furthermore, the seventh Translucent individual pointed out that it was a rare and golden opportunity for The Chosen One (The Sheela) to undertake three assignments, some of which involved going back in time to intervene in human history in order to try and change the course of some unfortunate events as they occurred in order to grant more human beings the opportunity to save their souls and avoid going to Gehenakumbo. If The Chosen One (The Sheela) managed to successfully undertake their assignments, the recompense was eternal life and permanent admission into Nebuparadiza to become a 'god', like themselves.

The sixth Translucent individual picked up from the seventh Translucent individual and continued to explain that the choosing and assigning tasks to The Chosen One (The Sheela) were done at a pomp and fearful ceremony called the Buite. He explained that the name Buite stood for 'The Jury of Consuming Fire or Court'. He also warned that Trump would soon appear before the Buite, which was chaired by Theo Lesa, who, according to the sixth Translucent individual, was the maker of everything that ever existed in heaven and on earth and other planets.

The sixth Translucent individual added that Trump would be called upon to appear before the Buite within the allocated 'Clap'. The Clap, it was explained to Trump, was the same as 'time' on earth because there was no such a thing as time in Nebuparadiza.

The sixth Translucent individual further explained that there was no time in Nebuparadiza because time was a form of prison originally designed in Nebuparadiza to control the affairs of human beings on earth. For instance, by controlling when they were allowed to go into the earth via a process called Bira (or birth), and also when to take them out of the earth, sometimes gently via a process called Odqi (e.g., dying peacefully in their sleep after attaining full old age) or violently if need be via a process called Kitr (e.g., through accidents, incurable diseases or natural disasters), or via another process called Tendr (e.g., through disappearance, often a time declared as missing individuals by the simple-minded human beings).

Trump was astounded to learn how the affairs of the inhabitants of the earth were controlled from this remote outer place called Nebuparadiza, when all the while the presidents, kings, queens, scientists and other key figures among the mortals were under the impression that it was themselves who were in control; yet they couldn't control processes such as Bira, Adqi, Kitr and Tendr.

The sixth Translucent individual also explained that as Trump was still in the body he adorned upon arrival in Nebuparadiza, he would put on a different body, just a level below theirs, upon being summoned to appear before Theo Lesa at the Buite, and that was one of the prerequisites for anyone to come into the presence of the holy Theo Lesa or else they would be consumed right away. It was further explained to Trump that the name for the Translucent beings or individuals was actually Ngeloi (known as Angel among the mortals on earth) and that Trump would also become a Ngeloi, albeit junior to the other Ngelois, if he succeeded in receiving approval to undertake assignments as The Chosen One (The Sheela) at the Buite.

In conclusion, explained the sixth Ngeloi, Trump's fate was not yet fully certain, and there was still a possibility he could be condemned to Gehenakumbo depending on the outcome of the court procession at the Buite.

At exactly the appointed Clap (time), which was not known to Trump, twenty strong Ngelois appeared and took Trump to the Buite for him to appear before Theo Lesa for his trial to determine his fate. Within a short Clap (time), Trump and the twenty strong special purpose Ngelois arrived at the Buite.

At the Buite, something immediately noticeable to Trump was that Theo Lesa had a different form from the other Ngelois present. In place of Theo Lesa, all Trump could see was a huge flame of consuming fire that had the shape of a Ngeloi, and no one could come close to him or else they would be consumed in an instant. Brimstone fire flared from Theo Lesa's nostrils, and he spoke in lightning and thunder, and there was an echoing sound each time he 'spoke' as evidenced by lightning and thunder.

The Buite (Jury of Consuming Fire) comprised a maximum of fifteen Marlenas (Judges) of varying seniority. The number of Marlenas who attended each trial session was determined by how sinful The Sheela (The Chosen One) was at the time of their death on earth. The more sinful The Chosen One (The Sheela) was deemed to be, the more serious the case and consequently the higher the number of the Marlenas in the Buite, and also, the higher the chances of being condemned to Gehenakumbo.

Trials at the Buite were conducted with relatively fewer Marlenas, five to seven Marlenas, if The Sheela (The Chosen One) was deemed to have been less sinful at the time of their death on earth. The opposite was true if The Chosen One (The Sheela) happened to be a hard core sinner at the moment they gave up their last breath on earth, in which case the number of the Marlenas who graced the Buite would be as high as fifteen, as was the case for Trump's trial, though he was unaware of this tiny yet important fact.

Though only a minor at the time of his death, things were taken so seriously in Nebuparadiza that Trump was categorised as a hardcore sinner and his death was noted as self-induced or suicide.

Trump stood anxiously and tried to pay attention to the court processions, but he was deeply troubled and had a feeling the outcome wasn't going to be at all pleasant. Theo Lesa, while vehemently breathing fire and sulpha, instructed Marlenas in detail before the start of the trial not only concerning their duties and responsibilities (as the jury) but also about the importance of the independence of their role from any chain of command or other influence, and the need for all the Marlenas to have an equal voice and vote regardless of the disparity in rank.

All sentencing proceedings for The Chosen Ones (The Sheela) convicted at trial or in the event of a guilty plea were conducted in the presence of Theo Lesa. Theo Lesa directed the Buite to sentencing guidelines and principles and had a casting vote in case of a deadlock. After deliberations, the Marlenas (jury) were invited to retire to consider their verdict, to decide if The Sheela (The Chosen One) was guilty or not guilty. The Sheela (The Chosen One), if dissatisfied with the outcome of their trial, had the right of appeal to Theo Lesa. Almost always, the outcome of the appeal went the same way as the Marlenas' initial verdict.

Having listened to the Buite's Court Clerk on directions on the law and summary of the evidence, the Marlenas were responsible for determining whether or not The Chosen One (The Sheela) was guilty or not guilty depending on the facts that were written in the 'Chiterball' (Book of Life).

Trump never lived a holy life during his time on earth, so upon hearing how seriously Theo Lesa and the Buite considered things, he didn't expect to be given a chance to undertake any of the assignments for him to try and alter his destiny; if anything he saw himself going to Gehenakumbo at the close of that session. He imagined total agony and infinite exposure to the heat of countless pits of fire and joining in with what he assumed would be insufferable screams of torture all around him, and he was absolutely horrified. Trump wasn't sure whether he was catastrophising and irrationally exaggerating his situation and blowing everything out of proportion.

All the deliberations of the Buite were conducted in an extra-terrestrial and interplanetary language far too complicated for Trump to grasp, not even a single word. At the Buite, it was serious business, and the sweet music that Trump was greeted with upon arrival in Nebuparadiza was not used as the medium of communication.

Trump waited nervously as the Marlenas deliberated his case based on his life history on earth as recorded in the Chiterball (Book of Life). After deliberating for a long Clap (time), the Marlenas (jury) finally reached a unanimous verdict and notified the jury bailiff, who notified the Court Clerk, who also notified Theo Lesa. The Marlenas returned to Court and The Sheela (The Chosen One), who happened to be Trump, returned to the dock. Theo Lesa then entered the courtroom in a blazing flame. All Trump could still see of Theo Lesa was a huge ball of fire in the shape of an incredibly huge Ngeloi.

The Court Clerk then asked the Marlenas' foreman to stand up and asked him, "Have you reached a verdict upon which you are all agreed? Please answer 'Yes' or 'No'." The answer was a resounding Yes. And the Court Clerk proceeded by saying, "In respect of each individual count, what is your verdict?" Accordingly, responses were provided for each count. Trump was found guilty on all the 307 counts brought against him.

The guilty verdicts were a mixture of criminal and summary offences including but not limited to: sitting on a brazier full of hot coal fire in a show that bore resemblance to a 'mad scientist's' crude experiment thereby causing unnecessary anguish to his parents who consequently subjected their maid to unnecessary tirade and harangue for not caring for their son; stealing a match-box to set fire to the family's grass thatched fence thereby causing panic in the compound as men and women made frantic efforts to quench the fire; attempted manslaughter in a sibling jealousy feat by cunningly misleading his sister Joanna to jump over the asbestos covering to the sewer hole knowing full well she was going to fall in and drown and die so that he could remain the only child in their family; depleting the family finances with hospital bills after he deliberately lured and caused his sister Joanna to fall into the sewer hole; inflicting wanton and deliberate pain on his sister which resulted from the cocktail of pathogens feasting on the variant faculties of her frail body following the accident; conceiving and concealing his pre-meditated murderous intentions against her; making determined effort not to confess despite being accorded numerous opportunities to do so e.g., one of the assigned angels on earth whispered to him countless times to confess and also appeared in his dreams and pleaded with him to confess but he remained adamant and hardened his heart against confession; notwithstanding his tender age, secretly peeping, or chirping, on the nakedness of the best friend to his mum, Manku, while the four men lowered her into the sewer as she grappled to rescue his younger sister who he had caused to drown on human waste; being indisposed to sympathy for his sister during attempts to resuscitate and revivify her after she was pulled out of the sewer hole; eavesdropping on adult conversation between his mum and her friend Manku; encouraging Manku's step daughter, Muzo, to continue peeping on his father while he was dressing and then asking her to narrate the explicit details of her father's genitalia so that he could compare the size with his own genitals; not disclosing his nightmares to his parents thereby indirectly and circuitously allowing his evil grandfather Dilaso to perpetuate his blood sucking missions at night; attempted manslaughter by causing a pile up of cars outside their home, which resulted in a terrible accident in which one widowed mum, unbeknown to Trump at the time, eventually lost her sight from the fragments of her shuttered windscreen; faking his alibi that he had been in the bathroom all the while following the accident; causing his mother Muswana to accuse the innocent driver of the red car (who was wrongfully charged with dangerous driving by the police) of racism as a result of Trump's bogus alibi which he persuaded his mother to believe; attempted suicide by conspiring with his friends, behind the back of their parents to undertake swimming lessons in a crocodile infested river; committing suicide by intentionally jumping into the rip currents of the river thereby bringing upon himself premature death, which was the principal reason for his indictment in the Buite etc. The list went on till it reached 307 guilty verdicts, one for each count.

In the interests of justice, which was the overarching principle in Nebuparadiza, the Court Clerk was mandated to give the accused the opportunity to defend themselves against the guilty verdict before Theo Lesa could pass final judgment.

In his new glorified body at the Buite, Trump was no longer the child that died of drowning on earth as that wouldn't have been fair for him to stand trial in Nebuparadiza based on the 'principle of incompetency due to maturity'. This principle was also imposed on human beings on earth by the Marlenas in Nebuparadiza.

In their limited capacity to grasp who the true rulers of the universe were, the mortals on earth understood the 'principle of incompetency due to maturity' as emanating from the highest courts in their land. In reality, it was the spiritual agents from Nebuparadiza commissioned by the Marlenas who caused cases that involved children and adolescents on earth to require specific expertise and consideration, and at the time of Trump's death, all this was well illustrated through case vignettes. For instance, in Dick vs. Kwesu Land (1909), the Supreme Court ruled that all criminal defendants must be competent to stand trial.

The test for competency announced by the Court in Dick was whether the defendant had a 'sufficient present ability to consult with their lawyer with a reasonable degree of rational understanding and whether they had a rational as well as a factual understanding of the proceedings against them'. This is commonly referred to as a two-prong test – whether the accused understood the charges and legal process against them and whether they could assist their lawyer in their own defence. Dick prompted changes in legislation throughout Kwesu Land and caused all states to enact legislation to comply with the Dick standard as applied to defendants in adult criminal court.

The spiritual forces from Nebuparadiza via the highest courts on earth (supreme courts) caused nations and states to typically apply the same Dick standard to all criminal court defendants, regardless of the defendant's age or whether they had dementia, schizophrenia or depression.

Further, the invisible agents from Nebuparadiza also caused various components of the 'principle of incompetency due to maturity' to be applied in the courts of the mortals on earth in order to determine the defendant's understanding of the proceedings, e.g., requirement for an understanding of the charges and the potential consequences of being found guilty of the charges; requirement for an understanding of the role of the various court room players (i.e., judge, jury, prosecutor, defence attorney, witnesses); and requirement for an understanding of some basic constitutional rights such as innocent until proven guilty, right to remain silent, etc.

The invisible agents from Nebuparadiza further instigated the human courts to determine that having a factual understanding of these issues, however, was not enough. The defendant was required to have a rational understanding of these issues and rationally discuss the case with their attorney. The invisible agents from Nebuparadiza further triggered the administrators of the human courts to determine that rational decision making may often be impaired by psychiatric illnesses, such as schizophrenia or major depression. Defendants who lacked a present ability to make rational decisions were to be referred by the courts of mortals for mandated treatment to 'restore' their competency before they could stand trial.

Trump was, therefore, as he stood trial in the Buite, at least ten times more intelligent than the most intelligent mortal or human being that ever lived on earth, the likes of William James Sidis, one of the most intelligent men to ever walk the earth. According to written records, Albert Einstein had an estimated IQ of 160, and Isaac Newton's estimated IQ was 190. These famous men are known as absolute geniuses around the world. But there once lived a person, William James Sidis, whose IQ was said to be between 250 and 300! William James Sidis was a child prodigy and an exceptional mathematician. He was a master at multiple dialects and a gifted author as well. But sadly, not many people have ever heard of him. William was born in New York City in 1898. His father, Boris, was an exemplary psychologist who earned four degrees from Harvard. His mother was also an MD. Since his parents were geniuses themselves, William James Sidis was expected to be brilliant, but his intelligence proved to be far more than ordinary. At the age of just 18 months, he was able to read The New York Times. By age 8, he taught himself Latin, Greek, French, Russian, German, Hebrew, Turkish and Armenian. In addition to those eight languages, he also invented his own and called it Vendergood. Very much aware of his intelligence, his father tried to enrol him in Harvard but was refused as William was only nine years old. Two years later, the institute accepted him, and William became the youngest person to be admitted to Harvard 1909. By 1910, his knowledge of mathematics peaked so much that he started lecturing his professors instead, earning him the title of 'child prodigy'. He completed his Bachelor of Arts degree at the age of 16.[18]

In a nutshell, the Marlenas, while carrying out Theo Lesa's mandate, ensured that the court proceedings on earth mirrored proceedings at the Buite in Nebuparadiza in order to ensure that justice was rendered 'without passion or prejudice'.

The major difference between mortal court proceedings on earth and Nebuparadiza lies in the fact that in the latter, The Chosen One (The Sheela) defended themselves after being convicted or simply put, after the pronouncement of the guilty verdict and not the other way round. Of course, there was no need for self-defence following a 'not guilty' verdict.

After the guilty verdict had been pronounced, it was now incumbent upon the Court Clerk to accord Trump the opportunity to defend himself, however, not against all the guilty verdict counts, but only against the paramount charge which in his case happened to be that of self-imposed death which was construed to be suicide by the Marlenas in the Buite.

Given the level of enhanced intelligence in his glorified new body, which was well above that of people like William James Sidis or Albert Einstein, there were no limits or restrictions to the extent of case law precedent in mortal courts on earth that Trump could refer to in his self-defence, and all this was admissible at the Buite.

Chapter 15
Self-Defence in the Unknown Court

In the human justice systems on earth, there are many reasons why some criminal defendants may wish to represent themselves in a criminal trial. Although it is usually wise to get a defence lawyer, sometimes it's unnecessary. Usually, the key to deciding if one needs a lawyer is to look at the punishment one is likely to face if convicted. The harsher the likely punishment, the more crucial it is that one is represented by an advocate or lawyer.

Defendants may choose to represent themselves for various reasons, one of them being self-represented defendants are not bound by lawyers' ethical codes. This means that a defendant who represents himself can delay proceedings and sometimes wreak havoc on an already overloaded system by repeatedly filing motions; although this approach is not advisable because it often backfires.

While self-representation may be possible in the justice systems of mortal beings on earth, it was the only option in Nebuparadiza upon being convicted by the Marlenas in the Buite (court). The unimaginable alternative to self-representation was the gnashing of teeth in the flames of Gehenakumbo. In other words, rejecting self-representation was tantamount to accepting the guilty verdict without attempting to put up a fight in self-defence, which would be foolish whichever way one looked at it given the quandary that surrounded the guilty verdict upon being pronounced against The Chosen One (The Sheela) in the Buite. Therefore, Trump had no option but to represent himself against his criminal conviction. After making his intentions known to the Court Clerk, the Buite reconvened to hear Trump's appeal to Theo Lesa against the guilty verdict passed down on him.

Trump opened his defence by contending that suicide on earth wasn't a criminal offence. "The term suicide," he asserted, "could be traced back to 1651 in human history. Its first occurrence was evidently in Sir Thomas Browne's

Religio Medici, written in 1635 and published in 1642. Before it became a common term, expressions such as 'self-murder' and 'self-killing' were used to describe the act of taking one's own life." Trump continued his defence, saying, "In Greek and Roman antiquity, suicide was accepted and even seen by some as an honourable means of death and the attainment of immediate salvation. Stoics and others influenced by them saw suicide as the triumph of an individual over fate. Socrates' decision to take his own life rather than violate the state's sentence of execution influenced many to see the act as noble."

On that point, one of the Marlena's interjected Trump's statement and pointed out that, "Socrates, however, also made clear that mortals belonged to the gods and could not end their lives unless they wished it so, meaning he knew that wasn't the correct way to die." According to the court proceedings in the Buite, the Marlena's interjection was noted by the Court Clerk, and Trump was allowed to proceed.

"Many of the early Christians," continued Trump, "knew they would likely die for their faith but chose to follow Christ at any cost. Those deaths were not typically considered 'suicide' since they were not initiated by the person but accepted due to their commitment to Jesus. However, one would argue that that was self-imposed death which can be equated, in some way, to the nature of my own death on earth on that fateful day through accidental drowning, which has been erroneously interpreted as suicide by the Marlenas here in the Buite."

Another Marlena interjected and pointed out that, "Augustine (AD 354–430) was a strong opponent of any form of self-murder (cf. *City of God* 1:4–26). He appealed to the sixth commandment and its prohibition against murder. And he agreed with Socrates that our lives belong to God, so that we have no right to end them ourselves. Over time, many in the church came to see self-murder as an unpardonable sin." The Court Clerk accordingly noted the Marlena's interjection and Trump was allowed to proceed.

"In the nineteenth century," continued Trump, "social scientists began to view suicide as a social issue and a symptom of a larger dysfunction in the community and/or home. Medical doctors began to identify depression and other disorders behind the act. Suicide became decriminalised so that the individual could be buried, his family not disinherited, and a survivor not prosecuted."

"Furthermore," Trump emphasised, "the Christian Bible, in the old testament, records five clear cases, without outright condemnation, of what could be deemed as suicide, and these were: When Abimelech was mortally wounded by a woman who dropped a millstone on his head, he cried to his armour-bearer to kill him so his death would not be credited to the woman (Judges 9:54). The mortally wounded King Saul fell upon his own sword lest the Philistines abused him further (1 Samuel 31:4). Saul's armour-bearer then took his own life as well (1 Samuel 31:5). Ahithophel hanged himself after his advice was no longer followed by King David's son Absalom (2 Samuel 17:23). And finally, Zimri set himself afire after his rebellion failed (1 Kings 16:18)." Trump then paused, supposedly for dramatic effect.

There being no further interjection from the Marlenas, Trump continued to defend himself by saying, "Additionally, some scholars consider Jonah to have attempted suicide (Jonah 1:11–15). And Samson destroyed the Philistine temple, killing himself and all those with him (Judges 16:29–30)."

On that point, another Marlena interjected and pointed out that, "Jonah's case could not be construed as attempted suicide because he was caught red-handed as the root cause for the storm that arose on the sea, and he would have been ejected into the sea anyhow; as for Samson his was an act of military bravery as opposed to suicide." The Court Clerk accordingly noted the interjection.

Trump continued, "Some consider Jesus' death to have been a kind of suicide since he made clear: No one takes my life from me, but I lay it down of my own accord (John 10:18)."

Another Marlena interjected and said, "As the divine Son of God, Jesus could only have been killed, by any means, with his permission." The Court Clerk accordingly noted the interjection.

Trump continued his self-defence, "The following principles of the Catholic Theology make it clear that suicide shouldn't result in automatic condemnation, 'We cannot be sure of the spiritual state of the person who commits suicide. This person may be suffering from grave psychological disturbances which can diminish the responsibility of the one committing suicide' (#2282). 'Mortal sin requires full knowledge and complete consent (#1859) and can be diminished by unintentional ignorance' (#1860). 'Thus, the Church should not despair of the eternal salvation of persons who have taken their own lives' (#2283)."

On that point, another Marlena interjected, "However, the Catholic Theology does not end at that, it further states that 'if the person was fully aware of his or her actions, without suffering grave psychological disturbances, this person committed murder, an act that is gravely sinful' (#2268). And that 'a person who commits a mortal sin and demonstrates persistence in it until the end goes to hell'

(#1037). Since a person who commits self-murder (suicide) cannot then repent of this sin, it is logical to conclude that this person cannot be saved from hell."

The Court Clerk noted the interjection and Trump's swift rebuttal or refutation was that, "The Catechism nowhere makes that conclusion explicit, at least not at the time of my death, which I have to add has been incorrectly classified as suicide by the Marlenas."

The hearing went on for a long Clap (i.e., time) until Trump finally rested his defence. It was now up to Theo Lesa to pass final judgement, taking into account the facts as presented by Trump in his defence as The Sheela (The Chosen One).

There were only two possible outcomes following an appeal against the Marlena's guilty verdict, and these were to either uphold the guilty verdict and condemn The Sheela (The Chosen One) to Gehenakumbo or overrule the guilty verdict and accord The Chosen One (The Sheela) another opportunity to alter their destiny subject to them successfully undertaking certain assignments; some of which were intended to alter the course of human history as recorded in Nebuparadiza. Failing such an assignment by the Chosen One (The Sheela) would result in a one-way ticket to Gehenakumbo without the right of appeal.

In Nebuparadiza, and of course in the affairs of the mortals on earth, Theo Lesa was both the Trial as well as the Appellate judge, and his decisions were final. Upon considering the facts presented by Trump in his defence, Theo Lesa ruled to uphold the guilty verdict passed by the Marlenas against Trump, and his decision was final.

Chapter 16
The Intervention

Just before Theo Lesa could pronounce the final sentence to condemn Trump to Gehenakumbo, the session was interrupted by an incredibly sweet sound of music that started in a low key and progressively increased in both rhythm and tempo until it grew louder and louder. The music wasn't vexingly loud. Rather, soothing and therapeutically loud.

The events that ensued following the intrusion of that sweet sound of music were nothing short of a spectacle. Theo Lesa paused, and a smoke-like substance with the aroma of incense started to slowly fill the courtroom as the sweet sound of music continued. It seemed as though the music was coming from the direction on the right-hand side of Theo Lesa. As Trump watched in wonder and awe, he saw the singer of the music walking into the courtroom majestically, yet slowly as he continued to sing.

The singer of the sweet sound of music, who seemed to have momentarily halted Trump's condemnation to Gehenakumbo, was enshrouded in some form of cloud, and as he got closer, Trump could see that he had the form of a Ngeloi except he seemed far much superior to all the other Ngelois that he had seen up to that stage, in stature, might and glitter. He was the most beautiful Ngeloi of them all, and unlike the other Ngelois, he wore a sympathetic and kind façade, and amid all that serious courtroom business, he smiled as he sang.

Suddenly, all the Marlena's prostrated themselves before him as he continued to sing. As he drew closer, Trump made a quarter turn and watched attentively to catch a better glimpse of this unique and incredibly gorgeous Ngeloi who had commanded so much respect and attention from all the Marlenas except for Theo Lesa, who remained seated in a ball of blazing fire.

When the incense-like smoke had disappeared, and the view was much clearer, Trump noticed that the beautiful Ngeloi was standing among seven golden lampstands and was dressed in a robe reaching down to his feet and with a golden sash around his chest. The hair on his head was white like wool, as white as snow, and his eyes were like blazing fire. His feet were like bronze glowing in a furnace, and his voice was like the sound of rushing waters. In his right hand he held seven stars. His face was like the sun shining in all its brilliance.

The beautiful Ngeloi walked slowly to where the stunned Trump was, and when he had come within inches to him, Trump fell at his feet, motionless. Then the beautiful Ngeloi placed his right hand on Trump and said, "Do not be afraid. I am the First and the Last. I am the Living One; I was dead, and now look, I am alive forever and ever! And I hold the keys of death and Hades. I am the Alpha and the Omega. The beginning and the end." And the beautiful Ngeloi started to sing again as he slowly turned towards the direction of Theo Lesa, who, in contrast, was a huge ball of burning fire.

To Trump's amusement, there was now something completely different about the song that the beautiful Ngeloi had started to sing. Trump could clearly hear the words as it was sung in an earthly mortal language that he was familiar with. "Wasn't it at Sunday school that I heard my teacher, Mrs Alex, sing that song?" speculated Trump serenely, and yes it was!

"Theo Lesa is gracious and full of compassion; slow to anger, and of great mercy;

Theo Lesa is good to all and his tender mercies are over all his works;

All thy works shall praise thee, O Theo Lesa; and thy saints shall bless thee;

Theo Lesa delighteth not in the strength of the horse; he taketh not pleasure in the legs of a man;

Theo Lesa taketh pleasure in them that fear him, in those that hope in his mercy;

O give thanks unto Theo Lesa; for he is good; for his mercy endureth forever;

Let mortals hope in Theo Lesa, for with Theo Lesa there is mercy; and with him is plenteous redemption;

Theo Lesa is merciful and gracious, slow to anger and plenteous in mercy;

Theo Lesa will not always chide, neither will he keep his anger forever;

Theo Lesa hath not dealt with mortals after their sins; nor rewarded them according to their iniquities;

For as the heaven is high above the earth, so great is his mercy towards them that fear him; As far as the east is from the west, so far hath he removed transgressions from mortals;

Enter into his gates with thanksgiving, and into his courts with praise;

Be thankful unto Theo Lesa and bless his name;

For Theo Lesa is good; his mercy is everlasting; and his truth endureth to all mortal generations;

Let thy mercy, O Theo Lesa, be upon mortals, according as they hope in thee;

Remember, O Theo, thy tender mercies and thy loving kindnesses; for they have been ever of old;

Remember not the sins of mortals, nor their transgressions according to thy mercy Remember thou the mortals for thy goodness' sake, O Theo; Surely, your goodness and mercy shall follow mortals all the days of their lives until they dwell in your house forevermore; the mortals that have trusted in thy mercy shall rejoice in thy salvation and will sing unto you O Theo Lesa because thou will deal bountifully with them..."

After the beautiful Ngeloi had finished singing, there was total silence in Nebuparadiza. Then the beautiful Ngeloi opened his mouth to speak and said, "I plead my blood to redeem him from condemnation. Have mercy on him." This was followed by further silence. Trump was so overwhelmed with a deep sense of guilt that he was coiled in a helpless heap, for he had now come to a full realisation of the gravity of his predicament, seeing the extent to which the beautiful Ngeloi had gone to try and save him.

After a prolonged period of 'awkward' silence, which seemed normal in that strange place, the 'ball of fire' that Theo Lesa was, stood up and at this, all the Marlenas in the Buite and other Ngelois including the mighty and exceedingly superior and beautiful Ngeloi prostrated themselves to the ground, and there was a loud voice that sounded like a trumpet, and Trump could clearly hear the words that were spoken:

"Sing to Theo Lesa, all you hosts of Nebuparadiza;

Tell of His glory among his creation and His wonderful deeds among all his creation;

For great is Theo Lesa, and greatly to be praised;

He also is to be feared above all gods;

For all the worlds will be filled with the knowledge of the glory of Theo Lesa as the waters cover the sea..."

It turned out the Court Clerk actually spoke the words. The tribute to Theo Lesa by the Court Clerk was followed by another moment of prolonged silence as all the hosts of Nebuparadiza, including the beautiful Ngeloi, remained prostrated. After this, the beautiful Ngeloi stood up and stretched himself full length. He was taller than any Ngeloi present in the courtroom; full of majesty and dignity. When he spoke, his voice was like many waterfalls flowing at the same time, but again, Trump could clearly hear what he was saying, and he said:

"They raise their voices, they shout for joy;

They all cry out concerning the majesty of Theo Lesa;

Therefore, glorify the name of Theo Lesa in the east, in the west, in the north and in the south;

You are Theo Lesa, the God of Nebuparadiza and all the worlds In the coastlands of the sea;

You are our God, and we give thanks to You;

You are our God, we extol You;

O magnify Theo Lesa with me,

And let us exalt His name together…"

After the beautiful Ngeloi had finished his accolades to Theo Lesa, he gestured to all the Ngelois to stand up, and they all stood up silently. The beautiful Ngeloi then gestured to the Court Clerk, who subsequently started walking, followed by all the Ngelois. They walked to form a circle around Trump so that he could be positioned inside the circle. When all the Ngelois were in place, the Court Clerk stopped and signalled to them to stop. They all then turned in a uniform fashion to face Trump, who didn't know what to make of that procession or parade.

Trump noticed that there was another group of Ngelois who weren't part of the circle; they were, in fact, a symphony orchestra about to perform a concert, and they had a variety of musical instruments from different instrument families ranging from bowed string instruments (violins, violas, cellos and double bass); woodwinds (flute, oboe, clarinet and bassoon); brass instruments (horns, trumpets, trombones and tubas); to percussion instruments (timpani, bass drums, triangles, snare drums, cymbals and mallet) etc.

During his lifetime on earth, Trump's parents never took him to watch a live symphony performance or concert though he watched it on TV on a few occasions as his father, Kennedy, was a great fan of classical music. He wondered whether he was about to witness a live symphony performance. What was even more confounding to him was whether he deserved to be accorded such a lavish display best reserved for royalties on earth, the likes of queen Elizabeth of England, especially that the outcome of the appeal against his guilty verdict was still unclear.

Talking about the symphony, the word is actually derived from the Greek word συμφωνία (symphonia), meaning 'agreement or concord of sound', 'concert of vocal or instrumental music', from σύμφωνος (symphōnos), 'harmonious'. The word referred to various concepts before ultimately settling on its current meaning, designating a musical form. In late Greek and medieval theory, the word was used for consonance, as opposed to διαφωνία (diaphōnia), which was the word for 'dissonance'. In the Middle Ages and later, the Latin form symphonia was used to describe various instruments, especially those capable of producing more than one sound simultaneously.[19]

Then without notice, as Trump endeavoured to decipher the meaning of that grandeur and extraordinary splendour, the orchestra started to play sweet soft music. The quality and beauty of the music was like no other music Trump had ever heard before. It was extremely soothing. All the Ngelois surrounding Trump started dancing with ecstatic jubilation. Although Trump was still spooked and didn't know what to make of anything, one undisputable thing was that that was a moment of extreme joy! Trump was invited to join in the celebrations, and in no time, he was lifted and tossed up and about by the Ngelois and was floating up and down ecstatically in a moment of continuous magical enjoyment. The only problem was that he wasn't too sure why everyone was so delighted.

Further, despite the exuberant mood all around him, Trump wasn't sure whether Theo Lesa, who a while ago had upheld the Marlena's guilty verdict and was about to condemn him to Gehenakumbo, was taking part in the celebrations because the consuming ball of fire that Theo Lesa was made of continued to burn no more no less amid the beautiful symphony music that kept blasting away.

After the jostling and celebrations and the orchestra symphony performance had ceased, Trump was brought forward from the centre of the courtroom to face Theo Lesa. The Court Clerk opened a huge Book, and the beautiful Ngeloi was now standing on the right-hand side of Theo Lesa. He was partially covered in the flames that radiated from Theo Lesa, but he was not consumed by the fire.

Theo Lesa spoke after the Book was fully opened, but Trump could not hear a single word. One thing for sure was that after the symphony orchestra concert and the jubilations that graced the occasion were over, Trump no longer felt as anxious or as fearful as before. He felt a sense of boldness about himself; he also felt extremely peaceful and joyful. When Trump checked out his body, it had changed and was now red in colour, like blood.

The Court Clerk translated the meaning of the words that Theo Lesa spoke to Trump. They meant, "Congratulations to you! There is always great joy in Nebuparadiza when the guilty Chosen One (The Sheela) from earth receives full pardon compared to the many righteous mortals who do not need pardon because they have lived sacred lives. My son here (i.e., the beautiful Ngeloi), has secured your pardon in full, and that's the reason why your body is now red in colour; you have been granted full pardon." The Court Clerk went on to explain that as a result of the intervention by the beautiful Ngeloi, Trump's past crimes had now been pardoned, and his condemnation to Gehenakumbo had been suspended, but not expunged. The Court Clerk explained that Trump now had a part to play in order to complete his redemption as The Chosen One (The Sheela). He had been granted special dispensation to enable him to try and change his fate.

Chapter 17
Seeing Things Hidden from Mortals

Following Trump's conditional pardon, the Court Clerk touched him on the face and said, "With the power vested in me by the almighty Theo Lesa, I now grant you '*Ubwyrukol'*," which literally meant Trump had now been granted supernatural sight to see and fathom things hidden from mortals. After the pronouncement by the Court Clerk, Trump noticed that the colour of his heavenly body had changed from red to the same heavenly colour as all the other Ngelois. There was now no palpable difference between him and them, except for the beautiful Ngeloi and Theo Lesa, who remained distinguished from the rest by virtue of their echelons in Nebuparadiza as commander and 2ic (second in command).

The Court Clerk then took Trump by the hand, led him through an open door and showed him the recorded history of the earth, other heavenly bodies and all the planets in the solar system since their creation.

From the recorded history, Trump was surprised to see that other races inhabited other planets besides planet earth, and each race had a unique colour unlike the human beings who were a mixture of colours, black, white, pink, red, etc. For instance, the Mardeduns race on Mars was blue in colour, the Vejs race on Venus was pink in colour, the Merions race on Mercury was zinc grey in colour, the Juleos race on Jupiter was strangely velvet in colour, the Nebwes race on Neptune was emerald-green in colour, the Satjunks race on Saturn was a blend of distinct colours as in a rainbow, the Ulikos race on Uranus was peach black in colour.

Trump was marvelled by what he saw. Only the earth had a variety of races; the other planets were inhabited by a single race. The Court Clerk then pointed to the sun in order to shift Trump's attention as if to say, "There are more wonders over there." Trump couldn't believe what he saw. There were beings seemingly made of hot or blazing iron who lived on the sun. The Court Clerk told Trump that the inhabitants of the sun were called the Muriro, which literally meant 'Hot beings' because they were made out of pure heat.

The Court Clerk explained that the major role of the Muriro race was to control and direct sun energy to all the four corners of the earth. "For instance," he pointed out, "summer on earth simply meant the Muriros or Hot men on the sun were working overtime and winter was down time following the same logic. Autumn and Spring were a mixture of shifts hence the changes in seasons as observed on earth." All this information was very different from Trump's earthly head knowledge about the sun which was limited to it being the star at the centre of the Solar System; a nearly perfect sphere of hot plasma heated to incandescence by nuclear fusion reactions in its core and radiating energy mainly as visible light and infrared radiation.

The Other earthly head knowledge Trump bore about the sun was that it was by far the most important source of energy for life on earth and that its diameter was about 1.39 million kilometres (864,000 miles), or 109 times that of the earth; that its mass was about 330,000 times that of earth and accounted for about 99.86% of the total mass of the Solar System. Trump also knew that roughly three-quarters of the sun's mass consisted of hydrogen (~73%); the rest was mostly helium (~25%), with much smaller quantities of heavier elements, including oxygen, carbon, neon and iron. And these were the only major facts Trump knew about the sun at the time of his death on earth. Till that eye-opening moment by the Court Clerk, Trump had no clue about the existence of the Muriro race or 'Hot men' as the inhabitants of the sun. He was pleasantly surprised at all the knowledge he had now come into, and it was just the beginning.

The Court Clerk then directed Trump's attention to the moon. With his new supernatural sight, Trump looked, and he could not believe his eyes. Following the Court Clerk's explanation, he came to understand that the moon was inhabited by a race of vicious rock-eating creatures that were made of bronze and steel, without skin, and they lived circa 1000 miles below the moon's surface. They were called the Muezee race or Muezees. The Court Clerk explained that Theo Lesa's original plan was for the Muezees to continue living 1000 miles below the moon's surface, but the Muezees rebelled and started digging their way to the moon's surface searching for human blood.

"Through their vast intellectual capabilities," the Court Clerk continued to explain to Trump, "a leading figure among the Muezees became aware of the human space explorations to the Moon after intercepting signals from NASA about their space programmes. He then convinced his fellow Muezees to believe, and stupidly so," continued the Court Clerk, "that they need human blood for them to live forever, or simply put, for them to inherit eternal life. That Muezee leading figure also convinced them to believe that human blood would enable them to transform their bodies into bodies like those of human beings, but they are unaware that human bodies perish and are susceptible to sickness, disease and old age. In short," concluded the Court Clerk, "by so doing, the Muezees have contravened Theo Lesa's original plan for the Muezee race. Their behaviour borders on attempted defilement of the sanctity of the human race on earth in their unrelenting quest to acquire human blood."

The Court Clerk then turned to Trump and told him that fighting and suppressing the Muezee rebellion would be one of his possible assignments as The Chosen One (The Sheela). In order to quell the Muezee rebellion, the Court Clerk continued to explain, Trump would have to lead a host of troopers whose details would be disclosed at a later stage to wage war against the Muezees in order to quell their rebellion.

Trump was then shown a panoramic historical view of the earth's creation by Theo Lesa. The only information he had about the earth's creation was what he was taught at Sunday school by Mrs Alex.

As Trump kept watching, it felt as though he was in a trance as vision upon vision about the creation of everything in existence in heaven and on earth flashed before him. He saw that in the beginning, before Theo Lesa created the earth, other planets and the heavens, the earth was formless and empty, darkness was over the surface of the deep and something that looked like a spirit hovered over the vast and endless expanse of the waters. From the recorded history of creation presented to him by the Court Clerk, Trump then saw and heard Theo Lesa say, "Let there be light," and light instantly appeared from nowhere. He then saw Theo Lesa looking on admirably upon seeing that the light was good, and Theo Lesa then separated the light from the darkness. Trump then heard Theo Lesa name the light 'day', and the darkness he named 'night'. He then saw that there was evening, and there was morning – the first day.

Following on, Trump saw and heard Theo Lesa say, "Let there be a vault between the waters to separate water from water." So, Theo Lesa made the vault and separated the water under the vault from the water above it. Theo Lesa called the vault 'sky'. And there was evening, and there was morning – the second day.

Trump then saw and heard Theo Lesa say, "Let the water under the sky be gathered to one place, and let dry ground appear." And it was so. Theo Lesa called the dry ground 'land' and the gathered waters he called 'seas'. The amused Trump then saw Theo Lesa admiring his creation again that it was indeed extremely very good.

Trump then saw and heard Theo Lesa further say, "Let the land produce vegetation: seed-bearing plants and trees on the land that bear fruit with seed in it, according to their various kinds." And it was so. The land produced vegetation: plants bearing seed according to their kinds and trees bearing fruit with seed in it according to their kinds. Yet again, Trump saw Theo Lesa admiring his creation, and he saw that there was evening, and there was morning – the third day.

Trump then saw and heard Theo Lesa say, "Let there be lights in the vault of the sky to separate the day from the night and let them serve as signs to mark sacred times, and days and years, and let them be lights in the vault of the sky to give light on the earth." And it was so. While completely subsumed in what he was watching, Trump saw Theo Lesa make two great lights – the greater light, which he called the sun he commanded it to govern the day; and the lesser light, which he called moon he commanded it to govern the night. Theo Lesa additionally made the stars and set them in the vault of the sky to give light on the earth, govern the day and the night, and separate light from the darkness. Yet again, Trump spotted Theo Lesa looking admirably at his creation that it was indeed exceptionally good. And there was evening, and there was morning – the fourth day.

After that, Trump then saw and heard Theo Lesa say, "Let the water teem with living creatures, and let birds fly above the earth across the vault of the sky." So, Theo Lesa created the great creatures of the sea and every living thing with which the water teems and that moves about in it, according to their kinds, and every winged bird according to its kind. Afterwards, Trump again saw Theo Lesa looking on marvellously that it was indeed very good. Trump then saw Theo Lesa blessing the great creatures of the sea, the birds and other living things and said, "Be fruitful and increase in number and fill the water in the seas, and let the birds increase on the earth." Trump noticed there was evening, and there was morning – the fifth day.

It seemed as though there was no end to the panoramic viewing of recorded history about creation that was being revealed to Trump by the Court Clerk. Following on from the previous viewing, Trump once again saw and heard Theo Lesa say, "Let the land produce living creatures according to their kinds: the livestock, the creatures that move along the ground, and the wild animals, each according to its kind." And it was so. Theo Lesa made the wild animals according to their kinds, the livestock according to their kinds, and all the creatures that move along the ground according to their kinds. Again, Trump saw Theo Lesa look commendably at his creation that it was undeniably very good.

Before the start of the next clip, Trump noticed something peculiar. There were two other individuals there besides Theo Lesa, both of whom he recognised; it was the beautiful Ngeloi and the Court Clerk. Trump heard the beautiful Ngeloi this time, speak to both Theo Lesa and another seemingly 'invisible' individual standing next to him, who was the Court Clerk, and he said, "Let us make mankind in our image, in our likeness, so that they may rule over the fish in the sea and the birds in the sky, over the livestock and all the wild animals, and overall the creatures that move along the ground." And the trio all gestured in agreement.

Furthermore, Trump saw Theo Lesa start to mould a creature in the image of the beautiful Ngeloi. It turned out to be an extremely huge human being, about 50 times taller and bigger than earth's tallest and biggest human being. Theo Lesa created the male first and then the female from the male's rib. Afterwards, Theo Lesa, the beautiful Ngeloi and the Court Clerk all joined hands and pronounced a blessing on the male and female human beings they had just created and said, "Be fruitful and increase in number; fill the earth and subdue it. Rule over the fish in the sea and the birds in the sky and over every living creature that moves on the ground." Theo Lesa continued, "I give you every seed-bearing plant on the face of the whole earth and every tree that has fruit with seed in it. They will be yours for food. And to all the beasts of the earth and all the birds in the sky and all the creatures that move along the ground – everything that has the breath of life in it – I give every green plant for food." And it was so. Trump then saw Theo Lesa, the beautiful Ngeloi, and the Court Clerk look on worthily at all they had created, and they all nodded in agreement to signify that it was extraordinarily and exceedingly very good. And there was evening, and there was morning – the sixth day.

The Court Clerk then brusquely switched off the recorded history about creation. Trump let the Court Clerk know that he was immensely appreciative of the opportunity to be considered worthy of being shown things hidden from all mortals on earth.

Chapter 18
Combat Ghosts from the Dead

After gaining a glimpse into the celestial wonders hidden from mortal beings, Trump was summoned to appear before the Buite again. In attendance was Theo Lesa, the beautiful Ngeloi, the Court Clerk and all the Marlenas. All the dignitaries were seated in a wide circle on highchairs that looked as though they were made of soft wool. Some form of mist oozed from the idiosyncratic and grandiose seats in the courtroom. Trump thought the scene wasn't as intimidating as before his reprieve from condemnation to Gehenakumbo by the beautiful Ngeloi.

The pious ceremony filled with pomp and magnificence was nevertheless reminiscent of the spectacle Trump had imagined while singing one of his favourite Sunday school songs during his lifetime on earth titled 'The Judgment Has Set' (originally composed by Franklin E Belden in 1886), which went like this:

The judgment has set, the books have been opened;
How shall we stand in that great day?
When every thought, and word, and action,
God, the righteous Judge, shall weigh?
How shall we stand in that great day?
How shall we stand in that great day?
Shall we be found before Him wanting?
Or with our sins, all washed away?
The work is begun with those who are sleeping,
Soon will the living here be tried,
Out of the books of God's remembrance,
His decision to abide.
O, how shall we stand that moment of searching,

When all our sins those books reveal?
When from that court, each case decided,
Shall be granted no appeal?

There was silence in the Buite as Trump waited to hear what was to follow or become of him. Finally, the Court Clerk stood up and pronounced six possible assignments for Trump to choose from for him to complete his redemption from Gehenakumbo as The Chosen One (The Sheela).

The Court Clerk read out loudly an array of possible assignments from a large book Trump later came to learn was called *"The Book of The Acts of The Chosen Ones (The Acts of The Sheela)."* Ahead of the pronouncements, the Court Clerk apprised Trump that for him to seal his place as a bona fide fellow of Nebuparadiza and become a Ngeloi, he had to undertake and successfully complete the tasks he would choose. At the time, he also explained to Trump that the Buite, and indeed Nebuparadiza, was going to avail him of the resources needed for his chosen missions.

Among the resources to be availed to Trump was an army from the souls of dead human beings called the 'Combat Ghosts'. The Combat Ghosts, the Court Clerk explained to Trump, were souls of dead men and women who either lived sinful or holy lives during their lifetime on earth. Both classes of Combat Ghosts were to be made available to Trump to help him undertake the missions he would opt for in The Acts of The Chosen Ones (The Acts of The Sheela).

The Christian Bible renders credence and independently attests to the distinction between the body and the soul that the Court Clerk alluded to in his description of the Combat Ghosts to Trump. The Book of Mathew 10:28 records, "Do not be afraid of those who kill the body but cannot kill the soul. Rather, be afraid of the One who can destroy both soul and body in hell."

Furthermore, the Court Clerk enlightened Trump that the Combat Ghosts from the dead holy men and women were kept in a special chamber in Nebuparadiza called 'Leeyhalim' where they rested in peace awaiting the final Clap (time) when Theo Lesa would accord them eternal life in a new world he was going to create at an appointed Clap.

"On the contrary," the Court Clerk continued to explain, "there is no rest for the Combat Ghosts of the dead evil men and women who instead of resting in peace in Leeyhalim in Nebuparadiza, are in a place called 'Gehenakumbo' where they are tormented day and night. They can only be retrieved from Gehenakumbo by either the beautiful Ngeloi or the Arch Ngeloi Gabriel if they were ever required to back up The Chosen One (The Sheela) in The Acts of The Chosen Ones (The Acts of The Sheela)."

The Court Clerk also put it to Trump that the choice of the class of Combat Ghosts (either from the dead holy or dead evil human beings) he hired in his preferred assignments in The Acts of The Chosen Ones (The Acts of The Sheela) was entirely up to him and predicated on how gruelling and arduous he considered each mission to be.

"Planning is a key ingredient to the success of every Chosen One (Sheela) who has ever undertaken a successful mission in The Acts of The Chosen Ones (The Acts of The Sheela)," advised the Court Clerk. The Court Clerk further counselled Trump that planning enabled The Sheela (The Chosen One) and his chain of command to understand and develop solutions to problems, anticipate events, adapt to changing circumstances, task organise their force and prioritise efforts. He also advised that Trump and the commanders he would select from the Combat Ghosts would be responsible for determining the appropriate mix of methodologies for planning based on the scope of the problem presented by each assignment or mission.

As the granular details of the key success factors in The Acts of the Chosen Ones (The Acts of The Sheela) were read out to Trump by the Court Clerk, all the Ngelois nodded their heads in mechanical unison akin to robots signifying affirmation to each and every instruction that was read out.

As the mission commander in The Acts of The Chosen Ones (The Acts of The Sheela), Trump learnt that he had overall responsibility for success or failure of his selected missions, including responsibility for planning and execution of each assignment. The Court Clerk assured Trump that regardless of the class the Combat Ghosts came from, either from the dead holy class or dead evil class, they would be loyal to him and obey his orders.

The Court Clerk also tasked Trump to choose two senior officials from the Combat Ghosts: his 2ic (second in command) and the assistant to both Trump and his 2ic whose rank would be that of Combat Ghost Sergeant. As second in command, Trump's 2ic was going to occupy a unique and privileged position to the mission and was going to be an expert responsible for inter alia, advising the Commander (Trump) and the Combat Ghost Sergeant while ensuring the planning process was integrated and completed.

On the other hand, the Court Clerk apprised Trump that the Combat Ghost Sergeant would be the backbone of the mission team. As the senior enlisted member of the mission, the Combat Ghost Sergeant was going to be responsible for the Team's day-to-day activities. The Combat Ghost Sergeant was also going to be responsible for advising Trump on all operational and training matters and also provide leadership, tactical and technical guidance to the Team. Further, the Combat Ghost Sergeant was going to be responsible, following Trump's approval, for assigning specific tasks and supervising team members' performance and ensuring military drills and rehearsals took place at all levels.

Trump listened intently as the mission instructions were read out to him; it would be a do or die mission. The incessant and comprehensive instructions from the Court Clerk would have been unbearable by human standards, but in Trump's new and glorified body for The Chosen Ones (The Sheela), he could absorb all the intricate details of the instructions that were being handed down to him without the need for him to note anything down.

However, Trump's main concern was how to successfully co-ordinate a mission composed of Combat Ghosts from the souls of those who died as evil men and women on earth if he decided to choose from that class. And the worst part of it all, he suspected, would be receiving advice from his 2ic and the Combat Ghost Sergeant. *Would it be credible strategic advice knowing fully well that these were the Combat Ghosts from some of the vilest men and women to have ever lived on earth?* he wondered.

According to the Association for Talent Development, "The ability to influence others is essential to a leader's success because they need to motivate their team, build consensus, and sway cynics or sceptics. It requires more than being a compelling speaker; it also requires what Aristotle said was fundamental to persuasion: credibility. According to Aristotle, for a leader to influence others, they must be viewed as a person of good character. Credibility is the audience's judgment about how believable the communicator is, adds psychologist Dan O'Keefe. And it's important because people often choose to respond to a persuasive message based not on the content but on their perception of the communicator[20]." Hence the cynicism that had started to play on Trump's mind.

Was the Buite and Nebuparadiza setting him up for failure by asking him to enlist the Combat Ghosts from people who died in shame and lacked credibility during their lifetime on earth? he pondered. These thoughts deeply troubled Trump, especially that the outcome of his chosen missions in The Acts of The Chosen Ones (The Acts of The Sheela) would determine his fate. Success in his chosen missions was going to result in him being confirmed as a Ngeloi with the promise to become a permanent citizen of Nebuparadiza and inherit eternal life. On the contrary, failure in any of his chosen missions would result in him being sent to Gehenakumbo in accordance with the guilty verdict reached by the Marlenas before he was salvaged from the brink of Gehenakumbo by the Beautiful Ngeloi.

Trump's view on leading and commandeering the Combat Ghosts from the dead holy men was completely different; he foresaw no impediments in coordinating the activities of this class of Combat Ghosts given they were souls from people who lived honourably and uprightly during their lifetime on earth. *All mortals on earth were wired to live meaningful lives*, Trump thought to himself, *and these are Combat Ghosts of men and women whose lives were so pleasing in the sight of Theo Lesa and the entire hosts of Nebuparadiza that upon succumbing to death, their souls were welcomed and kept in the Leeyhalim (special peaceful resting place) to await their well-deserved reward which was eternal life. I would have no difficulties working with these good Combat Ghosts.* Trump pondered and assured himself.

The Court Clerk seemed to have read Trump's deepest thoughts, including his apprehension in working with the Combat Ghosts from the dead evil men and women. In response, he touched Trump by his shoulder and gently said to him, "As earlier intimated, rest assured that all the Combat Ghosts will be loyal to you and obey your orders unquestioningly, whether from dead evil or saint. The success or failure of each mission will squarely rest on your shoulders," reassured the Court Clerk.

Chapter 19
Choosing the Acts (Assignments)

After the Court Clerk had finished reading out instructions and respective responsibilities for Trump and his senior Combat Ghosts, he closed the Book of instructions. Trump was called upon to select three assignments from the six available and presented to him. There was total tranquillity in Nebuparadiza in order to accord Trump the opportunity to carefully select his preferred missions.

According to the Innovation Decision Model, in order to make the best decision as fast as possible, it is imperative to choose the right decision-making style. The time available to complete the decision-making process for a specific decision is probably the most important criteria in choosing the most appropriate style; it is advisable to pay careful attention to this criterion (time available) as it is the factor most manipulated to pressure a poor decision. While it is desirable to get the positive consequences of a good decision as soon as possible, more time usually leads to a more effective analysis of the available information. In most cases, there is more time available for making a decision than first believed. While more time may be available, the decision maker should not overanalyse the situation as this tends to lead to what is commonly called 'analysis paralysis'. Innovation Decision further advises that it doesn't make sense to spend a lot of time or effort on a $10 decision, nor too little effort on a million-dollar decision. The decision maker should assess the value of a decision's outcome and expect to spend 0.5% to 2% of that value in making a good decision. A higher value decision requires a more consultative or collaborative decision making style[21].

Although his was a high-value decision with so much at stake and required him to adopt a more consultative decision-making style, Trump had no one else to consult in picking the three missions out of six. One would think perhaps the opportunity for him to choose his preferred missions should have been delayed till after he had selected his Combat Ghosts in order for him to consult with his top two Combat Ghosts, i.e., his 2ic (second in command) and the Combat Ghost Sergeant.

Since Trump was not accorded the opportunity to consult, deciding on the three assignments proved to be a huge challenge for him because it was a decision he could not have afforded to bungle.

Innovation Decision further advises that the bigger the challenge, the greater the required level of commitment or acceptance from those implementing the actions resulting from the decision. Failure to implement the decision is a common problem for those involved in decision making. Using an inclusive style can build acceptance and commitment to the execution of a decision. Alas, yet again, Trump had no one else to 'involve' in the decision-making process and the Combat Ghosts, upon being selected, were going to be required to implement decisions they did not have the opportunity to input to at the initial stage.

The Court Clerk informed Trump that silence in the Buite would continue until he signalled to them that he had reached a decision. During that moment of silence, Trump's internal decision-making process fluctuated between identifying goals for his mission, eliminating choices by setting standards without worrying so much about finding the best or the easiest options, at the same time constantly aware of his biases, to trying hard not to rush in order to make the right decision. After what seemed like an eternity, Trump finally picked the three missions he had opted to undertake in his Acts of The Chosen Ones (The Acts of The Sheela) in order to complete his redemption from Gehenakumbo.

When he was ready, Trump signalled the Court Clerk that he was done selecting his assignments. Per procedure in the Buite, Trump was ushered into the middle of the courtroom surrounded by the Marlenas with the beautiful Ngeloi and the Court Clerk positioned and seated in front of him. He noticed that there was something different about the whole set-up and arrangement in the Buite this time. The 'burning and consuming ball of fire' was not present. In other words, Theo Lesa was not present at that particular meeting. Instead, the beautiful Ngeloi sat in the position hitherto occupied by Theo Lesa.

The beautiful Ngeloi was seated on the throne, high and exalted, and the train of his robe filled the Buite. Above him were what appeared to be special-purpose Ngelois, each with nine wings: With three wings, they covered their faces, with three, they covered their feet, and with three they were flying. The special-purpose Ngelois constantly sang praises to the beautiful Ngeloi as their voices bounced off each other: "Divine, divine, divine is the beautiful Ngeloi almighty; Nebuparadiza and all the worlds are full of his glory." At the sound of the voices of the special purpose Ngelois, the doorposts and thresholds of the courtroom shook, and the Buite was filled with smoke and the smell of sweet incense.

Trump was surmounted with the weight of anxiety and the gravity of the mission that lay ahead of him; he started to tremble and could not utter a single word. One of the special-purpose Ngelois, who was perched above the beautiful Ngeloi, sluggishly flew to Trump with a burning substance in his hand which he had taken with tongs from the altar that lay in front of the beautiful Ngeloi. With it, he touched Trump's mouth and said, "See, this has touched your lips; need I remind you again that all your guilt and wrongdoing from your previous life on earth has been absolved and taken away and your sins atoned for? You are The Chosen One (The Sheela), be bold and take courage."

At the mention of those words, Trump felt strong and stood upright. After that, Trump heard a voice from the Court Clerk as though emanating from a very loudspeaker that repeatedly echoed, "Sheela, Sheela, Sheela, Oh Sheela. The Chosen One, tell the Buite the names of the missions thou hast chosen to undertake in The Acts of The Chosen Ones (The Acts of The Sheela)."

After the Court Clerk had called upon Trump to state his preferred missions, a huge book was opened by one of the special purpose Ngelois. The Court Clerk informed Trump that it was called *'The Book of the Acts of the Chosen Ones or The Book of The Acts of The Sheela'*. The Court Clerk further informed Trump that the missions he had selected would be recorded in that Book and that if he were to succeed in his undertakings, his name would be eternally sealed in the Book. "Conversely," continued the Court Clerk, "your name would be purged from this Book permanently as though you hadn't even attempted any mission if you were to fail in any of your chosen missions." After a moment of silence, Trump informed the Buite that he had elected to undertake the following assignments (known as 'Acts' in Nebuparadiza):

Act/Assignment 1: Lead an army of Combat Ghosts from the dead evil men and women from Gehenakumbo to repress the Muezee rebellion in their quest to dig their way to the surface of the moon in search of human blood.

Act/Assignment 2: Lead an army of Combat Ghosts from the dead saints' men, and women from Leeyhalim to save some of the people that perished in sin during some of the worst pandemics in human history e.g., some of the 50+ million victims of the swine flu.

Act/Assignment 3: Lead an army of Combat Ghosts from the dead saints' men, and women in order to try and stop the origin of sin and death.

Trump's first mission in The Acts of The Chosen Ones (The Acts of The Sheela) was, therefore, to lead an army of Combat Ghosts of the souls from the dead evil (both men and women) from Gehenakumbo to repress and crush the Muezee rebellion to stop them digging their way to the surface of the moon in search of human blood in their quest to live forever.

The Buite approved the 'Acts' or missions that Trump selected, and they were duly recorded by the Court Clerk in *The Book of The Acts of the Sheela (The Book of The Acts of The Chosen Ones)*.

Chapter 20
Assembling Team Combat Ghost

The Court Clerk reminded Trump that for each mission (Act), he was at liberty to pick a blend of Combat Ghosts from each class (i.e., from dead saints and dead evil). He responded that for his first mission, he was inclined to pick Combat Ghosts from one class only, from the class of the dead evil men and women. Trump's predilection, or preference, was annotated against his first mission in *The Book of The Acts of The Sheela (The Book of The Acts of The Chosen Ones)*.

Because Trump had opted to select his first team of Combat Ghosts from one class only (the dead evil), the task of retrieving individual members of his team from Gehenakumbo (hell) was assigned to the Arch Ngeloi by the name of Gabriel. This was done out of respect for the souls of the Combat Ghosts from the dead saints whose retrieval from their peaceful resting chamber in Nebuparadiza, called Leeyhalim, would have involved the indulgence of the beautiful Ngeloi.

The Court Clerk informed Trump that before selecting his team of Combat Ghosts from the dead evil for his first mission or 'Act', he would be accorded the opportunity to preview their individual life histories for him to make an informed decision. To narrow it down, Trump was also required to pick a category of death through which the dead evil men and women were removed from earth to Gehenakumbo; all of which were violent deaths predominantly because these were evil men and women. The Court Clerk showed Trump the various death categories on record, ranging from death by murder, death by assassination, death by beheading, death by firing squad, death by lethal injection, to death by hanging and the list went on. Trump opted for the class of Combat Ghosts that were sentenced to death by hanging.

The Court Clerk then asked Trump why he had opted for that particular death category (death by hanging), to which he responded that it took a certain level of 'discipline', albeit despicable, to consistently pursue a wrong course of action that eventually resulted in one's demise or death. And because death by hanging was excruciatingly more painful, justified Trump, that in itself spoke volumes about the courage, audacity and bravery of the criminal in question before their death hence his attraction to that class of Combat Ghosts because he was going to need those qualities in his team to succeed in The Acts of The Chosen Ones (The Acts of The Sheela). He also added that pursuing a particular path without compromising, however evil that path or course of action might have been, signified possession of a particular trait of character that would help him to succeed in The Acts of The Chosen Ones (The Acts of The Sheela). Trump further added that such unwavering traits were inversely comparable to the admirable traits displayed by martyrs who died for various noble causes, such as refusing to renounce their faith in the face of death.

The Court Clerk was enthralled with Trump's response and probed him further by asking if he could name one such person who opted to die rather than compromise. Without hesitation, Trump mentioned the name of Cassian, who was a teacher in Imola, Italy, in 363. Formerly the bishop of Brescia, he became a schoolmaster after his banishment from that place. As a Christian teacher of pagan pupils during Christian persecution in the Roman Empire, Cassian was in a dangerous position. By refusing to make a sacrifice to the pagan gods, he angered the local officials, who sentenced him to death and turned him over to his students as his executioners. Why this should be the case and why they seemed happy to carry out the sentence is not entirely clear from historical accounts. But Cassian's death was torturous because of it: the only instruments the students had at their disposal were small and non-lethal. The boys employed their tablets to bash Cassian and their styluses (pointed iron instruments for writing) and penknives to make a multitude of cuts and punctures all over his body for an agonisingly extended time. Conscious through the long process, Cassian encouraged them to strike him forcefully, as he was eager to die for his faith[22].

Lastly, Trump added that the other reason he wished to select his first team of Combat Ghosts from the vilest dead evil was that they were souls from dead people who were not born criminals. They were capable of doing good during their lifetime but chose to commit evil deeds instead.

Trump's remarks on the Combat Ghosts from the dead evil men and women not being born 'evil' would be supported in part by an article featured in the

Oxford University Press, 'Academic Insights for the Thinking World'. According to the article, clinical studies of the defendants at the Nuremberg trials (in 1945–1946) undertaken by several psychiatrists and psychologists revealed that these men had no recognisable mental impairments that could account for the horrendous actions they had orchestrated. They all knew the difference between right and wrong. Further, Evolutionary psychology has confirmed that human beings have the potential for aggressive violence, but the universal capacity for doing harm does not explain why only some go on to perpetrate extraordinary evil. There is no gene for genocide, and indeed human beings have an innate resistance to killing their own kind. What Steven Pinker has called the 'better angels of our nature' generally subdues the demons of violence with which human beings are wired. Further, the experiments carried out by the social psychologist Stanley Milgram have been held to prove that any person at any time can be made into a murderer.

After the probing by the Court Clerk was over, Trump readied himself to preview the life histories of some of the vilest dead men and women whose every detail was recorded in Nebuparadiza since the creation of the universe by Theo Lesa. The Court Clerk made it clear to Trump for the second time that the reason was for him to make an informed decision on whom he wanted to be part of his team. Without much ado, the Court Clerk switched on the panorama of recorded history for the Combat Ghosts belonging to the class (dead evil) that Trump had opted to engage in his first assignment. As the clips continued to play, Trump could not believe how evil some people had chosen to live their lives. As he watched intently, one thing that dazed him was the astronomical level of shady and dark secrets that human beings kept from each other. It didn't matter whether they were married or single, gay or straight, rich or poor, educated or uneducated, men or women, believer or pagan; they were all like filthy rags because of what they did in secrecy. Some of the people held in high regard and honoured during their lifetime on earth as holy men and women actually lived opposite lives in private. Many of them made it a habit to commit evil deeds with unbridled impunity. For some, their secrets were exposed during their lifetime on earth, and they either repented or became worse; whereas a good number of them took their secrets to the grave and were now paying a high price in Gehenakumbo, having initially thought they had escaped reprimand or punishment.

Everything was recorded in Nebuparadiza, and there was nothing that was hidden to Theo Lesa and his Ngelois, as Trump was now witnessing first-hand in his privileged capacity as The Chosen One (The Sheela); only chosen by Nebuparadiza once every 1000 years, and he was grateful to be in that privileged position.

After viewing and reviewing, fast-forwarding and rewinding, querying and probing the recorded life histories of various Combat Ghosts from his preferred category of the dead evil men and women who died by hanging, Trump finally managed to select a team of 1000 (one thousand) Combat Ghosts to assist him in his first assignment in The Acts of The Chosen Ones (The Acts of The Sheela). It was both a tortuous and torturous exercise partially due to the gruesome nature of the crimes that resulted in the capital punishment of the people represented by the Combat Ghosts from Trump's preferred class (those who died by hanging).

Due to the horrific and grisly nature of the evil deeds that were committed by people represented by the one thousand Combat Ghosts that Trump selected during their lifetime, only the details of four Combat Ghosts, the first three and the last one, have been highlighted below as they have been deemed to be least disturbing; all of whom died by way of hanging.

Trump's first choice of Combat Ghost was Meroldack Chipok. He was 45 years old at the time of his death and resided at 1911 Trull Street, Dorchester, in Boston. Chipok was charged with the murder of a widower of 82 years old named Jon Burnett, who ran a convenience shop which was part of his home at 7011 Sussex Street in the suburbs of Boston on Friday night, 8th of November 1957. The crime was discovered the following morning when his employee, 18-year-old Jane John, could not open the door and, on looking through the letter box, saw Mr Burnett lying on the floor. Jane called the police, who forced the door and discovered Mr Burnett's badly beaten body, the skull fractured from multiple baseball bat blows. Inspection of the crime scene revealed some size 11 bloody footprints in the foyer and a woman's silk stocking under the body. Chipok was arrested three days later, initially denying any involvement in the crime, claiming to have been with his girlfriend that night. Police found blood on Chipok's jacket, trousers and shoes. In a statement, Chipok said, "I went to the convenience store on Friday night about eleven. When I knocked at the door, Mr Burnett answered it. I was rather surprised because I did not expect an answer. My idea was to find out if anyone was in and then get in by the best possible means. The first thing I did was push him back. Then he started yelling and struggling with me. There was a baseball bat in my right hand, which I had brought in case I had to force an entry. I knew that if I struggled with him too long, somebody would hear us, so I hit him with the baseball bat. But instead of knocking him out as I expected, he continued to struggle, so I kept on hitting him. In the end, he fell to the floor and dragged me down with him. Then he went quiet, but I could hear he was still groaning like a frog, and I took some keys out of his pockets and tried them in the door, and I left the keys in the keyhole. There were a lot of keys, but I dropped some. I went and tried all the drawers to see if there was any money. I had a hasty look around in panic but couldn't find much money, only a bit. Mr Burnett was still moving and groaning, and then he started as if to get up. I didn't want him to see me, so I switched off the light and made for the door. Then I thought it would be better to leave the light on so that someone would see it, probably a police officer on duty and go and check. I wanted this so that he wouldn't lose too much blood. Then he started to get up again. He had been struggling to get up all the time, but he couldn't get a footing. It was too slippery in the blood. The last thing I saw was Mr Burnett up on his knees. Then I left by the front door. I meant to leave the door open, but there was someone outside posting a letter, so I slammed it shut. I didn't intend to do the old man any harm. I didn't even intend to touch him or do what I did'. Chipok then admitted to searching the store for other valuables such as jewellery and also to wearing women's silk stockings over his hands to avoid leaving fingerprints. He was committed for trial by the local magistrate on 12th of November and duly appeared at East Boston before Mr Smith Williamson on the 10th and 11th of March 1958. He was prosecuted by Mr B.J. Spinks and Mr W.V. Black and defended by Mr C. Cupid and Mr L. Flywheel. Chipok's defence was that he was suffering from 'impaired mental responsibility' and had been driven to the 'terrible deed' by force beyond his control. Mr Cupid, Q.C. told the jury that 'The defence is not that this man did not kill the unfortunate shop owner. That tragic fact is true. The defence is that when the accused did it, he was suffering from an abnormality of the mind which impaired substantially his mental responsibility for what he did when he killed Mr Burnett'." If the jury accepted this defence, said Mr Cupid, they could not convict Chipok of murder. Quoting the 1957 Homicide Act, he told them. "The law says that in such a case you must bring in a verdict of manslaughter. He may be a most dangerous man because of his abnormality," said Mr Cupid. On questioning from Mr Cupid, Dr Miles said that he believed Chipok knew what he was doing, but he was suffering from 'mental illness'. He considered that mental abnormality substantially impaired the 45-year-old Chipok's mental responsibility when he killed Mr Burnett, he further stated that his remorse for his actions was 'imperceptibly shallow'. In contrast, Dr V. Banda, Senior Medical Officer said that in his opinion, Chipok was not suffering from any abnormality of the mind. He disagreed with Dr Miles's statement, saying that in his opinion, Chipok did not have a psychopathic personality. The Jury deliberated for five days. On the final day, after one hour and thirty minutes, the jury emerged for the fifth time. Chipok was called to the dock to hear his verdict. It was a guilty verdict of capital murder in the furtherance of theft. Chipok rose and gripped the rail of the dock as Mr Justice Williamson put on the black cap and pronounced the sentence of death, telling him that he would 'suffer death in the manner authorised by law', as the new wording of the death sentence had become since the passing of the Homicide Act of 1957. As Chipok was taken to the cells, he gestured and smiled to friends in the crowded public gallery. On the appointed day, Chipok was hanged per his death sentence.

Following his selection to be part of Trump's team, the Court Clerk recorded Meroldack Chipok's name in *'The Book of Summoned Combat Ghosts from the Dead Evil'*.

Trump's second choice of Combat Ghost was a female who went by the name of Jude Arran during her lifetime on earth. Jude was 28 years old when she was hanged in 1755 for the murder of her father by poisoning. She was unusual in the annals of female criminals of the time – she was middle class and well educated. Her father, Mr Archibald Arran, was a prosperous accountant in North Berwick at the time of his murder. So, Jude lived a comfortable lifestyle at the family home in Abbotsford Road. Arran had imprudently advertised a dowry of £12,000 – a huge sum for those days, for the man who married Jude. This attracted a plethora of paramours or suitors, all of whom were promptly rejected except one, a lawyer named John Adair, who was initially acceptable. John was the son of a Scottish aristocrat and therefore seen as a suitable match for Jude. By all accounts, he was not a physically attractive person but seemed to have taken Jude in completely. All went well, to begin with, but then problems arose when it was discovered that John was still married, having wed one Mary Abercrombie in 1745 in Scotland. Jude's father became very unhappy about John and began to see him for what he was. To get over Arran's hostility, John persuaded Jude to give her father powders which he described as an ancient 'love potion' and which he assured her would make Arran like him. He knew what the powders contained but ostensibly didn't mind letting his girlfriend murder her father to get the £12,000 dowry. Ironically, Archibald Arran's estate came only to around £7,000. Under the law at the time, this would have automatically passed to him if they married. Jude seemed to be totally taken in by John and administered these powders, which were, in fact, arsenic, in her father's tea and gruel. He became progressively more ill. The servants had also become ill from eating some of the leftover food, although they all recovered. None of this seemed to register with Jude, that the powders might be the cause of the problem. When her father was seriously ill, and near death, Jude sent for the local physician who advised her that she could be held liable for poisoning him, so she quickly burned John's love letters and disposed of the remaining powders. Jean, the housemaid, had the mind to rescue some of the powder from the fire when Jude tried to destroy the evidence and took it to a chemist for analysis who found arsenic. Arsenic is a cumulative poison and only kills when the levels have built up in the body. Arran realised he was dying and asked to see Jude, telling her that he suspected she was poisoning him. She implored for his forgiveness, which he indeed gave her, even though she did not admit her crime to him. He finally succumbed to the poison and died. It was some time before Jude was arrested, however. As soon as he got wind of her likely arrest, John deserted her, escaped abroad and died penniless in German in late 1759. An inquest was held, finding that Archibald Arran was poisoned and accused Jude of administering it. On Friday, the 16th of August, the coroner issued a warrant for the arrest of Jude and for her committal to the county gaol of Oxford. Jude defended herself with the help of two counsel, although her case was hopeless. She made an impassioned speech for her own defence in which she totally denied administering poison but did admit that she had put a powder into her father's food, she claimed, "Which had been given me with another intent." The servants gave evidence against her, telling the court that they had seen her administering the powders to her father's food and drink and trying to destroy the evidence. Not surprisingly, at the end of the two-day trial, the jury convicted her of murder, and she received the mandatory death sentence. She was hanged on Monday the 12th of December 1755 from a gallows consisting of a wooden beam placed between two trees.

On being selected to be part of Trump's team of Combat Ghosts, the Court Clerk recorded Jude Arran's name in *The Book of Summoned Combat Ghosts from the Dead Evil.*

Trump's third choice of Combat Ghost was a man who went by the name of Matthew Bruce during his lifetime on earth, born on the 19th of June 1841 at

Boston in Lincolnshire and was generally known as Matt. He met Susan, who was working as a barmaid at a hotel in Burslem in the Staffordshire Potteries, and they soon fell for one another. He married her in 1864 and, with financial help from his father, purchased the Sunshine Hotel. He soon established himself and was held in very high regard locally. Matt and Susan had been married for some five years, having two children whilst running the hotel. Initially, all went well, but Matt began drinking heavily, and the marriage started to fall apart to the point where in early 1869, Susan left him and moved to Boston in Lincolnshire to live with his father. In February of 1869 Matt believed that Susan had been seeing another man and decided to initiate divorce proceedings. Matt's father had taken Susan's side, which probably didn't help the situation. Matt sold up in Burslem and moved to Liverpool, where he drank heavily. He purchased a revolver from a gunsmith in Liverpool and sent it to Liverpool station for his collection. On the afternoon of Saturday, the 11th of January, Matt went to the station and enquired whether his parcel had arrived, which at this time it hadn't and also bought a ticket to Boston. He departed for Boston, travelling as far as Grantham before returning to Liverpool later in the afternoon by which time the gun and ammunition had reached the station. He stayed the night in Liverpool before setting off for Boston on the Sunday, now armed. Jack Mike, the inspector of the Great Northern Railway at Liverpool station, knew Matt and was aware of the marital problems. Examining the package, he realised that it contained a gun and immediately sent a telegraph to Matt's father in Boston. Matt tried to see Susan on the Sunday but was refused admission to the house. He returned the following morning, but Susan was out. Sadly, Matt found Susan at home at around 3 o'clock on the Monday afternoon and immediately shot her from behind, the bullet penetrating her rib cage passing through her lung and lodging in her aorta, injuries which caused a very rapid death. Family members and servants heard the shot and raced to the drawing-room to find Matt standing over Susan's dying body. He made no effort to escape and told one of them to fetch a constable. He handed the gun to his brother, David, telling him, "You have no notion, David, how I loved that woman, but I could not stand the jealousy." He was arrested at the house by Constable James and admitted the shooting, telling the constable, "I did it and am only sorry that I have not shot Mr Maurice and Mr Duncan, who have had connection with my wife." An inquest into Susan's death was held the following day presided over by the Coroner, Mr Swig. Elizabeth Jenkins, the housemaid, described the events of the fatal afternoon to the coroner and the inquest jury as follows. She was in the kitchen when she heard the shot and rushed out to see Susan collapse in the breakfast room around 3 p.m. She ran into the yard for help, and by the time she returned, Susan was dead. Matt was standing by Susan's body. On the material day, Matt's brother David arrived at the house at around 3.15 p.m. and asked Matt to give him the revolver, which he did. He had said to his brother, "Oh, Matt, why have you done this?" Matt replied, "It's no use now, David, it can't be helped. It's done." David told the coroner's jury that he was aware of Matt's jealousy of Susan. After a brief retirement, the jury brought in a verdict of wilful murder against Matt, and he was remanded to prison to appear before Boston magistrate's court. Matt made a lengthy statement in his defence detailing Susan's unfaithfulness to him over the previous year. He was committed for trial by the magistrates to the Lincolnshire Lent Assizes. His trial opened at Lincoln Assize Court on Wednesday the 13th of April before Mr Justice Guild. The prosecution was led by Mr Sergeant Bright, assisted by Mr Winehouse, with Mr Kareem and Mr Muhammad facing a seriously uphill struggle to mount a credible defence. Insanity was the only real option open to them, in view of the prisoner's admissions and the physical evidence. Mr Kareem did his best to argue that the excessive drinking combined with his all-consuming jealousy was sufficient to unbalance Matt's mind. The jury did not accept this and brought in a guilty verdict. The judge sentenced Matt to hang, and he was removed to one of Lincoln Castle's two male condemned cells to await execution. He was quite resigned to his fate' although he was concerned about the future of his two children. There would be no reprieve, and the hanging was set for Easter Monday, the 1st of April 1871. In the Condemned Cell, Matt wrote a lengthy and penitent letter to a friend over the weekend telling the friend how he had found God. He received the sacrament from the prison chaplain, the Rev. Robertson on Sunday afternoon, who arrived at 8 am on the Monday morning and stayed with Matt for some 35 minutes. Behind the Assize Court, the New Drop gallows was erected in the Castle Yard. The normal procession then started off across the Castle Yard with Matt escorted by two warders, walking unaided and with a firm step. At the foot of the gallows, Rev. Robertson read the burial service, and Matt thanked him and one of the accompanying warders before climbing the steps up to the platform where his legs were strapped. Here he said, "Goodbye, Father, God Bless you. God forgive my poor dear father. God bless my poor children." His final words as the hangman was hooding him and adjusting the noose were, "Lord have mercy on my soul." When the trap doors were released, Matt dropped through the trap leaving just the still, taut rope in sight of the officials on the platform. His death was instantaneous. There was no agonised struggling and writhing, no choking sounds. The whole process was far less distressing for all concerned. The prison surgeon, Dr Dimbleby examined the body and certified death. Jealousy has often been a motive for murder, and it certainly was again in this case.

On being selected to be part of Trump's team of Combat Ghosts, the Court Clerk recorded Matthew Bruce's name in *The Book of Summoned Combat Ghosts from the Dead Evil.*

Trump's third choice of Combat Ghost was a woman who went by the name of Emily. She was born Emily Jackson around 1765 to a teacher at Asenby, some four miles south of Thirsk in North Yorkshire and even as a child exhibited criminal tendencies. Like many girls of her era, she went into domestic service as a teenager, initially working for a family in Thirsk but was soon sacked for stealing. She continued her criminal career with a series of minor thefts and scams and by 1775 had moved to Leeds. In 1779, after knowing him for just two weeks, she married Michael Willoughby, a porter, but the marriage did not rein in her activities, and the couple had to move regularly to avoid arrest. They had three children. By 1796, Emily was living in Marsh Lane, Leeds. She started dressmaking and took to telling fortunes, claiming to have supernatural powers that she used to great effect. She made and sold potions to cure various ailments and ward off evil spirits. There was still a popular belief in the power of witchcraft at this time, and Emily found she could cash in on it. It was probably far more profitable and certainly less risky than stealing, a crime she could easily be hanged for. Emily poisoned four people in 1800, although she was never tried for or convicted of these murders. The victims were two Quaker sisters who lived above their candy shop with their aunt. Emily sold them medicines which were, in fact, poison mixtures and having killed them, she robbed the house and shop. When the neighbours asked why the three women had died, she told them that they had caught the bubonic plague. Amazingly, there was little suspicion about the cause of death. So, Emily just walked away from the crime with her booty. Emily frequently used a 'Mrs Jackson' to help her in her scams. This non-existent lady was the initial fount of all Emily's 'wisdom' and was always consulted on behalf of Emily's clients. They were told that the money she took from them was, of course, to go to Mrs Jackson. In 1803, Mary invented a new alter ego called 'Mrs Brighton' to help her in her plans. Living in the Bramley area of Leeds at this time was a comfortably off but childless middle-aged couple, George and Samantha Lovelace. Samantha suffered from a pulsating in the breast whenever she laid down and was also having psychological problems, claiming to be haunted by a black cat and other spirits. She was told by her doctor, Dr Aziz, that she was under some sort of spell and that he was unable to help her. At Whitsun in 1803, the Lovelace's were visited by their nephew who suggested obtaining help from Emily Jackson, who he said would be able to rid her aunt of the spirits that were possessing her. As a result, a meeting was arranged between the Lovelace's and Emily outside the Okay pub. Emily asked for an item of underclothing which she would send to Mrs Brighton in Scarborough, who would be able to help. George Lovelace took a flannel petticoat to Emily, who promised to send it to Mrs Brighton and told George to come and see her the following week. This he did, and Emily showed him the letter from Mrs Brighton. 'Mrs Brighton' directed that Emily should go to the Lovelace's house and sew three guinea notes (£1) and some gold coins she had sent, one into each corner of Samantha's bed, where they were to be left for fifteen months. George was to give Emily three guinea notes to return to Mrs Brighton. The notes were duly sewn into the bed, and George was instructed to visit Emily regularly to receive further instructions from Mrs Brighton. The next instruction was that George should nail two horseshoes to the door. George was soon to receive a letter from Mrs Brighton instructing him to take Emily a further two guinea notes and purchase a cheese to be sent to her by Emily. The letter was to be burnt after it had been read. The next letter requested a small quantity of china and silverware be sent to her, together with some tea and sugar. Again, the letter was to be burnt. A further request was for a bed and bed clothes as Mrs Brighton could not sleep in her bed due to the battle she was having with the spirits that had taken over Samantha. Again, the letter was to be immediately burnt after it had been actioned. The next letter predicted an illness in the Lovelace house affecting one or both of them. It instructed Samantha to take half a pound of honey to Emily, who would mix it into some special medicine Mrs Brighton had made. Also, the Lovelace's were to eat puddings for five days, into each of which they were to mix a daily marked packet of powder that Mary would give them. Samantha went to see Emily, who did as the letter instructed, and she left with the honey and the packets of powder. On the 4th of April, another letter arrived instructing the Lovelace's to eat the puddings on the 10th of April. Interestingly, it said that only sufficient pudding was to be made for each day, nobody else was to be allowed to eat any of it and that if there was any leftover, it must be immediately destroyed. It also said that should George or Samantha become ill, they were not to get the doctor because he would be unable to help. Unsurprisingly this letter, like its predecessors, was to be burnt. So, the scene for the final act was now set. The Lovelace's would poison themselves and kindly destroy all the evidence of Emily's involvement. To begin with, eating the puddings produced no ill effects, but on the fifth day, they tasted different and caused George and Samantha to have severe stomach cramps and vomiting. As directed, a doctor was not consulted, and Samantha, who continued to eat the honey, died on the 23rd of April 1807. George did consult a doctor who suspected that Samantha could have been poisoned, but no post mortem was carried out. George began to slowly recover somewhat as he was no longer eating the puddings. Emily had been very clever up to this time. Through Mrs Brighton she continued to demand items of value from the Lovelace's but not more than she assessed that they could afford, given George's successful business. Her real problem was that George had lived rather than died as planned. George decided at length to examine the little silk purses that contained the guinea notes and gold coins that Mrs Brighton had asked to have sewn into Samantha's bed clothes, surely, they should still contain the notes and coins that had been placed in them. Instead, they contained rose flower leaves and copper coins. Now it seems that the penny had finally dropped with George. He arranged a meeting with Emily on the ruse of buying another bottle of medicine and took assistance with him, in the form of Constable Alan. Emily had brought a bottle of liquid containing oatmeal and arsenic with which she presumably hoped to silence her principal accuser. As soon as she saw the constable, she tried to make out that George Lovelace had bought the bottle for her. He was not impressed by this charade. Emily was now taken into custody, and when the constable searched her house, he was able to recover many of the items sent to Mrs Brighton by the Lovelaces. She appeared before the magistrates the following day charged with Samantha's murder. They committed her for trial at the Yorkshire Lent Assizes of 1809, which opened at York Castle on Thursday the 16th of March before Judge Pence Samuel. Evidence of the handwriting on Mrs Brighton's letters being identical to Emily's was given and how Emily had sent the letters to Scarborough and had them mailed back so that they would bear the correct postmark. A thorough search by constables in Scarborough had revealed, predictably, that there was no

Mrs Brighton. Forensic evidence was provided by Mr Charles, who had analysed the remains of the honey and found that it contained mercuric chloride, which was extremely poisonous, and this was consistent with the symptoms displayed by the Lovelaces. Emily's defence was straightforward denial of any involvement with the death. Sir Pence Samuel summed up and told the jury that they had to satisfy themselves on three points to bring in a guilty verdict. These were that Samantha had died from poisoning, that the poison had been administered with the knowledge and contrivance of Emily and that it had been done in the expectation of causing Samantha's death. He reminded them that although there was a strong case against Emily for having systematically defrauded the Lovelaces, this did not make her automatically guilty of murder. The evidence of criminality and murder was so overwhelming that it did not take the jury long to deliver its verdict. Following the usual procedure Emily was asked if she had anything to say as to why a sentence of death should not be pronounced on her. Breaking into floods of tears, she pleaded her belly, in other words, claimed to be pregnant. As a result, the judge ordered the court doors to be locked and immediately empanelled a jury of matrons to examine her. They found her not to be pregnant, and so he proceeded to sentence her to be hanged and afterwards dissected on the following Monday. She was forty forty-five at this time and had an infant child with her in prison until she was condemned.

On being selected to be part of Trump's team of Combat Ghosts, the Court Clerk recorded Emily Jackson's name in *The Book of Summoned Combat Ghosts from the Dead Evil.*

These were the first three Combat Ghosts that Trump had picked from the souls of the dead evil to help him undertake his missions in The Acts of The Chosen Ones (The Acts of the Sheela).

Unlike on earth, there was no night or day in Nebuparadiza because there was no time there. This meant that Trump continued the selection of Combat Ghosts until he picked his last Combat Ghost to make a team of one thousand strong Combat Ghosts.

Trump's final pick and 1000th choice of Combat Ghost went by the name of Julie Walker during her lifetime on earth. Julie was a forty-one-year-old widow who was convicted of drowning her one-year-old grandson, Nigel Wagstaff, after a quarrel with her son-in-law. She lived with her daughter Lisa and Joel Scofield in Hammersmith, London. Joel had accused his mother-in-law of breaking the door of the hen house, which she denied, and this led to an acrimonious quarrel, with Joel telling Julie that she would have to go or they would. On Monday, the 27th of March, Julie did leave and took young Nigel with her. She went to the house of a friend, a Mrs Melvin, who put them up for the night. Julie left with the baby the following morning, telling Mrs Melvin that she had not decided whether to return to Hammersmith. In the end, she didn't, and wandered the streets all day instead. In the evening, she went back to Hammersmith and met a Mrs Ferguson who knew both her and Lisa. Mrs Ferguson took the exhausted Julie to her home and then went out to get some beer for them. She asked Julie to take the baby home to his mother before she left later in the evening. Julie told her that the baby was all right and that he loved his granny and she loved him. Joel received a highly disturbing letter on the same evening suggesting that Julie had drowned herself and the baby. The letter read "Joe, I have left Mrs Melvin, if you or your wife had come there you would have found the child. It is the only thing I can do to make your heart ache as you have made mine, so long." Joel immediately went to the police with the letter. Julie, however, was still alive and was seen on Friday the 30th of March in Great Queen Street, where she pushed a note through the letter box of the house her younger daughter Janet worked. The note read, "Come at once as I have done murder, and I want you to give me into the hands of justice." Later Julie went to the door and spoke to Janet, who had not seen the note. Janet sent for the police, and Julie told them that she had taken the child. She was arrested and taken before a magistrate who committed her for trial and remanded her to Newgate. However, there was no body to show that a murder had occurred, only Julie's partial confession. The body of baby Nigel was found a week or so later in the river Thames by a waterman called Victor James near Millwall Dock. There were no external injuries, and the cause of death was drowning. Julie was visited by her daughter in Newgate, who told her more of the circumstances of the boy's death. She said that she had been crossing Albert Bridge over the River Thames but could not find anywhere to sit down. She leaned against the bridge parapet and lost her grip on Nigel, who fell into the river below. Her trial, held at the Old Bailey on Tuesday the 9th of June, before Mr Justice Beckham was a relatively brief affair and the jury quickly convicted her. However, given her age, her recent widowhood, her known love for the baby boy and the provocation of her son-in-law, they added a recommendation for mercy. Once again, this was not endorsed by the trial judge, even though he was reported as saying that she 'had committed the act under some perversity of mind'. Sir Ashcroft Wilson, the Home

Secretary, saw no reason to interfere with the course of the law in this rather sad case. Julie was the last woman to be hanged on the old gallows set up in one of Newgate prison's yards. The hanging took place at 9.00 a.m. on Tuesday the 30th of June 1874. A pit had been dug under the gallows to allow for the longer drop. The body was left on the rope for an hour to ensure total death before being taken down for inquest and burial within the prison.

On being selected as the final and 1000th member of Trump's team of Combat Ghosts, the Court Clerk recorded Julie Walker's name in *The Book of Summoned Combat Ghosts from the Dead Evil.*

Chapter 21
The Stubborn King and His Kingdom

After assembling his team of one thousand Combat Ghosts, Trump's next step was to organise and marshal his troops in readiness for his first mission in The Acts of The Chosen Ones (The Acts of The Sheela). Success in Trump's first mission was going to be the litmus test for progressing to the next, and failure meant instant cancellation of successive missions; revocation of The Chosen One (The Sheela) status, which was just below that of a Ngeloi; crystallisation of his guilty verdict; and instant condemnation to Gehenakumbo. His second battalion of Combat Ghosts to undertake his second mission was predicated on his triumph in his first mission.

Trump planned to pick the second cohort of Combat Ghosts from the souls of the dead saints and none from the dead evil he decided to use in his first mission. As recorded by the Court Clerk, Trump's first mission in The Acts of The Chosen Ones (The Acts of The Sheela) was to wage war against the Muezee kingdom to quash their rebellion against Theo Lesa.

The Muezee Kingdom was located 1000 miles beneath the moon's surface along a beautiful river that flowed with mercury. It was created some 300 years before Theo Lesa created the earth. It was an orderly kingdom that was ruled by a great and wise King named Nguzoo, who was obedient to Theo Lesa. All the kingdom inhabitants were content with their lot and way of life. Unlike the mortal beings on earth, the inhabitants of the Muezee Kingdom had no possibility of becoming Ngelois; neither were they designed to inherit eternal life. However, the Muezee race had a long but fixed life span that was recyclable or extended to 700 years, depending on how they lived their first 300 years.

Each Muezee had two phases of life: the first phase of 300 years and the final conditional phase of 400 years. The first life span expired exactly on the last and 300th day. Depending on how they lived their first phase, they would then be brought back to life for another 400 years as a reward for having lived an immaculate and obedient first phase of their life. Much like human beings on the earth, the Muezees also had cognitive abilities that distinguished them from animals, and they possessed the ability to distinguish between right from wrong, and good from evil.

According to an article that Natalie Wolchover authored on 'What Distinguishes Humans from Other Animals?'[23], there's no consensus on the question of what makes human beings special from animals. The biggest point of contention is whether human beings' cognitive abilities differ from those of other animals 'in kind', or merely in degree. On the other hand, Charles Darwin supported the hypothesis that human beings were similar to animals and merely incrementally more intelligent due to their higher evolution. According to Marc Hauser, director of the cognitive evolution lab at Harvard University, in a recent article in Scientific American, 'mounting evidence indicates that, in contrast to Darwin's theory of a continuity of mind between humans and other species, a profound gap separates our intellect from the animal kind'. Hauser and his colleagues have identified four abilities of the human mind that they believe to be the essence of our 'humaniqueness' mental traits and abilities that distinguish us from our fellow earthlings, and these are:

1) Generative computation, which allows humans to generate a practically limitless variety of words and concepts. Humans do so through two modes of operation recursive and combinatorial. The recursive operation allows humans to apply a learned rule to create new expressions. In combinatorial operations, humans mix different learned elements to create a new concept.

2) Promiscuous combination of ideas, which Hauser explained, 'allows the mingling of different domains of knowledge such as art, sex, space, causality and friendship thereby generating new laws, social relationships and technologies'.

3) The use of mental symbols, which are the humans' way of encoding sensory experiences. They form the basis of humans' complex systems of language and communication. Humans may also choose to keep mental symbols to themselves or represent them to others using words or pictures.

4) Abstract thought, which is the contemplation of things beyond what humans can sense. Researchers have also found some of the building blocks of human cognition in other species, but these building blocks make up only the cement footprint of the skyscraper that is the human mind. The evolutionary origins of human cognitive abilities thus remain rather hazy.

The Muezee race was so sophisticated that they possessed all the human beings' cognitive abilities listed above and beyond, albeit with nuances. Therefore, being a ruler over such a kingdom was not the easiest of tasks for King Nguzoo. If there's anything that can be learnt from history, it's the fact that most of the things never remain the same. Over time, one of King Nguzoo's senior army officials by the name of Razin started sowing seeds of rebellion among the Muezee 'people' in the second and final phase of King Nguzoo's 400 years, shortly before his death; having lived an immaculate first phase of 300 years.

Razin's discontent was ignited after he accidentally intercepted a signal from earth regarding exploring the moon, orbit and space by human beings. He discovered there were beings that lived on another planet called earth. As time went by, Razin gathered more data and information about the nature of earth's inhabitants akin to an undertaking in empirical research.

The term empirical was originally used to refer to certain ancient Greek practitioners of medicine who rejected adherence to the dogmatic doctrines of the day, preferring instead to rely on the observation of phenomena as perceived in experience. Later empiricism referred to a theory of knowledge in philosophy that adheres to the principle that knowledge arises from experience and evidence gathered specifically using the senses. In scientific use, the term empirical refers to gathering data using only evidence that is observable by the senses or using calibrated scientific instruments. Early philosophers described as empiricist and empirical research have in common the dependence on observable data to formulate and test theories and come to conclusions.

Through his empirical research filliped by the signals he had been intercepting between the planet earth and the satellites in the orbit, Razin compiled and recorded all his findings in his 'compendium' of empirical research about human beings.

According to Razin's propaganda, one of his striking discoveries was the fact that unlike them, the Muezee race, the human race was unfairly conferred (by Theo Lesa) with the privilege or possibility of inheriting eternal life and or even becoming a Ngeloi depending on how well they lived their life on earth. He argued that this wasn't the case with the Muezee race who's final 400 years following the initial phase of 300 years was the very most they could ever hope to live without any possibility of ever existing in perpetuity thereafter. Moreover, Razin protested that Theo Lesa unfairly imposed stringent and shifting requirements on the Muezees for transitioning into the final phase of their lives, which meant that only a few Muezees went on to live another 400 years after their initial phase of 300 years.

Through his research, Razin also concluded and complained bitterly to his blinkered followers that, unlike them (the Muezees), human beings were unfairly created with bodies that housed 'a portion' of Theo Lesa called the soul, or spirit, also known as 'the breath' of Theo Lesa. According to Razin's findings, this soul resided inside the bodies of human beings and continued to exist forever after their physical bodies had long died. "How can that be fair?" whined and remonstrated Razin to his fellow Muezees.

Razin also argued that through his partiality and 'nepotism', Theo Lesa only created the Muezees as an afterthought; and didn't love the Muezee race as much as he loved the human race hence the reason why he created them like disposable objects with a finite life span; with no hope or the possibility of ever becoming a Ngeloi or achieving a state of living in perpetuity, also known as eternal life.

According to written records, eternal life traditionally refers to continued life after death, as outlined in Christian eschatology. For instance, *The Apostles' Creed* testifies: "I believe…the resurrection of the body, and life everlasting." In this view, eternal life commences after the second coming of Jesus and the resurrection of the dead, although in the New Testament's Johannine literature, there are references to eternal life commencing in the earthly life of the believer, possibly indicating an inaugurated eschatology. According to mainstream Christian theology, after death but before the Second Coming, the saved live with God in an intermediate state, but after the Second Coming, experience the physical resurrection of the dead and the physical recreation of a New Earth. The Catechism of the Catholic Church states, "By death the soul is separated from the body, but in the resurrection, God will give incorruptible life to our body, transformed by reunion with our soul. Just as Christ is risen and lives for ever, so all of us will rise at the last day."

Though oblivious to the hard facts, that is the sort of life Razin yearned for and wished for the Muezees to inherit if at all there was fairness in the privileges supposedly equally and bountifully endowed by Theo Lesa on the whole of his creation, be it on the moon, sun, earth and other planets.

Further, according to findings from his research, Razin's other conclusion amongst countless other inferences, some of which bordered on innuendo, was that the soul or Theo Lesa's breathe in humans resided in a red like fluid inside the human body called blood. Based on these findings, Razin was absolutely convinced that the human blood was the holy grail that would enable the Muezees to capture or trap the soul or the breath of Theo Lesa to enable them to live forever. As he continued his 'forbidden' research aided by his newfound ability to intercept signals from the earth, Razin also concluded that not only had the humans been to the moon once or twice, but also that the moon continued to be of great interest to human beings on earth in their quest to gain new knowledge and create opportunities for themselves as well as to inspire the next generation of human beings. He also discovered that travelling to the moon provided human beings with grounds to test technologies that would take them to Mars and other planets and allow them to build a sustainable and reusable architecture.

The final conclusion Razin drew from his discoveries was that although human blood was some sort of 'holy grail', it was very much within their reach given human beings had plans to visit the moon again; and that seemed to have been the motivation for the rebellion that Razin funnelled against the 'unfair' Theo Lesa.

To address this perceived injustice, Razin embarked on organising 'dark corner' meetings aimed at inciting rebellion against King Nguzoo and indirectly against Theo Lesa. His message was intended to galvanise the Muezees to dig their way to the surface of the moon to set up traps to capture human beings on their visit to the moon in order to suck blood from their bodies to enable the Muezee 'people' to live forever. He continued to orchestrate pockets of rallies for like-minded Muezees, and within a short time, his ideological 'live forever' propaganda spread like wildfire in summer.

According to One Earth Future Foundation on the subject of 'Why do people choose to rebel?'[24], in many ways, answering the question of why people rebel is central to understanding civil wars. Unlike countries, rebel groups have no standing armies to fight with. Neither do most rebel groups have well-developed government bureaucracies to finance and support their front-line troops. Thus, rebel groups must rely primarily on voluntary participation and support, especially early in a conflict. Civil wars erupt and grow when people are willing to join or support a rebel organisation. However, where people choose not to join a rebel group, attempted rebellions quickly wither, and stability returns to a country. A number of explanations have been offered for why people rebel, many of which have been discredited. Civil wars and rebellions are neither driven by ancient hatreds between ethnic groups nor simply by opportunistic greed.

Instead, scholars argue that people rebel out of a sense of relative deprivation in which they believe that they lack the economic benefits or social position or some other benefit that they deserve. In addition, potential rebels may be deterred from rebelling if they have significant economic opportunities and responsibilities that they would have to give up. Together, these issues show that providing inclusive governance and economic opportunity should reduce the motives and opportunity to rebel.

Imbedded within those mentioned above are some of the reasons that would help explain the rebellion brewing and gathering momentum right under the nose of king Nguzoo of the Muezee 'people'.

As Razin's 'live forever' ideology continued to take root at an unprecedented pace, it was clear even to the most obstinate and indecisive Muezees that his propaganda was extremely effective. He had a huge following among the Muezee 'people' whom all bought into the idea that Theo Lesa had discriminated against them in favour of the human race whose souls continued to live after the death of their bodies, which was merely a shelter of the 'real deal' thing (the soul) that resided inside of them. Effectively speaking, Razin managed to do something that had never been done before in the Muezee kingdom since its creation by Theo Lesa. The only way to rectify the injustice committed against the Muezee race, Razin repeatedly 'preached', was to go against Theo Lesa's order for them to remain 1000 miles below the moon's surface in pursuit of human blood.

At the time of King Nguzoo's death, the Muezee kingdom was completely divided, and Razin had a following of circa 90% of the entire Muezee population. Therefore, he was the natural successor to King Nguzoo following the expiry of his final 400 years. Upon ascending to the throne, Razin, now King, vowed to go against everything else that Theo Lesa had commanded. The level of defiance championed by Razin following the death of King Nguzoo could only be equated to that of Adolf Hitler's violation or rebellion against the Treaty of Versailles.

According to history, the Treaty of Versailles signed in July 1919, eight months after the guns fell silent in World War I, called for stiff war restitution payments and other punishing peace terms for defeated Germany. Having been forced to sign the treaty, the German delegation to the peace conference indicated its attitude by breaking the ceremonial pen. As dictated by the Treaty of Versailles, Germany's military forces were reduced to insignificance, and the Rhineland was to be demilitarised. In 1925, after a European peace conference held in Switzerland, the Locarno Pact was signed, reaffirming the national boundaries decided by the Treaty of Versailles and approving the German entry into the League of Nations. The so-called 'spirit of Locarno' symbolised hopes for an era of European peace and goodwill, and by 1930 German Foreign Minister Gustav Stresemann had negotiated the removal of the last Allied troops in the demilitarised Rhineland. However, just four years later, Adolf Hitler and the Nazi Party seized full power in Germany, promising vengeance against the Allied nations that had forced the Treaty of Versailles on the German people. In 1935, Hitler unilaterally cancelled the treaty's military clauses and in March 1936 denounced the Locarno Pact and began remilitarising the Rhineland. Two years later, Nazi Germany burst out of its territories, absorbing Austria and portions of Czechoslovakia. In 1939, Hitler invaded Poland, leading to the outbreak of World War II in Europe.

Similar to the 'popularity card' that was played by Hitler when he unilaterally annulled the military clauses of the Treaty of Versailles that Germany signed with the allied nations, Razin's defiant spirit against Theo Lesa's dictates and 'impositions' proved to be popular with his nationals based on the tantalisingly misty promise of eternal life to his citizenry which was also predicated on the outcome of another factor: ambushing or trapping human beings on their visit mission to the moon to deprive them of their 'prized' possession which happened to be their blood.

Unlike human beings, the Muezee race was such a unique species that they wore no clothes, and their bodies never grew old. No human being would survive on the type of food that the Muezees ate and depended on for survival. In a way, it would be a misnomer to describe food for the Muezees in the strictest sense of what constitutes food from a human beings' perspective.

The Muezees' food was composed of an assortment of rocks made of clusters or mixtures of minerals. For instance, diamonds (made of carbon atoms) were the hardest food substance that the Muezee people ate; and was also their most preferred meal for dinner. Despite diamonds being their hardest meal, their teeth crushed it as easily as human beings would chew an apple or a piece of chicken. Graphite (also made of carbon atoms and used in pencil lead by human beings on earth) was among their softest food and was mainly eaten as a snack. Further, Rubies (formed of a mineral called corundum comprised of aluminium oxide) were one of their most colourful food. Furthermore, the Muezee people relied on Mercury for water, and their bodies were composed of about 65% Mercury. The functions of Mercury included helping digestion, absorption, circulation, the creation of a saliva-like substance called Mateh to help chew their food, transportation of nutrients to other parts of their bodies, and maintenance of their body temperature at a constant high of 200 degrees Celsius.

Whereas in very high doses, some forms of mercury have caused increases in several types of tumours in rats and mice, mercury posed no such problems to the Muezee 'people'. Although no human data currently ties mercury exposure to cancer, the data available is limited to completely rule out the likelihood of mercury exposure causing cancer.

And finally, Emerald, formed of a mineral called beryl whose chemical formula was a complex mix of beryllium, aluminium, silicon, and oxygen and whose colour came from additional traces of chromium and vanadium was eaten as the main breakfast by the Muezee 'people'.

This is but a succinct description of the 'people' or race called the Muezee, against whom Trump chose to wage war in an attempt to crush the rebellion fomented against Theo Lesa by King Razin; which was going to culminate in Trump's debut mission in The Acts of The Chosen Ones (The Acts of The Sheela) to complete his redemption and become a Ngeloi and live forever thereafter in the beautiful Nebuparadiza.

Chapter 22
The Natural Disaster Weapons

After successfully enlisting his team of 1000 Combat Ghosts for his first assignment in The Acts of The Chosen Ones (The Acts of The Sheela), Trump was asked by the Court Clerk to select weapons he would use in the battle against the rebel King Razin and his Muezee Kingdom. To signify that the previous chapter had now been closed, a trumpet was blown by one of the Ngelois though Trump couldn't figure out who exactly did it.

The Court Clerk signalled to Trump to enter through what looked like a door, and he obliged. Upon entering, he noticed the place was full of tiny containers which looked like very small briefcases. The Court Clerk informed Trump that they were inside a weapons armoury, and each small square box contained a weapon called Nebuparadiza Natural Disaster Weapon (NNDW). He pointed to a blue case and said it contained a NNDW (Nebuparadiza Natural Disaster Weapon) called Hurrica. He explained that the Hurrica NNDW worked by churning out huge storms and could spell instant disaster for any adversary of the mighty and fearsome Theo Lesa; the ruler of Nebuparadiza, and the universe. The Court Clerk added that Trump could invoke the powers locked in the Hurrica NNDW by shouting the secret word 'hubah!' followed by the password 'hindr!'. He further explained that the Hurrica NNDW had compressed power equivalent to the seven most violent hurricanes on earth.

Startled as he was, Trump hesitantly contributed to the conversation by affirming that in his former life on earth, humans feared hurricanes for their lashing winds, torrential rains, and inundating storm surges. He continued by saying according to what he knew from various sources such as news channels during his lifetime, hurricanes were also potentially lethal tempests known for causing extensive damage and that he was therefore in no doubt as to the scale of the power that was contained in the Hurrica NNDW.

The Court Clerk then pointed to a colourless case that resembled water and said it contained an NNDW called Tornah and that during the war, its catastrophic powers could be unleashed by shouting the secret word 'hossa' followed by the password 'hiber'. He explained further that on being set loose, the Tornah NNDW caused a violent rotating column of air to flow from the thunderstorm it created to the targeted object or enemy forces and that it had the compressed combined force that was equivalent to seven most calamitous Tornadoes on earth.

Trump was even more astounded as he said he sort of knew something about Tornadoes from his Geography lessons during his lifetime on earth. He said Tornadoes were also called twisters and were known to be one of nature's most powerful and destructive forces on earth, to which the Court Clerk nodded in acknowledgement.

Following on from the Tornah NNDW, the Court Clerk introduced yet another powerful weapon called the Volca NNDW, packaged in a khaki container. He took time to explain to Trump that the Volca NNDW had power equivalent to the seven most active Volcanoes on earth if their combined lava was to explode from a single mountain vent yet from seven different magma reservoirs. He further added that there were different categories of the Volca NNDW weapon in that armoury that operated similarly but to varying degrees. The Court Clerk finished by saying that the cataclysmic powers of the Volca NNDW could be unleashed by bellowing the secret word 'makari!' followed by the password 'dacaes'.

Following on, the Court Clerk introduced another weapon called the Tsu NNDW, which was packaged in a shiny white container. Its white colour was so unique that Trump could not associate it with any other white colour he had seen during his lifetime on earth. The Court Clerk paused to allow Trump to finish admiring the shiny white container that housed the Tsu NNDW. He then continued to explain that on being unleashed, the Tsu NNDW generated massive waves of liquid mercury that flowed like a tempestuous river running down mountain gorges at a speed over 200 miles per hour and could rise as high as 300 feet en route to destroying the targeted nemesis. The Court Clerk further added that the Tsu NNDW had compressed devastating power equivalent to the seven most powerful Tsunamis on earth. Trump added that he very well remembered the danger posed not only to life but also to infrastructure by Tsunamis during his life time on earth. He further said that from his school lessons, he knew that

Tsunamis were very difficult to detect far out at sea mainly because waves did not begin to gain size until they had reached shallower waters and that as a result, Tsunamis struck with very little warning often resulting in a huge loss of human life. Furthermore, Trump said he recalled watching documentaries showing how after a tsunami had struck, contaminated water and food supplies posed a risk to people's health; and landscapes that previously constituted picturesque beaches or seaside towns became a wasteland. The Court Clerk nodded in acknowledgement and concluded by stating that during war, the catastrophic powers of the Tsu NNDW could be unleashed by shouting the secret word 'Makant' followed by the password 'wafwa'.

The Court Clerk then introduced another weapon called the L'unquak NNDW, packaged in a golden case. He explained that it had compressed power equivalent to the seven most destructive earthquakes on earth and that its devastating effectiveness lay in its capability to generate temblors that could strike and rattle enemy territory. The Court Clerk further said the L'unquak NNDW caused the ground of the enemy territory to split along targeted areas in order to swallow the enemy forces, deplete their resources, and bring any survivors to submission. To sum it up, he instructed Trump that during the war, the L'unquak NNDW could be galvanised into action by shouting the secret word 'vuvu!' followed by the password 'Ojuku'.

The Court Clerk introduced the next weapon called the L'ighi NNDW, which was stored in a velvet case. He explained to Trump that the L'ighi NNDW had compressed electric current equivalent to the seven most powerful bolts of lightning on earth. Trump, who was cautiously becoming acquainted with the Court Clerk augmented that, "Lightning killed as many as 2,000 people on planet earth every year. Hundreds more people were struck but survived, usually with lingering and debilitating symptoms," to which the Court Clerk added, "from here in Nebuparadiza where we can see everything, the reality is actually worse than that…but let's not dwell." He then directed Trump to unleash the destructive electric current contained in the L'ighi NNDW by shouting the secret word 'edule' followed by the password 'pakr'.

Following the Court Clerk's revelations about the NNDWs (Nebuparadiza Natural Disaster Weapons), it was as though 'scales' had fallen off Trump's eyes, and his perception had deepened, and he could now see clearly. It dawned on Trump that there was a lot that human beings didn't know on earth despite the advancements in technology, scientific inventions and discoveries. It was as though the extent of things hidden from mortals could be summed up in the following two verses from the Christian Bible: 1) 'the secret things belong to the Lord our God, but the things revealed belong to us and to our children forever that we may follow all the words of this law' (Deuteronomy 29:29); 2) 'God gave them a spirit of stupor, eyes that would not see and ears that would not hear, down to this very day' (Romans 8.11).

The Court Clerk showed Trump countless other supernatural weapons, most of which were too complicated. However, Trump grasped how they operated because of his upgraded status from a mortal being to The Chosen One (The Sheela); a state just one level below that of a Ngeloi.

The last and final Nebuparadiza Natural Disaster Weapon (NNDW) that the Court Clerk introduced to Trump from the first armoury was called the Fylod NNDW. The Fylod NNDW was contained in a box with a colour Trump had never heard about during his lifetime on earth, called Nu. The Court Clerk described the Fylod NNDW as containing compressed devastating power equivalent to the seven most dangerous flash floods on earth. Trump contributed what he knew about flash floods during his lifetime on earth. "According to what I know," Trump said, "flash floods are among the most hazardous weather disasters on earth, causing power outages, damage to infrastructure, triggering landslides, and they can be very deadly. They occur when water has inundated normally dry land, and it can happen in a multitude of ways, such as through excessive rain, a ruptured dam or levee, rapid melting of snow or ice, or even an unfortunately placed beaver dam that could overwhelm a river spreading over the adjacent land called a floodplain. I also know that coastal flooding occurs when a large storm or tsunami has caused the sea to surge inland." The Court Clerk was impressed with the level of Trump's knowledge and nodded in acknowledgement.

According to research into weather patterns, most floods on earth take hours or even days to develop, giving residents time to prepare or evacuate. Others generate quickly and with little warning. Floods cause more than £30 billion in damage worldwide annually, and in the U.S.A. alone, losses average close to $8 billion a year.

After he had finished showing Trump all the weapons in the first armoury, the Court Clerk told him that he intended to show him weapons in other armouries as well so that he could make a knowledgeable decision regarding the weapons he wanted to use during The Acts of The Chosen Ones (The Acts of

The Sheela) in which his first mission was to wage war against King Razin. The Court Clerk explained that he chose to start with the first armoury because some of the weapons were similar to the natural disasters Trump was familiar with from earth. He further pointed out that other armouries contained weapons associated with natural disasters on other planets and heavenly bodies (such as the sun) that Trump had never heard of during his lifetime on earth.

Trump was eager to see other peculiar weapons, and the Court Clerk was more than happy to show off the weapons. He gestured to Trump to enter through another door, and they were in the second armoury.

The second armoury contained a plethora of small balls of various sizes. Each one of them contained a unique weapon associated with a natural disaster that Trump had never heard of. The Court Clerk explained that 95% of the weapons in that second armoury were associated with natural disasters familiar to the sun's inhabitants and were collectively called 'Solar Finkunkerz'. The term Solar Finkunkerz, the Court Clerk explained, was the umbrella term for disturbances in the 'normal' activities of the sun, which were interpreted as natural disasters by the inhabitants of the sun. He further apprised Trump that ever since Theo Lesa created the sun, Nebuparadiza has only had to use the Solar Finkunkerz weapons once to suppress a rebellion from the Muriro 'people' (who were the inhabitants of the sun).

The Muriro rebellion, the Court Clerk, explained, was all about the changing weather patterns on earth and the resultant extra work the Muriros were required to undertake in order to maintain an optimal level of atmospheric temperature for the mortal beings on earth following their irresponsible behaviour in damaging natural filters such as the ozone layer. Specifically speaking, the Court Clerk explained that the extra work required of the Muriros involved moderating the level of heat and radiation to planet earth to prevent human beings and their planet from melting. To protest against extra work, the Muriros resolved to deliberately destroy the mortal beings altogether by deliberately increasing the amount of radiation from the sun, which was contrary to one of Theo Lesa's principal laws in metaphysics, which required all his living creations to co-exist; and above all operate in an orderly fashion. The Court Clerk told Trump that in their attempt to destroy the mortals, the Muriros hatched a secretive plan to increase the intensity of UV radiation rays reaching human beings on earth.

According to science, the sun sends energy to earth in a few different ways: visible light that humans can see, infrared radiation that humans can feel as heat, and rays of UV radiation that humans can't see or feel. Fortunately, the earth's atmosphere protects humans from most UV radiation. While humans need some exposure to sunlight to help their bodies make vitamin D, too much UV is dangerous. There are three types of UV rays:

1. Ultraviolet A rays (UVA). The atmosphere does little to shield humans from these rays – most UVA radiation reaches the earth's surface and cause problems for human such as skin ageing, eye damage and lowering the ability of their bodies to fight off illness and also contribute to the risk of skin cancer in humans.

2. Ultraviolet B rays (UVB). The earth's atmosphere shields humans from most of UVB rays, and the amount of UVB rays that reach the earth's surface depends on latitude, altitude, time of year and other factors. UVB rays cause problems to humans such as sunburns, skin cancer, skin ageing and snow blindness (a sunburn to the cornea that causes a temporary loss of vision).

3. Ultraviolet C rays (UVC). These rays do not reach the earth's surface because they are completely absorbed by the atmosphere, and their harmful effects are minimal.

The Court Clerk continued to explain to Trump, "As you can see, the UV radiation that reaches the earth's surface is mostly UVA, and some UVB and these are the two types of harmful UV radiation that the Muriros secretly planned to increase with the evil intent to wipe out the human beings from earth."

Trump was grateful to the Court Clerk for taking time to reveal some of the top secrets only privy to the inhabitants of Nebuparadiza and concealed from mortal beings. To inspire him, the Court Clerk emphatically mentioned that the Muriro rebellion was crashed through an assignment that was undertaken by Trump's predecessor from the earth, another Chosen One, in The Acts of The Chosen Ones (The Acts of The Sheela) and was similarly backed by a battalion of Combat Ghosts; the only difference being his predecessor's team of Combat Ghosts was a mixture drawn from the dead saints and dead evil in equal proportion. The Court Clerk also added that the Sheela in question was now a Ngeloi in Nebuparadiza following victory in his chosen missions as recorded in *The Book of The Acts of The Chosen Ones (The Book of The Acts of The Sheela).*

In closing, the Court Clerk said he hoped Trump had been inspired by the success story of his predecessor for him to follow suit and triumph in his chosen missions in The Acts of The Chosen Ones (The Acts of The Sheela).

Talking about inspiration, according to an article that was authored by Scott Barry Kaufman and published in the Harvard Business Review titled 'Why Inspiration Matters', "In a culture obsessed with measuring talent and ability, we often overlook the important role of inspiration. Inspiration awakens us to new possibilities by allowing us to transcend our ordinary experiences and limitations. Inspiration propels a person from apathy to possibility and transforms the way we perceive our own capabilities. Inspiration may sometimes be overlooked because of its elusive nature. Its history of being treated as supernatural or divine hasn't helped the situation. But as recent research shows, inspiration can be activated, captured, and manipulated, and it has a major effect on important life outcomes." Further, according to Psychologists Todd M. Thrash and Andrew J. Elliot, inspiration has three main qualities, and they have noted these core aspects of inspiration as evocation, transcendence, and approach motivation. First, inspiration is evoked spontaneously without intention. Inspiration is also transcendent of our more animalistic and self-serving concerns and limitations. Such transcendence often involves a moment of clarity and awareness of new possibilities. Furthermore, Thrash and Elliot note, *"The heights of human motivation spring from the beauty and goodness that precede us and awaken us to better possibilities."* This moment of clarity is often vivid, and can take the form of a grand vision, or a 'seeing' of something one has not seen before (but that was probably always there). Finally, inspiration involves *approach motivation*, in which the individual strives to transmit, express, or actualise a new idea or vision. Thrash and Elliot further argue that, "Inspiration involves both being inspired *by* something *and acting on* that inspiration[25]."

After learning of his successor's victory against the Muriro rebellion on the sun, Trump felt emboldened and inspired to succeed in his chosen missions so that he could become a Ngeloi and inherit eternal life. He remained attentive as the Court Clerk continued to show him various other Solar Finkunkerz weapons, some of which were used by the victorious Chosen One (The Sheela), whom the Court Clerk had alluded to as having received the great recompense of becoming a Ngeloi and inheriting eternal life having won the battle for Theo Lesa in The Acts of The Chosen Ones (The Acts of The Sheela).

Among the Solar Finkunkerz weapons introduced to Trump by the Court Clerk was one called the 'Solar Muvwi weapon', which was packaged in a brown ball. He explained that upon being unleashed, the Solar Muvwi weapon operated by discharging large protons generated from the sun's atmosphere to the targeted object (in this case, the nemesis of Theo Lesa – the Muezee 'people') and could inflict extensive and irreparable damage.

The other Solar Finkunkerz weapon introduced to Trump by the Court Clerk was called the 'Solar Emaz weapon', which was packaged in a red ball with sparkling spots dotted all around. He explained that upon being launched, the Solar Emaz weapon released gargantuan emissions of highly concentrated heat energy generated from the sun's surface and had the potential to vaporise Theo Lesa's enemies upon being targeted however resistant or formidable their lines of defence maybe; and the emissions could travel faster than the speed of light.

After that, the Court Clerk introduced another Solar Finkunkerz weapon to Trump called the 'Solar Windzer weapon' packaged in a bronze ball. He explained that the 'Solar Windzer weapon' contained high-energy gamma rays capable of inflicting severe harm against Theo Lesa's enemies upon being targeted. Not being one to shy away from the conversation on subjects he knew something about, however modest, Trump threw in what he knew and said, "During my time on earth, I learnt that gamma rays are a form of radiation known as 'ionising radiation' because they remove electrons from atoms. I also learnt that radiation could damage a human being's DNA which could lead to cancer." The Court Clerk acknowledged Trump's contribution as being correct and added that, "The other positive side to radiation on earth is that it has been harnessed by human beings to treat diseases such as cancer."

As was rightly pointed out by the Court Clerk to Trump, according to an educational article published on 'Let's Talk Science[26]', radiation in the form of Gamma rays can be used to treat cancer. Radiation therapy, or radiotherapy, uses high-energy gamma rays to kill cancer cells and shrink tumours. Gamma Knife Radiosurgery is a special form of radiotherapy. It uses beams of gamma rays to treat injured brain tissue by damaging the DNA of dangerous cells. This technique is one of the most accurate and precise radiosurgery systems. It can focus on a small area and avoid damaging surrounding tissues. It can also target cells in the middle of the brain without cutting into the surrounding brain. In fact, only one mm of additional tissue around the tumour is destroyed.

After the Court Clerk had finished showing Trump all the Solar Finkunkerz weapons from the second armoury, he proposed moving to the third armoury. Trump responded that he had seen enough weapons for him to make an informed decision on the appropriate weapons he intended to use in The Acts of The Chosen Ones (The Acts of The Sheela). Being someone who 'uprooted' himself from earth, Trump also added that the Solar Finkunkerz weapons in the second armoury were so outlandish and didn't appeal to him as much as the weapons in the first armoury. For that reason, he said he had therefore made up his mind to settle for the NNDWs (Nebuparadiza Natural Disaster Weapons) in the first armoury. He justified his decision as primarily being, "Because I am well familiar with the natural disaster weapons in the first armoury as they are closely associated with the natural disasters on earth, where I came from."

The Court Clerk insisted on showing Trump the weapons in other armouries so that he could have a wide range of weapons to choose from, but he responded by saying, "I would be most grateful, your worship, if you inclined your ear to your humble servant's request to allow me to settle for the weapons in the first armoury…I beg of you." The Court Clerk was obliged to fulfil The Chosen One's preferred choice of weapons, and Trump's request was accordingly granted, and the decision sealed. It was going to be so without any qualms.

The Court Clerk then opened another Book called '*The Book of Ntobolo*' in which the weapons that Trump had decided to use in The Acts of The Chosen Ones (The Acts of The Sheela) were noted down together with the associated secret words and passwords. The names of the Nebuparadiza Natural Disaster Weapons (NNDWs) that the Court Clerk recorded in *The Book of Ntobolo* in no particular order were as follows: the Volca NNDW, the Hurrica NNDW, the Tornah NNDW, the L'unquak NNDW, the Tsu NNDW, the L'ighi NNDW and the Fylod NNDW.

Chapter 23
The Wings Warehouse

Although he hadn't brought up the issue yet, Trump wondered what mode of transportation he would use during his conflict with King Razin in The Acts of The Chosen Ones (The Acts of The Sheela) because he didn't have wings like the Ngelois. He relied on the Court Clerk to carry him around on that highly purposed tour.

After Trump's preferred weapons (NNDWs) had been recorded in *The Book of Ntobolo* and the Book closed, he was led through another door into a strange room that was full of wings. Trump knew his lingering question was about to be answered. He had spotted different wings on different Ngelois, and they were now in the wings warehouse. The Court Clerk informed Trump that the name of that wings warehouse was called the 'Katih'. He explained that his role was restricted to presenting the advantages and disadvantages associated with each set of wings in the Katih warehouse. After that, it was up to Trump as The Chosen One (The Sheela) to use that information to decide on the set of wings he deemed most appropriate to use in the battle against King Razin.

As The Chosen One, Trump could make decisions required of him by the Court Clerk because he now had a new mind and had both understanding and discernment far more superior than any other human. It was a gift that came with being The Sheela (The Chosen One). Not only was Trump required to choose wings for himself, but he also had the mandate to choose wings for all his Combat Ghosts (i.e., for his second in command, for his Combat Ghost Sergeant, and for the rest of the nine hundred and ninety-eight Combat Ghosts, in short, for the entire squad). This was also meant to connote that The Sheela (The Chosen One) was accorded full control or total authority, so to say, over their assignments in The Acts of The Chosen Ones (The Acts of The Sheela).

Upon coming to a halt in the Katih warehouse, the Court Clerk proceeded to not only introduce the wings to Trump but also to describe their unique characteristics in order for him to make an enlightened decision.

The first set of wings to be introduced by the Court Clerk was called 'Egta wings'. He explained that the Egta wings had long primary feathers spread out widely to catch vertical columns of hot air (called thermals) to enable The Chosen One (The Sheela) or whoever was using them to rise much higher in the air. The Court Clerk then mentioned that birds with the Egta wings on earth included eagles, most hawks and storks.

The next set of wings that the Court Clerk introduced was called 'Albaes wings'. He explained that the Albaes wings were long and narrow to enable the Chosen One (The Sheela), or whoever was using them, to fly for a longer time without flapping their wings. The disadvantage with the Albaes wings, the Court Clerk pointed out, was that they made the flier to be more dependent on wind currents than the Egta wings. He gave examples of birds with the Albaes wings on earth, including the albatrosses, gulls, and gannets.

The Court Clerk introduced the 'Lysa wings', which were longer than the Albaes wings and narrower. He explained that the Lysa wings were well-adapted for the strong, constant winds like the winds that blew over parts of the oceans on earth, and their major advantage was that they could easily withstand strong winds.

The Court Clerk then introduced another set of wings called 'R'blaspar wings', which he explained were good for short bursts of high speed and allowed fast take offs and tight manoeuvring. "While the R'blaspar wings allow high speed," the Court Clerk explained, "the speed cannot be maintained." He gave examples of birds with such wings on earth as crows, ravens, blackbirds, sparrows and thrushes (he mentioned the American Robin as an example). Trump added that the common ravens he had seen on earth were acrobatic flyers; and that it was not infrequent to see ravens doing rolls and flip-flops with their wings. The Court Clerk nodded in affirmation. One could only speculate that Trump was thrilled at the thought of the sort of gymnastics he would perform if the R'blaspar wings were to be mounted on his shoulders.

The next set of wings the Court Clerk introduced was called 'Elical wings', which he said were incredibly fast, and unlike the R'blaspar wings, they could also maintain speed. Again, for the sake of Trump's benefit, the Court Clerk was quick to mention the names of birds with such wings on earth, and the list included swifts, ducks, falcons, terns, and sandpipers.

There were a plethora of other wings in the Katih warehouse and the Court Clerk carefully described their unique characteristics to Trump and gave him a chance to ask questions.

The final set of wings the Court Clerk presented to Trump was called 'Ver'g wings'. They were smaller than the other wings, but he stressed that they were quick and adapted for fast movement. He also told Trump that a good example of a bird with such wings on earth was the Ruby-throated Hummingbird, which at times appeared to float in space while sipping nectar and hovering from flower to flower.

After the Court Clerk had finished introducing and describing the different types of wings and their characteristics, Trump was invited to select the wings for himself and also for his team of Combat Ghosts. The irony was that Trump had not yet seen the team of Combat Ghosts that he had selected though the Court Clerk informed him before the weapons selection process and tour of the armouries that the Arch Ngeloi Gabriel had travelled to Gehenakumbo to retrieve a total of 1000 (one thousand) Combat Ghosts from the souls of the dead evil in accordance with Trump's preference. He also informed Trump that to the Combat Ghosts in question, being selected from Gehenakumbo out of the many damned souls, there was not only an honour but also a great respite from the daily torment they were subjected to. The exact words that the Court Clerk used to describe the experience of the souls of the dead evil in Gehenakumbo were: "In Gehenakumbo, there is no peace unto the wicked, they are like the tossing sea for it cannot be quiet, and its waters toss up refuse and mud."

The task of selecting wings for himself wasn't an easy one to start with, given there were so many different types of wings in the Katih warehouse. Trump was spoiled for choice. Based on advice from the Court Clerk, he narrowed down the decision influencing factors for selecting the best wings to 1) their unique characteristics 2) the type of bird the wings were associated with on earth. This methodology somehow made the wings selection process more focused. Of all the birds that the Court Clerk had mentioned, Trump had great respect for the eagle. After ticking off the decision influencing factors as advised by the Court Clerk, Trump then employed the elimination process.

The R'blaspar Wings were first to be eliminated. The reason Trump gave was that although they were good for short bursts of high speed and allowed fast take offs and tight manoeuvring, speed could not be maintained using these wings, and he supposed that would constitute a weakness when confronted with enemy fire.

Next to be discounted were the Ver'g wings. According to Trump, though they were specially adapted for incredibly fast movement, he thought their relatively small size would present a logjam in the efficient execution of the mission in the battle that lay ahead.

Using the same process, Trump eliminated all the other wings except for the Egta wings, which were his preferred choice in his capacity as The Chosen One (The Sheela) and commander of the mission in The Acts of The Chosen Ones (The Acts of The Sheela). His fascination with the Egta wings was brought on because of their long primary feathers that spread out effortlessly. Trump thought the unique characteristics of the Egta wings would enable him to rise much higher before launching strikes against the Muezee army or when escaping from enemy attack. The other enchantment with the Egta wings was they shared similar characteristics with the eagle's wings. During his lifetime on earth, Trump heard copious metaphorical lessons and examples referring to the eagle, and he thought he could learn a lot from the eagle's determination.

According to an article by Mirlande Chery titled 'The Seven Characteristics of An Eagle and Why They Are Vital for Good Leadership'[27], an eagle will never surrender to its prey, no matter its strength or size. It will always put up a fight to win its prey or regain its territory. Eagles are such remarkable hunters that they can prey on goats much larger than themselves by throwing them off the side of a cliff. Further, eagles are known to be fearless; and Trump thought good leaders are supposed to be fearless too. They face problems head-on. Others take note of their passion and determination and draw strength from it. Eagles also have an extremely powerful vision; the eyes of an eagle are specially designed for long-distance focus with clarity; the eagle's eye is one of the strongest in the entire animal kingdom (four to eight times stronger than that of the average human) and can spot a rabbit 3.2 km away. An eagle's eyes are roughly the same size as those of a human being. In fact, as an eagle descends to attack its prey, the muscles in its eyes continuously adjust the curvature of the eyeballs to maintain sharp focus throughout the approach and attack.

These are just a few reasons why Trump opted for the Egta wings, primarily because of their association with the eagle. The Court Clerk enquired whether

Trump was absolutely sure with his choice of the Egta wings, and he responded in the affirmative.

Following Trump's decision, the Court Clerk opened another book called *'K'taboul'*, which was the 'Book of Wings for The Chosen Ones (The Sheela) and their Combat Ghosts'. Trump's choice of wings was duly recorded in the K'taboul. Amongst the things that were so palpable and vividly noticeable to Trump was the number of different types of Books in that heavenly place called Nebuparadiza. Despite all the Ngelois and their seniors (i.e., the Court Clerk, the beautiful Ngeloi, and the omnipotent, omnipresent and omniscient Theo Lesa) being all-knowing and imbued with infinite memory and intelligence, yet everything had to be recorded in those sacrosanct, hallowed, consecrated and sacred Books. Following an enquiry by Trump as to why almost everything had to be recorded in the respective books, the Court Clerk responded that it was done not only for the sake of future reference but also to ensure that justice prevailed.

The word 'justice' reminded Trump of his Sunday School teachings during his lifetime on earth, one of them being: "Let judgment run down. Let the execution of justice be everywhere like the showers that fall upon the land to render it fertile; and let righteousness in heart and life be like a mighty river, or the Jordan, that shall wind its course through the whole nation and carry every abomination into the Dead Sea. Let justice and righteousness prevail everywhere and sweep their contraries out of the land."

In Nebuparadiza, the significance of writing and recording of life events as opposed to committing everything to memory was fully impressed on Trump. He wondered whether that Was one of the secrets to being a 'god', i.e., the art of recording and writing down vital events as they unfolded. Trump also wondered whether systematic and impeccable record keeping was one of the distinctive features of how those heavenly hosts in Nebuparadiza treated crucial events compared to how mortal beings approached critical life events.

According to Mark Murphy, New York Times bestselling author, a contributor to Forbes, and Founder of Leadership IQ (a research and training firm), "Neuroscience explains why you need to write down your goals if you actually want to achieve them[28]." Mark writes that Neuropsychologists have identified what they call the 'generation effect', which basically says individuals demonstrate better memory for the material they've generated themselves than for material they've merely read, and that's where writing things down comes in. Writing things down happens on two levels: external storage and encoding. External storage is easy to explain: you're storing the information contained in your goal in a location (e.g., a piece of paper) that is very easy to access and review at any time. But there's another deeper phenomenon happening: encoding. Encoding is the biological process by which the things we perceive travel to our brain's hippocampus, where they're analysed. From there, decisions are made about what gets stored in our long-term memory and, in turn, what gets discarded. Writing improves that encoding process. In other words, when you write it down, it has a much greater chance of being remembered.

After the Court Clerk had finished recording Trump's preferred wings in the K'taboul (Book of Wings for The Chosen Ones (The Sheela) and their Combat Ghosts), he without warning uttered some forceful and authoritative words in an alien language that sounded more like Greek when spoken by someone chewing or cracking particles of glass with their teeth. He said, "*afiste to na ginei*," meaning 'let it be done' and immediately after uttering those words, the Egta wings (the wings that Trump chose for himself) grew on his shoulders. He now had wings! They were huge and magnificent. Upon seeing his beautiful wings, Trump immediately jumped up in excitement and instead of coming down afterwards, he flew away in what looked like a reflex action. In the moments that ensued, Trump flew up and down and all over the place as the Court Clerk looked on in contentment. Trump couldn't believe what had just happened to him.

After the flying 'practice' episode was over, the Court Clerk voiced out some more alien words, "*Káne ton san theó*," meaning 'make him like a god'. As though that wasn't enough, the Court Clerk uttered some more alien words, "*Eísai tóra stratiótis*," meaning 'you are now a warrior or soldier'. Immediately after the Court Clerk had pronounced those final set of words, Trump's mentality, the shape of his body, and his strength all metamorphosised instantaneously. He felt courageous and solid. In short, he felt robust and very strong. It was as though he had experienced a rebirth. He also felt as though he's always had wings. The period when he had no wings was selectively and supernaturally erased from his 'memory', for lack of a better term, leaving only the sections of his 'memory' that were deemed necessary for his imminent mission in The Acts of The Chosen Ones (The Acts of The Sheela), which was to wage war against King Razin and his Muezee Kingdom in order to quell their rebellious doings.

Upon becoming Theo Lesa's 'warrior with wings', Trump performed sophisticated aerodynamic gymnastics and salient manoeuvres to test his new 'warrior with wings' status. After he had finished, the Court Clerk opened another book called '*Mushkakoolou*', which literally meant 'The warrior's Creed'.

Chapter 24
The Warrior's Creed

From the pages of the Mushkakoolou Book, the Court Clerk read out aloud to Trump on what it meant and took to be a true warrior for the mighty Theo Lesa; who for the first time he described as 'The Man of War'. He judiciously explained to Trump the qualities that were demanded of all The Chosen Ones (The Sheela) upon their transformation into 'warrior with wings status' and also what it took for such a warrior to succeed in The Acts of The Chosen Ones (The Acts of The Sheela) missions.

Trump listened raptly and keenly as the Court Clerk continued his lecture: "Theo Lesa's warrior is completely focused, disciplined, and aggressive not out of selfishness, but on behalf of others. To be Theo Lesa's warrior, you need to figure out and master what triggers your 'beast mode' and make it part of your routine as you undertake your assignments in The Acts of The Chosen Ones (The Acts of The Sheela)."

The Court Clerk paused briefly and then continued, "Every warrior of Theo Lesa has a ritual they follow before going into battle, and when you find yours, you make yourself that much more likely to emerge victoriously. No successful military campaign performed in the name of Theo Lesa begins with a vague objective. You need a clear vision of victory to aim for. Failure in any of your missions will ruin your chances of becoming a Ngeloi and inheriting eternal life. I charge you to take full responsibility for what is happening on your missions. If a team member has not understood one of your instructions, you, as a commander, cannot blame them. There is no such thing as a bad team, just bad leaders."

The Court Clerk paused again and asked Trump if he had any questions at that stage, to which he responded, "No," and the Court Clerk proceeded, "believing is important. It is difficult to sell a plan to your team if you don't believe in it. If you want to maintain leadership of your team, never give the impression that you don't understand or don't approve of the decision from the Buite or indeed Theo Lesa's decision for that matter, for instance, your mandate to trounce the rebellion by the Muezee Kingdom. If you don't fully understand the reasoning behind Theo Lesa's and the Buite's decision to attack King Razin and his rebellious Muezee 'people', then ask now so that you too can 'believe' and trust the decision taken by the Buite and Theo Lesa."

"Beware of your ego," warned the Court Clerk while looking straight at Trump, as though trying to detect his reaction. He then continued reading from the Mushkakoolou Book, "Even though you are The Chosen One (The Sheela) leading the Combat Ghosts of mortal beings who led evil lives on earth, on the battlefield you as their leader can't be a show-off who knows everything and won't take any advice from either your deputy commander or your Combat Ghost Sergeant or any ordinary Combat Ghost within your team. Contrary to popular belief among the mortal beings on earth," continued the Court Clerk, eager to make a point, "you will not lose credit in the eyes of your team if you admit you don't know everything, if anything, this will only reinforce your position as their leader."

The Court Clerk asked if Trump had any questions, and when the answer was 'no' again, he proceeded to read out further instructions, "Before you move on the battlefield, whether under attack or not, you always have to ensure that part of the team cover for the team that is moving and the objective is to ensure the security of every member of the operation. Keep things simple because complexity is the enemy of execution; the simpler a plan, an instruction or a strategy is to understand, the more your team will be inclined to act. Inversely, the more it is complex and obscure, the more suspicion will take over, and the less your team will be inclined to act."

The Court Clerk continued reading to the attentive and responsive Trump: "Remember to set priorities for yourself and the team and to act on them. There will be moments on your mission when you and your team will feel swamped by demands, challenges and uncertainties. The most important thing is to remain focused, calm and to be able to stop to consider the options at hand. Everything cannot always be done or resolved immediately. But rather than remain in uncertainty and indecision or be submerged by challenges, you should be able to take a short break, take a step back and determine the most important priority to be considered at that moment, set up a plan to resolve the problem and act until the problem is resolved and then move on to the next challenge."

"Where possible or necessary," the Court Clerk continued reading from the Mushkakoolou Book, "try and decentralise command because it may sometimes be difficult in the case of enemy contact or complications to communicate speedily and efficiently with the chain of command to adapt the mission to the new circumstances. In such circumstances, allow your Combat Ghosts to make their own decisions as long as they know their responsibilities and have a clear idea of what is expected of them. Decentralising command effectively means that the mission and its limits have been formally defined by you and your deputy Combat Ghosts, who have an overview of the mission, but the details of the execution are left to the Combat Ghosts on the field who are in contact with its reality."

The Court Clerk stopped and then continued, "Plan, because no plan resists the first contact with the enemy. The more precautions are taken to anticipate problems and catastrophes, the higher the chances of success in The Acts of The Chosen Ones (The Acts of the Sheela). It is thus your responsibility to plan for a maximum number of scenarios and alternative plans to adapt to a situation that can change at any moment. The plans must be clearly explained to all your Combat Ghosts who the members of your team are, and then, you, as the leader, must ensure that everyone understands all aspects of the various options."

The Court Clerk then melodramatically said to Trump, "Pay attention to this next instruction," and then continued, "endeavour to lead downwards and upwards, and that means if a plan, a decision or a strategy decided by you and your deputy Combat Ghosts doesn't make sense or cannot work on the field, your army of Combat Ghosts on the field must pluck up the courage to contact you as leaders requesting to consider the reality they face so that a plan may be varied or quashed altogether. As much as you must ensure that your deputies and army of Combat Ghosts understand the aim of the mission and its objectives, the Combat Ghosts carrying out the tasks in partnership with you must just as much make sure that you as a leader are aware of the innumerable hitches that can crop up and all this with the greatest mutual respect."

The Court Clerk flipped to the next chapter of the *Mushkakoolou* book and continued, "There is nothing worse than indecision. When faced with a difficult situation on the battlefield and you and your army of Combat Ghosts are under heavy attack and at risk of losing the battle, you can't decide to wait to see how things turn out because that would create real danger in letting a situation degenerate due to a lack of firmness and decisiveness on your part as The Chosen One (The Sheela)."

The Court Clerk paused again before introducing another cardinal point, "Discipline brings freedom," he said. "The more you study your plans with discipline and detail, the easier it will be for you and your army to react when faced with an unexpected situation on the battlefield. The more the rules of engagement or instructions for your mission are known and clear to your army of Combat Ghosts, the easier it will be for them to make their own decisions on the field. Discipline and commitment require personal investment and effort from the onset but will liberate your troops to fight a good fight for you and your mission. Indiscipline should not be tolerated considering the consequences it will lead to."

"If you fail in any of your three assignments in The Acts of The Chosen Ones (The Acts of The Sheela)," admonished the Court Clerk sanctimoniously in a rather supercilious manner, "you will surely be condemned to Gehenakumbo in fulfilment of the guilty verdict that was pronounced against you by the Buite and upheld by Theo Lesa. The beautiful Ngeloi secured your provisional pardon to accord you the opportunity to try and change the course of your destiny, and you shouldn't scupper the opportunity."

After receiving a thorough lecture and instructions on leadership in his capacity as The Chosen One (The Sheela) from the Court Clerk, Trump felt more confident and geared for the battle against King Razin.

The Court Clerk recorded that Trump had received full instructions on leadership from the Mushkakoolou Book in another book called '*The Book of Ifipope*'.

Chapter 25
Meeting the Combat Ghosts

After *The Book of Ifipope* had been closed, Trump was led back to the Katih warehouse where he had earlier picked a set of Egta wings for himself, which enabled him to fly freely without relying on the Court Clerk to carry him around. Upon arriving at the wings warehouse, the Court Clerk told Trump that as commander of the missions in The Acts of The Chosen Ones (The Acts of The Sheela) he also had the responsibility to select appropriate wings for his Combat Ghosts. This was inter alia because the Combat Ghosts had no access to Nebuparadiza because they were Ghosts of the souls from the dead evil men and women who had been condemned to Gehenakumbo. Combat Ghosts from the dead evil could only be granted relief from Gehenakumbo to take part in The Acts of The Chosen Ones (The Acts of The Sheela) missions; in this case as allied forces with Trump to wage war against the Muezee Kingdom for their rebellious activities against Theo Lesa.

The Court Clerk advised Trump on the importance of using the 'right tools' for any task and that choosing the right wings for his team was crucial to his success in the battle against King Razin.

"You're only as good as the tools you use," goes the old saying, which has stood the test of time. According to Alex Weitzel in his article titled 'The Importance of Providing the Right Tools at Work', "There are thousands of tools out there and the challenge for managers is to find the right ones to implement in the workplace to aid their employees. Whether physical equipment is needed to perform a task or different applications to facilitate processes at work, it is important for the business to have the correct tools available for their employees to do their work effectively. Having the right tools is imperative to successful completion of the task at hand. In addition, the right tools allow employees to complete their task efficiently, which affords employees opportunities to expand their range of capabilities. When employees aren't provided with the correct tools, they are forced to rely on what is readily available to them. This can lead to inefficient, slow work that might also result in incorrect completion of a task, which companies would obviously like to avoid. Employees might not feel comfortable telling management that they need better devices or more of them, so it's a good idea for the manager to take initiative and check with them instead of waiting for feedback which may not be forthcoming as it depends on a number of other factors such as the prevailing work culture, their back ground or their temperament[29]."

The final tutoring to Trump by the Court Clerk was that as The Chosen One (The Sheela), his wings had to be unique or different from the ones he would choose for his Combat Ghosts. That effectively meant he couldn't choose the Egta wings because that's the type of wings he had picked for himself. After reviewing the characteristics associated with each type of wings in the Katih warehouse, Trump decided to choose the Lysa Wings for his Combat Ghosts. The reason he gave for choosing the Lysa Wings was that they were well adapted for strong and constant winds, and if his army of Combat Ghosts were to be subjected to the adverse battleground or atmospheric conditions during the fight, he was convinced that was the type of wings that would endure adverse conditions and help him win the battle.

The Court Clerk duly recorded the Lysa wings in the K'taboul Book, which was the 'Book of Wings for The Chosen Ones (The Sheela) and their Combat Ghosts' to denote finalisation of the wing's selection process for The Chosen One (The Sheela) and his squad.

It was almost time for Trump to embark on his mission. Preparations for the war against King Razin and his Muezee Kingdom with the backup of the Combat Ghosts were coming together and forming shape.

The Court Clerk informed Trump that the NNDWs (Nebuparadiza Natural Disaster Weapons) that he had chosen from the first armoury were ready for collection at a special location that was called 'Inchde'. The word Inchde literally meant 'meeting place for a special mission ordained by Theo Lesa'. Inchde was a place just outside Nebuparadiza that was specially designated as the place for The Chosen One (The Sheela) to meet their army of Combat Ghosts from Gehenakumbo for the first time.

The Court Clerk directed Trump that upon meeting his team of Combat Ghosts, his first task was to fill the two positions of 2ic (i.e., second in command)

Combat Ghost and the Combat Ghost Sergeant and confer authority upon them to operate in those senior roles. The Court Clerk accompanied Trump to the Inchde to meet the Combat Ghosts.

Upon arriving at the Inchde, Trump was shown another door, and upon entering, he and the Court Clerk were ushered into the magnificent presence of numerous semi-transparent beings who had the form or shape of human beings. They were the Combat Ghosts of the souls from the dead evil retrieved from Gehenakumbo by the Arch Ngeloi Gabriel as backup soldiers for Trump in The Acts of The Chosen Ones (The Acts of The Sheela). They were 1000 (one thousand) of them in total, a mixture of both men and women.

The Court Clerk introduced Trump to the Combat Ghosts and the Combat Ghosts to Trump. After the introductions were over, the Court Clerk uttered some more strange 'Greek' sounding words that were now familiar to Trump, and he said, "*Lávete fterá tóra,*" which plainly meant 'receive wings now'! Immediately after pronouncing those words, the wings that Trump had chosen for the Combat Ghosts, the Lysa wings, supernaturally appeared on the shoulders of the Combat Ghosts. The form of the Combat Ghosts also changed. They were now less transparent and slightly more visible.

Just like what had happened to Trump after receiving his Egta wings, the Combat Ghosts were catapulted into the 'flying mode', and they started flapping their wings up and down and began hovering all over the place. This continued until all the Combat Ghosts could fly naturally and smoothly to denote that the practice session had achieved its intended goal.

The Court Clerk handed over the NNDWs (Nebuparadiza Natural Disaster Weapons) that Trump had selected, including various other weapons. He told Trump that it was entirely up to him to assign them to his army of Combat Ghosts, except for the NNDWs, which could only be operated by him as The Chosen One (The Sheela), as all the secret codes were entrusted with him and not the Combat Ghosts.

It was now time for Trump to appoint his 2ic (i.e., second in command). After careful consideration, he opted for a Combat Ghost who went by the name of General Suby during his lifetime on earth as his 2ic. General Suby was one of the evillest generals ever to have lived on earth. It was therefore not a surprise that he died a violent death, as though in fulfilment of the words that were spoken by Jesus of Nazareth, "For all they that take the sword shall perish with the sword."

During his career as a top soldier, General Suby's war strategy and paradigm were that 'war was meant to be waged against both civilians and soldiers of the enemy nation'. Before setting off for war General Suby always divided his army into two groups. The first group was comprised of elite troops (the equivalent of the Navy Seals in the USA) whose priority was to fight enemy troops on the battlefield and another group of less specialised infantries who were tasked to fight a different type of 'strange' war that impinged on an unethical and morally bankrupt paradigm that specifically targeted civilians (especially women and children) during the war. Their mandate couldn't have been any clearer as it was spelt out loudly by General Suby himself that they were to murder and rape civilian men and women and children in their homes, marketplace or wherever they could be found away from the battlefield.

General Suby's strategy was centred on weakening his enemies on the battlefield by targeting and hitting them where it hurt the most, which he identified as their treasured civilian family members. The idea was to cause nemesis forces on the battlefield to lose concentration and eventually lose the battle upon learning of the catastrophes that had befallen their family members left at home in their supposedly 'secure' confinements away from the battlefield. While murder, rape and other human rights violations were collateral damage or unintended consequences of most wars, General Suby's military strategy was to intentionally employ these evil acts as weapons to win the wars he fought.

When his time to exit earth came knocking, General Suby was taken away violently. He died a woeful and wretched death at the hands of his trusted soldiers. After he was surprisingly shot dead by two of his most trustworthy soldiers who were secretly opposed to his abhorrent military tactics against civilians (especially women and children being family men themselves), they commanded 12 junior soldiers to each shove sharp pieces of wood into his anus and one of those long sharp objects protruded through his left shoulder. One of the renegade soldiers who took part in the unceremonious killing of General Suby later confessed, before being sentenced to death, that the aim in inflicting the diabolical punishment on General Suby was for the sharp piece of wood that he thrust through his backside to pop out through his mouth in disdain of all the evil orders they were made to obey which resulted in the superfluous death of innocent women and children as well as unarmed civilian men. The Court Clerk recorded the name of Trump's 2ic, General Suby, in the appropriate Book.

The next task was for Trump to elect his Combat Ghost Sergeant (third in command). After careful consideration, he chose a Combat Ghost who went by the name of General Benj during his lifetime on earth. Like General Suby, General Benj also died a horrible death. One could rightly conclude that both General Suby and General Benj died horrendous deaths because the blood of their innocent victims (mostly women and children) was screaming out for retribution from their graves. As the ancient universal saying goes, "You reap what you sow or what goes around comes around," also called 'Karma' in Buddhism.

According to John Edwards, director of CLA's School of Psychological Science and OSU's Contemplative Studies Initiative, "Karma, however, is deeply personal and to the unfamiliar, karma sounds like a system of justice governed by the cosmos. In the Buddhist point of view karma is a psychological phenomenon. It happens because of the way the mind works. It's not some general force that exists in the universe. It's not the hand of God. The basic idea is that your own behaviours and actions lead you to experience the world in a certain way[30]."

Like General Suby, General Benj's ordeal preceding his death was quite horrific. Upon being captured by enemy forces in the Battle of Badon (also known as the Battle of Mons Badonicus) in 500 AD, he was thrown alive in a highly concentrated sulphuric-acid-like chemical and his body dissolved without a trace.

The Court Clerk recorded the name of General Benj as the Combat Ghost Sergeant (third in command) in the appropriate Book and closed it thereafter. The Court Clerk was now only left with giving or showing Trump the direction to the Muezee Kingdom, which was located 1000 miles beneath the moon. From their position, the Court Clerk drew Trump's attention (and that of his senior Combat Ghosts Generals Suby and Benj) to the Solar System which was visibly very clear, and Trump and his Combat Ghosts could all see the sun, the eight planets with their moons, and lots of other smaller objects such as dwarf planets, asteroids and other Near Earth Objects (NEOs), and comets. He explained to Trump and his two top Combat Ghosts that the Muezee Kingdom was located underneath the moon, also called Luna, which he said was the earth's only natural satellite and was the fifth largest moon in the entire Solar System.

To get to the Muezee Kingdom, directed the Court Clerk, Trump and his army of Combat Ghosts were to enter through an abyss or chasm which was located in a secret place only known to the residents of Nebuparadiza (i.e., Theo Lesa, the beautiful Ngeloi, the Court Clerk and the Ngelois). The secret entrance leading to the Muezee kingdom was called 'Muarule', which meant 'hard to find'. The Court Clerk gave Trump, in the hearing range of his two deputies, directions to the exact location of the secret entrance (Muarule) on the moon, which led through the rocky caves to the Muezee Kingdom.

The final instruction from the Court Clerk was that in the unlikely event that the rebel King Razin and his army put up a strong fight, or unexpected resistance, and Trump was on the verge of losing the battle, he could call the Court Clerk (via the secret channel for which he shared the secret code and other details with him) to summon one-off assistance from the Arch Ngeloi, Gabriel. The Court Clerk reminded Trump that help from the Arch Ngeloi Gabriel could only be requested and accessed once in all the three assignments that were to be undertaken in The Acts of The Chosen Ones (The Acts of The Sheela). He also reminded Trump that he was required to successfully undertake all the three separate assignments he had selected to complete his redemption, become a Ngeloi and inherit eternal life.

Upon being asked if he had any questions before the Court Clerk could depart, Trump answered that he had none and that all the instructions were clear. The Court Clerk wished Trump and his Combat Ghosts well and reminded him of what was at stake. He also informed Trump that after the battle against King Razin was over, he would meet him at that same place, at Inchde, to welcome and lead him back to the Buite (courtroom) in Nebuparadiza to be given orders and instructions for his next mission in The Acts of The Chosen Ones (The Acts of The Sheela). This was, of course, based on the assumption that he would triumph against King Razin. Needless to say, the opposite (i.e., condemnation to Gehenakumbo) was true if he were to lose the battle against the rebel King Razin. Shortly thereafter, the Court Clerk disappeared (vanished), and Trump was now firmly in charge.

Chapter 26
Military Strategies

Upon assuming the reigns of authority over his army of Combat Ghosts, Trump's first move was to privately confer with his deputies, General Suby and General Benj to map out suitable military strategies as the rest of the Combat Ghosts waited for further instructions. The trio deliberated on several military strategies, mainly focusing on their merits and demerits. General Suby drew on his vast military experience gained during his long military career on earth and alluded to several military tactics that won him countless battles over and over again, albeit in a callous, heartless and brutal manner.

The first military strategy that General Suby proposed was called 'Operation Pseudonakuru', which was centred on: 1) ambuscading, bushwhacking, or taking the enemy by surprise, i.e., attacking when least expected and 2) cutting off enemy supplies and/or damaging their key infrastructure such as weapon armouries before launching a vicious attack. He quoted several examples of battles that he won during his decorated military career on earth using the Operation Pseudonakuru military strategy. According to his graphic description of the strategy to Trump and General Benj, the enemy was completely taken by surprise at the sudden 'apparition' of the invading force, leaving them no time to organise themselves. This, coupled with the fact that their supplies were cut off, left the enemy zero chances of winning the war.

Rob Johnson (author and lecturer in the History of War at Oxford University) called this military tactic as the 'Envelopment' in his article themed 'Ten of the Greatest Battlefield Tactics'[31]. According to Rob, "The unexpected appearance of enemy troops on a flank or from behind can damage an army's morale, and if a force is encircled, it can be deprived of supplies or attacked from any side. Ultimately, if completely cut off, it must cut its way out, surrender or fight to the death." Rob further states that, "The 'Envelopment' is the classic example of manoeuvre warfare and has produced some of the most decisive victories in history. The tactic was employed at Stalingrad in Operation Uranus, beginning on 19th of November 1942. With the Germans pinned down and unable to manoeuvre, the Soviets delivered a heavy artillery bombardment from 3,500 guns on Romanian and Italian positions on either side of the city, then unleashed several armoured formations, including three tank corps. They combined mobility and speed with devastating firepower, driving deep behind German lines to cut off and then defeat the entire German army in Stalingrad."

General Benj was not one to be outfoxed, he immediately pointed out that the major flaw with the Operation Pseudonakuru (Envelopment) military strategy was that it assumed the enemy would be oblivious to the planned attack, which wasn't always the case. He pointed out that according to his military experience, most armies had access to a network of sophisticated intelligence information which was ingeniously secreted or hidden away from their nemesis. He also added the ancient saying he learnt while on earth, "Assumption is the mother of all foolishness."

To add gravitas to General Benj's criticism of the Operation Pseudonakuru (Envelopment) military strategy, one would infer that over reliance on 'assumptions' is what might have led to the disastrous outcome of the infamous invasion of Cuba by the USA. An article that was authored by Vincent Dueñas titled *'Bay of Pigs: A Case Study in Strategic Leadership and Failed Assumptions'*[32], would certainly have rendered legitimacy to General Benj's assertions.

According to Vincent Dueñas, "The Bay of Pigs invasion was President John F. Kennedy's most controversial foreign policy mistake, and it serves as a useful case study in strategic miscalculation and faulty critical analysis. The failures in the planning and conduct of the operation highlight the leadership challenges and inherent difficulty in attempting to covertly overthrow another government deemed hostile to National Security interests. Planned initially during President Dwight D. Eisenhower's administration and executed by President Kennedy's administration, the Bay of Pigs was devised as an attempt to foment a popular uprising against the government of the newly triumphant Cuban dictator, Fidel Castro. Operation Zapata was a covert effort led by the Central Intelligence Agency (CIA) to organise and train expatriate Cubans as a direct-action force to invade Cuba and establish a base of operations that would incite a general revolt against Castro. The CIA had been responsible for the successful, covert *coups d'état* in Iran under Operation Ajax in 1953, and in Guatemala under Operation Success in 1954, proving a U.S. aptitude for this type of operation. To maintain plausible deniability, President Kennedy wanted it to be executed under the auspices of rich Cuban dissidents who were willing to pay for the cost of the invasion themselves. In the end, the operation was overly complex, based on multiple unsubstantiated assumptions, and underwent too many last-minute changes, which ultimately rendered it impossible for the operation to comply with an absolute requirement that the U.S. maintain plausible deniability of its participation. On the key topic of covert action, Kennedy did not differ from Eisenhower on the philosophy of its usefulness to combat communism. A key difference, however, was Kennedy's lack of experience or understanding of covert operations. As a result, he endorsed Operation Zapata's somewhat hastily and relied heavily on advisors for key analysis and critiques. When viewed in hindsight, advisors failed to communicate to President Kennedy key information about the operation. Furthermore, the impacts of decisions he was making to critical components of the operation seem to have not been discussed or considered. In understanding the shortfalls that plagued the operation what emerges is a patchwork of restraints and assumptions at the strategic level which directly impacted the tactical situation and led to what Jim Rasenberger eloquently called 'the brilliant disaster'. Rasenberger described this as the perfectly planned failure by intelligent men all committed to the defence of democracy. The restraints, identified as strategic priorities, embodied the factors which President Kennedy and the operation needed to put in place in order to set the parameters for how the invasion was to be conducted. The assumptions embodied the accepted knowledge of the situation that could not be verified, but were thought to be generally understood, on which all other decisions were predicated upon. A litany of failed assumptions, arising from several sources ultimately doomed the operation to failure. These fundamental assumptions, such as the belief that the advice to the President was thoroughly and completely vetted by relevant agencies, that each advisor actually believed in the likelihood of success they purported, and the belief that the situation in Cuba itself was well-defined, were all deeply flawed. In hindsight, they amplify the need for executive leadership to conduct vigorous critiques of the operation each time changes were made. The phenomenon of groupthink pervaded the operation and led to the acceptance of conditions that made the tactical situation unwinnable. The real lesson to be gleaned from this example is that strategic leadership must not be content in merely believing that because an operation is justified and well-planned that those characteristics can be counted on as a guarantor of success."

After the trio had debated General Suby's Operation Pseudonakuru military strategy at length with 'heavy punches' exchanged between the two generals, Trump indicated he would reserve his decision for later and suggested they explore other military tactics. Before that and not wanting to take anything for granted, Trump thanked both generals for their detailed knowledge and insight. The merits and demerits of the strategies discussed up to that point were all recorded by Trump in a special compact book that was part and parcel of the weapons that the Court Clerk had delivered to him at their farewell meeting at Inchde, just outside Nebuparadiza.

General Benj proposed another military strategy called 'Operation Bungayama'. Much like General Suby when he introduced the Operation Pseudonakuru military strategy, General Benj went into great detail about the wars he had won during his lifetime on earth using the Bungayama military strategy. He explained that Operation Bungayama military strategy was fulcrumed on deception and involved the infiltration of the enemy territory for the sole purpose of sowing seeds of doubt as to the efficacy or reasons behind the rebellion within the enemy camp. In this case, he suggested sowing doubt among the Muezee 'people' regarding the reality of the eternal life 'propaganda' that Razin used to foment rebellion against King Nguzoo (before his death) and ultimately against Theo Lesa. If they were to succeed in casting doubt among a quarter of Razin's most influential individuals, argued General Benj, that would be sufficient for the tide of rebellion to falter.

General Benj's Operation Bungayama military strategy is similar to the military strategy that Rob Johnson mentioned in his *'Ten of the Greatest Battlefield Tactics'* article which he called 'Deception'. According to Rob, "To work, Deception has to establish significant doubt in the minds of the enemy so that they alter their plans. During World War I, the Royal Navy struggled to find a solution to U-boat attacks in the Atlantic. Yet it was noticed early on that the Germans preferred to surface and use the less sophisticated main armament on the foredeck to sink their victims. Named after their home port, Queenstown in Ireland, a number of 'Q-ships' were deployed – civilian vessels with concealed armaments. With holds packed with wood to enable them to float even when torpedoed, they were deliberately sent into areas where U-boats were known to be operating. As the U-boat surfaced, side panels were dropped to clear the line of fire for concealed guns – a technique used by HMS *Baralong*, which sank U-27 after it surfaced to attack a merchantman off south-west England."

Trump paused for a moment and acknowledged that that was a brilliant military tactic. He pointed out that the only principal huddle was that the Operation Bungayama military strategy was predicated on them being able to successfully infiltrate the Muezee army in the first place and that called for camouflaging themselves in order to look like the Muezee 'people' who looked anything but like them. Both Generals expressed surprise at that revelation because they believed that they somehow looked like the Muezee 'people'. Trump was quick to dismiss that assumption because only he was privy to the detailed description of the Muezee 'people' by the Court Clerk. Further, Trump pointed out that of all the powers imbued on him by the Buite, creation wasn't one of them, so he was unable to recreate any of his soldiers in order for them to look like the Muezee to infiltrate them. He then directed that they explore other military tactics to broaden their options.

General Suby was swift to suggest another military tactic he previously employed during his military career on earth, it was called 'Operation Dabosenge'. He explained that the Operation Dabosenge military strategy was hinged on gathering vast amounts of intelligence information about their enemies before launching an attack based on their intel, such as their intentions and military capabilities, weaknesses and strengths and current location etc.

In Rob Johnson's article (Ten of the Greatest Battlefield Tactics), this military tactic is analogous to what he referred to as the Intelligence military tactic. According to Robson, "Battlefield victory may swivel or depend on accurate timely intelligence information about the enemy, particularly regarding their intentions and their capabilities. In March 1941, naval intelligence learnt through its successful code-breaking that a strong Italian fleet had set out to attack a British convoy. The nearby fleet commander, Admiral Andrew Cunningham, concentrated his forces, and after aerial attacks he disabled an Italian cruiser. The Royal Navy's radar assisted in locating the stricken Italian vessel and its escorts. Cunningham decided to bring to bear maximum firepower by approaching at night. In the subsequent action, the Italians, who possessed no comparable intelligence assets, lost two more heavy cruisers and two destroyers."

After a carefully calculated pause as though waiting to surmise Trump's likely response, General Benj concurred with General Suby and added that since the entire Nebuparadiza had vested interest in ensuring that King Razin's rebellion was crushed to bring about orderliness not only on the moon but also on other planets, releasing intelligence information about the Muezees was in their best interest. He urged Trump to send the request to the Court Clerk without delay. Trump acknowledged the wisdom contained in the words put to him by his generals but was quick to point out impediments to progressing those ideas; the chief one being he had no access to the Court Clerk or anyone else in the Buite or Nebuparadiza before the commencement of the battle against King Razin. Trump was very careful not to mention the name of Theo Lesa in the process. Besides, the Court Clerk had categorically mentioned to Trump that the only other time he would meet him was at the end of his first mission in The Acts of The Chosen Ones (The Acts of The Sheela); whether triumphant or defeated.

General Benj was used to not taking no for an answer. It was therefore not a surprise when he pushed back by insisting that if there was any other way, Trump needed to contact the Court Clerk before setting off for war so that they could access the much-needed intelligence information about King Razin and the Muezee 'people' and kingdom. Obtaining the intelligence information, he insisted, was necessary to ensure the war against King Razin was not protracted as it would enable them to critically analyse the Muezee army to enable them to move into strategic and strong tactical positions before launching the attack.

The Operation Dabosenge military tactic proposed by General Benj is similar to the military tactic Rob Johnson referred to as the 'Strategic Offence and Tactical Defence' based on good intelligence information. Robson wrote that, "In war, it's advisable to advance into a region that's strategically valuable and, once there, to defend a strong tactical position and force the enemy to make a costly attack." He gives the example that, "Babur, the ruler of Kabul, set out to defeat Lodi, the sultan of Delhi, but he had just 12,000 men against 100,000, and though his force was armed with gunpowder weapons, their slow rate of fire made his men vulnerable to Lodi's cavalry. Babur advanced rapidly to Panipat near Delhi, knowing this sudden threat to his opponent's capital would prevent him from seeking refuge behind its walls. He selected the battlefield carefully and formed a barrier of wagons, and Lodi's men made a series of fruitless assaults. Having inflicted heavy losses, Babur counter-attacked, then resumed his offensive into India."

General Suby backed up General Benj's military tactic on the significance of moving into strong strategic locations. He pointed out that the importance of strategic locations was that it was key to them knowing where they would be able to concentrate their military might for maximum results in the enemy territory.

Rob Johnson referred to another military tactic that highlighted the importance of strategic location, and he called it 'Concentration'. He wrote that, "The German strategist Clausewitz regarded the concentration of force as the highest principle of war. This required the accumulation of resources at the precise point and moment where a battle would be decided. In World War I, the German strategy of using air squadrons defensively in 1917 enabled them to marshal their reserves, strike only where they were needed, prioritise their resources and preserve the lives and therefore the experience of their pilots. Jagdgeschwader (Flying Circus) formations were assembled to counter Allied sorties at strategic points on the front. These proved effective and built a reputation for success that was epitomised by Von Richthofen, the Red Baron."

It was now clear to Trump that his two Generals were siding with each other and without fault of their own. It was precisely because they had valuable experience with the deployment of various military tactics during their military careers. He was grateful for their contributions towards the formulation of bespoke military strategies against the Muezees, but he was also not blinded to the fact that he was the boss and there was so much at stake for him to do anything stupid to ruin his chances of becoming a Ngeloi and inheriting eternal life. For instance, he was resolute in his belief that attempting to contact the Court Clerk to request intelligence information was not only stupid but dumb. The Court Clerk's instructions were clear when he told him that he was only allowed to make one contact with Nebuparadiza during the war, which was a single one-off SOS to request for the assistance of the Arch Ngeloi Gabriel, and he wasn't going to jeopardise that.

General Suby suggested he had one final military tactic he wanted to table, and Trump permitted him to do so. It was called 'Operation Buffalo Wozer'. The Operation Buffalo Wozer military tactic had similar tenets to the Deception military tactic in that it was based on deceiving the enemy by putting up a false 'façade' in order to win the war.

The first part of the Operation Buffalo Wozer military tactic involved sending a sizeable number of soldiers onto the battlefield while tactically holding back a relatively larger and more powerful battalion in order to entice the enemy into fully committing their army and other resources based on the mistaken assumption that the invading force had also done the same. Then, depending on how the war was progressing, unleash the fresh battalion held back to inflict maximum assault on the enemy to win the war.

The Operation Buffalo Wozer military tactic is comparable to Rob Johnson's 'Committing the Reserve' military tactic. According to Rob, "One of the principles of war is to achieve one's objectives with an economy of effort, so that a reserve force is preserved to meet the unexpected, reinforce a threatened part of the front or press home to certainty a successful action. At Austerlitz in 1805, Napoleon chose a deployment that would tempt the opposing Austro-Russian force to attack him on his right. In doing so, he knew he would be able to overextend his enemies. Although under significant pressure, Napoleon held his reserve back until he was absolutely certain the allies were committed, then he struck. His troops smashed the allied centre, beat off a counterattack and then curled around the isolated allied left. It was a decisive victory, won by the precise commitment of resources at the critical moment."

Both Trump and General Benj hailed the Operation Buffalo Wozer military tactic as both dazzling and splendid. General Benj pointed out that the major weakness with that military tactic was that a lot depended on the probability of success. To start with, if the initial battalion were to be completely overwhelmed or annihilated by a comparably larger and mightier enemy army, there was a risk that ushering in the reserve battalion might not achieve the intended objective in that it only formed a fraction of the entire army and the benefits of synergy, which occurred when two or more entities interact or cooperate to produce a combined effect that is greater than the sum of its separate parts would have been lost eventually leading to defeat.

According to various scholarly articles, there are many ways in which synergy helps management including creating better effects and results, generating better solutions to problems and achieving organisational vision and mission. Synergy isn't only achieved when two entities work together for a common goal. Methodologies can have synergy too. That's what's called hybrid methodologies. It's taking two different ways to do something and using parts of one and parts of the other for an innovative way to manage a project[33].

Trump allowed for one more military strategy before they could collectively decide, and General Benj jumped on the opportunity. He introduced another military tactic called 'Operation Barba Amarilla'. He explained that this military tactic had its roots in psychological warfare. The enemy forces were made to believe they were losing the war by concentrating fire power on identified 'weak links or least resistant sections' in their chain of operation, thereby forcing them to retreat and eventually surrender.

According to General Benj, the Operation Barba Amarilla military tactic was not only a potent juggernaut, but it was also a double-edged sword in that the quick wins gained boosted the morale of the invading forces while the retreating soldiers within the enemy camp sent the opposite message to their comrades in arms that they were on the verge of losing the war thereby causing them to become demoralised in the process. General Benj further added that sustained attack buoyed by retreating soldiers was an attestation to the fact that 'defeat is a state of mind'.

To add weight to General Benj's statement that defeat is often a time a state of mind, according to one of the best martial artists to have ever walked the earth, Bruce Lee, "Defeat is a state of mind; no one is ever defeated until defeat has been accepted as a reality." Bruce defined defeat not as a mistake or failure but as an attitude of giving up or a depressive attitude, a loss of energy[34].

In Rob Johnson's 'Ten of the Greatest Battlefield Tactics', the Operation Barba Amarilla military strategy would be identical to the 'Shock Action' military tactic. According to Rob, "Often, at the critical moment in a battle, the shock action of a charge or a brief increase in the intensity of fire is enough to break an enemy force. The sudden assault has often been delivered by 'heavy' troops – infantry, cavalry or tanks, designed specifically to punch their way through an enemy line. The impact of that charge, indeed, sometimes the very spectacle of it, can prove too much for the troops on the receiving end. This was the case at the Battle of Arsuf during the Third Crusade (1189–1192). The Europeans under Richard the Lionheart had marched under a rain of arrows for hours, as Saracen archers tried repeatedly to goad them out of their tight formation. Then, suddenly, the knights charged at Saladin's infantry and light cavalry. The effect was dramatic – the Saracens broke and fled or were crushed by the sheer weight of the attack."

After the proposition of military strategies was over, Trump and his deputies turned their attention to selecting the most befitting military strategies. They continued deliberating until they were all fully conversant and agreeable with the merits and demerits of the military strategies that had been proposed. It was up to Trump to show leadership and decide on the appropriate military strategies to deploy. He started by summarising the military tactics that had been proposed and then analysed them further. He also ensured to ask the generals many questions for clarity on anything he was unsure about.

First to be tackled was the Pseudonakuru military tactic which involved taking the enemy by surprise. Trump pointed out that the major weakness with the Pseudonakuru military tactic was that it assumed that the enemy would be unaware of the planned attack. He alluded to the obvious fact that after fomenting the uprise and causing the Muezee kingdom to rebel against king Nguzoo and the mighty Theo Lesa, surely Razin should have expected some form of retribution and to think otherwise would be stupid of them. Therefore, while the Pseudonakuru military tactic was good, Trump was bothered by its inherent risks.

Next to be torn apart was the Buffalo Wozer military tactic based on enticing the enemy into fully committing their military resources based on the smoke screen impression that the invading army had also done so; then causing the enemy to bear the full brunt of the bait. Trump decried that while it was a superb tactic, the risk lay in the many unknowns about the strength and capabilities of the enemy forces and how well they fought against the initial battalion intended to entice them into fully committing their resources.

Trump then analysed the Operation Dabosenge military tactic, which involved gathering large amounts of intelligence information about the enemy before launching an attack. He pointed out that the major weakness with the Dabosenge military tactic was that he had no access to vast amounts of intel on which he could rely before launching an attack.

Following on, Trump considered the Bungayama military tactic, which involved infiltrating the enemy camp to weaken the propaganda or ideology behind the rebellion before launching an assault. He concluded that both the Dabosenge and the Bungayama military tactics would be ineffectual in their situation and the two generals agreed with him for the asserted reasons.

The final military tactic Trump considered and discoursed was the Barba Amarilla military tactic. This tactic was effectively a psychological warfare that focused maximum force on identified weak points within the enemy camp, forcing a segment of the opposing forces to flee or retreat. The idea that underpinned this tactic was that the fleeing soldiers unintentionally communicated the wrong signal to the entire army that they were 'out on a limb' and fighting on their back foot, and the end result? The enemy would lose the will to continue fighting, choosing to either flee or surrender. Trump concluded that he was very much in favour of the Barba Amarilla military tactic.

At the end of their detailed discussions and analyses, Trump and his two generals were all agreeable on three military strategies, which were: the Pseudonakuru, the Buffalo Wozer, and the Barba Amarilla military strategies.

Trump then informed his two generals of the order in which the strategies would be deployed. He emphasised that the key to winning the war against King Razin lay in taking the Muezee 'people' completely by surprise, and that's where the Pseudonakuru military tactic fitted in well, he stressed as the generals listened intently. General Suby, however, warned that they were to exercise caution in deploying the Pseudonakuru military strategy by not being over-reliant on the assumption that King Razin would be completely in the dark about 'probable' punishment from Nebuparadiza to crush the Muezee rebellion.

The mainstay of the Pseudonakuru military tactic was to gain quick wins without wasting many resources by launching a surprise attack against the Muezees. While Trump and his generals acknowledged the risks associated with this military strategy, they were nevertheless all agreeable that they did not want a convoluted war with King Razin hence the fascination with the Pseudonakuru military tactic.

Trump directed that upon arriving at Muarule and gaining access to the abyss that led to the Muezee kingdom, they were to deploy the Buffalo Wozer military tactic, which entailed sending in the first half of the battalion of Combat Ghosts to invade the Muezees while holding back the other half. The initial battalion was intended to entice King Razin to fully commit his military resources, following which the reserve battalion of Combat Ghosts would be unleashed onto the battlefield to get the job done and win the battle.

Trump informed his generals that the reserve army of Combat Ghosts would be stationed close to Muarule (entrance on the Moon leading to the Muezee kingdom) to await a signal from the advance battalion before joining so that the timing was right. Trump emphasised that getting the timing right was going to ensure their resources were used efficiently.

Trump further informed his generals that both the first and reserve battalion of Combat Ghosts were to deploy the Barba Amarilla military tactic in tandem with the Pseudonakuru and Buffalo Wozer military tactic to ensure maximum force was targeted on perceived weak areas within the enemy stronghold to compel them to surrender early in the battle.

Furthermore, Trump ordered that the first battalion of Combat Ghosts to be tactfully ushered onto the battlefield, in line with the Buffalo Wozer military tactic, was going to be led by General Benj. Trump and General Suby were going to remain behind with the second battalion of Combat Ghosts to wait for a signal before storming the battlefield. The two generals were both pleased with the military strategies agreed upon and adopted.

Chapter 27
The War Speech and Military Training

After all had been said and done, General Suby ordered all the Combat Ghosts to attention in readiness for Trump's speech before going to war. Trump stood up, full of authority, mighty and tall, befitting someone on Theo Lesa's noble and sacrosanct mission. He addressed the 1000 strong squad of his Combat Ghosts army and said, "My fellow soldiers, I stand before you today as a warrior of Theo Lesa. I urge you all to stand firm on your wobbly legs, some of you. This is Theo Lesa's battle, and he will ensure we have the victory. Theo Lesa will give us the courage and confidence to put up a good fight and defeat the rebellious King Razin and his wayward Muezee kingdom. Theo Lesa will be our strength and song in this battle, and his name will be exalted throughout the entire universe. Theo Lesa is a warrior; 'The Man of War' is his name. The deep waters will cover king Razin and his army, and they will sink like a stone. Theo Lesa will cast The best of King Razin's officers into deep waters, and they will drown in this battle we are about to take to them. Theo Lesa's right hand is majestic in power and will shatter his enemies. In the greatness of his majesty, Theo Lesa will hurl down those who oppose him to send the message that there can be no other god but Theo Lesa. He will unleash his burning anger to consume his enemies like stubble. By the blast of Theo Lesa's nostrils, the waters will pile up against his enemies. King Razin and his rebellious kingdom have boasted against the mighty Theo Lesa and said, 'We will lay traps, pursue and overtake the mortals and suck their blood to inherit eternal life in defiance of Theo Lesa's unjust and tyrannical rulership of the universe. We will divide the spoils; we will gorge ourselves on the mortals on their visit to the moon, we will draw our sword and destroy mortal beings and suck their blood', but I hereby assure you today," continued Trump, "Theo Lesa will give us victory against the ungrateful and mutinous Muezee 'people'. They will sink like lead in the mighty waters. Who among their gods is like the mighty Theo Lesa? Who is like him – majestic in piety, awesome in glory, working wonders? Theo Lesa will stretch out his right hand as we fight his battle, and their very ground will swallow the disobedient King Razin and his defiant Muezee 'people'. In Theo Lesa's unfailing love, he will lead the obedient ones among the Muezees to safety. In Theo Lesa's strength, he will guide those opposed to King Razin and heal and restore the Muezee kingdom for their sake. The inhabitants of the entire universe will hear and tremble; anguish will grip them and deter them from rebelling against the sacred dictates of Theo Lesa. Their leaders will hear about our victory for Theo Lesa, and they will be terrified and seized with trembling and melt away; terror and dread will fall upon them. By the power of Theo Lesa's arm, they will be as still as a stone until those who obey his commands and fear him pass by. Theo Lesa will reign forever and ever. I hereby charge you, to fight with tenacity and conviction, for victory belongs to Theo Lesa and us."

Following his charismatic and powerful address to his army of Combat Ghosts, Trump checked his plan to see what was to follow. According to his blueprint, the next step was to equip his army with swords and shields. The Court Clerk had instructed Trump that this was to be done after agreeing on the appropriate military strategies with his senior Combat Ghosts, General Suby and General Benj.

Trump issued the command for the 'release' of swords and shields for his Combat Ghosts by repeating the secret codes that the Court Clerk had confided in him. He screamed some strange words in the presence of all the Combat Ghosts and said, "*Lávete ta ópla*," meaning 'receive the weapons'! Immediately after Trump's command, blazing iron swords appeared in the right hand of each Combat Ghost and a shield in their left hand, thereby equipping them for war against King Razin. As directed by the Court Clerk, the secret weapons of mass destruction called NNDWs (i.e., Nebuparadiza Natural Disaster Weapons) could only be operated by Trump because he was The Chosen One (The Sheela); as only he knew all the secret codes.

After equipping his army, Trump signalled to the Combat Ghost Sergeant, General Benj, to take the army through the military drill in preparation for war. As the drill instructor, General Benj's role inter alia involved indoctrinating the Combat Ghosts, as new recruits, into the customs and practices of military life. Following the order, General Benj saluted Trump and took command of the troops. His voice was piercingly sharp and firm, befitting the decorated general he once was while a mortal being on earth.

General Benj explained to all the Combat Ghosts that the primary purpose of the military drill was to teach them a precise and orderly way of doing things during the war and that drill increased skill and coordination. He further said the drill would accustom the Combat Ghosts to group response and that the other purpose served by the drill was to promote teamwork and discipline. Furthermore, General Benj explained that drill was to be conducted with precision. Hence perfection was the only acceptable standard. He also stressed that military drill was meant to cultivate full alertness in the mind of each Combat Ghost not only during the drill but at all times during the war.

General Benj continued to lay the foundation as to the essence of military drill. He said drill consisted of certain movements by which each squad of Combat Ghosts was to move to ensure orderliness, obedience to orders and commands and precision during the war. These attributes, pointed out by General Benj, were important if they were to triumph against King Razin and his army. Therefore, it was critical that each Combat Ghost in the squad or platoon did their part exactly as they were supposed to do. General Benj explained certain drill terms to the Combat Ghosts including:

1) Alignment, which he explained was a straight line upon which several teams were formed.

2) Base, which he explained was the element on which a movement was regulated.

3) Cadence, which he explained was the uniform rhythm by which a movement was executed.

4) Centre, which he explained was the middle point or element of command etc.

After the military drill lecture, General Benj proceeded to induct the Combat Ghosts in military formations and manoeuvres during war. To start with, he divided the Combat Ghosts into four groups and then into two groups thereafter and ensured they were matching and responding to his drill commands.

According to military scholars, a drill command is an oral order of a military leader. The precise movement is affected by how the command is given. Some of the rules that commanders follow in commanding the drill include:

1) When at halt, the commander should face the troops when giving a command. In a command that sets the unit in motion (marching from one point

to another), the commander should move simultaneously with the unit to maintain proper position within the formation.

2) When marching, the commander should turn his/her head in the direction of the troops upon giving a command.

Military drill instructions and practice continued until Trump, General Suby, and General Benj were all satisfied and reassured that the Combat Ghosts were alert and able to respond to instructions promptly. Trump then ordered General Benj to call the troops to attention to mark the end of the drill session.

The next and final session was to be led by General Suby. It was a session in sword fighting techniques to prepare the Combat Ghosts to fight in a smart, adroit and skilful manner. It was a session in swordsmanship. General Suby explained that when using the sword, great power was necessary to instantly put down the enemy.

According to sword scholars[35], swordsmanship is defined as the art of killing an opponent with a sword. Throughout the centuries, many techniques and styles have emerged, developed, and perfected. All medieval warriors acquired numerous sword fighting techniques, and they were able to beautifully execute ducks, parries, dodges, and traps; they made use of notably graceful foot and handwork simultaneously with equally outstanding medieval fighting techniques. The sword scholars further explain that defence for sword fighting techniques was just as necessary, and the primary trick of fighters during the medieval times was to avoid where the enemy's strike/attack would fall; they could easily do so by sidestepping, slipping, ducking, or dodging and these were commonly followed by parries, blocks, deflections and counterattacks. Deflecting an enemy's blow was possible: instead of blocking an enemy's attacks, a medieval fighter could catch the full force of the blow via his weapon or shield.

General Suby gave examples of some core sword fighting techniques which included: Striking, which he said referred to the utilisation of swords to inflict physical harm to the enemy and that it was made up of three parts, namely thrusting, cutting, and slashing. He emphasised that timing was also needed and that this was one of the most important sword fighting techniques that a swordsman needed to perfect. General Suby also stated that, according to earthly history, the masters during the medieval period focused on promoting aggression to control one's reaction during combat.

According to General Suby, distance was another vital sword fighting technique referring to the proper positioning and distance to be observed when engaged in a sword fight. General Suby also touched on some offensive techniques, which according to sword scholars include:

1) The Lunge, which is probably the most basic move when it comes to the offensive sword fighting techniques; this is because it only involves assaulting the enemy by stepping forward while taking a striking position.

2) Feinting, which is one of the very useful sword fighting techniques since this provokes the enemy to make a mistake or to lunge, allowing the fighter to attack first.

3) Disengage, which is a sword fighting technique to also trick the opponent by targeting and attacking a certain spot. After doing so, the fighter moves in a circle-like arc to target and fully attack a different spot.

Furthermore, General Suby touched on defensive techniques, which according to sword scholars include:

1) The Riposte, which is one of the defensive sword fighting techniques that is referred to as a counter-attack executed by a defender after lunging; the defender will either strike back with a parry or lunge.

2) Parrying is another defensive technique that is specifically a counterattack to lunging. It allows the fighter to block the enemy using the sword – this will cause the opponent to be pushed back while the fighter continues to retain their current position.

3) Circle Parrying is also one of the useful defensive sword fighting techniques wherein the user's sword is bent in a circular fashion to be able to catch the tip of the enemy's sword before deflecting it.

General Suby inducted the Combat Ghosts in several other offensive and defensive techniques in swordsmanship, which he learnt during his fierce military career on earth rightly earning him the code name of 'notorious stealthy killer' amongst his peers.

Further, to accelerate learning from the rigorous and demanding training sessions, General Suby paired the Combat Ghosts with different opponents, most of whom had picked up unique fighting styles during the sessions; some were south paw while others were orthodox fighters. According to boxing experts[36], to have an orthodox stance means to stand with your left foot in the front and right foot in the back. To have a southpaw stance means to stand with your right foot in the front and left foot in the back. In general, one would always have their strongest hand in the back. The reason being the back hand has more room and distance to throw a harder punch, whereas the front hand is for throwing fast jabs to set up bigger punches. From a technical standpoint, having one's weak hand in front would make it more likely for it to connect with punches than to have the weak hand all the way in the back.

Trump considered the training session in swordsmanship as key to winning the war against King Razin, so he was in no hurry to call off the training. He deliberately allowed the training session to continue until he was absolutely satisfied that all the Combat Ghosts could use their swords competently. Even after the Combat Ghosts had grown in confidence and proficiency in sword fighting techniques, Trump ordered repeat sessions to be undertaken. The repeat sessions were shrewdly well-spaced to allow the fighting skills to take root to comprehensively prepare the Combat Ghosts for dogmatic, obstinate and intransigent combat against the Muezee army.

According to Zig Ziglar, "Repetition is the mother of learning, the father of action, making it the architect of accomplishment." T.S. Elliot (The Dry Salvages) had this to say on the value of repetition, "We shall not cease from exploration; and the end of all our exploring will be to arrive where we started; and know the place for the first time." Further, according to an article that Robert F Bruner authored from the University of Virginia titled 'Repetition is the First Principle of All Learning', the deepest 'aha's' spring from an encounter and then a return. Repeating the encounter fuses it into one's awareness. One of the biggest mistakes a teacher can make is to forego the return or repetition. The learning process is one of slow engagement with ideas; gradually, the engagement builds to a critical mass when the student actually acquires the idea. Repetition matters because it can hasten and deepen the engagement process. If one cares about the quality of learning, one should consciously design repetitive engagement into courses and daily teaching. To do this well is harder than it seems[37].

Trump and his generals understood the importance of repetition hence the reason they focused on repetitive training sessions for the Combat Ghosts without the need to quickly rush through. Special attention was attached to ensuring the Combat Ghosts were sleek in the art of using hands when executing their sword manoeuvres; were relentless in seeking victory; were accurate in their strikes, and able to absorb and deflect the enemy strikes.

The type of swords that the Combat Ghosts were armed with were very different from the swords that Trump had seen dangling on the hip side of the soldiers during his lifetime on earth. While on earth, Trump's father occasionally took him to watch army processions during special occasions such as the graduation ceremonies for army and police recruits or during events held to celebrate their country's national Independence Day. The main difference was that earthly swords couldn't be used in the fight against the Muezees precisely because of the material that the Muezee 'people' were made of. That's the reason why the Combat Ghosts had to be equipped with fiery blazing swords that could cut through steel or, indeed, any metal.

One would be right in saying the fight between Trump's Combat Ghosts and King Razin's Muezee army wasn't going to be a 'bloody battle' because neither of the two factions had blood running through their veins in the manner that human beings understand biology. What blood was to the bodies of human beings on earth is what mercury was to the bodies of the Muezee 'people'. All this was done in Theo Lesa's unfathomable, impenetrable and inscrutable wisdom as he created the different species in the entire universe.

After the Combat Ghosts had successfully completed their swordsmanship combat lessons, Trump ordered them to attention. He then called upon the Combat Ghost Sergeant, General Benj, to induct them in the interpretation of commands or orders that would be issued via the playing of the bugle before, during, and after the war. This was because, during the early years of his military career, General Benj was a bugler for his army unit, during which time he gained significant experience as he played various bugle calls depending on the occasion.

Bugle calls are musical signals that announce scheduled and certain non-scheduled events on a military, battlefield or ship. Scheduled bugle calls are prescribed by the commander, and non-scheduled calls are sounded by the direction of the commander[38].

The first verifiable formal use of a brass bugle as a military signal device was the Halbmondbläser, or half-moon bugle, used in Hanover in 1758. It was U-shaped (hence its name) and comfortably carried by a shoulder strap attached to the mouthpiece and bell. A defining feature of a bugle call is that it consists only of notes from a single overtone series. Historically, bugles, drums, and other loud musical instruments were used for clear communication in the noise and confusion of a battlefield. Naval bugle calls were also used to command the crew of many warships. Bugle calls typically indicated the change in the daily routines of camp. Every duty around the camp had its own bugle call, and since cavalry had horses to look after, they heard twice as many signals as regular infantry. 'Boots and Saddles' was the most imperative of these signals and could be sounded without warning at any time of day or night, signalling the men to immediately equip themselves and their mounts. Bugle calls also relayed commanders' orders on the battlefield, signalling the troops to Go Forward, To the Left, To the Right, About, Rally on the Chief, Trot, Gallop, Rise up, Lay down, Commence Firing, Cease Firing, Disperse and other specific actions[39].

General Benj played various and distinctive bugle calls to the Combat Ghosts and carefully explained the meaning of each bugle call, including:

1) Drill Call, to send signal for the Combat Ghosts to turnout for drill;
2) Assembly Call, to signal that the Combat Ghosts had to assemble at a designated place;
3) Fatigue Call, to signal that the Combat Ghosts had to ready themselves for fatigue duty;
4) Charge Call, to signal to Combat Ghosts to execute a charge or dash forward into harm's way with deadly intent.

After General Benj had finished his bugle call lessons and Trump was satisfied that the Combat Ghosts were conversant with the meaning of each bugle call, he assigned the role of bugler to the Combat Ghost who went by the name of Talanqui while on earth. Corporal Talanqui served as a bugler in the French Army before being captured and tortured to death during the French Revolution of 1830. Upon being assigned the role of bugler, Corporal Talanqui rehearsed different bugle calls with the Combat Ghosts until Trump, and his deputies were absolutely satisfied that the signals were being interpreted correctly. Trump and his troops were now ready for war against King Razin and his Muezee army.

Given there was no time in the cosmic space where Trump and his army were based, at Inchde, just outside Nebuparadiza, it would be right to assume Trump couldn't have known just how long the military training took to fully prepare for war against the Muezee kingdom. In earthly terms, it would be approximately six months.

According to research, in the USA (and other parts of the world), not all military basic training are created equally, and how long you'll have drill instructors yelling at you depends on your service branch. For instance, Army Basic Combat Training (BCT) lasts nine weeks. This length doesn't count time spent in reception, nor does it count the time spent for job training if you attend an OSUT unit, which combines basic and job training into one combined course. Air Force basic training at Lackland AFB in Texas is eight weeks, plus one week of in-processing, called zero week. Until recently, Air Force basic training was only six weeks, the shortest basic training of any of the military branches. However, the Air Force recently redesigned their basic training program, tacking on two extra weeks in the process. Navy basic training is seven weeks, plus one week at the beginning called processing week, which isn't officially part of basic training, but because you will still have drill instructors yelling at you and telling you what to do, it might as well be. The Marine Corps has the longest basic training – 12 weeks, not including four days of in-processing time. Counting the half week spent in forming (in-processing), one would spend a total of seven and a half weeks in Coast Guard basic training at Cape May, the shortest basic training of all the services[40].

Therefore, it would not be preposterous to conclude that having spent the equivalent of six months in military training, the Combat Ghosts were thoroughly prepared for the mammoth task that lay ahead of them. The military training also significantly improved their chances of succeeding in the war against King Razin, and it was a great morale booster, especially since it was Trump's first assignment in The Acts of The Chosen Ones (The Acts of The Sheela).

Chapter 28
Good Angels, Bad Angels

On Trump's orders, General Suby had word with General Benj, who communicated what had been agreed to Corporal Talanqui. After readying himself, Corporal Talanqui took the bugler and sounded a loud Assembly Call, and all the Combat Ghosts assembled in front of Trump and his deputies. Trump stood up and congratulated the Combat Ghosts for having successfully completed their military training. He also reminded them that they were now at a point of no return. He encouraged his troops to fight valiantly and skilfully for Theo Lesa.

Trump emphasised that 'failure was not an option', a phrase associated with Gene Kranz and the Apollo 13 Moon landing mission. Although Kranz is often attributed to having spoken those words during the mission, he did not. The origin of the phrase is from the preparation for the 1995 film Apollo 13 according to FDO Flight Controller Jerry Bostick, "In preparation for the movie, the script writers, Al Reinert and Bill Broyles, came down to Clear Lake to interview me on 'What are the people in Mission Control really like?'" One of their questions was, "Weren't there times when everybody, or at least a few people, just panicked?"

My answer was, "No, when bad things happened, we just calmly laid out all the options, and failure was not one of them." I immediately sensed that Bill Broyles wanted to leave and assumed that he was bored with the interview.

Only months later did I learn that when they got in their car to leave, he started screaming, "That's it! That's the tag line for the whole movie: Failure is not an option[41]."

Trump continued to issue final instructions until he came to the message one would think the Combat Ghosts were all longing to hear: what was in it for each one of them for taking part in The Acts of The Chosen Ones (The Acts of The

Sheela) if they were to succeed as well as the consequences for being terminated on the battlefield.

The Court Clerk had already informed Trump while in Nebuparadiza on the benefits and consequences of participating in The Acts of The Chosen Ones (The Acts of The Sheela) for the Combat Ghosts. He then gave Trump strict instructions to deliver the message to the Combat Ghosts after their military training, just before heading into war with King Razin. The time was now ripe for Trump to incentivise his troops.

According to one theory of human motivation called the 'incentive theory'[42], actions are often inspired by a desire to gain outside reinforcement. The incentive theory is one of the major theories of motivation and suggests that behaviour is motivated by a desire for reinforcement or incentives. The incentive theory emerged during the 1940s and 1950s, building on the earlier drive theories established by psychologists such as Clark Hull. Rather than focusing on more intrinsic forces behind motivation, the incentive theory proposes that people are pulled towards behaviours that lead to rewards and pushed away from actions that might lead to negative consequences. In other words, differences in behaviour from one person to another or from one situation to another can be traced to the incentives available and the value a person places on those incentives at the time. There have been many psychological questions unanswered by the Incentive theory of motivation. For example, the Incentive theory fails to explain the motivational process when an individual tries to fulfil needs although there is no apparent incentive present, for example, being paid very little to work or having an occupation that doesn't match one's eligibility. Additionally, the incentive theory doesn't explain the motivation of behaviours when there is no incentive available, such as helping a family stranded in a house on fire.

Trump summarised the benefits for the victors and the consequences for the losers in the battle against King Razin as follows: "The victorious Combat Ghosts in the Acts of The Sheela (The Acts of The Chosen Ones) will be sent down to planet earth to dwell among the mortal beings as Angels of Light (or good angels) whose job is going to be that of influencing humans to live lives that were pleasing in the sight of Theo Lesa for them to inherit eternal life at the end of their journey on earth."

Trump gave a detailed job description for the good angels or Angels of Light on earth. It included duties such as influencing human beings to love one another wholeheartedly as this would deter them from vices such as murder, hatred, envy, robbery, deceit, selfishness, greediness etc. Suffice to say, it was a long list of good deeds. The other section of the job description for the Angels of Light contained duties also bordering on good deeds and included: influencing mortals to live joyful and peaceful lives; influencing mortals towards forbearance, kindness, goodness, faithfulness, gentleness and self-control and the list continued. In short, Trump's message was that the victorious Combat Ghosts would be promoted and permanently removed from Gehenakumbo to become Theo Lesa's invisible messengers for good on planet earth.

"The reason why Theo Lesa has chosen to employ the victorious Combat Ghosts as Angels of Light on earth," Trump explained, "is predominantly because of their first-hand dreadful experience in Gehenakumbo. Their nasty experience in Gehenakumbo will qualify and enable the Angels of Light to strive with erring and stubborn human beings to help them live uprightly in the sight of Theo Lesa for them to inherit eternal life after their life on earth comes to an end."

As Trump explained the significance of possessing first-hand experience to the prospective Angels of Light, he recalled a story told by one of his Sunday school teachers, Mr Charlie. He decided to repeat it to the Combat Ghosts, most of whom had no idea what Sunday school was partly because of the horrible lives they led on earth. It was the story of the Richman and Lazarus. "There was a rich man who was dressed in purple and fine linen and lived in luxury every day. A beggar named Lazarus was laid at his gate, covered with sores and longing to eat what fell from the rich man's table. Even the dogs came and licked his sores. The time came when the beggar died, and the angels carried him to Abraham's side. The rich man also died and was buried. In Hades, where he was in torment, he looked up and saw Abraham far away, with Lazarus by his side. So he called to him, 'Father Abraham, have pity on me and send Lazarus to dip the tip of his finger in water and cool my tongue, because I am in agony in this fire'." But Abraham replied, "Son, remember that in your lifetime you received your good things, while Lazarus received bad things, but now he is comforted here and you are in agony. And besides all this, between us and you a great chasm has been set in place, so that those who want to go from here to you cannot, nor can anyone cross over from there to us." He answered, "Then I beg you, Father, send Lazarus to my family, for I have five brothers. Let him warn them, so that they will not also come to this place of torment." Abraham replied, "They have Moses and the

Prophets; let them listen to them." "No, Father Abraham," he said, "but if someone from the dead goes to them, they will repent."

"According to the Sunday school story I have just told you," summed up Trump, "Father Abraham actually refused to grant the rich man's request of sending someone from Hades or Gehenakumbo to go and warn his loved ones on earth so that they didn't have to suffer similar punishment. In this case," contrasted Trump, "Theo Lesa has chosen to do something different by his promise to permanently remove the victorious Combat Ghosts from Gehenakumbo. He will instead transform them into Angels of Light and send them down to earth to take on a new noble role of warning the wayward mortals to turn away from the impending doom and misery that lies ahead if they remain adamant and refuse to change their evil ways."

After detailing the benefits or incentives for winning the war against King Razin, Trump turned to detail the consequences for being terminated (i.e., killed in earthly language) in the Acts of The Sheela (The Acts of The Chosen Ones). He explained that, "The Combat Ghosts who will be terminated during the war will also be sent down to planet earth, however, unlike the Angels of Light who will be tasked to lead human beings into righteous paths; the defeated Combat Ghosts will instead become Dark Angels." Trump explained that the role of Dark Angels on earth, "Will involve performing grim and moribund duties of recruiting more souls for Gehenakumbo. This will be done by luring human beings to commit all manner of evil against their fellow human beings in defiance of Theo Lesa's commandments for human beings to love and care for each other. It will be similar to the insurrection fomented by King Razin among the Muezee 'people'."

Trump detailed the job description for the Dark Angels to the Combat Ghosts, unsurprisingly, it included duties they were mostly familiar with from their time on earth, such as: "Swaying mortals to gravitate towards sexual immorality, impurity and debauchery, idolatry, witchcraft; hatred, discord, jealousy, rage, selfish ambition, dissensions, factions and envy; drunkenness, orgies, racism etc.," and the list continued.

Trump explained that, "In the end, Theo Lesa will hold the Dark Angels accountable for their evil influence among the mortals and their final punishment in Gehenakumbo will far exceed the torment they suffered before their removal from Gehenakumbo to take part in The Acts of The Sheela (The Acts of The Chosen Ones)." He stressed that the only way to avoid the unfortunate eventuality of being transformed into one of the Dark Angels on earth was to put up a good fight and defeat King Razin and his Muezee army. He also pointed out that after being retrieved from Gehenakumbo to take part in the Acts of The Chosen Ones (The Acts of The Sheela), the defeated or terminated Combat Ghosts could not be returned to Gehenakumbo directly according to Theo Lesa's order of things, hence the provisory route of becoming a Dark Angel in the first instance before being returned to Gehenakumbo to suffer greater torment than the initial punishment.

Trump further explained that although the punishment for being terminated or defeated in the battle against King Razin seemed less harsh than what the Combat Ghosts had initially been subjected to in Gehenakumbo, in the grand scheme of things, the opposite was true. He said this was the case because the punishment was merely delayed to an appointed time when Theo Lesa would finally destroy the earth and create a new one in which the upright mortals would put on immortal bodies and live forever.

To let them in on something they had no way of knowing, Trump told the Combat Ghosts that while he was in Nebuparadiza, the Court Clerk informed him that at the appointed time, when Theo Lesa will destroy the earth together with the Dark Angels and all the evil doers, The beautiful Ngeloi, the great prince who protects Theo Lesa's obedient followers on planet earth (those whom the Angels of Light lead), will arise with great power and strength. There will be a time of distress such as has not happened from the beginning of all nations and all creation until then.

"But at that time," explained Trump, "every mortal being whose name is found written in Theo Lesa's Book of the *Faithful Mortals* will be delivered." He also mentioned that the Court Clerk further apprised him that, "On that fearful day, multitudes who sleep in the dust of the earth will awake; some to everlasting life, initially in Nebuparadiza for a thousand years and then back to the new earth after the old earth has been destroyed; while others will awake to shame and contempt and everlasting torment in Gehenakumbo together with the Dark Angels who had deceived them into committing all manner of evil while on earth." He continued by saying, "On that sacred and frightening day, the mortals who are wise will shine like the brightness of the heaven, and those who in obedience to the leadings of the Angels of Light led immaculate lives including leading many to righteousness, will shine like the stars forever and ever."

There was total silence among the Combat Ghosts after Trump had finished talking. After a moment of hesitance, General Suby asked Trump if the Court Clerk had shown him anything else besides what he had just explained to them while he was in Nebuparadiza, especially regarding the appointed time or the end time he had referred to when Theo Lesa would destroy the earth, the Dark Angels as well as their followers and how it was all going to be.

Trump raised his voice to catch the attention of the Combat Ghosts and stressed that he spoke of what he had seen while in Nebuparadiza and that indeed he had been shown images of the end time by the Court Clerk. He explained that the same end-time vision and images were shown to all the fortunate mortals selected to take part in the Acts of The Sheela (The Acts of The Chosen Ones). He then said, "I saw a great white throne and Theo Lesa was seated on it. The earth and the heavens fled from his presence, and there was no place for them; then I saw the dead, great and small, standing before Theo Lesa's throne, and books were opened, and another book was opened, which was *The Book of life*; I saw the dead being judged according to what was recorded in the books, and each mortal was judged according to what they had done. Then I saw death, the Dark Angels and Gehenakumbo all thrown into a lake of fire which was the final death; anyone whose name was not found written in The Book was thrown into the lake of fire."

Trump posed, and then proceeded, "Afterwards, I was shown a new earth for the first earth had passed away, and there was no longer any sea; and I also saw the Divine City, Nebuparadiza, prepared as a bride beautifully dressed for her husband; and then I heard a loud voice that said look! Theo Lesa's dwelling place is now among the mortals, and he will dwell with them forever. He will wipe away every tear from their eyes, and there will be no more death or mourning or crying or pain for the old order of things has passed away."

Trump finished by stating that what he had just told the Combat Ghosts was a true testimony of what the Court Clerk had shown him in Nebuparadiza. He repeated the message that in Theo Lesa's great mercy, he had accorded the Combat Ghosts a rare opportunity to take part in The Acts of The Sheela (The Acts of The Chosen Ones). He reminded them that if they put up a good fight and subjugated the rebellious King Razin and his army, they would live forever as Angels of Light on earth because Theo Lesa's mercies were from everlasting to everlasting. He also added that, on the other hand, losing the battle against King Razin would have the opposite effect and involved luring mortals to commit all manner of evil to ensure they were condemned to Gehenakumbo after death.

Trump then shed light on another issue, he said from what he had gathered from the Court Clerk, most mortal beings on earth were unaware that their evil acts were not caused by mere flesh and blood, neither were their evil deeds brought on by the insatiable desires of their human bodies to commit evil, rather, they were spurred on and influenced by the unseen Dark Angels who were the rulers, the authorities, the powers of the dark world, the spiritual forces of evil from Gehenakumbo. All the Combat Ghosts listened keenly to Trump. One thing for sure was that there was so much at stake in the war against King Razin.

According to an article by Terence Nichols from the University of St Thomas on the subject of 'Angels and Satan'[43], angels in Christian belief are messengers and agents of God. The Hebrew word *malak* (messenger) is translated by the Greek term *angelos* (messenger), and by the English 'angel'. In Christian belief, however, there are good (i.e., Angels of Light), and evil angels (i.e., Dark Angels); Satan is considered a fallen angel, who is associated with other evil angels by Jesus (Matthew 25:41). Angels appear frequently in the Old Testament as God's messengers or agents. Thus, an angel of the Lord appears to Hagar (Genesis 16), telling her that she will conceive a son by Abraham. In Genesis 18, three angels appear as men to Abraham, telling him that he and his wife Sarah will have a son in one year. Angels are the messengers of destruction in Genesis 19, warning Lot and his family to flee from Sodom, which is about to be destroyed by God. An angel of the Lord is said to go before the Israelite army in battle (Exodus 23:20, 23). Again, in 2 Samuel 24, an angel of God is sent to destroy the people in Jerusalem (2 Samuel 24:16). In Job, Satan appears among the 'heavenly beings' (probably angels) who consult with God in his heavenly court. Tobias, the son of Tobit, is helped by the angel Raphael in his journey to find a wife. Angels are also frequently mentioned in the Psalms, for example: "Bless the Lord, O you his angels, you mighty ones who do his bidding, obedient to his spoken word" (Ps. 103:20). Finally, the archangel Michael is said to be Israel's great prince and protector (Daniel 12:1). In the Old Testament, angels frequently appear as men and are not recognised as angels until they announce themselves as angels – this is true, for example, of the angel who appears to Samson's parents (Judges 13), or of Raphael, in his journey with Tobias (Tobit 5–12). Angels play a prominent role in the New Testament also. An angel of God tells Joseph in his dream that the child of Mary is conceived by the Holy Spirit

(Matthew 1:20–21). In Luke's infancy narrative, the angel Gabriel appears first to Zechariah, then to Mary, and announces to her that she will conceive a son by the Holy Spirit (Luke 1:19–38). Angels appear to the shepherds bringing the good news that a Messiah and Saviour has been born in the City of David (Luke 2:9–14). Again, before his crucifixion, Jesus says: "Do you not think that I cannot appeal to my father and he will at once send me more than twelve legions of angels?" (Matthew 26:53). Though some early theologians, (e.g., Augustine) thought that angels might have some kind of material bodies, the contemporary Christian consensus is that angels are spirits. Christian theology explains Satan as a fallen angel. Jesus is reported as saying in Luke: "I watched Satan fall from heaven like a flash of lightening" (Luke 10:18). The account in Revelations 12, concerning the battle of Michael and his angels with the dragon and his angels, has been taken in Christian tradition as the story of Satan's fall from heaven. Angels, therefore, are thought by Christians to be capable of freely choosing for or against God. Satan points to a personal force for evil that is older and greater than humanity. The evil angels who are said by Jesus to accompany Satan are mysterious. Jesus, in fact, passed on the authority over demons to his disciples: "Then Jesus summoned his twelve disciples and gave them authority over unclean spirits, to cast them out, and to cure every disease and every sickness" (Matthew 10:1).

Writing on the same subject of angels from a Muslim perspective, Muhammad H. Muhawesh writes that The Quran refers to angels as the direct servants of God. One of their primary purposes is to relay the message of God unto mankind. Their every action is completed to fulfil the will of God, and they do not possess the capability to deviate from this responsibility. According to Muslims, the role of angels differs very little from the concept of the holy beings held by most Christian sects. Perhaps the primary distinction between the Islamic and Christian understanding of angels is the scale on which they operate within our daily lives. Muslims believe that every human has, among others, two angels that accompany him from the point of his conception; to the point in which his soul exits his body (death. These two angels are responsible for recording the good and bad deeds that their respective host commits. However, it is not just simple legislation these angels record. They are responsible for registering how the sins or good deeds a man commits affect his persona, his soul, and, to an extent, even his physical appearance. There are numerous examples of this occurrence in the holy Quran. The dictation of the Quran itself was received by the prophet Muhammad from the angel Gabriel, who was conveying the message directly from God. The responsibilities of angels exceed relaying divine messages to God's chosen messengers and recording the actions and nature of mankind. Angels are, in fact, responsible for maintaining the perfect equilibrium of nature and all of God's divine laws. They are behind every drop of rain that falls from the clouds, every storm that brews above us, and even the micro ecological miracles of bacteria and germs. It must be noted that the angels are not working autonomously. In fact, their every action is willed by God, and they do not even possess the capability to act on free will. Angels have many other roles according to the teachings of Islam. There are guardian angels that protect us from daily mishaps; there are angels who protect us from the whispers of the devils, and there are angels who are charged with causing us to die. However, Muslims believe that angels do not perform evil acts when they bring us death or calamities since they are only performing tasks that God ordains.

The existence of a being that is bent on misguiding the righteous is a theme common to many faiths. According to Muhammad H. Muhawesh, Islam holds a somewhat unique perspective on the devil's origin, role, and nature. Unlike Christians, Muslims do not believe that Satan was a fallen angel; instead, he is a creature God created from fire among a species of creatures referred to in the Quran as Jinn (Quran 7:13). Members of this species possess the capability to commit sin just like their human counterparts. This is an important distinction, as Islam rejects the idea that angels have the capability to sway from their designated path from God. Furthermore, the Quran states that angels are created solely from light instead of clay, like humans, or fire-like Jinn (Qur'an 7:12–18). The Islamic perspective on the fall of Satan centres on the creation of Adam. The Quran states that when God created Adam, He commanded all of his angels to submit to His new creation. Iblis was present with the angels and commanded by Allah to prostrate himself to Adam. *Iblis* is the name of a Jinni that God allowed to reside among the angels. The story is recounted in Chapter seven of the Quran: 7:12. And WE indeed created you and then WE gave you shape; and then WE said to the angels, "Submit to Adam;" and they all submitted. But *Iblis* did not; he will not be of those who submit. 7:13. God said, "What prevented thee from submitting when I commanded thee?"

He said, "I am better than he. Thou hast created me of fire while him hast thou created of clay." 7:14.

God said, "Then go down; hence, it is not for thee to be arrogant here. Get out; thou art certainly of those who are abased." 7:15.

He said, "Respite me till the day when they will be raised up." 7:16.

God said, "Thou art of those who are respited." 7:17.

He said, "Now, since Thou hast adjudge me to be erring, I will assuredly lie in wait for them on Thy straight path;" 7:18. "Then will I surely come upon them from before them and from behind them and from their right and from their left, and Thou wilt not find most of them to be grateful." 7:19.

God said, "Get out hence, despised and banished. Whosoever of them shall follow thee; I will surely fill Hell with you all." (Quran 7:12–19).

The Quran makes a clear distinction between *Iblis* (the actual name for Lucifer in Arabic) and angels, as *Iblis* boasts of his composition of fire and the Quran states on numerous occasions that angels are created of pure light. When *Iblis* refused to prostrate himself to Adam because Adam was created of clay and *Iblis* of fire is seen by Islam as the root of all feelings of supremacy and hence the cause of all evil. Out of spite and quest for revenge, *Iblis* swore to misguide mankind and lead them to hell. *Iblis* uses his many followers from among the Jinn and people who may or may not be aware that they serve his cause to misguide people. The Quran makes it clear that *Iblis* is humanity's number one enemy and that we must guard ourselves against him and his soldiers (Quran 6:142).

The differences in the understanding of angels between Christianity and Islam are striking. Christians have assumed that there are good and evil angels, that Satan is a fallen angel, and that therefore angels are capable of freely choosing for or against God. On the other hand, Muslims believe there are only good angels and that Satan, and his evil followers are *jinn*. The *jinn* are a class of creatures not found in Christianity: invisible beings (made of fire) capable of choosing for or against God and, therefore, need salvation, just as humans do.

Chapter 29
The Silence of God

Following Trump's final message to his army of Combat Ghosts on the benefits and consequences of fighting in The Acts of The Sheela (The Acts of The Chosen Ones), the team was ready to wage war against King Razin.

Corporal Talanqui received orders and played the First Sergeant's Call on his bugle to signal that the Ghost Combat Sergeant (who was also the First Sergeant), General Benj, was about to form company in readiness for war. After a brief drill to bring the Combat Ghosts to attention, General Suby reminded them, one more time, that they needed to obey and follow the commands and orders at all times in order to succeed in the battle against King Razin. After speaking, he handed the Combat Ghosts back to Trump for further directives.

Trump informed his army that they were going to fly in the western direction towards the moon in a V formation with General Suby and General Benj positioned at the front of the V shape, whereas he was going to be positioned at the rear end of the V formation, in the Centre. In the earthly setup, a V formation is the symmetric V-shaped flight formation of flights of geese, swans, ducks, and other migratory birds. The V formation possibly improves the efficiency of flying birds, particularly over long migratory routes. All the birds except the first fly in the upwash from one of the wingtip vortices of the bird ahead. The upwash assists each bird in supporting its own weight in flight, in the same way a glider can climb or maintain height indefinitely in rising air. According to research, in a V formation of 25 members, each bird can reduce induced drag and increase their range by 71%. The birds flying at the tips and at the front are rotated in a timely cyclical fashion to equally spread flight fatigue among the flock members. Canada geese, ducks and swans commonly form a skein in V formation. V formations also improve aircraft fuel efficiency and are used on military flight missions[44].

Trump and the Combat Ghosts were geared for war, armed with shields in their left hands and blazing swords in their right hands. Corporal Talanqui played the Charge Call on his bugle when everyone was ready. General Suby and General Benj were the first ones to fly off, and each one of them was followed by an equal number of 499 Combat Ghosts. When everyone was airborne, the V shape formation fell into place with Trump at the rear end in the middle. They flew West towards the moon's direction where the Muezee kingdom was located.

The flying spectacle or display was reminiscent of the images that might have flushed through the mind of Reverend Sabine Baring-Gould (1834–1924) of Lew Trenchard in Devon, England, who was an Anglican priest, hagiographer, antiquarian, novelist, folk song collector and eclectic scholar, when he authored the text to the song called 'Onward, Christian Soldiers':

"Onward, Christian soldiers, marching as to war,
With the cross of Jesus going on before.
Christ, the royal Master, leads against the foe;
Forward into battle see His banners go!
At the sign of triumph Satan's host doth flee;
On then, Christian soldiers, on to victory!
Hell's foundations quiver at the shout of praise;
Brothers, lift your voices, loud your anthems raise.
Like a mighty army moves the church of God;
Brothers, we are treading where the saints have trod.
We are not divided, all one body we,
One in hope and doctrine, one in charity.
Crowns and thrones may perish, kingdoms rise and wane,
But the church of Jesus constant will remain.
Gates of hell can never 'gainst that church prevail;
We have Christ's own promise, and that cannot fail.
Onward then, ye people, join our happy throng,
Blend with ours your voices in the triumph song.
Glory, laud, and honour unto Christ the King,
This through countless ages men and angels sing."

Though Trump was at the rear end of the V formation with his deputies at the front, he was instructed to land first on the moon by the Court Clerk, followed by the nine hundred and ninety-eight Combat Ghosts and General Suby and General Benj were to land last. That's what exactly happened. This was not only because Trump was The Chosen One (The Sheela) and team leader of the squad, but it was also because it was only him who knew where the exact entrance to the Muezee kingdom was located on the moon. It was, therefore, a great relief when he landed on the very spot. The name of the secret spot was called 'Muarule'.

Within the secret place called Muarule, there was an invisible door leading to the Muezee Kingdom, only known by Theo Lesa, the beautiful Ngeloi, The Court Clerk and the Ngelois in Nebuparadiza. While still at Inchde (just outside Nebuparadiza), Trump was given directions and the passcodes to the invisible door leading to the Muezee Kingdom by the Court Clerk. He was instructed not to share the details with anyone else.

After all the Combat Ghosts had landed, the Combat Ghost Sergeant, General Benj, ordered the bugler, Corporal Talanqui, to play the Assembly Call for the Combat Ghost troops to assemble at Muarule. When all were assembled, in a firm yet hushed voice, Trump shouted the secret passcode to the invisible door at Muarule, and he emphatically said, "*Ánoixe*," (meaning open) but nothing happened, and nothing moved anywhere. This was followed by a spell of silence, as Trump wondered what to do next. Surely, he couldn't have gotten the passcode wrong?

After a spell of deafening silence, Trump decided to repeat the passcode: '*Ánoixe*' and yet still nothing happened as all the Combat Ghosts waited unwearyingly in silence, with their shields and blazing swords ready for the challenge that lay ahead except the door at Muarule was momentarily proving a challenge and refusing to open. Trump decided to try again. This time, he raised his voice up a notch and emphatically commanded the door to open as he repeated the passcode: "*Ánoi – xe!*" His voice was greeted by silence yet still in a scene akin to the sentiments contained in Andrew Peter's song 'The Silence of God':

"The silence of God, it's enough to drive a man crazy; it'll break a man's faith
    It's enough to make him wonder if he's ever been sane
    When he's bleating for comfort from Thy staff and Thy rod
    And the heaven's only answer is the silence of God
    It'll shake a man's timbers when he loses his heart
    When he has to remember what broke him apart
    This yoke may be easy, but this burden is not

When the crying fields are frozen by the silence of God
There's a statue of Jesus on a monastery knoll
In the hills of Kentucky, all quiet and cold
And He's kneeling in the garden, as silent as a Stone
All His friends are sleeping and He's weeping all alone
And the man of all sorrows, he never forgot
What sorrow is carried by the hearts that he bought
So when the questions dissolve into the silence of God
The aching may remain, but the breaking does not
The aching may remain, but the breaking does not
In the holy, lonesome echo of the silence of God."

Trump shouted the secret code to the invisible door at Muarule two more times, but he was still greeted with silence, so he decided to wait and do nothing. If there was one thing that sustained his belief that the invisible door would eventually open, it was that he was fully convinced that he had followed all the orders. According to research, "Doing the right thing can be a great confidence booster even in the absence of tangible results." As the silence persisted, Trump took solace in the fact that the Court Clerk did not tell him how long it was going to take for the invisible door to open. He was nevertheless of the view that it should have opened the first time he commanded it to open.

Noticing that his boss was in a quandary, General Suby comfortingly moved closer to where Trump was standing as though to communicate the silent message, "I am your friend, and I am right here, I will stand by you until the silent mystery unravels." According to an article that was published by the British Psychological Society (BPS), Friendships play a vital role in helping people get through substantial challenges in life. Until now, little research has been carried out into the role friends and, in particular, best friends play in building resilience to adversity – surviving and thriving in the face of difficult times. The new preliminary study by Dr Rebecca Graber, University of Brighton Senior Lecturer in Psychology, provides long-term statistical evidence of the enormous benefit these valued social relationships have on adults' resilience[45].

As Trump stood there next to General Suby clueless on what to do next, suddenly, a thudding vibration started, and the ground on which they were standing started to shake vigorously. Whilst all the commotion was taking place, some thick dust started to rise from one particular position, which turned out to be the exact spot where the invisible door Trump had eagerly waited to open was positioned.

The fractious noises continued and sounded like metal plates that were in the process of violently separating from each other. Precipitously, there was a huge bang, and a chasm opened up. What followed was completely mind-boggling! Trump and all his Combat Ghosts got sucked into the hollow and cavernous opening. Spookily, they found themselves inside the doorway that led to the Muezee Kingdom. They had finally entered through the invisible door, albeit via a sudden great pull thrust.

Chapter 30
Inside the Invisible Door

The Muezee kingdom was a distance of circa 1000 miles from their current position. Trump turned to Generals Suby and Benj and reminded them of the military tactics they had agreed upon. The idea behind the aide-mémoire (reminder or prompt) was to reaffirm the military strategies approved at Inchde with his deputies who were part of his 'inner circle' before he could address the rest of the Combat Ghosts.

According to John C Maxwell, author, speaker, and pastor who has written many books primarily focusing on leadership, 'a leader's potential is determined by those closest to him' (The Law of Inner Circle). Further, countless scholars have often said nobody does anything great alone. Great leaders surround themselves with great people precisely because Mother Teresa observed, "You can do what I cannot do. I can do what you cannot do. Together we can do great things." That is the power of the Law of the Inner Circle. Every leader needs a team of people they can totally trust and discuss their intimate plans and fears without holding back.

Upon reconvening his inner circle, Trump's initial task was to reconfirm the first military strategy they would use called Operation Pseudonakuru. This aimed to ensure they took King Razin and his army by 'storm', i.e., unawares. He, however, sounded the warning against placing too much reliance on the assumption that King Razin and his rebel minions would be completely in the dark regarding the planned attack on their kingdom.

Trump repeated the spirit of the Operation Pseudonakuru military tactic and emphasised that only the first half of their well-equipped troops led by General Suby would burst onto the Muezee plains and launch the preliminary attack. The other battalion (second half) headed by Trump and General Benj was going to be held back in reserve at their current position, which was within the vicinity of

Muarule. Trump continued his address and repeated his earlier message that their reserve force would only be unleashed onto the battlefield after receiving a signal from Gen Benj that King Razin had fully committed his army and other resources. He also emphasised that the main goal for the 'fresh' second battalion (reserve) when ordered to join the war was to bring the battle to a brutal end by launching a vicious attack on the Muezee army presumably fighting on tired legs at that point. He further added that both battalions (first and second) were to employ the Barba Amarilla military tactic in conjunction with the Pseudonakuru and the Buffalo Wozer military tactics and target maximum force on identified weak offensive and defensive positions within the enemy strongholds in order to compel them to retreat and surrender early in the battle.

After his impromptu inner circle meeting with his two deputies, Trump addressed the rest of the Combat Ghosts. Before his address, Corporal Talanqui acting on General Benj's order played the Assembly Call on his bugle once again, and all the Combat Ghosts gathered around Trump for a refresher or recap of the military tactics they were going to employ.

Trump opened his address by stating the obvious (in that the Combat Ghosts had already heard it before). He repeated his earlier keynote message that the secret to early victory was to take the rebel King Razin and his Muezee kingdom completely by surprise. Like any good leader, he assured his army that Generals Suby and Benj and himself had strong conviction that King Razin and his Muezee fighters would be caught unaware by their sudden attack following the Pseudonakuru military tactic. He directed that once inside the Muezee Kingdom, the first thing the initial battalion (headed by General Benj) was supposed to do was cut off the mercury supply for the Muezee 'people' (which was their version of water) as well as the mineral supplies (food for the Muezees) by positioning troops of Combat Ghosts around the sources of these supplies.

Further, Trump reiterated how their chosen military strategies were going to be implemented and how the game changer would come about after their reserve and fresh second battalion of Combat Ghosts was ushered onto the battlefield to fight enemy soldiers fighting on tired legs. He also indicated the trigger point for their reserve army to join the battle, via a signal from General Benj to Trump or General Suby that King Razin had fallen for their trick and had fully committed his troops and resources, unaware of their booby trap. Upon receiving the signal, Corporal Talanqui was going to play the Charge Call on his bugle for the reserve battalion headed by General Suby under Trump's overall command to burst onto the battlefield 'like a rancorous current of water that has broken through the barriers of a dam to cut down the Muezee soldiers and win the war'.

Finally, Trump re-emphasised to General Benj that upon cutting off the mercury and mineral supplies for the Muezees, he was to command the Combat Ghosts to concentrate their firepower on identified weak pockets of resistance within King Razin's line of defence in the first place. He also repeated, for the third time, that after 'locking horns' with the enemy soldiers fighting along identified 'weak zones', General Benj was to catalyse the Combat Ghosts to fight heroically with the sole aim of crushing any resistance swiftly to break the 'hearts' of their enemies and cause them to either flee or surrender. This, according to Trump, was going to send the signal within the enemy camp that they were engaged in a losing battle in line with the Barba Amarilla military tactic, which was effectively psychological warfare.

In Trump's judgement, affirmed by both General Suby and General Benj, it wasn't going to be necessary to use the NNDWs (Nebuparadiza Natural Disaster Weapons) that had been assigned to him because of his strong conviction that king Razin and his army would be caught unawares with their guard down. The other reason the trio decided against using NNDWs at that stage was to reign in collateral damage (i.e., inadvertent casualties and destruction inflicted on civilians in the course of military operations).

Trump decided enough words had been spoken. It was now time for action and putting their military strategies into practice. Per their plan, the Combat Ghosts were divided into two groups, the first battalion headed by General Benj and the second battalion (reserve) headed by General Suby; both battalions under Trump's overall command.

On Trump's orders, Corporal Talanqui raised his bugle and played the Charge Call, which signalled to the first battalion of Combat Ghosts to execute the charge or gallop forward into harm's way with deadly intent. Shortly after the Charge Call, a total of 500 Combat Ghosts headed by General Benj, in line with the Pseudonakuru military strategy, readied themselves. Armed with blazing swords and shields, the first battalion stretched their wings and flew through the dark abyss taking 'fire' and 'destruction' to King Razin and his rebellious cronies.

According to an article published by the Public Broadcasting Service (PBS) titled *'Going to War: The emotions of war'*[46], war is the most destructive and pitiless of all human activities. And yet the experience of war has a profound and strangely compelling effect on those who fight. Combat kills, maims, and terrifies, but it can also reveal the power of brotherhood and a selfless sense of purpose. It's an experience that changes soldiers, and those changes last a lifetime. Most who join the military and go to war are as young as 18, 19 years old, and many have never been away from home. They have little experience of the world, let alone war, death, and killing. For them and all soldiers, combat is a complex mix of emotions that define the experience of war and shape the experience of coming home. War is many things, and it is unrealistic to pretend that it being exciting isn't one of them. War offers soldiers raw life: vibrant, terrifying, and full blast. According to Sebastian Junger, "War is insanely exciting. It is the worst thing in the world, inflicting both physical and emotional injuries, yet the people who have been through it often miss it terribly." This exhilaration is related to the brain's physiological response to trauma and stress centred in the amygdala – the fight, flight, or freeze part of the brain – triggering adrenaline flow, pushing up pulse and blood pressure levels dramatically, and flooding the heart, brain, and major muscle groups. "There's nothing like it in the world," one Afghanistan veteran told Junger. "If it's negative 20 degrees outside, you're sweating. If it's 120, you're ice cold. It's an adrenaline rush like you can't imagine." The capacity for self-sacrifice among human beings is nowhere more evident than in the bond between soldiers during the war. Sebastian Junger calls this brotherhood the 'core experience of combat. The willingness to die for another person is a form of love and is a profound and essential part of the experience'. Some combat veterans have felt that their lives never mattered more than when they were in combat. This sense of meaning and purpose grows out of protecting and being protected by their comrades in arms. Psychiatrist Jonathan Shay tells us that, "The terror and privation of combat bonds men in a way that the word 'brother' only partly captures. Men become *mothers* to one another in combat." Young soldiers in combat inevitably confront killing. They take life away from others and breach one of the most fundamental moral values of their society, often with long-term consequences. Karl Marlantes often felt satisfaction when his unit killed the enemy, fighting for survival in Vietnam. He felt haunted by those deaths in later years, as do other combat veterans. Barbara Van Dahlen, PhD, Founder and President of Give an Hour, a U.S. based non-profit that provides free mental health care to those who serve and their families, believes young soldiers should be better prepared emotionally for the realities of war, even though no one can fully prepare for the experience of combat. While killing an enemy combatant might be unavoidable, the act of killing is understandably troubling and potentially psychologically destructive. Understanding this reality can help warriors heal emotionally from the psychological consequences of war.

The major distinction between earthly wars and the wars that The Chosen Ones fought in The Acts of The Sheela (The Acts of The Chosen Ones) lay in the fact that the agents of Nebuparadiza, in this instance Trump and the Combat Ghosts, were not mortal beings. They were supernatural beings who had embarked on mysterious and perplexing battles in their afterlife experience, which no 'flesh and blood' on earth could ever fully comprehend or even start to imagine. To the 'unsophisticated' beloved family members to these poor departed souls left behind on earth, they were still buried six feet under the ground, and for the affluent, in some of the most expensive caskets or coffins that money can buy evinced by the overpriced tombstones erected in the ground above their lifeless and decomposed bodies with comforting, and in some cases, hilarious epitaphs (inscriptions) splashed right across the cold and 'sombre' tombstones ranging from:

Here lies an Atheist, all dressed up and nowhere to go,

Here lies Jacob Yeast, pardon me for not rising,

Go away, I'm asleep,

Now I know something you don't…to raised four beautiful daughters with only one bathroom and still there was love.

The magnitude of the afterlife's unknowns and mysteries is inextricably compounded by the various beliefs among mortals on what happens to human beings after death. For instance, Atheist views on life after death vary depending on individual beliefs. Some Atheists don't believe in any sort of life after death, but others believe in the existence of spirits, the afterlife, or reincarnation.

Bardo, the intermediate state, is the time between death and rebirth where Buddhists experience different phenomena. Buddhists believe in reincarnation, the cycle of death and rebirth. Since Buddhists don't believe in the existence of souls, reincarnation means taking on another body in their next life. However, being in this reincarnation cycle is considered a suffering experience, and the goal is to escape this cycle by reaching Nirvana. Nirvana is seen as an end to suffering and to some, as a heavenly paradise.

Christian belief in the afterlife depends on what denomination they're a part of, but most believe in the resurrection of Jesus, the existence of the afterlife, and that moral choices you make on earth affect whether you end up in Heaven or Hell. Catholic Christians believe in Purgatory, a place where the dead destined for Heaven must first go if they need purification for their sins.

Hindus believe in reincarnation after death and that the atman, or soul, receives a new body and life depending on Karma or good and bad actions taken in their previous life. They believe you can be reincarnated as humans and animals, insects, and plants. The goal is to be released from the reincarnation cycle and achieve Moksha, liberation from the cycle. After being freed from the cycle, it's believed they return to be with Brahman.

Jewish afterlife beliefs depend on the individual's beliefs. Jews focus more on their life on earth, but most Jews believe there is an afterlife, but it can come in many forms. Some Jews believe in a reincarnation cycle, while others believe in the World to Come, a heaven-like paradise.

Muslims believe that death is the end of physical life on earth, but the soul lives on. The soul goes to the Angel of Death to wait for Judgment Day. On Judgment Day, their actions during their time on earth will be judged to determine whether they go to Jannat, paradise or Jahannam, Hell.

Spiritualists believe that the afterlife, or spirit world, is a realm where spirits evolve. They believe souls live on and take their consciousness with them. They believe souls can interact with those living on earth through mediums in the spirit world and physical world[47].

As for Trump and the Combat Ghosts, whatever belief they held on 'life-after-death' came to an end the moment they crossed over to this new world and were now living their reality by partaking in The Acts of The Sheela (The Acts of The Chosen Ones).

Chapter 31
Incursion into the Revolutionary Kingdom

General Benj and the 499 Combat Ghosts flew boldly through the tunnel leading to the Muezee Kingdom but became slightly more cautious as they approached the Kingdom. Before starting off, Trump informed Gen Benj that the shining mercury river that flowed through the Muezee kingdom and beyond could be seen on approach to the Kingdom. This was according to the information relayed to him by the Court Clerk. General Benj was, therefore, in no doubt that they had neared the Muezee Kingdom upon seeing 'twinkles' on the horizon as they flew through the dark abyss.

When they were a short distance from the Muezee kingdom, General Benj ordered 100 Combat Ghosts to be stationed along the mercury river, which supplied the Muezee 'people' with mercury (their version of 'water') in order to cut off the supply. He ordered a further 100 Combat Ghosts to be stationed around the quarry where the Muezee 'people' extracted their food which was an assortment of mineral deposits ranging from precious minerals to base metal for the same reason. The remaining 299 Combat Ghosts were given orders to attack the Muezee army by way of ambush under the command of General Benj. The plan was to quickly identify weak pockets of resistance in the Muezee army as directed by Trump (following the Barba Amarilla military tactic) and then concentrate fire power on those areas.

In a shocking and unsettling twist of events, unbeknownst to Trump and the Combat Ghosts, King Razin and his Muezee army had long anticipated the attack. The only thing they didn't know was the actual moment of 'visitation'. After ascending to the throne on the back of the promise to accord his blinkered loyal follower's eternal life once they got hold of human blood, King Razin and his followers slowly but consistently started to dig their way to the surface of the moon. They were, however, not aware of the secret tunnel or route via Muarule to their Kingdom that the special agents used from Nebuparadiza (the Combat Ghosts) led by Trump, who was The Chosen One (The Sheela); aided by General Suby and General Benj to quell the rebellion engineered by Razin amongst the Muezee 'people'.

Something alerted King Razin and his army that the moment they had dreaded for so long was now upon them. It was the door opening process at Muarule after Trump's several attempts to open it. Paradoxically, the commotion, the shaking of the ground and the eerie noises that preceded the opening of the secret door at Muarule was inadvertently picked up by King Razin and his army. It was a tell-tale sign which they instinctively and portentously correctly interpreted as not only being unusual but also a sign of something dangerous skulking in the shadows of their tranquil Kingdom. In response to the disconcerting occurrences whose reverberations reached the shores of his Kingdom, King Razin immediately ordered his army to arm themselves and to hide in the trenches that were dotted around the field where the invaders were most likely to land before launching an attack on his kingdom. King Razin's military orders were intended to defend the Muezee Kingdom and protect their 'intellectual property', which constituted 'the means of attaining eternal life by acquiring human blood'.

Consequently, the 299 Combat Ghosts under General Benj's command walked right straight into King Razin's well laid out 'spider web' as they were unaware of the trap that awaited their arrival. As soon as General Benj and his troops ventured onto the Muezee fields with 'deadly' intent, they were met with equal and opposite firepower. King Razin's army burst out from their trenches with boisterous, barbaric, squawky and cackly screams, which could have only spelt doom and death to the assailants for the wanton incursion into the 'royal' Muezee Kingdom!

The distressing uproars, clatters, jangles and blares from King Razin's army were also a bold declaration of war whose aim was to thwart, confound and wipe out the intruders. General Benj and his soldiers were completely besieged by a militia of 'cold-blooded' brutes who rushed at them from all directions with weapons that included burning rocks, blazing spears and arrows, swords to mention but a few. Lethal objects and instruments of destruction rained incessantly on the Combat Ghosts from all directions who, through a tapestry of impulsive reaction and good military training, managed to put up formidable resistance from the unexpected vicious counterattack that King Razin and his army mounted.

As opposed to being in the driving seat of the battle in accordance with their brilliantly crafted military strategies, General Benj and his army were caught on the back foot with no room to implement any of the tactics logically. Upon seeing their comrades come under precipitous heavy attack, the 200 Combat Ghosts who were mandated to cut off the mercury and mineral supplies for the Muezee army had no other option but to abandon their positions and join the fight. The battle rapidly descended into a bitter and nasty fight accompanied by deafening clamour and sparks of fire from the clashing of the blazing swords coupled with bangs and thunderous clatters from the burning rocks and spears that were being hurled continually at the Combat Ghosts, and there was dust everywhere.

Drawing on lessons learnt from their six months long military training, General Benj and his army of Combat Ghosts put up a spirited and gallant fight, having overcome the shock of the counter-ambush attack that King Razin splendidly mounted. The situation they found themselves in was completely unexpected as their neatly hewn military strategies had all pointed to a swift victory over the rebellious King Razin and his army.

General Benj assiduously and vigorously commanded his troops as the war progressed. Like a bare-knuckle boxing coach, he constantly barked orders urging the Combat Ghosts to fight on, and the response was positively correlated to his orders. Under extreme pressure and intense fire, the Combat Ghosts kept alive the prize that lay ahead of them if they were to succeed in that royal battle which was billboarded *'The Acts of The Chosen Ones' (The Acts of The Sheela)*, ordained by the mighty and fearsome Theo Lesa.

Chapter 32
Heroic Episodes

When the battle was nearing its climax, it became clear to some prominent Combat Ghosts that the relentless military orders that hitherto came from Gen Benj had ceased. It was an abrupt end, but given the confusion, it wasn't clear why or when the orders came to an end. However, what was clear was that the lack of orders was harming the morale and performance of the Combat Ghost warriors.

One such prominent and notable Combat Ghost went by the name of Sepov during his lifetime on earth. He was a rebel killed during the Tatar rebellion of 1552–1556. The Tatar rebellion was an uprising against Muscovite Russia, aimed to restore the Kazan Khanate, which Moscow had conquered in October 1552. The rebel armies mostly consisted of Tatars, Chuvashes, Cheremises, Mordvins and Udmurts. Russian troops under Andrey Kurbsky and Alexander Gorbatyi-Shuisky opposed the 'rebels' and thousands died on both sides, and Sepov (now a Combat Ghost), was among the dead rebels.

Upon noting the disquieting and nerve-wracking situation and the void that had developed in the chain of command caused by Gen Benj's abrupt silence, Sepov took charge and started to issue commands and orders not only to direct the fight but also to encourage and rally his fellow Combat Ghosts to continue fighting to the very bitter end.

King Razin and his Muezee forces put up a determined and brave fight and eventually started to turn the tide of the battle in their favour as the number of the Combat Ghosts on the battlefield kept depleting.

As Trump had forewarned, Combat Ghosts terminated during the war were immediately hurled down to earth, where they became Dark Angels. Whereas the Combat Ghosts who got terminated (killed) disappeared from the battlefield and reappeared in another realm and form on earth, the bodies of the Muezee rebels were littered all over the battlefield though relatively fewer compared to the number of Combat Ghosts who had been terminated.

Ingeniously, as part of their preparation for probable 'future' confrontation, King Razin had also hatched a plan similar to Trump's Operation Pseudonakuru military strategy. The battle with the Combat Ghosts might have been raging, but smartly he hadn't fully committed all his military resources to the battlefield. The battalion of King Razin's army that had countered the attack by the Combat Ghosts was the one he had 'planted' in the trenches. He still had more soldiers hidden in the surrounding hills and mountains, ready to pounce upon being ordered to engage.

As a result of King Razin's own version of the 'Pseudonakuru military tactic' what followed next was completely horrifying. As though to add 'salt to the wound' in a battle, he seemed to have the upper hand. King Razin then issued orders for the reserve forces he had held back to pour onto the battlefield in order to finish off their resolute and obstinate adversaries. He was eager to send a crystal clear message to Theo Lesa that all they were fighting for was justice. According to King Razin and his zealous adherents, all they were asking was to be accorded the same opportunity as the human beings; the prospect to inherit eternal life after death. That was the root cause of the rebellion that King Razin had successfully fomented against Theo Lesa, and he was now in pole position to win that campaign.

During his rebel days on earth, Sepov was a vicious and ferocious savage, and his heroism proved true during the Tatar rebellion when he fought against the mighty Russian forces. He was nicknamed 'the blood hound' by his colleagues for his killer instincts and his wit and ability to read the situation and use initiative to resolve complex and dangerous military situations. Therefore, he was fighting hard at the same time, trying to use his initiative to crack the cocoon they were in contrived by no other than the insurgent King Razin.

It is said that 'initiative' in a chess position belongs to the player who can make threats that cannot be ignored, thus putting the opponent in the position of having to spend turns responding to threats rather than creating new threats. Initiative in a military context is whether or not you have the choice to take the offensive (i.e., make threats that cannot be ignored), forcing your opponent to respond before they are prepared. Ideally, your enemy will waste effort and resources on responding to your threat rather than getting closer to reaching their objective, either physically or metaphorically. Seeking to have the initiative in battle is seeking to have an advantage. Every commander in battle seeks an advantage over their adversary. Commanders must understand when they do or do not have the initiative. This is critical to being in control of their own destiny. Without this understanding, it is difficult to weigh risk in taking fleeting opportunity and pressing harder against the enemy, or to recognise when your force is being dragged along by its nose. Understanding whether you have the initiative is not as clear cut as a methodology or a discernible indicator and warning. It requires commanders at all levels to discuss whether they believe they have the initiative and why they have formed their opinion. Is the enemy imposing friction on me? Are we constantly surprised or pinned down by the enemy? Is the enemy where we think they are? Is our plan working? Does the plan need to change? Is a transition required or approaching? All questions that commanders must constantly ask themselves and their subordinates to understand whether they honestly believe they have the initiative[48].

Having assumed the role of 'shadow commander' for the first battalion of the Combat Ghosts, it became apparent to Sepov that General Benj had either fled the battlefield or had been terminated. He concluded that the former was almost impossible, for there was no way General Benj could have abandoned his troops. Besides, there was nowhere else to run to in the 'death trap' of the Muezee plains, Sepov convinced himself. Unbeknownst to Sepov and his fellow Combat Ghosts who continued fighting according to the script, albeit in the absence of orders from General Benj (but from the self-imposed commander Sepov), it was the shocking truth that General Benj was no more!

General Benj got terminated (killed) after being struck by a flurry of highly charged blazing rocks and arrows as the battle grew more intense. His termination wasn't accidental, the Muezee soldiers specifically targeted him on orders from King Razin. This was part of King Razin's military tactic of winning the war upon discovering from the intel gathered during the battle that General Benj was the ringleader of the Combat Ghosts. The military tactic that King Razin applied to successfully orchestrate the termination of Gen Benj was called 'Ichkuria military tactic' among the Muezee military top brass. It was based on the idea that 'the quickest way to kill the tail is to kill the headfirst'.

During the battle's early stages, General Benj evaded numerous attacks targeted at him by being inconspicuous while issuing orders. However, as General Benj upped the intensity of his orders in response to the tempo of the battle, instead of ensuring he was safe at the same time that he was issuing orders, he inadvertently placed more emphasis on the latter, thereby exposing himself to the assault that took him out.

Upon being terminated, General Benj exploded into some dark smoke and was hurled down to earth, where he became a Dark Angel. Despite being Trump's third in Command and having courageously served in the crusade that Theo Lesa ordered, there were no exceptions to the rule or way of escaping the consequences for being terminated in The Acts of The Chosen Ones (The Acts of The Sheela).

As intimated by Trump on numerous occasions, General Benj's new assignment as a Dark Angel on earth was to operate among the mortals as one of the invisible agents whose mission was to deceive and recruit gullible and unwary mortals for Gehenakumbo pending final destruction by Theo Lesa. Alas, therefore, General Benj was among the first cohort of Combat Ghosts to be terminated in The Acts of The Sheela (The Acts of The Chosen Ones).

Chapter 33
Fighting in Retreat

Upon noticing King Razin's troops pouring onto the battlefield in large numbers from some unknown source, Sepov realised it was time to turn to Plan B. The alternative plan B that Sepov devised was about finding means, albeit in the confusion of the battle, to alert Trump and General Suby about the unfortunate turn of events. Trump and General Suby and the second battalion of reserve Combat Ghosts were still waiting close to Muarule for a signal from General Benj before joining the war. This conformed with the Pseudonakuru military strategy, but little did they know that the Combat Ghost Sergeant, General Benj, was no more.

Sepov's conundrum or enigma was how to send the signal to Trump and General Suby, given the dangerous circumstances they were in. After evaluating and sifting through various options, he made up his mind that the only way to do so was to withdraw some of the Combat Ghosts from the battlefield by cunningly continuing fighting while slowly withdrawing or reversing into the direction leading to the secret tunnel through which they came. Notwithstanding that they were in the middle of a hot war and as dangerous as that might have been, Sepov cleverly liaised with ten carefully selected Combat Ghosts and instructed them to fight in retreat. When they were all on the same 'wavelength' as to what he meant and was trying to achieve, he ordered them to continue fighting while slowly moving back towards the escape route.

The 'superior' order that eventually came full square to the ten Combat Ghosts whom Sepov chose to fight in retreat was that upon reaching the entrance to the secret tunnel, they were to allow one Combat Ghost to escape in order to alert Trump and General Suby and the second battalion of Combat Ghosts to join the battle right away. The Operation Pseudonakuru military strategy had failed to hold water largely due to the wrong assumptions on which it was based. The magnitude of the miscalculation was so catastrophic that the first battalion of Combat Ghosts walked right straight into the snare expertly laid by King Razin. This was against the backdrop of Trump's supposedly carefully planned ruse, which was meant to ensnare King Razin and his army, but tables had turned.

Having firmly bought into Sepov's Plan B, the ten Combat Ghosts continued to fight skilfully while slowly retreating from the battlefield, juggling both the offensive and defensive fighting techniques learnt during their preparatory military training at Inchde. Overall, whatever that first battalion of Combat Ghosts lacked (largely attributable to their diminishing headcount), they surely made up in fighting skills; thanks to the intense military training they had undergone. The fact that Sepov and the ten Combat Ghosts were in 'intentional-retreat-mode' meant they were fighting twice as hard as the other Combat Ghosts in a battle in which they were clearly outnumbered. The closer they got to the escape or exit route, the more they had to dig in to parry off attacks and also counterattack at the same time.

The fighting in retreat tactic that Sepov hatched was evocative or redolent of the British retreat in World War II to Dunkirk. According to an article titled 'Dunkirk was a victory for morale but ultimately a humiliating military defeat'[49], authored by Gerard Oram (Director of Programmes for War and Society, from Swansea University), although Dunkirk is one of the proudest moments of World War II that led to the evacuation of 338,226 troops and other personnel from the beaches of northern France (which took place between 26th of May and 4th of June 1940), Dunkirk was only a victory for morale but ultimately a humiliating military defeat; and people quite often now forget the catastrophic defeat that led to 'Operation Dynamo'. On 10 May 1940, the British Expeditionary Force (BEF), totalling approximately 400,000 at the height of the campaign and commanded by Lord Gort, was deployed in Belgium, alongside its allies, as part of a defensive line against German invasion. But by 13 May, German units had pierced French defences and crossed the River Meuse near Sedan, close to the Belgian border in northeast France. Within a week, German panzer divisions had reached the French coast south of Boulogne, trapping the BEF and the French 1st Army in a small pocket around the channel ports, cutting them off from the main Allied force. The British retreat to Dunkirk was controversial. But poor planning, intelligence, leadership and communications had left the allies in a desperate situation. Prime minister Winston Churchill had promised the French that the BEF would participate in a coordinated counterattack against the German flank. However, Lord Gort was preparing to evacuate his troops, apparently with the blessing of the secretary of state for war, Anthony Eden. The BEF staged a fighting retreat to the coast to escape annihilation, and rescue plans were hastily made, including appeals for owners of 'self-propelled pleasure craft between 30 and 100 feet' to contact the Admiralty. Exhausted troops converged on Dunkirk. Naturally, there was panic and chaos on the beaches. The town and port were bombed, and time was running out. Crucial time was bought by those covering the retreat. At Lille, the French 1st Army fought German forces to a standstill for four days, despite being hopelessly outnumbered and lacking any armour. The French forces forming a perimeter defence around Dunkirk were killed or captured. British forces covering the retreat also paid a high price. Those who were not killed in the fighting became prisoners of war. But even that was no guarantee of safety. At the village of Le Paradis, 97 British troops who had surrendered were massacred by the SS. At least 200 Muslim soldiers of the French army met with the same fate. As the quays of Dunkirk had been destroyed, the evacuation had to take place from the shore itself, justifying the foresight of the Admiralty to co-opt the small ships. These small craft transported troops to larger vessels of the Royal Navy and French Navy under frequent harassment from the Luftwaffe. Remarkably, however, Hitler was persuaded to halt the advance on land in favour of airstrikes against the men on the beaches. The limitations of isolated air operations and the deteriorating weather that reduced the number of sorties (missions) flown probably saved many British and French lives. The BEF was rescued, but this was far from a victory. More than 50,000 men had been lost (killed, missing or captured), and an enormous number of tanks, guns, and trucks had been left behind, too.

Owing to the determined and dogmatic fight put up by King Razin's troops, Sepov lost three Combat Ghosts from the ten he had originally selected to fight in retreat and was now down to seven soldiers. The seven soldiers, however, continued to fight as though it was still ten of them fighting with the secret intent to send SOS to Trump and others. The closer they got to the secret exit route, the more intense the fighting became. It was as though King Razin and his troops had second-guessed Sepov's undercover 'Plan B' and were determined to stymie their efforts to alert Trump and the reserve Combat Ghosts from joining the war. As Sepov and the undercover Combat Ghosts neared the exit route, three more Combat Ghosts were terminated in the blink of an eye leaving only four from the original 'special' team of ten.

One of the brutal advantages that the Muezee mutineers held over the Combat Ghost soldiers was that they fought dirty. Whereas the Combat Ghosts chiefly relied on their blazing swords and shields and skills such as the ability to fly and flip over to attack and duck fiery pebbles and other deadly objectives that were directed at them, the Muezees had no fighting pattern and employed unpredictable stratagems and wiles that incorporated all manner of weapons that maimed and terminated (killed), and they came from any direction.

Some of the weapons used by the Muezee soldiers were:

i) Blazing swords. Their swords were different from the ones that the Combat Ghosts used. The swords for the Muezee army were fast-moving weapons that could stab and slice and delivered the most damage for the least effort.

ii) Lances. The force of an advancing Muezee soldier concentrated through the point of a lance which gave it incredible power. But it was a one-shot weapon, often shattering on impact and was no use up close, nevertheless effective.

iii) Burning spears, Axes, Mace. Burning spears were used in large defensive blocks, and they provided an antidote to Combat Ghosts' charges.

iv) Flaming Bows. Muezee soldiers had three types of bows: recurve bows, crossbows, and longbows used to thrust and propel burning arrows and had range and capacity to terminate. The force of their impact could not only terminate but also incapacitate and shatter morale, although the morale of the Combat Ghosts remained intact primarily driven by the tantalising ultimate prize for winning the war, which was going to culminate in eternal respite from Gehenakumbo.

v) Trebuchet. These weapons were used to repeatedly fling burning rocks into the advancing Combat Ghosts, but given the confusion on the battlefield, some Muezees ended up being terminated by friendly fire from their own camp.

vi) Daggers. The Muezee soldiers used these to punch through the gaps in the armours of the Combat Ghosts. King Razin also used Daggers and his army against incapacitated Combat Ghosts (e.g., those with clipped off wings) in order to finish them off and dispatch them on a one-way ticket to mortal land (earth) were they became Dark Angels.

Some of the weapons and fighting methodologies employed by King Razin's army in battle bore a resemblance to those used in the medieval warfare among mortals on planet earth. According to historical facts, medieval warfare was mostly decided by sieges, and here a different sort of weapon mattered. Loades refers to the trebuchet as the 'weapon par excellence for the siege'. By flinging rocks repeatedly at a single point, it could hammer a hole in a castle's defences, letting the attackers in. Traction trebuchets were in use from the start of the Middle Ages. The arrival of the counterweight trebuchet in the thirteenth century increased their power, making even great castles vulnerable. In July 1304, the garrison of Stirling Castle surrendered to Edward I rather than face Warwolf, Edward's massive counterweight trebuchet. Further, historians believe daggers were used to kill Richard III at the Battle of Bosworth Field. After only two years in power, King Richard III of England was killed in 1485 at the Battle of Bosworth Field, when a force loyal to his rival, Henry Tudor (Henry VII), crushed his reckless cavalry charge. Richard's death at age 32 marked the end of the 330-year-old Plantagenet dynasty and the beginning of the reign of the Tudors, who vilified him as brutal and corrupt. Based on Richard's remains, DeVries believes that his helmet was cut off with daggers, exposing him to the attacks that killed him[50].

Following the termination of another Combat Ghost from his original 'special team' of ten, Sepov was now down to three Combat Ghosts who bravely fought side by side with him and were within a throw stone distance from the secret exit route. Effectively, they were now within reach of a solution to help them tilt the battle in their favour. It was all dependant on them being able to tap Trump and the reserve Combat Ghosts to join the war, and the stakes couldn't have been higher. But as the 'heat' from the war intensified on the plains of the Muezee Kingdom, leading to the termination of more Combat Ghosts outside the 'special team' charged with the responsibility to call for help, Sepov and his fellow Combat Ghosts from the first battalion were on course to being obliterated.

Oddly, the timing for the SOS couldn't have been righter because all signs were now pointing to the fact that King Razin had fully committed his troops and other military resources to the battle in line with his own version of the 'Pseudonakuru' military strategy. The Combat Ghosts were outnumbered by far, yet victory still remained a tantalising reality for King Razin.

Just as one of the Combat Ghosts from Sepov's 'special team' was about to enter the secret tunnel and exit the battlefield to call for support, deadly objects started to rain on them at an unprecedented rate. It was at a level of firepower concentration that Sepov and his Combat Ghosts (especially those tasked to fight in retreat) had not experienced to that point. They were compelled to switch to the survival mode and had to do more defending than attacking to achieve their secret goal rooted in Sepov's Plan B.

The whole battlefield was on fire as the fighting intensified, and things changed so fast. One thing led to the other, and by the time Sepov captured a rare opportunity to assess their chances of executing 'Plan B' given they were now so close to the entrance to the secret tunnel, it sadly dawned on him that all the remaining three Combat Ghosts from his 'special team' had been terminated. He was now vulnerable to becoming the next victim. His reaction to the grim and sombre reality he faced was to ignore the impending doom, and he fought even harder than before.

Undeniably Sepov's 'ingenious' Plan B had come at a huge cost. He was now the only Combat Ghost, by default, who even had the faintest chance of escaping to sound the alarm if he were to survive that level of sustained attack from their Muezee foes. The Plan he had efficaciously sold to his fellow Combat Ghosts ended in the termination of all his ten comrades from the 'special team'. Despite being a brave warrior and de facto commander whose contribution was desperately needed on the battlefield by his fellow Combat Ghosts who were under heavy attack and were depleting faster than 'diarrhoea', the benefits of him escaping to call for help by far outweighed the benefits of him continuing to fight a losing battle.

Chapter 34
The Point of No Return

In the treacherous moments that followed, Sepov thought to himself...*If it's not me to deliver the SOS message to Trump and the reserve Combat Ghosts, then who?* Besides, he was the only one closest to the secret exit route, albeit dangerously so. Sepov had encountered a situation famously known as the 'point of no return'. In the 'Rubicon Theory of War', Dominic D.P. Johnson and Dominic Tierney explain how the path to conflict reaches the point of no return based on an illustration. In 49 BC, Julius Caesar halted his army on the banks of the Rubicon River in northern Italy. According to Suetonius, he paused in momentary hesitation before sweeping across the waters towards Rome with the immortal phrase '*Alae iacta est*' (The die has been cast). By violating an ancient Roman law forbidding any general to cross the Rubicon with an army, Caesar's decision made war inevitable. Ever since 'crossing the Rubicon' has come to symbolise a 'point of no return' when the time for deliberation is over, and action is at hand. When people believe they have crossed a psychological Rubicon and perceive war to be imminent, they switch from what psychologists call a 'deliberative' to an 'implemental' mindset, triggering several psychological biases, most notably overconfidence. These biases can cause an increase in aggressive or risky military planning[51].

While the first battalion of Combat Ghosts under Sepov's de facto command was contending with 'hell' fire that was switched on full throttle by King Razin and his army and were almost subsumed in the menacing shadows of the precarious state of affairs which relegated them to fighting for survival, Trump and the reserve Combat Ghosts were still waiting for the signal before joining the war.

After what seemed like a very long wait, Trump conferred with General Suby, and they both agreed that the signal had taken much longer than anticipated. General Suby suggested something might have gone terribly wrong, but the apparent delay did not so much fluster boss Trump, so he proposed they give it another wait so as not to foil their plans. "Besides, I have a lot of confidence in General Benj," he retorted, without knowing that General Benj had been terminated.

After another prolonged wait, there was still no signal from General Benj. Yet another wait followed this, and the signal tarried still. Finally, both Trump and General Suby agreed that it was time to do something to ensure their military plans remained on track. Instead of joining the battle before receiving the signal, Trump suggested they send out a team of five spy Combat Ghosts to go and check out the situation and report back without joining the battle or getting too close to the battlefield. Following General Suby's consent that it was a brilliant idea, five spy Combat Ghosts were appointed and tasked with the mission to spy and report back. They were also given orders to neither join the war nor get too close to the battlefield. The five Combat Ghosts complied and took off on a spy mission.

Meanwhile, Sepov had come within just a few metres of the exit outlet on the battlefield, but he was heavily surrounded by the dogged Muezee soldiers determined to take him out. In earthly terms, it would be absolutely right to say all Sepov needed were 'a few split seconds' to step into the secret exit tunnel and escape, but as soon as he made the final move to escape, a barrage of flaming spears and blazing rocks overwhelmingly pierce and fall on him and he had no chance of survival.

It is said that 'a cat has nine lives' and Sepov had fully lived and finally exhausted all his nine lives; he was now down to zero lives and quickly wafted into the negative. The euphoric Muezee soldiers watched with contentment as Sepov exploded into some dark smoke and disappeared. Of the initial 500 Cohort of Combat Ghosts that Trump had sent out in accordance with the Pseudonakuru military strategy, only 299 were still standing and fighting but were all surrounded by King Razin's savagery minions.

That marked the end of a special and brave warrior by the name of Sepov, who had given his whole in what turned out to be a very challenging battle to support Trump in his quest to triumph in his first mission in The Acts of The Sheela (The Acts of The Chosen Ones).

Sepov's selflessness, bravery, helplessness (because he couldn't control everything that was happening on the battlefield, no matter how much he tried), and his unfortunate end would be summed up in the poignant, distressing, sad and emotional words once written about a Warrior's Life:

"The force that rules our destinies is outside of ourselves and has nothing to do with our acts of volition. In view of my total lack of control over the forces which decide my destiny, my only possible freedom in that ravine consisted in tying my shoelaces impeccably. As average men, we would never know that it was something utterly real and functional – our connecting link with intent – which gave us our hereditary preoccupation with fate. The course of a warrior's destiny is unalterable…the challenge is how far he can go within those rigid bounds; how impeccable he can be within those rigid bounds. If there are obstacles in his path, the warrior strives impeccably to overcome them. If he finds unbearable hardship and pain on his path, he weeps, but all his tears put together could not move the line of his destiny the breadth of one hair. In the life of a warrior, there is only one thing, one issue alone which is really undecided: how far one can go on the path of knowledge and power. That is an issue which is open, and no one can predict its outcome. Power comes only after we accept our fate without recriminations. All paths are the same: they lead nowhere. They are paths going through the bush, or into the bush. I have learned that the countless paths one traverses in one's life are all equal. Oppressors and oppressed meet at the end, and the only thing that prevails is that life was altogether too short for both[52]."

The Muezee soldiers close to the scene were delighted with themselves for having terminated the brave warrior Sepov. Just to make sure he was no more, they waited until the smoke into which he burst had completely disappeared before switching their energies to the battlefield. About that same time, four of the five spy Combat Ghosts that Trump had sent out emerged from the secret tunnel. The 5th Combat Ghost hadn't yet emerged as she flew a few metres behind the four. It was as though the four Combat Ghosts were 'flying blindly' and forgot Trump's instruction of not getting too close to the battlefield because they literally popped out straight into enemy fire.

As soon as the Muezee fighters who had terminated Sepov startlingly saw the four Combat Ghosts appear from the secret tunnel, they flung all their deadly objects and weapons at them, which included red-hot blazing rocks, burning spears, pebbles and other terminal devices. They stood no chance of survival and got terminated instantly. The Muezee soldiers watched the four spy Combat Ghosts explode into a spectacular dark smoke that had become a familiar spectacle to King Razin and his soldiers. The four unfortunate Combat Ghosts, on account of failure to follow orders, were violently transitioned into Dark Angels upon termination without even putting up a fight. It was another clear sign that the battle had indeed turned ugly.

The fifth 'lucky' spy Combat Ghost kept alive the instruction to not get too close to the battlefield. Instead, she only peeped and spied from afar to see what was going on and witnessed first-hand the fateful incident that befell her four comrades. She then did what any sage soldier would do in that situation; she applied 'emergency brakes' and fled immediately, having seen enough of the ugly scenes. They say curiosity killed the cat, and she wasn't going to fall for it.

Upon arrival, having flown at break-neck speed, the 5th spy Combat Ghost who had a fluky escape instantly testified to both Trump and General Suby the horrible and downhearted scene she had witnessed on the battlefield. She told them she couldn't see everything due to the gravity of the situation, which resulted in the extermination of the four spy Combat Ghosts; adding that the four had no chance to defend themselves as they walked straight into enemy fire. Despite the escapee spy Combat Ghost alluding to the fact that she didn't see all the happenings on the battlefield, the fact that her fellow spy Combat Ghosts got terminated on arrival was enough intel for Trump and General Suby to realise their initial plan had gone awfully wrong, and they wondered why no one had called for assistance.

Consequent to the dual's critical meeting, General Suby ordered Corporal Talanqui to play the Assembly Bugle Call, following which all the Combat Ghosts gathered at once. Trump informed the 2nd battalion of Combat Ghosts held in reserve that their initial strategy had 'most likely' gone awry and they needed to join the war without delay. He encouraged each one of them to fight for their future and for the prize that had been promised. He also told them that the battle was very much theirs in as much as it was for Theo Lesa. Trump further explained that the delay in receiving the signal from General Benj wasn't deliberate but was because their Comrades had unfortunately been overwhelmed by the enemies of Theo Lesa and of the five spy Combat Ghosts who had been sent to check out the situation four of them got terminated on arrival. "Our initial military strategy has failed to achieve its intended results," commiserated Trump to the Combat Ghosts on parade.

Following the calamitous outcome from their military strategies, Trump made an executive decision to employ the NNDWs (Nebuparadiza Natural

Disaster Weapons) upon joining the war in order to address the situation and hopefully avert what sounded like looming defeat. He explicated that the major risk in using NNDWs lay in the fact that they had the potential to destroy whoever stood in their path, be it Combat Ghosts or civilians among the Muezee 'people'. He also warned that the NNDWs posed a threat to the Combat Ghosts of being terminated by 'friendly fire' in the same manner as the natural disasters on earth would wreak havoc indiscriminately.

Further, Trump stressed that to avoid 'friendly fire' terminating anyone of them, there was heightened need for all the Combat Ghosts to strictly follow instructions and fight around the NNDWs that would be targeted at Muezee fighters. He stated that upon him unleashing each NNDW, he expected confusion and panic to ensue among the enemy soldiers and that their role in the midst of the pandemonium was to take advantage of the situation and mercilessly hack down the fleeing and muddled Muezee rebels.

Trump also emphasised that once the NNDW had ripped through the enemy camp and they were charging to destroy their adversaries, it was paramount to ensure they did not expose themselves to enemy attacks in the process. He also informed his troops that he had instructed Corporal Talanqui to play the Alarm Bugle Call before each NNDW could be unleashed, mainly to alert them to stay out of the path of the 'enemy destroyer' NNDW. Trump further admonished that they could avoid the possibility of being terminated by 'friendly fire' from the NNDWs altogether as long as they fought tactfully and listened for the Bugle Call.

Furthermore, Trump informed his squadron that Corporal Talanqui was not going to engage in combat fighting and would be under the protection of four Combat Ghosts throughout the war for him to carry out the important task of sending warning signals via bugle calls just before the unleashing of each NNDW. He added that the playing of Bugle Calls was also intended to send confusion in the enemy camp as they would neither guess nor realise its significance.

During that critical meeting, General Suby explained that the requirement to fight around the NNDWs, as directed by Trump, conformed with what he called the 'Bull Horn' offensive military tactic. The tactic was so-called because the attacking formation took the shape of the horns of a bull. The Combat Ghosts would spread out in that formation on the battlefield with Trump and Corporal Talanqui at the centre. General Suby further directed that the Combat Ghosts along the Bull Horn formation were supposed to close in and strike down their enemies following the unleashing of each NNDW.

After Gen Suby's orders, Trump took the opportunity to show off the unique cases from Nebuparadiza, which contained the NNDWs he had alluded to. He did this to assure his troops that they had fire power and to stir courage in each one of them. The intention was to remind them that they were on Theo Lesa's mission, and he had bountifully endowed them with weapons of mass destruction intended to help them in their quest to emerge victorious in The Acts of The Chosen Ones (The Acts of The Sheela). Trump further explained that all the NNDWs could be let loose on their Muezee enemies after shouting the secret codes the Court Clerk entrusted with him at Inchde.

The first case to be displayed was bluish in colour, which Trump explained contained the Hurrica NNDW weapon, which could churn out huge storms and could spell instant disaster for any adversary of Theo Lesa. The other weapons that Trump showed off to the Combat Ghosts in successive order were the Tornah NNDW: packed in a colourless case that resembled water, this weapon, he explained could cause violently rotating columns of air and was equivalent in force to seven Tornadoes on earth. Next was the Volca NNDW: packaged in a khaki-like case which Trump explained was the equivalent of seven Volcanoes put together. The Tsu NNDW followed this: Trump explained it could generate massive waves of overwhelming volumes of liquid mercury and could approach the Muezee rebels at speed in excess of 100 miles per hour and could rise more than 300 feet to destroy their enemies. Trump then introduced the L'unquak NNDW: packaged in a golden case, he explained that it was equal to the seven most destructive earthquakes on earth and was capable of generating temblors that could strike and rattle the Muezee territory causing the ground to split and swallow their adversaries, leaving survivors with no option but to surrender. Next to be displayed was the L'ighi NNDW: packaged in a velvet case, this weapon, Trump explained, had an electric current equivalent to the seven most dangerous and powerful lightning on earth. The final weapon Trump showed off was the Fylod NNDW: packaged in an attractive casing whose colour was called Nu. He equated this weapon to the seven most violent and fast running Flash floods put together on earth.

After Trump had finished showing off the NNDWs, General Suby took over command and issued the instruction that upon hearing the Bugle Call from Corporal Talanqui, they were all to fly in a V formation just like before when they flew from Inchde to the moon, with Trump at the centre of the V formation. Upon arrival at the outlet into the Muezee kingdom, continued General Suby, they were to halt and wait for the Charge Bugle Call, following which they were to bravely charge onto the battlefield in a Bull Horn shape formation, and they were to listen for the Alarm Bugle Call which was to proceed the unleashing of each NNDW.

After General Suby had finished issuing the instructions that Trump approved, Corporal Talanqui played the Charge Bugle Call, and they all took off in a V formation. As they flew through the tunnel leading to the battlefield, Corporal Talanqui continued to play the bugle according to the instructions given to him to play the bugle throughout their flight to the assembly point just before the exit onto the battlefield on the plains of the Muezee Kingdom.

Some schools of thought claim music play a huge role in boosting soldiers' morale. For instance, in a campaign to boost the morale of its conscripted soldiers, the Korean Defence Ministry released four new rap and pop songs that were recorded by soldiers who were also famous performers. Among the performers were Private Yoon Kye-sang, a former member of the boy band g.o.d., Private Hong Kyung-in, a former actor, and Private Park Kwang-hyun, a former actor and singer. The songs carried lyrics offering reasons for their service. One song, titled 'My Fellow Soldiers', contained rap lyrics that said, "Why am I here in the Army uniform…An immature person who has not experienced difficulty…I became a soldier." A female performer also participated, Jinju, a pop star, performed 'Real Man Sung By Friends', a remake of 'Real Man', which had been popular among Korean soldiers for decades. The song was about a girlfriend asking her boyfriend to join the Army to become a 'real man'. The Defence Ministry said it expected soldiers to sing these songs for fun and during training. The ministry said it planned to produce CDs with the new songs and distribute them to military radio and television stations. Music videos were also planned[53].

After flying for a while, the Combat Ghosts at the tips of the V formation were the first to arrive at the exit point. According to the orders from Gen Suby, after all the Combat Ghosts had landed, Corporal Talanqui played the Assembly Call on his bugle, and all the Combat Ghosts gathered in front of Trump. Trump repeated the instructions briefly. Following the impromptu meeting, Corporal Talanqui played the Charge Bugle Call, which signalled to the Combat Ghosts to join the war; to join their comrades (the first battalion) on the battlefield in the war against the Muezee rebels in The Acts of The Chosen Ones (The Acts of The Sheela).

As planned, the Combat Ghosts exited the secret tunnel onto the battlefield in a Bull Horn shape formation with Trump at the centre and General Suby at the helm on the far right of the formation. It was as though the Muezee soldiers had anticipated the arrival of Trump's reserve force as they almost immediately engaged them in a vicious fight like hungry wild dogs.

What rapidly emerged was a vicious and acrimonious military tussle in a dog-eat-dog kind of scenario. The atmosphere in the Muezee Kingdom was filled with ominous and deafening chilly clamours emanating from the clashing of parched nemesis swords and shields, and also from the collision and strikes from rocks, pebbles, daggers, arrows and spears and everything that constituted weapons and other instruments of war from King Razin's radical Muezee mutineers and Trump's Combat Ghost warriors.

Chapter 35
The First Natural Disaster Weapon

When Trump and the second battalion of 500 Combat Ghosts joined the war, there were only 179 surviving Combat Ghosts from the original 500 strong 1st Battalion under Gen Benj's command. A total of 321 Combat Ghosts had been terminated, including the lead Combat Ghost, General Benj. The Operation Pseudonakuru military tactic had lamentably failed to climax and achieve its intended goals.

When viewed from the optimistic concept of the 'glass being half full as opposed to being half empty', the reduced number of Combat Ghosts presented both threats and opportunities for team Trump. Threats in that they had lost many troops from the initial squad, and that in itself increased the risk of being completely overwhelmed by the larger and well equipped Muezee side under the command of King Razin. Opportunities lay in the fact that given Trump had comparatively fewer troops than King Razin, his NNDWs (Nebuparadiza Natural Disaster Weapons) had a higher probability of hitting and destroying the Muezee soldiers than his own Combat Ghosts.

In this situation, the befitting definition of probability being 'the branch of mathematics concerning numerical descriptions of how likely an event is to occur, or how likely it is that a proposition is true. The probability of an event is a number between 0 and 1, where, roughly speaking, 0 indicates impossibility of the event and 1 indicates certainty. The higher the probability of an event, the more likely it is that the event will occur'. With fewer troops on the ground, the Probability of Trump's NNDW terminating a Muezee soldier was roughly 0.6 or 60%, i.e., higher.

As the battle intensified, Trump decided to abandon the Bull Horn military tactic due to poor visibility on the battlefield. He also feared he was more likely to be terminated from his current position because King Razin's elite fighters were fighting from the centre, and their weapons were much more sophisticated. Also, given he was the custodian of the NNDWs, for which only he knew the secret codes, he believed the battle would be lost if he were to be terminated. Besides, there was also the indisputable fact that he was the 'key man' being The Chosen One (The Sheela) who needed to be the last man standing if it all boiled down to that.

Amid the battle mayhem and pandemonium, Trump somehow managed to signal to General Suby to take centre stage while he dropped back and moved far right where most Muezee fighters were concentrated. He also correctly read the situation and concluded that the Muezee fighters on the far back right side of the battlefield were not a branch of the elite side that had taken centre stage and were fighting in front of King Razin, who continuously yelled orders urging them to fight on.

As the war became fiercer and wilder, King Razin unintentionally leaked a valuable piece of intel in an attempt to 'milk' each and every ounce from the 'fighting spirit' in his troops to bear tangible results on the battlefield. While barking orders to his troops to urge them on, he involuntarily added, "Help is on the way." That last portion of King Razin's statement seemed to be loaded with unsolicited intelligence information which fell within the hearing range of both Trump and General Suby, but they didn't know what to make of it, opting to ignore it and continue fighting.

"Advance and hold, Advance and hold, Advance and hold," was King Razin's fighting mantra to his Muezee warriors, and they literally ensured they were advancing and holding as they mercilessly ploughed their way through the defence lines of the Combat Ghosts who admirably stood their ground and put up a spectacular and brave fight despite their dwindling numbers.

Both Trump and General Suby took turns issuing commands and orders to the Combat Ghosts as they desperately sought to gain the upper hand, but they faced an uphill battle as the trajectory of the fight was heavily skewed in favour of King Razin. The situation remained unchanged for a while, and that fact alone played a major role in bolstering the confidence of the Muezee army. For the first time ever since its creation by the infallible Theo Lesa, the Muezee kingdom was filled with bangs, and bone-chilling noises never witnessed before. Trump had now significantly withdrawn from the centre of the original 'Bull Horn' formation and was positioned far back on the right-hand side of the battlefield and was preparing to unleash his first NNDW (Nebuparadiza Natural Disaster Weapon).

Upon noticing that the conditions were right, Trump ordered Corporal Talanqui to play the Alert Bugle Call, which he did. As expected, the deafening sound from the Bugle Call injected considerable confusion into the unsuspecting Muezee camp, who neither knew where the sound came from nor what it meant.

History is laden with a plethora of literature supporting the blowing of a trumpet before and during ancient wars, holy crusades and ceremonies. One such instrument is called a shofar[54]. A shofar is an ancient musical horn typically made of a ram's horn, used for Jewish religious purposes. Like the modern bugle, the shofar lacks pitch-altering devices, with all pitch control done by varying the player's embouchure or mouthpiece. The shofar was used to announce the new moon and the Jubilee year. The first day of Tishrei (now known as Rosh Hashana) is termed a 'memorial of blowing', or 'day of blowing', the shofar. Shofars were used for signifying the start of a war. They were also employed in processions as musical accompaniment and were inserted into the temple orchestra by David, The Shofar is mentioned seventy-two times in the bible in various contexts and functions. In the revelation of Sinai, the very strong sound of a Shofar, which shocked the people, was heard among the sounds and bolts, Exodus (29, 16–19):16… "And it came to pass on the third day in the morning, that there were thunders and lightnings, and a thick cloud upon the mount, and the voice of the trumpet exceeding loud; so that all the people that was in the camp trembled." 17… "And Moses brought forth the people out of the camp to meet with God; and they stood at the nether part of the mount." 18… "And Mount Sinai was altogether on a smoke, because the LORD descended upon it in fire; and the smoke thereof ascended as the smoke of a furnace, and the whole mount quaked greatly." 19… "And when the voice of the trumpet sounded long, and waxed louder and louder, Moses spoke, and God answered him by a voice." The role of the Shofar in the description of receiving the Torah at Mount Sinai may be the strongest expression of the magic, supernatural, enchanted nature of the Shofar, which had such an impact on the imagination of people through the ages. In the description of the conquests of Joshua and the People of Israel, the walls of Jericho came tumbling down after blowing the Shofars. And so it is written in the book of Joshua (6, 1–20) about the conquest of Jericho and falling of its walls: "1 Now Jericho was tightly shut up because of the Israelites. No one went out and no one came in. 2 Then the LORD said to Joshua, 'See, I have delivered Jericho into your hands, along with its king and its fighting men. 3 March around the city once with all the armed men. Do this for six days. 4 Have seven priests carry trumpets of rams' horns in front of the ark. On the seventh day, march around the city seven times, with the priests blowing the trumpets. 5 When you hear them sound a long blast on the trumpets, have all the people give a loud shout; then the wall of the city will collapse…' In various places in the Bible the Shofar is conceived as an instrument, used by God himself: 'Then the LORD will appear over them; his arrow will flash like lightning. The Sovereign LORD will sound the trumpet…' (Zechariah 9:14)."

As the dying sound of the bugle was still reverberating, Trump swiftly grabbed a golden NNDW case and shouted the cryptic code 'vuvu!' followed by the password 'Ojuku!' to unleash the L'unquak NNDW (Nebuparadiza Natural Disaster Weapon), which had power equivalent to the seven most powerful and destructive earthquakes on earth. Upon being released, the L'unquak NNDW spawned and set off heavy and ghastly seismic activity that rattled and shook the ground violently, causing billows of sulphuric fire to viciously leak out to the surface through the cracks that had opened up in areas that had a high concentration of Muezee soldiers. King Razin watched helplessly as his troops fell into the fiery cracks amid shrieks, yells, and yelps of anguish.

Looking at what had just happened, Trump and Corporal Talanqui stole glances at each other, which could have only implied 'job well done'. The single blow that was thrashed out via the L'unquak NNDW weapon consumed almost a quarter of the Muezee revolutionaries fighting on the right side of the battlefield.

In keeping with earlier instructions, circa 90% of the Combat Ghosts fighting on the right-wing side of the battlefield remembered what to do upon hearing Corporal Talanqui's Alert Bugle Call and tactically stayed out of the 'killer' L'unquak NNDW's path of destruction. They also readied themselves and dashed into the bewilderment that ensued to slaughter the perplexed Muezee soldiers while simultaneously protecting themselves from rival fire. Regrettably, around 10% of the Combat Ghosts on that same right side of the battlefield where the L'unquak NNDW inflicted untold destruction and chaos failed to correctly interpret the meaning and significance of the Alert Bugle Call that had been signalled and fortuitously got destroyed by 'friendly fire' together with the Muezee rebels.

The terminated Combat Ghosts were cast down to earth to dwell among the mortals as Dark Angels pending their final destruction. Their role had also mutated in accordance with their earmarked obnoxious, grim, horrid and callous new assignment of recruiting gullible, trusting, and pliant mortal beings for Gehenakumbo.

Although the L'unquak NNDW wreaked havoc among the Muezee fighters, Trump wasn't so impressed by the fact that in so doing, some of his Combat Ghosts got destroyed in the process. When a window of opportunity presented itself, Trump enquired of Corporal Talanqui if he too had noticed the fatal incident to which he nodded 'yes' but was quick to point out that the Combat Ghosts in question got destroyed due to their disobedience to straightforward instructions on what to do upon hearing the Alert Bugle Call. Trump was also of the same view that the unfortunate Combat Ghosts got destroyed by 'friendly-fire' due to their 'insanity' and disobedience to superior orders.

In parallel, throughout human history, disobedience in the face of armed conflict is nothing new. The reasons for disobedience vary from fear of death, taking a political stand against a government or leader, personal notoriety or fame, to moral and legal objections to the conflict. If there is a duty to disobey, it is found in the context of the *jus in bello*, the laws governing conduct during war. The Nuremberg Tribunal provides perhaps the best example. The so-called Nuremberg defence was the defence raised by Nazi leaders tried at the Nuremberg International Military Tribunal arguing unsuccessfully that they could not be held liable for criminal acts ordered by superiors. A similar defence was raised in the Vietnam-era case, United States v. Calley. In that case, First Lieutenant William Calley argued he could not be held responsible for the slaughter of hundreds of unarmed civilians (the My Lai Massacre) because his unit had been ordered to clear the village. The Court of Military Review held: The acts of a subordinate done in compliance with an unlawful order given him by his superior are excused and impose no criminal liability upon him unless the superior's order is one which a man of ordinary sense and understanding would, under the circumstances know to be unlawful, or if the order in question is actually known to the accused to be unlawful (U.S. v. Calley, 48 C.M.R. 19, 27 (1974)) This has been referred to as the 'manifestly unlawful' test. Under the manifestly unlawful standard, the legal duty to disobey is strongest when the superior's order is unlawful on its face[55].

In contrast to the 'manifestly unlawful' test, there was nothing illegal to disobey about Trump's order to his Combat Ghosts to stay out of the destructive path of the NNDWs upon hearing the Alert Bugle Call. The Combat Ghosts that complied with Trump's 'safety-first' order avoided destruction, and after the L'unquak NNDW had torn through King Razin's army and the ground had patched up immediately rushed onto the battlefield to strike down the confused Muezee fighters, some of whom were now in retreat owing to the calamity that had befallen their 'chums in arms'.

Trump and General Suby were highly enlivened by the devastating results of the L'unquak NNDW and sensed the possibility of a tidal shift in their favour. They were enthused to urge their soldiers to fight on all the more. Everything seemed to be going swimmingly for team Trump and all that just after unleashing a single NNDW which was very reassuring and a huge confidence booster.

Chapter 36
First There's Calm, Then Disaster Strikes

As most generals know, one cannot overstress the importance of confidence, especially during a hot war. According to an article by the University of Akron on 'Army Leadership', confidence is the faith that leaders place in their abilities to act properly in any situation, even under stress and with little information. Leaders who know their capabilities and believe in themselves are confident. Self-confidence grows from professional competence. But too much confidence can be as detrimental as too little confidence. Both extremes impede learning and adaptability. Bluster, loudmouthed bragging or self-promotion is not confidence. Truly confident leaders do not need to advertise their gifts because their actions prove their abilities. Confidence is important for leaders and teams. A leader's confidence is contagious and quickly permeates the entire organisation, especially in dire situations. Military leaders can help their soldiers control doubt in combat while reducing team anxiety. Combined with strong will and self-discipline, confidence spurs a leader to do what they must in circumstances in which it would be easier to do nothing[56].

The level of confidence exuded by both Trump and General Suby after unleashing the L'unquak NNDW (Nebuparadiza Natural Disaster Weapon) was truly contagious and powered up their troops in the way that turbines use the driving force of water to set electrons in motion to generate alternating current or electricity. One of the well-documented facts about electricity is that it is consumed as soon as it is produced, and it is transmitted at a very high speed, close to the speed of light (300,000 km/s)[57]. This is the best analogy of the rate at which team Trump tapped into the confidence of their superiors following the unleashing of the L'unquak NNDW.

Then without warning, Trump and General Suby and undoubtedly all the troops on both sides astonishingly felt some form of seismic activity beginning to develop a short distance from the battlefield. The vibrations started on a low note but increased in intensity at a very fast rate, mainly concentrated at the back right side of the battlefield where Trump and some of his Combat Ghosts were positioned and engaged in fierce combat. It soon became clear that it was actually a violent earthquake that had developed seemingly from nowhere, and it was brutally ripping up the ground and spitting billows of fiery lava and was headed towards Trump and his Combat Ghosts. Coincidentally, the level of seismic activity from the mysterious, monstrous earthquake was almost equal in strength to the earlier earthquake unleashed via the L'unquak NNDW by Trump, which had consumed almost a quarter of the Muezee rebels, including some of his Combat Ghosts.

The peculiar and extra-terrestrial earthquake from some unknown source was swift and ferocious. Within a short time, it cracked and tore open the ground where some of the Combat Ghosts were positioned. Trump was bemused and astounded to see his troops and some of the Muezee fighters get swallowed in red hot flames within the blink of an eye. It was a catastrophe he could not have anticipated because, as far as he was aware, it was only him who had access to the Natural Disaster Weapons on the battlefield.

What was even more upsetting to Trump was that some of the advantages he had achieved via the L'unquak NNDW had now been reversed by the bizarre, wacky and zany earthquake that voraciously and ravenously claimed some of his Combat Ghosts. Worse still, he had no clue where it originated.

Chapter 37
From Best Friends to Worst Enemies

After the dust had settled and Trump had picked himself up, only then did he realise the horror of 'what-the-hell' was going on. Another army surrounded them, but it wasn't the Muezee army. It was an alien army that was in the process of joining the war. It was this alien bunch of soldiers that had unleashed the earthquake that had just destroyed some of his Combat Ghosts as well as some of the Muezee rebels in the process.

Like a bulb after flicking on a switch, it immediately dawned on Trump as to the meaning of King Razin's words he had eavesdropped (with General Suby) urging his Muezee soldier's to fight on because 'help is on its way'. He immediately conjectured that the 'help' King Razin had accidentally mentioned at the time had now arrived and the risk of him losing the fight dubbed The Acts of The Sheela (The Acts of The Chosen Ones) had exponentially increased. The counterfeit earthquake from the alien army took out a sizeable chunk of his Combat Ghosts.

Unbeknown to both Trump and General Suby, at the start of the war, King Razin had rightly suspected there could be more enemy forces joining the battle in due course, so he proactively sent for assistance to Theo Lesa's 'public enemy' number one, who went by the name of M'nshbwa (which meant the cast out). King Razin considered M'nshbwa as Theo Lesa's Chief rebel of all time, having been part of Theo Lesa's inner circle before things went terribly wrong.

M'nshbwa was once a Ngeloi in Nebuparadiza who was a well-respected Marlena (Judge) and a bonafide member of the Buite (Court). He rebelled after his request to be appointed the fourth in command in the hierarchy of Nebuparadiza (after the Court Clerk) was turned down by Theo Lesa. His main argument was that he deserved recognition by way of promotion owing to the successful assignments he had previously undertaken on behalf of Theo Lesa, especially the mission to crush the infamous rebellion by the Muriros on the Sun. At the time of the Muriro rebellion, M'nshbwa was the special Ngeloi whom the Court Clerk assigned to go and assist The Chosen One (The Sheela) who had been tasked to quell the Muriro rebellion in The Acts of The Chosen Ones (The Acts of The Sheela) in the year 1002 (way before Trump was born). The Sheela at the time, who went by the name of Mulah was overwhelmed and was on the verge of defeat when he requested one-off assistance from Nebuparadiza. Because the Arch Ngeloi Gabriel was on another assignment, the natural pick by the Court Clerk was M'nshbwa due to his fighting prowess and feats in similar other assignments.

At the time of the Muriro rebellion, Mulah and his Combat Ghosts nearly lost the battle in his first mission of The Acts of The Chosen Ones (The Acts of The Sheela) that he undertook for Theo Lesa only to be rescued and the Muriro rebellion completely crushed after M'nshbwa was engaged. To his credit, that wasn't the only successful mission that M'nshbwa had undertaken on behalf of Theo Lesa, and in asking and later on demanding for a promotion, he argued that the peace that was prevalent amongst the inhabitants of the planets and numerous other heavenly bodies that Theo Lesa had created was partly due to his heroism and astute military skills. It was because of the successful outcomes from M'nshbwa's perilous crusades that strengthened his resolve to initially request for a promotion and later demand for it from Theo Lesa.

According to an article authored by Mikaela Kiner, founder and CEO with uniquelyHR titled '6 Unspoken Rules of Promotions That No One Tells You About'[58], "One major sign that the boss is considering you for promotion is they will assign you a stretch assignment. It's a nod that management recognises your diligence, skill and talent and has confidence in your ability to take it to the next level." Kiner explains that, "A stretch assignment might be deliberately created to advance talented employees, or it may be the result of organisational growth, an unexpected vacancy, or a new product or initiative. Whatever prompted you to earn the nod, you'll recognise a stretch assignment because it seems a bit lofty." Kiner further explains, "The assignment should help you do one or more of the following: Build new skills, increase your visibility, try out a new discipline or geography, or gain an experience like managing people that you haven't had before." While this may seem a bit intimidating, Kiner assures: "Leadership will only ask you to take on a stretch assignment if they believe that you can do the work and that it will develop your skills."

Though this was not in human settings and comparisons may be unwarranted, one would be tempted to infer that M'nshbwa was entirely right in looking out and asking for promotion from the establishment based on his track record of successful military campaigns in Nebuparadiza. He insisted that Theo Lesa must create a special position for him so that his inner circle would include the beautiful Ngeloi and The Court Clerk and himself. Put another way, M'nshbwa effectively demanded a mini restructure to transform Nabuparadiza's senior leadership team from a trio to a quartet.

The more M'nshbwa focused on his accomplishments, the more he grew in his delusions of grandeur until he crossed the fine line between confidence and megalomania. His grandiosity, sense of self-importance, egotism and conceitedness propped him to start considering his accomplishments as being above those of the Court Clerk and the beautiful Ngeloi whom he accused of receiving overtly unearned favours from Theo Lesa. As time (Clap) went by, M'nshbwa gained a small following among some of the Ngelois who were sympathetic to his grievances.

In response to his unbecoming and indecorous behaviour, Theo Lesa ordered the Court Clerk to court-martial M'nshbwa. Following the hearing of M'nshbwa's case, Theo Lesa ruled that besides the top three, himself, the beautiful Ngeloi, and The Court Clerk, all the Ngelois were equal in rank, and no one had the right to exalt themselves above others. The only punishment imposed on M'nshbwa was the denial of his promotion and a final warning for him to fall back in line with the chain of command and responsibility.

Subsequent to the outcome of the court-martial not to grant his request and what he misconstrued to be a mortifying and unfair verdict, M'nshbwa abdicated Nebuparadiza in mutiny against Theo Lesa. He also took with him all the Ngelois who agreed with him and were sympathetic to his grievances. M'nshbwa and his renegade Ngelois went and occupied a 'no-man's' section that stretched between Gehenakumbo and Nebuparadiza. Theo Lesa opted to tentatively not take any further action or wage war against the mutinous and defiant M'nshbwa and his followers on advice from both the beautiful Ngeloi and The Court Clerk. To this fallen Ngeloi and former star of Nebuparadiza, M'nshbwa, King Razin had sent an SOS missive asking for support or back up in the war against Trump and his army of Combat Ghosts.

Because of his bitterness, heinous and contemptible animosity against the establishment in Nebuparadiza, joining forces with King Razin to oppose Trump and his Combat Ghosts was something M'nshbwa embraced wholeheartedly. He took it as a covert operation to indirectly wage war against Theo Lesa. M'nshbwa responded in the affirmative and sent a sizeable force in response to King Razins request for assistance in the war against Trump and the Combat Ghosts, and of course, against the 'mastermind' Theo Lesa.

Fearing for his own fate and ensuring maximum and lasting damage to Theo Lesa's military crusade against King Razin, M'nshbwa granted one of his senior general's full powers and ability to discharge counterfeit Natural Disaster Weapons that he had brought with him from Nebuparadiza on abdication. This senior general assigned to assist King Razin is the one who detonated the deadly 'alien' earthquake that ripped through the side of the battlefield where Trump had gained significant grounds after setting off the L'unquak NNDW (Nebuparadiza Natural Disaster Weapon).

To the followers of the chronicles from the Christian Bible, the account of the counterfeit earthquake that M'nshbwa's senior general ignited would be deemed a close shave to the facts surrounding the story of Moses and Pharaoh in the Christian Bible as recorded in the book of Exodus (7–8) when Moses and Aaron confronted the Pharaoh in Egypt demanding that he free God's people, the Israelites, from slavery. Moses and Aaron performed miracles to confirm their message, and on three occasions, Pharaoh's magicians were able to duplicate the miracles. God spoke to Moses through a burning bush and charged him to speak to Pharaoh on His behalf (Exodus 3). During that commissioning, God granted Moses the ability to perform miracles (Exodus 4:21). Knowing that Pharaoh would demand a sign, God instructed Moses and Aaron to throw down Aaron's staff upon their first meeting with the ruler. Aaron did so, and his staff turned into a snake. Pharaoh immediately summoned his magicians, who could turn their own staffs into snakes. In what must have been an ominous sign for Pharaoh's court, Aaron's snake devoured the magicians' snakes (Exodus 7:8–13). Twice more, Pharaoh's magicians were able to perform miracles to match the signs of Moses and Aaron. The first plague that Moses called down upon the Egyptians was a plague of blood. The magicians could also turn water to blood as Moses had done to the Nile River (Exodus 7:14–22). The second plague was a horde of frogs sent among the Egyptian people, and the magicians summoned their own frogs as well – adding to the problem rather than alleviating it (Exodus

8:1–7). After this, however, the magicians' power stopped, as they could not replicate any further plagues, and they acknowledged they were witnessing 'the finger of God' in Moses' signs (verse 19)[59].

Chapter 38
The Second Natural Disaster Weapon

After losing some of his Combat Ghosts to the counterfeit earthquake set off by M'nshbwa's commander of the armed forces sent to support King Razin, Trump decided to take revenge without delay. The urgency was partly prompted by the fact that M'nshbwa's army was still a distance from the battlefield, and the risk of accidentally terminating his Combat Ghosts in the process was relatively low. Accordingly, Trump ordered Corporal Talanqui to play the Alert Call on his bugle, and he complied right away. This time round, one would have hoped that all the Combat Ghosts would be alert and know exactly what to do upon hearing the Alert Bugle Call, i.e., continue fighting but stay out of harm's way and strike down the enemies after the NNDW (Nebuparadiza Natural Disaster Weapon) has reaped through enemy camp.

Following the sounding of the bugle, Trump took out the colourless NNDW box and bellowed the secret code 'hossa!' followed by the password 'hiber!' to release the Natural Disaster Weapon called the Tornah NNDW, which was equivalent in force to seven most powerful Tornadoes on earth. Trump's act of calling out the secret codes caused a powerful and vicious rotating column of air to form accompanied by lightning which was encapsulated in a thunderstorm as it aggressively made its way towards the direction of the approaching M'nshbwa army. Trump and some of the Combat Ghosts looked on admirably, anxiously confident of the desired outcome while they continued to fight.

Upon seeing the 'natural' calamity that was headed their way, the commander of the M'nshbwa army swung into action with his own 'magical' version of the Natural Disaster Weapon, and it didn't disappoint. The M'nshbwa army commander unleashed an equally violent Tornado directed at the battlefield and headed towards Trump's side of the battlefield (right-wing). The unnerving occurrences took all the warring forces on the battlefield completely by surprise.

Trump, General Suby, the Combat Ghosts, as well as King Razin and his Muezee insurgents, were all set on alert as the Tornado that was let loose from the direction of the M'nshbwa forces raged towards them. The monster storms caused all sorts of mixed reactions amongst the bewildered fighting factions on the battlefield and the approaching M'nshbwa army. For a moment, they all seemed to have divided their attention between fighting and watching out for the killer storm that was headed their way. The weaklings among the Muezee and M'nshbwa soldiers succumbed and scampered in all directions while the Combat Ghosts, thanks to their gruelling military training, remained rooted to the battlefield.

From an onlooker's perspective, it would seem as though the two, almost evenly matched, 'hungry' rival Tornadoes became uncontrollable upon being discharged by Trump and the commander of the M'nshbwa armed forces as they failed to avoid each other's path of destruction, so it seemed. The two fast-moving, and furious tornadoes from opposite directions clashed in the middle ground in the space between the backside of the battlefield and the approaching M'nshbwa soldiers and exploded into lightning and thunder as they forcibly tussled with each other, thereby breeding a deadly and chilly cold anthem of all sorts of mayhem.

The combined force of the nemesis tornados released a powerful storm that spiralled out of control and indiscriminately annihilated several soldiers from each of the tripartite warring sides of Trump's Combat Ghosts, King Razin's Muezee rebels and the M'nshbwa interlopers. The destruction and confusion persisted as the hybrid gigantic storm produced from the clashing of the two rival tornadoes continued on its deadly warpath as it reeled on the battlefield like a drunk and demented man. The fighters and their weapons were tossed about helplessly, causing some to violently smash into fellow soldiers from the same camp, whereas others were impaled to sharp weapons on the battlefield.

It was as though the two rival Tornado Natural Disaster Weapons had metamorphosed into some form of Frankenstein. In Shelley's Gothic story, Victor Frankenstein builds the creature in his laboratory through an ambiguous method based on his discovered scientific principle. Shelley describes the monster as eight feet (240 cm) tall and terribly hideous but emotional. The monster attempts to fit into human society but is shunned, which leads him to seek revenge against Frankenstein.

For the spell that Trump's Torna NNDW with its disparate M'nshbwa Tornado spiralled out of control, an armchair critic would suspect that Trump's NNDW had turned against him in a way. However, Trump viewed the situation differently despite what he had just witnessed. It was more crucial to him that he had access to this supernatural power which he could call into action at any time for it to do his bidding than bemoaning the loss he had suffered.

After the mother of all storms had subsided, it became evident to all the commanders that they had each suffered heavy casualties. For instance, of the 1000 Combat Ghosts that Trump had enlisted to help him quash the Muezee rebellion in The Acts of The Sheela (The Acts of The Chosen Ones), he was only left with circa 350 Combat Ghosts on the battlefield, 650 of them had been terminated and transitioned into Dark Angels on earth in what would be deemed some form of tentative respite from Gehenakumbo where they suffered constant and perpetually excruciating pain. The exact number of casualties from each side following the Tornado-tag-of war was anyone's guess and difficult to determine especially while the battle was still raging.

Comparably, although military sources provide the primary statistics of war losses and casualties during World War I, the verification of the recorded figures has been highly problematic for several reasons. After the war, political leaders of new states tended to publish high figures of losses to show other nations how damaging the war had been for their people. But no one can say how many Poles or Czechs were killed with any degree of certainty. Some writers, though, tried to do just that. They first derived the number of Czech or Polish soldiers killed while wearing the Russian, German or Austro-Hungarian army uniforms based on the percentage of soldiers of each nationality within each imperial army. They then added these numbers to obtain, for example, the total Polish war dead. First, the definition of Polish territory varied between the three imperial armies and did not coincide with Polish frontiers established in 1919. From what part of Poland did Polish soldiers come? This evaluation assumed that Polish soldiers' mortality rate was exactly the same as those of German or Russian soldiers. But this was just a hypothesis. Second, War loss statistics were highly sensitive data. During the war, figures indicating the numbers of soldiers killed or wounded in action were arguments in political and military debates. High numbers of useless losses were invoked against commanders in chief, for example, against Robert Nivelle (1856–1824) and Sir Douglas Haig (1861–1928) in 1917; such bloodletting was a major reason behind calls for their removal. Public opinion was shocked by the death of thousands on the first days of the Somme, the Chemin des Dames or Passchendaele, and the home population's morale was at stake. Hence the armies were eager to conceal too high of losses in order to safeguard themselves from controversy. For this reason, the main source of information was likely biased by commanders' and their staffs' temptation to minimise war losses. Further, Military statistics only registered officers and soldiers, not civilians. This makes such figures useless in counting the losses of civilian populations and a small part of military losses after discharge. Some soldiers died from their wounds or illness after leaving the army. It would be fair to count them among war losses[60].

Drawing a parallel from the challenges experienced in compiling the numbers of the war dead from World War I (and also World War II) and the difficulties in accounting for civilian casualties, undoubtedly King Razin had suffered more casualties because the war was fought on his home turf, on the plains of his Muezee kingdom, and the safety of the Muezee civilians was not guaranteed. This meant that among the Muezee dead were not only the soldiers who, out of their own volution, had enlisted to fight for King Razin, but were also the obedient Muezees who wisely chose not to rebel against Theo Lesa but still ended up being killed as collateral damage. Some contemporary schools of thought argue that one of the main reasons powerful nations have 'deliberately' waged war away from 'home' is to avoid civilians being killed as collateral damage; and the evidence is there for all to see whatever the level of cynicism.

Fortunately, in the aftermath of the Tornado galore massacre, General Suby was among the Combat Ghosts who were still standing and fighting, which was very reassuring to Trump, notwithstanding the heavy losses they had suffered.

Chapter 39
The Third Natural Disaster Weapon

The surviving M'nshbwa soldiers whom the clash of the opposing Tornadoes had momentarily disoriented were now switched on and advancing towards the battlefield. Upon seeing their tenacious spirit, Trump opted to capitalise on the ancient saying, "There is no time like the present." He decided to take advantage of the window of opportunity presented by the gap between the battlefield and the advancing M'nshbwa army to unleash another NNDW (Nebuparadiza Natural Disaster Weapon).

According to plan, Trump ordered Corporal Talanqui, who had also survived the Tornado ordeal, to play the Alert Bugle Call, and he swung into action without delay. Soon after the Bugle Call, Trump reached for the velvet box that contained the Natural Disaster Weapon called the L'ighi NNDW. Back then, in Nebuparadiza, during the weapon handover ceremony, the Court Clerk told Trump that the L'ighi NNDW had power equivalent to the seven most powerful bolts of lightning on earth, combined. According to research, lightning kills as many as 2,000 people on planet earth every year, with hundreds more survivors suffering lingering and debilitating symptoms.

To usher the L'ighi NNDW weapon into action, Trump repeated the secret codes entrusted to him by The Court Clerk by hollering the words 'edule!' followed by the password 'pakr!' After an ostensibly calculated pause, powerful lightning struck, followed by deafening thunder right in the middle of the approaching M'nshbwa army. This was followed by a deep and heavy bang that vigorously shook the very ground on which they were standing, instantly killing a good number of the M'nshbwa soldiers.

According to an article that Ravji Desai authored in The SWADDLE newsletter, Lightning can injure or kill people in three major ways. One of the most popular but least common, the direct strike, is when a ray of lightning strikes a person in an open area straight from the sky. It's the deadliest, but it 'hardly ever happens', American meteorologist, Ron Holle, tells The Washington Post. Another kind is the contact strike, also called conduction, during which the lightning travels in wires, water pipes, and through metal surfaces. It's likely to mostly injure people indoors using electrical appliances, handling a metal object, or taking a shower. Both contact and direct strikes make up 3–5% of all lightning-related deaths and injuries. The biggest danger, when lightning strikes, manifests in the form of ground currents, in which the electricity from the lightning spreads out in the form of a deadly current on the ground, gradually getting weaker as it moves away from the point of contact. This spreading out forms an arc on the ground, almost as far as 60 feet from where the lightning originally hit, and the most common way people get injured by lightning is through these ground currents. If a person is standing anywhere in the arc, it's likely the current from the ground travels up the person's body through their leg, impairing or completely stopping the person's heart or breathing, then moving down the other leg and out. It can cause cardiac arrest, severe burns, permanent brain damage, memory loss and personality change. Further, according to lightning injuries expert Dr Mary Ann Cooper, Lightning injures more people than it kills; 90% of people hit by lightning survive, possibly with long-lasting neurological damage. In terms of how a person gets hurt by a lightning strike, lightning flows on a person's skin and enters their body through a contact point to travel through the nervous or cardiovascular systems. The bigger the body, the more space the lightning has to travel inside the body, and the more damage it does to the human or animal. According to National Geographic, some safety precautions that reduce the risk of being struck by lightning include avoiding being on the phone, in contact with metal surfaces or concrete walls, directly touching plumbing or electrical systems during a thunderstorm, or being near windows or doors[61].

The L'ighi NNDW weapon proved successful as it took out more than a quarter of the M'nshbwa soldiers. Following the strike, General Suby ordered the Combat Ghosts within his hearing range to rash in the direction of the surviving M'nshbwa soldiers (who were still confused) following the devastating strike from the L'ighi NNDW that hit their cavalcade, killing several of them. Yet, the survivors continued to advance towards the battlefield.

It seemed as though Trump's team was on the verge of turning the tide in their favour. Trump, however, was still wary of retaliation; and speak of the devil, within a short space of time, there was a huge reciprocal lightning and thunder that hit the left side of the battlefield indiscriminately terminating several Combat Ghosts as well as Muezee soldiers. Talk about 'smacking down' the gauntlet on the frosty plains of the Muezee Kingdom, the M'nshbwa army was up for a 'good' fight! Forget about the Muezee guerrillas, it now dawned on Trump that the M'nshbwa warriors were a force to reckon with because they had answered all the challenges he had thrown at them up to that point.

Lamentably, the counterfeit lightning discharged by M'nshbwa's top general that struck the left-wing side of the battlefield also took out Trump's loyal commander and his second in command, General Suby. Upon being terminated, General Suby exploded into a cloud of black smoke and was flung down to earth to dwell among the mortal beings as a Dark Angel. Trump realised that his deputy had been terminated because he couldn't see him anywhere following that lightning assault from the M'nshbwa forces. The second sign of General Suby's demise was that his overtone commands to the Combat Ghosts had come to a sudden end after the confusion had slightly subsided.

General Suby's termination was a huge loss to Trump and his team. Trump, however, had already made up his mind to fight to the very bitter end. It was Billy Graham who once said, "Courage is contagious, when a brave man takes a stand, the spines of others are often stiffened," and Trump's decisive and courageous stance emboldened his troops to put up a spirited fight too despite losing a good number of their comrades-in-arms.

If Trump had a way of rendering tribute to his loyal and valiant warrior by the name of General Suby, it would be along the lines of the eulogy that was penned down by William Shakespeare for Julius Caesar:

"Friends, Romans, countrymen, lend me your ears;

I come to bury Caesar (*General Suby*), not to praise him;

The evil that men do lives after them,

The good is oft interred with their bones,

So let it be with Caesar (*General Suby*)...The noble Brutus (*M'nshbwa*)

Hath told you Caesar (*General Suby*) was ambitious:

If it were so, it was a grievous fault,

And grievously hath Caesar (*General Suby*) answered it...

Here, under leave of Brutus (*M'nshbwa*) and the rest,

(For Brutus (*M'nshbwa*) is an honourable man;

So are they all; all honourable men)

Come I to speak in Caesar's (*General Suby's*) funeral…
He was my friend, faithful and just to me:
But Brutus (*M'nshbwa*) says he was ambitious;
And Brutus (*M'nshbwa*) is an honourable man.…
He hath brought many captives home to Rome,
Whose ransoms did the general coffers fill:
Did this in Caesar (*General Suby*) seem ambitious?
When that the poor have cried, Caesar (*General Suby*) hath wept:
Ambition should be made of sterner stuff:
Yet Brutus (*M'nshbwa*) says he was ambitious;
And Brutus (*M'nshbwa*) is an honourable man.
You all did see that on the Lupercal
I thrice presented him a kingly crown,
Which he did thrice refuse: was this ambition?
Yet Brutus (*M'nshbwa*) says he was ambitious;
And, sure, he is an honourable man.
I speak not to disprove what Brutus (*M'nshbwa*) spoke,
But here I am to speak what I do know.
You all did love him once, not without cause:
What cause withholds you then to mourn for him?
O judgement! thou art fled to brutish beasts,
And men have lost their reason…Bear with me;
My heart is in the coffin there with Caesar (*General Suby*),
And I must pause till it come back to me."

After Trump had convalesced from the loss of his beloved top soldier, General Suby, to his astonishment, he noticed that another fresh bunch of M'nshbwa soldiers had appeared on the opposite horizon and was on its way to join the fight in support of King Razin. The writing was on the wall, Theo Lesa's nemesis, M'nshbwa, was not leaving anything to chance and wanted to use Trump's war against the Muezees in The Acts of The Sheela (The Acts of The Chosen Ones) as a preparatory battle for his eventual showdown with Theo Lesa. Therefore, he was giving it his whole and taking it personally by rendering maximum assistance to King Razin to ensure that the imminent victory against Trump and his Combat Ghosts, ultimately against Theo Lesa, was decisive.

Chapter 40
Asking for Help

Studying the situation without falling prey to analysis paralysis, Trump knew he needed to act without hesitation. He decided to unleash another NNDW (Nebuparadiza Natural Disaster Weapon), aiming towards the approaching menacing sword brandishing M'nshbwa ruffians. It was a delicate situation. However, through it all, Trump still kept alive the Court Clerk's 'insurance' or one-off offer for assistance from the Arch Ngeloi Gabriel direct from Nebuparadiza if he ever needed backup during the war with King Razin. The caveat the Court Clerk attached to the backing was that it could only be requested as a one-off assistance in all the three assignments that Trump had chosen to undertake during The Acts of The Chosen Ones (The Acts of The Sheela).

As the ancient saying goes, "Things are always unknown till they are known." When the Court Clerk extended the offer for one-off assistance from the Arch Ngeloi Gabriel, Trump thought he had enough military resources at his disposal and didn't envision the possibility of a desperate situation arising during The Acts of The Chosen Ones (The Acts of The Sheela). And you guessed it! his response to that generous offer by the Court Clerk was surprisingly lukewarm. Notwithstanding Trump's ungracious reaction, the Court Clerk nevertheless still left the offer open.

Due to his tepid reaction to the Court Clerk's offer, Trump was at the outset reluctant to request support from Nebuparadiza. But so much had changed since the start of the war against King Razin. Over half of his Combat Ghost troopers had perished, including his two deputies, General Suby and General Benj. Akin to 'adding salt to a wound', Trump was now fighting against three disparate battalions of the Muezee contingent and two separate combat units from Theo Lesa's 'public enemy' number one, M'nshbwa. He was undeniably in a perilous and desperate predicament, and the prospects of him winning the first phase of his military campaign in The Acts of The Chosen Ones (The Acts of The Sheela) appeared gloomy and lacklustre.

Despite his detached response towards help at the time it was extended to him by the Court Clerk, Trump now felt completely justified in soliciting assistance from Nabuparadiza's special agent, the Arch Ngeloi Gabriel, via the Court Clerk. After all, Trump rationalised, asking for allied succour, or support, was exactly what King Razin had resorted to doing by having two separate units of M'nshbwa forces involved in the war; and it was due to that allied military assistance that the battle was heavily skewed in favour of the rebel trailblazer King Razin.

Instead of being despondent, the turn of events paradoxically fuelled Trump's ambition to win by any means possible in The Acts of The Chosen Ones (The Acts of The Sheela). And if that failed, he resolved to do whatever was necessary to win. Summoning for assistance from Nebuparadiza hence became very appealing to Trump. Besides, he had few options in the tight corner he found himself with the bandwagon of Combat Ghosts despite their gallant efforts and fighting proficiency. Having overcome his 'go-no-go' dilemma, Trump fired off a covert signal to The Court Clerk requesting the assistance of the Arch Ngeloi Gabriel. To do so, he had to follow strict instructions that were surreptitiously given to him at Inchde by the Court Clerk.

After successfully sending the SOS signal to the Court Clerk, Trump ordered Corporal Talanqui to play the Alert Bugle Call, following which he swiftly took out one of his invaluable NNDW cases and screamed the secret code 'Makant!' followed by the password 'wafwa!' to let loose the Natural Disaster Weapon called Tsu. The Tsu NNDW rolled into action after Trump finished uttering the secret codes. It generated and churned out massive and violent volumes of liquid mercury directed at the approaching M'nshbwa soldiers on the opposite horizon. The velocity of the dark ice cold and thick liquid mercury was over 100 miles per hour after rising to a height of circa 300 feet as each and every atom and molecule rallied and rushed to carry out Trump's directive to drown and terminate the M'nshbwa antagonists. During the NNDW weapon handover ceremony just outside Nebuparadiza, at Inchde, to be precise, the Court Clerk explained to Trump that the Tsu NNDW weapon was equal to the combined force of the seven most devastating Tsunamis on earth.

From a distance, Trump could see that some elements within the seemingly gigantic, mighty and powerful M'nshbwa army had started scurrying, darting and scampering in all directions in an attempt to avoid the highly charged current of liquid mercury waves born out of the destroyer Tsunami in the name of the Tsu NNDW (Nebuparadiza Natural Disaster Weapon). The executioner Tsunami rushed at the M'nshbwa soldiers at such an astronomical speed that there was no room to circumvent or sidestep its wide arc.

The Tsu NNDW caught its intended prey within the blink of an eye and killed a large number of the M'nshbwa soldiers. Better still, this time around, it seemed as though the M'nshbwa army did not have a readily available response in their quilt of counterfeit Natural Disaster Weapons. Upon seeing the extraordinary results that emanated from the firing off of the Tsu NNDW, Trump decided to increase the 'dosage'. He asked Corporal Talanqui to play another Alert Call on his bugle for him to unleash the Tsu NNDW weapon for a second time for maximum impact.

As grave as the situation might have seemed in light of the failed military strategies and the wabbly, wonky and rickety assumptions on which they were founded, the 'repeat-action strategy' of the NNDWs might have been the 'low-lying fruit' that Trump had neglected to employ. Could that oversight have accounted for the reason why the battle against King Razin had protracted? Was the battle being lost because Trump had unleashed his NNDW weapons at spaced intervals, thereby giving a chance to his enemies to respond with their counterfeit Natural Disaster Weapons? there was no easy solution or explanation to the quandary that team Trump faced.

As the saying goes, "If at first you don't succeed, try, try and try again." Robert the Bruce, king of Scotland, is meant to have told his troops this shortly before defeating the English at Bannockburn in 1314. The idiom, said to have been inspired by a humble spider stoically weaving his web as Bruce hid from his English pursuers in a cave. The legend of Bruce and spider is world-famous. It is said that in the early days of Bruce's reign, he was defeated by the English and driven into exile. He was on the run, a hunted man. He sought refuge in a small dark cave and sat and watched a little spider trying to make a web. Time and time again, the spider would fall and then climb slowly back up to try again. Finally, as the Bruce looked on, the spider managed to stick a strand of silk to the cave wall and began to weave a web. Robert the Bruce was inspired by the spider and defeated the English at the Battle of Bannockburn. The legend as it is now told was first published by Sir Walter Scott in 'Tales of a Grandfather' in 1828, more than 500 years after the Battle of Bannockburn. Caves across

Scotland and Ireland are said to be the legendary cave of Bruce and the spider: the King's Cave at Drumadoon on Arran; King Robert the Bruce's Cave in Kirkpatrick Fleming near Lockerbie; Bruce's Cave, Uamh-an-Righ, Balquhidder Glen; Bruce's Cave on Rathlin Island[62].

Trump's 'second try' with the Tsu NNDW weapon was so successful that a significant number from the second battalion of the M'nshbwa soldiers who were set to join forces with King Razin's Muezee army were dealt a devastating blow. More than half of them got terminated (killed) even before setting foot on the battlefield, and this was a huge dose of a morale booster to Trump and the remnant of his Combat Ghosts who were still very spirited as they fought on.

Just when Trump thought fortunes had started to permanently tilt in their favour, lo and behold another shocking and menacing scene unexpectedly greeted them. A third regiment of M'nshbwa special forces appeared on the opposite other horizon, and the agony of the apparition was such that there was no way for Trump to safely unleash his NNDWs (Nebuparadiza Natural Disaster Weapons) without unintentionally wiping out some of his own Combat Ghosts in the process as there was no clear path past his troops. This was because the remaining NNDWs could only travel in a straight line. It seemed as though Trump had reverted to square zero. He felt overwhelmed and despondent and thought it was now all over. He was convinced there was no way he could win that battle without support from the Arch Ngeloi Gabriel from Nebuparadiza. He also wished he had asked for help much earlier than he did.

An article by Miguel Montaner in the Harvard Business Review suggests that most people are reluctant to ask for help for several reasons. "As research in neuroscience and psychology shows, the social threats involved, which include uncertainty, risk of rejection, the potential for diminished status, and inherent relinquishing of autonomy activate the same brain regions that physical pain does. And in the workplace, where staff are typically keen to demonstrate as much expertise, competence, and confidence as possible, it can feel particularly uncomfortable to make such requests. However, studies also show that it's virtually impossible to advance in modern organisations without assistance from others. Cross-functional teams, agile project management techniques, matrixed or hierarchy-minimising structures and increasingly collaborative office cultures require staff to constantly push for the cooperation and support of their managers, peers, and employees. Individual staff's performance, development, and career progression depend more now than ever on their seeking out the advice, referrals, and resources they need. In fact, estimates suggest that as much as 75% to 90% of the help co-workers give one another is in response to direct appeals[63]."

Trump's only hope of ever winning the fight in his first mission in The Acts of The Sheela (The Acts of The Chosen Ones) was now dependant on the arrival of the assistance he had solicited from Nebuparadiza via The Court Clerk. The difficulty was that the help had delayed, and worse still, there was no confirmation it was on its way as Trump helplessly witnessed an increasing number of his gallant Combat Ghosts succumb to the ruthless allied militia and mercenaries under the secure command of King Razin and Theo Lesa's 'public enemy' number one, M'nshbwa. The 'unholy matrimony' of convenience between King Razin and M'nshbwa had 'correctly' reeked and sensed victory and was leaving nothing to chance in the quest to overrun the invading army of Combat Ghosts that Trump led.

Despite facing the threat of total annihilation, Trump continued to issue directives to his Combat Ghosts with impunity. He urged them to fight on even though their position seemed defenceless as they were surrounded by King Razin's Muezee army backed by M'nshbwa's armed forces. Simply put, Trump and his remaining Combat Ghosts were in dire straits and on a slippery slope towards extinction.

Trump questioned whether that was Theo Lesa's plot in the first place; asking him to drink from a poisoned chalice by fighting a losing battle whose outcome was foreknown. He wondered why Theo Lesa had not been 'man enough' to send him to Gehenakumbo right away following the guilty verdict against him by the Buite (Court) which was primarily based on what was construed as his 'unholy' death on earth or suicide. He also wondered what the point was in sending him on a comical 'master-and-puppet' mission around Theo Lesa's own creations if his role in The Acts of The Chosen Ones (The Acts of The Sheela) was relegated to that of a defeated foe from inception.

Meanwhile, the reticence (silence) from Nebuparadiza continued; and that was not the first time that Trump had to endure 'the silent treatment' from Nebuparadiza during The Acts of The Sheela (The Acts of The Chosen Ones).

Some counsellors define 'the silent treatment' as a refusal to communicate verbally with another person. According to an article featured in the Medical News Today newsletter on the subject, "Is the silent treatment a form of abuse?[64]" People who use the silent treatment may even refuse to acknowledge the presence of the other person. People use the silent treatment in many types of relationships. It can sometimes be a form of emotional abuse. This is the case when one person controls and manipulates the other with it. People use the silent treatment for several reasons which include:

i) Avoidance: In some cases, people stay silent in a conversation because they do not know what to say or want to avoid conflict.

ii) Communication: A person may use the silent treatment if they do not know how to express their feelings but want their partner to know that they are upset.

iii) Punishment: If a person uses silence to punish someone or to exert control or power over them, this is a form of emotional abuse.

In most cases, silent treatment is not a productive way to deal with a disagreement. Research indicates that both men and women use silent treatment in relationships. However, clear and direct communication is essential for healthy relationships. Using silent treatment prevents people from helpfully resolving their conflicts. When one partner wants to talk about a problem, but the other withdraws, it can cause negative emotions such as anger and distress. According to a 2012 study, people who regularly feel ignored also report lower levels of self-esteem, belonging and meaning in their lives. Because of this, silent treatment can impact the health of a relationship, even if the silent person is trying to avoid conflict. A person with a partner who avoids conflict is more likely to continue a dispute because they have not had an opportunity to discuss their grievances.

Further, according to Pastor Chris Noland, Silence is one of the most difficult things to bear. There is a lot that silence can communicate. For instance, a husband is always concerned and worried when his wife is silent. There is an awkwardness that comes when you walk into a completely silent room. When a child has disappointed their parents, and no word is spoken, the silence cuts deep into the child's heart. Yes, silence is a very powerful thing. To illustrate his point further on the impact of silence, Pastor Chris Noland quotes the example found in the Book of Revelation 8:1, which says, *"When the Lamb opened the seventh seal, there was silence in heaven for about half an hour."* Jesus is opening the seventh seal. This seventh seal reveals God's awesome and terrible wrath that is about to be poured out on the earth during the last half of the tribulation period. This silence is very strange and powerful. Previously, John witnessed a lot of noise in heaven. Multitudes were gathered around the throne and worshipped God continually. The raptured church is there, the elders are there, the angels are there, the creatures are there. Sounds of praise and music fill the air. Lightning and thunder proceed from the throne of God. Then, the Lamb of God opens the seventh seal. As He opens the seal, all of heaven is hushed. There is absolute total silence. There is no time in heaven, yet John is still within the limits of time, and he describes the silence as lasting for half an hour. All of heaven is silent becomes the opening of the seventh seal reveals what is to come. The wrath of God is about to be poured out upon the earth in a way that has never been seen before, and there are no words left to say[65].

Given it was too risky to attack the newest and third cohort of the M'nshbwa soldiers that had appeared on the opposite horizon, Trump decided that he wasn't going to engage them just yet because he couldn't afford to accidentally terminate any more of his soldiers who were now considerably few in number. He instead chose to direct the vengeful might of his NNDWs (Nebuparadiza Natural Disaster Weapons) at the group of M'nshbwa soldiers that had already been sapped, weakened and destabilised by the Tsu NNDW weapon he had twice unleashed earlier. When he attacked the target group with the Tsu NNDW, over a quarter of them were terminated. Trump's plan was now to completely get rid of that group of the M'nshbwa army which was 'out on a limb' in line with the Bungayama military strategy for which the main aim was to focus on the weakest link in the enemy chain of defence or resistance to psychologically send fear in the enemy camp.

Accordingly, Trump asked Corporal Talanqui to play the Alert Call on his bugle. Shortly after the bugle, Trump reached for his khaki NNDW case and passionately cried out the secret code 'makari' followed by the password 'dacaes' to unleash his brand new NNDW (Nebuparadiza Natural Disaster Weapon) called the Volca NNDW. This was the weapon that the Court Clerk lavishly praised as possessing the combined destructive energy equivalent to the seven most active, deadly, and borne consuming volcanoes on earth.

Upon launching the Volca NNDW, there was the usual ominous pause followed by a loud and vehement explosion on the side of the battlefield where there was a high concentration of the M'nshbwa mercenaries. The same group had already been struck twice and weakened by the Tsu NNDW. When the Volca NNDW exploded, it scattered streams of boiling lava with temperatures over 4,000 degrees Fahrenheit, instantly consuming whoever was unfortunate not to escape its wrath. Only a handful of the M'nshbwa soldiers from the targeted group managed to circumvent the Volca NNDW weapon. Unfortunately, approximately 20 of Trump's Combat Ghosts and a couple of Muezee soldiers were also victims. It was a 'bittersweet' situation for Trump, who was still pleased that he had managed to annihilate a large number of enemy soldiers, although some of his own soldiers got terminated by friendly fire in the process.

The odds were stacked against Trump winning the war. There was still no response from Nebuparadiza or any sign to acknowledge Trump's request for assistance. Trump decided to send a follow-up signal for backup to The Court Clerk as his Combat Ghosts dug deeper to hang on to the fight, but they were being terminated much faster than at any time since the start of the battle as they were heavily surrounded. Like locusts succumbing to Fenitrothion and Malathion (the most used materials for swarm control, the former being generally recommended against the Desert Locust), Trump helplessly watched his Combat Ghosts disappear from the battlefield in explosions of dark smoke straight down to earth where they became Dark Angels.

Despite the ruinous effects of the Volca NNDW weapon, afterwards, only less than a hundred Combat Ghosts were still standing and fighting in what seemed like a Goliath versus David duel. As the battle got more ugly, Corporal Talanqui, who had played a major role as a bugler in The Acts of The Chosen Ones (The Acts of The Sheela), got caught in crossfire and was terminated. Upon seeing what had just happened, Trump raised his hands in despair, but there was no way of surrendering in The Acts of The Sheela (The Acts of The Chosen Ones), however hopeless the situation was proving to be. During his induction with the Court Clerk, there was no mention of the procedure to follow if Trump and his Combat Ghosts got overwhelmed and decided to surrender to their enemies to avoid being terminated. "Was that omission by the Court Clerk deliberate?" Trump speculated amid the hullabaloo and battle pandemonium.

Without wasting anymore Clap (time), upon seeing approximately 13 more Combat Ghosts get terminated and tossed down to earth as Dark Angels, Trump decided it was time to surrender to save the few remaining Combat Ghosts and indeed himself, although he didn't know what was to become of him and his army after surrendering to Theo Lesa's enemies.

But before Trump could fully stretch his hands in surrender, suddenly, there was a mighty wind that tore into the mountain that stood closest to the battlefield, but it seemed as though all the other fighters were oblivious to the strange occurrence. After the wind, there was an earthquake that shook the battleground, but, again, it seemed as though only Trump felt the shaking as the other fighters were neither startled nor concerned.

Finally, Trump dropped to his knees to give up the fight and expected to be terminated any time despite not being in a fighting stance. He wondered whether the strange rattling and noises that only he might have heard was the method typically used by Nebuparadiza to notify The Chosen Ones (The Sheela), that they had lost the battle in The Acts of The Sheela (The Acts of The Chosen Ones).

Unexpectedly, in all the mayhem, the despondent Trump heard a quiet voice from an invisible source as though it was a whisper and it said, "Stand up Dear Chosen One, Stand up Dear Sheela, you who are highly esteemed, consider carefully the words I am about to speak to you, for I have been sent to you." And when the voice said this to Trump, he quickly stood up, trembling in the heart of the battle bedlam and chaos. The voice continued, "Do not be afraid, Dear Chosen One, Dear Sheela. Since the moment you asked for assistance from Nebuparadiza through the Court Clerk, your words were heard, and I have come in response to your request for assistance. Do not be afraid, you who are highly esteemed." The quiet voice continued further, "Peace be with you! Be strong; be strong Dear Chosen One, be strong Dear Sheela."

Trump then felt something touch his forehead, but it was invisible, it touched his forehead again, but he could see nothing still. When it touched him for the third time, he again heard the same quiet voice say, "Dear Chosen One, Dear Sheela, open your eyes and see." Trump looked and was dumbfounded. He noticed that the hills and mountains surrounding the battlefield were full of black and purple horses and bronze chariots with wheels of fire that were burning continuously. There was a Ngeloi mounted on each horse and another inside each chariot. The Ngelois were adorned in shiny red and sparkling blue apparel with blazing swords of fire in their right hands. Further, Trump noticed that standing beside him was the quiet voice that had been speaking to him, now in the form of a Ngeloi, it was the Arch Ngeloi Gabriel, who was mighty and exceeding in strength. It was the same distinguished Ngeloi he had seen back in Nebuparadiza.

The Arch Ngeloi Gabriel spoke to Trump and said, "Well done, Dear Sheela, Well done, Dear Chosen One. You have fought a good fight; you have persevered to the very end. As it was in the beginning, so shall it ever be; good will always triumph over evil! You will not have to fight this battle alone from this stage onwards. Take your position and stand firm, and I will make it known to you that there is no other ruler greater than Theo Lesa, and there will never be." The Arch Ngeloi Gabriel then prostrated himself to the ground, with his hands raised and spread out as though in prayer. Afterwards, the Arch Ngeloi Gabriel stood up and issued orders to the Ngelois, who were mounted on black and purple horses and in bronze chariots of fire with blazing swords in their right hands. With his voice full of authority, the Arch Ngeloi Gabriel emphatically shouted, "Strike down these rebels!"

Immediately after issuing the decree (order), the whole squad of Ngelois surrounding hills and mountains, including the Arch Ngeloi Gabriel, became invisible. They vanished into the furore and kerfuffle that was running amok on the battlefield packed with the antagonistic warring factions who were busy striking each other down. The special agents from Nebuparadiza under the command of the Arch Ngeloi Gabriel, unseen, selectively struck down the Muezee and M'nshbwa soldiers to the exclusion of the Combat Ghosts who couldn't believe what they were witnessing as they were not privy to the revelation that had been given to Trump by the Arch Ngeloi Gabriel. The sleek underground job undertaken by the Arch Ngeloi Gabriel, and his crew was analogous to a rapture, except the fallen Muezee and M'nshbwa soldiers were not disappearing. Instead, their bodies were strewn across the battlefield.

Trump and the Combat Ghosts watched in awe, reverence and wonderment as their enemies fell one by one in their dozens, hundreds, thousands and so on and so forth from the highly ranked officer to the very junior officer amongst them. The entire battlefield was littered with the bodies of 'dead' enemy soldiers, and those who tried to escape suffered the same fate too. There was no way of escaping the fury and wrath from Nebuparadiza, which arguably they had brought upon themselves by rebelling against Theo Lesa.

At the point that the Arch Ngeloi Gabriel and the 'death' squad of Ngelois intervened in the war in response to Trump's request for support in The Acts of The Chosen Ones (The Acts of The Sheela), there were only 37 Combat Ghosts from the original 1000 Combat Ghosts who had survived the onslaught from the Muezee insurgents and the M'nshbwa mercenaries. Trump and the surviving 37 Combat Ghosts could not believe what was happening as they stood still watching their enemies helplessly succumb in agony and anguish to an invisible force. And all this was after King Razin, and the chief rebel M'nshbwa had won the war in principle except that Trump and the 37 Combat Ghosts tenaciously held on and continued fighting against all odds before the Arch Ngeloi Gabriel came to their rescue in the dying moments.

The slaughter by the Arch Ngeloi Gabriel and his squad of Ngelois continued, killing King Razin and the commander of the M'nshbwa army in the process, at which point the remaining Muezee and M'nshbwa soldiers surrendered, lay flat on the ground, and distanced themselves from their weapons.

Judging from a distance, the rescue mission by the Arch Ngeloi Gabriel, which was planned in Nebuparadiza and carried out 1000 miles beneath the moon's surface to suppress the Muezee rebellion, closely depicts Moses' pre-victory words of encouragement to the Israelites as recorded in the Christian Bible when he said, "Do not be afraid. Stand firm and you will see the deliverance the Lord will bring you today. The Egyptians you see today you will never see again. The Lord will fight for you; you need only to be still" (Exodus 14.13–14); Or as Jesus said to his disciples on the value of perseverance in Mathew 24:13, "But the one who perseveres to the end will be saved."

References

1. https://www.nbcnews.com/better/health/science-behind-why-we-can-t-look-away-disasters-ncna804966

2. https://culteducation.com/group/1104-psychics/27981-psychology-the-truth-about-the-paranormal.html

3. https://www.bbc.co.uk/news/magazine-14490790

4. https://en.wikipedia.org/wiki/Witchcraft_accusations_against_children

5. https://afineparent.com/be-positive/parent-child-relationship.html

6. https://www.webmd.com/mental-health/addiction/high-functioning-alcoholic#1

7. A Neuroscientific Look at Speaking in Tongues – The New York Times (nytimes.com) (https://www.nytimes.com/2006/11/07/health/07brain.html)

8. https://en.wikipedia.org/wiki/Kaffir_(racial_term)

9. https://www.abuaminaelias.com/the-definition-of-faith-in-islam/

10. https://www.psychologytoday.com/gb/blog/so-happy-together/201702/time-together-and-time-apart

11. http://swedenborgstudy.com/books/H.Lj.Odhner_Spirits-Men/index.htm

12. https://futurism.com/the-truth-behind-the-biggest-eureka-moments-in-science

13. https://www.reallymoving.com/blog/october-2019/how-to-look-after-your-mental-health-during-your-move

14. https://bryankramer.com/the-core-ingredient-in-trust-is-vulnerability

15. https://www.theresiliencecentre.com.au/boundaries-why-are-they-important

16. https://www.parents.com/kids/development/behavioral/age-by-age-guide-to-lying

17. Here's how your life flashes before your eyes, according to these 7 near-death experiences – National | Globalnews.ca (https://globalnews.ca/news/3223245/heres-how-your-life-flashes-before-your-eyes-according-to-7-people-who-had-near-death-experiences/)

18. https://www.npr.org/2011/01/23/132737060/meet-william-james-sidis-the-smartest-guy-ever?t=1621084947893

19. https://en.wikipedia.org/wiki/Symphony

20. https://www.td.org/insights/importance-of-credibility-for-managers

21. https://medium.com/persona-global/4-phases-of-innovative-decision-making-af1a017d359d

22. https://www.britannica.com/list/murder-most-horrid-the-grisliest-deaths-of-roman-catholic-saints

23. https://www.livescience.com/33376-humans-other-animals-distinguishing-mental-abilities.html

24. https://oneearthfuture.org/opinion-insights/why-do-people-choose-rebel

25. https://hbr.org/2011/11/why-inspiration-matters

26. https://letstalkscience.ca/educational-resources/stem-in-context/gamma-rays-helper-or-hazard

27. https://www.linkedin.com/pulse/7-characteristics-eagle-why-vital-good-leadership-ms-mirlande-chery

28. https://www.forbes.com/sites/markmurphy/2018/04/15/neuroscience-explains-why-you-need-to-write-down-your-goals-if-you-actually-want-to-achieve-them/?sh=464fb4507905

29. https://teambay.com/tools-at-work

30. https://edge.oregonstate.edu/2017/08/23/the-science-of-karma

31. https://www.dailymail.co.uk/home/moslive/article-1267536/Ten-greatest-battlefield-tactics-Rob-Johnson.html

32. https://thestrategybridge.org/the-bridge/2017/5/2/bay-of-pigs-a-case-study-in-strategic-leadership-and-failed-assumptions

33. https://projectmanager.com

34. https://brucelee.com/podcast-blog/2017/10/18/68-defeat-is-a-state-of-mind

35. https://sportsaspire.com/sword-fighting-techniques-styles-moves

36. www.expertboxing.com

37. https://www.researchgate.net/publication/228318502_Repetition_is_the_First_Principle_of_All_Learning

38. https://www.bands.army.mil

39. https://en.wikipedia.org/wiki/Bugle_call

40. https://www.military.com/join-armed-forces/length-of-basic-training-and-your-first-paycheck.html

41. https://en.wikipedia.org/wiki/Failure_Is_Not_an_Option

42. https://www.verywellmind.com/the-incentive-theory-of-motivation

43. https://www.stthomas.edu/cas/encounteringislam/dialogues/angelsandsatan/

44. https://en.wikipedia.org/wiki/V_formation

45. https://www.sciencedaily.com/releases/2017/04/170420113921.htm

46. https://www.pbs.org/tpt/going-to-war/themes/combat-experience

47. https://frazerconsultants.com/2017/03/is-there-an-afterlife-different-religious-views-on-death

48. https://cove.army.gov.au/article/taking-the-initiative-battle

49. https://theconversation.com/dunkirk

50. https://www.history.com/news/medieval-weapons

51. Dominic D.P. Johnson and Dominic Tierney: ('The Rubicon Theory of War' pg. 7)

52. http://www2.hawaii.edu/~jjudd/energy/partIII/sorcererway/warrior1.5.htm

53. https://koreajoongangdaily.joins.com/news/article/article.aspx?aid=2608062

54. http://www.shofarot-israel.com/index.php/the-shofar/biblicaltime/

55. https://www.justsecurity.org/34612/duty-disobey

56. https://www.uakron.edu/armyrotc/MS1/22

57. http://www.hydroquebec.com/learning/transport/parcours.html

58. https://www.glassdoor.com/blog/unspoken-rules-promotions/

59. https://www.gotquestions.org/Pharaohs-magicians-miracles.html

60. https://encyclopedia.1914-1918-online.net/article/war_losses

61. https://theswaddle.com/how-lightning-strikes-kill-injure-thousands-of-people-every-year

62. http://www.sath.org.uk/edscot/www.educationscotland.gov.uk/scotlandshistory/warsofindependence/bruceandspider/

63. https://hbr.org/2018/05/how-to-get-the-help-you-need

64. https://www.medicalnewstoday.com/articles/silent-treatment

65. https://chrisnoland.org/2014/01/22/when-heaven-is-silent-revelation-81/